Rob Niven qualified from St Andrews and Manchester Universities in Medicine. He spent most of his medical career in Manchester, with a brief sojourn in Leicester. After becoming a consultant and specialising initially in Occupational Lung Disease, he developed the first Severe Asthma Service in the North West, but against the national norm, with support from so many regional colleagues, he encouraged the development of a regional network of self-supporting colleagues, delivering care to patients with the severest forms of asthma. Some still see it as a model for the delivery of specialist care.

He became known for developing or progressing a number of novel medical innovations and concepts, publishing 150 scientific medical papers, chapters and educational programmes.

Later he worked with SIGN and the British Thoracic Society, to modernise the National Guidelines for the Management of Asthma.

Having planned a period of easing down into retirement on a part time contract, the pandemic blocked these plans and he spent the first 15 months working full time on the front-line for respiratory admissions.

Retirement to the Isle of Arran, beckoned however, from where the planned series are inspired by Colin Douglas who wrote books on medical life in the 1980s, as well as the spirituality and serenity of the island and the desire to have a new challenge. Encumbered by a late diagnosed of dyslexia, which explained much of his academic limitation, with writing being the hardest challenge.

Rob considers himself one of the most fortunate souls alive, to have done a career, which he loved and to have survived long enough to have an opportunity to write about the funny, the sad and the sometimes gross reality of life in hospitals over the last forty years.

This work is dedicated to the patients, colleagues, family and friends who made a wonderful life of a lung specialist possible.

Whilst many of the stories are based on real events, the characters in the book are fictional; though, they are inspired by the patients, friends and colleagues I met along the way. *The House-Dog's Tail* is a work of fiction, created around the autobiographical skeleton of my medical career.

The last few years have been challenging for many reasons within the NHS and I would like to thank and praise all those who continue to strive to improve care for all medical problems, within a society, which has lost touch with reality of the personal truth of medical professionals and the sacrifices of their lives. My ambition is to redress this balance a little, allowing the reader to see a more personal side of the past and present of a medical career.

Rob Niven

A LIFE OF BREATH

THE HOUSE DOG'S TAIL

AUSTIN MACAULEY PUBLISHERS™

LONDON • CAMBRIDGE • NEW YORK • SHARJAH

Copyright © Rob Niven 2023

The right of Rob Niven to be identified as author of this work has been asserted by the author in accordance with sections 77 and 78 of the Copyright, Designs and Patents Act 1988.

All rights reserved. No part of this publication may be reproduced, stored in a retrieval system, or transmitted in any form or by any means, electronic, mechanical, photocopying, recording, or otherwise, without the prior permission of the publishers.

Any person who commits any unauthorised act in relation to this publication may be liable to criminal prosecution and civil claims for damages.

This is a work of fiction. Names, characters, businesses, places, events, locales, and incidents are either the products of the author's imagination or used in a fictitious manner. Any resemblance to actual persons, living or dead, or actual events is purely coincidental.

A CIP catalogue record for this title is available from the British Library.

ISBN 9781528996884 (Paperback)
ISBN 9781528996891 (ePub e-book)

www.austinmacauley.com

First Published 2023
Austin Macauley Publishers Ltd®
1 Canada Square
Canary Wharf
London
E14 5AA

I would like to acknowledge all my colleagues and patients, who have contributed to the fictional characters created within the book. If you recognise a part of yourself, I only hope I have done your part justice.

I would especially like to thank Mundy Walsh for her Alpha reading and advice and those who have helped me improve the final work, specifically good friends, Jemma Haines (MBE) and Rae Garrard, who contributed invaluable editing advice.

Finally, to my two boys, who sacrificed a lot in the life left behind after the medical career absorbed so much of my time and energy, especially when they were young and for their unflinching encouragement, knowing me well enough to expect that some parts of the stories will come with a tinge of embarrassment. I hope I have not disappointed you too much!

Table of Contents

Chapter 1: Getting Covid: Day Zero — 13

Chapter 2: The House Officer Year: Day 1 — 19

Chapter 3: Getting Covid: Day Zero, Discussions of Virus Transmission — 33

Chapter 4: The House Officer Year: Day 1 (Part II) — 39

Chapter 5: Getting Covid: Day Zero (Part III) — 56

Chapter 6: The House Year: Day 2 and the First Weekend — 65

Chapter 7: Getting Covid: Evening Zero — 74

Chapter 8: The House Year: First Weekend (Part II) — 76

Chapter 9: Getting Covid: Day 1 — 86

Chapter 10: The 'House' Year: Disasters and Dreams — 94

Chapter 11: Getting Covid: Night 2 and Other Stories — 98

Chapter 12: The House Year: Dealing with Infamy — 105

Chapter 13: The House Year: Doctors Get Sick Too (Pre-Covid) — 119

Chapter 14: Getting Covid: Day 2 — 126

Chapter 15: The House Year: First Mess Party — 128

Chapter 16: Getting Covid: Day 3 — 136

Chapter 17: The House Year: Trouble on Board — 143

Chapter 18: The House Year: All Change — 149

Chapter 19: Getting Covid: Day 3 Anxious Patients — 154

Chapter 20: The 'House' Year: Surgical House 'Dog'	160
Chapter 21: The House Year: Crisis, What Crisis?	170
Chapter 22: The House Year: On the Receiving End and Life's Little Crises	183
Chapter 23: The House Year: Switchboard to the Rescue	192
Chapter 24: Getting Covid: Days 3 and 4	200
Chapter 25: The SHO Years: Life with Wayne	204
Chapter 26: Getting Covid: Night 4, Night Sweats	220
Chapter 27: The SHO Years: Learning Lessons	222
Chapter 28: The SHO Years: Success Out of Disaster	228
Chapter 29: The SHO Years: More Accidents and Incidents	236
Chapter 30: Getting Covid: Having Covid Day 1—The Perils of Doing Nothing	241
Chapter 31: The SHO Years: More Life Events	243
Chapter 32: The SHO Years: Wind-Ups Failing	245
Chapter 33: The SHO Years: Inappropriate Resuscitation	254
Chapter 34: The SHO Years: More Crazy Resuscitation Attempts	261
Chapter 35: Getting Covid: Having Covid Day 1	267
Chapter 36: The SHO Years: Specialist Respiratory Clinics	276
Chapter 37: The SHO Years: Second Year SHO: Who Is Dating Whom?	283
Chapter 38: Having Covid Day 2: Low Oxygen Levels	287
Chapter 39: The SHO Years: Wrong Diagnoses	289
Chapter 40: The SHO Years: Bad Times at the End of a Good Year	300
Chapter 41: The SHO Years: SHO Year 3: Life in Leicester	302
Chapter 42: The SHO Years: Traumatic Times Ahead	309
Chapter 43: The SHO Years: Inexplicable Events	313

Chapter 44: Getting Covid: Illness, Day 4	319
Chapter 45: The SHO Years: Life & Career Progression	320
Chapter 46: The SHO Years: More Interviews	326
Chapter 47: Getting Covid: Covid Illness Day 5: Dealing with Fear	330
Chapter 48: The SHO Years: SHO Year 3/Registrar: Promotion, Day One	337
Chapter 49: The SHO Years: More Clinic Events	343
Chapter 50: Getting Covid: Post-Covid Day 9: Potential Recovery	354
Chapter 51: End of the Junior Years and Sliding Doors: Part II	359
Chapter 52: Getting Covid: Day 10: Worst-Case Scenario	365

Chapter 1
Getting Covid: Day Zero

Jamie stared at the mug with suspicion. It was his alright, it had that 'I'd rather be watching Man City' logo and it was where he had left it, before he went for his first Covid-19 vaccine.

But now, it was full of steaming black tea. His drink!

It was on his newly white Formica-topped desk. The rich wood desks, he had as a new consultant twenty years before in a single office, long gone to maximise space in a hospital, too small to fit the increasing number of employees.

The whole room was benched around, making space for eight desktop computers and phone pods. He dreaded the concept that they might add plastic dividers to depersonalise the space even more, like the restaurants that followed guidance to separate space, leaving a de-humanised dining experience.

Three of Jamie's colleagues were on the telephone, doing clinic consultations in the new virtual world of modern health provision. Two doctors and a physiotherapist, all chittering concurrently. It made the room feel like a call centre, more than a medical consultation room.

"It is really essential you get outside and exercise. This two-stone weight gain you have told me about, is a much greater risk to your long-term health than Covid is, especially if you get vaccinated in the next two months." Tim Coffey one of his medical consultant colleagues, was in full flow.

It was January 2021. Jamie had just had his vaccination as soon as he had the first invite. There was just a slight ache where the potentially life-saving few drops of scientific magic now resided, twitching his immune system gently.

Jamie looked at his desk, idly listening to the repetitive phrases of lifestyle advice and reassurance, that had become central to the thousands of telephone-calls Jamie and the team were making every day.

He eyed the pictures of his current dog (Isla), a cocker spaniel, and the older image of the springer (Jura), which had been part of his life with Heather, his ex-partner.

The curls of steam from the black tea obscured his view, just as much as the blurry, damp eyes, as he remembered the now deceased Jura. He had loved her presence so much. Due to Heather and his separation, Jamie felt he had been deprived of the six years of time with the dog. For the latter three years, Isla had brought back the joy he got from walking and watching either of them chase squirrels and rabbits, with the crazy, unrestrained, but eventually unsuccessful fervour of all spaniels.

Jamie tugged his attention back to the mug of tea. His concern was emanating from the fact that he hadn't actually made it for himself. He hadn't clicked the kettle on, or thrown the tea bag in the cup in that rather flamboyant action, resembling a basketball dunk, he routinely used.

Dan Ashton, his Severe Asthma colleague and newly appointed 'boss', had made it for him, with the best of intentions. However, Jamie hadn't drunk a cup of tea that anyone else had made, since the pandemic had taken proper hold of their lives and his own views on the transmission of the virus had crystalised.

Dan knew Jamie didn't actually enjoy having injections or blood tests or medical procedures performed on himself. It had been a natural, supportive gesture that Dan had a cup of tea ready for the older consultant's return. Jamie, appreciated it and it was that appreciation, that left him in a natural predicament.

As it happened, the vaccine had been done smoothly and professionally, and Jamie had been fine. He had as expected, barely felt the needle. He had chosen instead to look around the soulless area converted from cardiology clinic to become the vaccination centre for their huge hospital. The pale green walled area, had been further segmented, with blue wall dividers. How had hospitals become so absent in personality and soul, he wondered as the nurse tapped on the computer? There were no paper records. He noted her colourless finger nails and the bland pale blue uniform of tunic and trousers. Shapeless and sexless, were the words that came to his mind.

"Did you wait your full ten-minutes in the 'pen'?" Dan had already had his jab and was guessing the sort of answer he would get, knowing his friend and colleague's frustration with mindless rules.

"What do you think? I think I managed two." Jamie turned to look at his colleague.

Dan's question had referred to the expectation that all staff would wait ten minutes after the Covid-jab.

The 'holding pen' was a converted patient waiting area and had been even more congested with plastic chairs, than their team office. Jamie could even smell strong, second-hand garlic on the breath of one of his newly vaccinated colleagues, such was their proximity. So much for social distancing!

"Everyone just sits there looking at the walls and not making eye contact, just like on the underground."

Jamie could remember the day, when he would know more than half of the working population of the hospital by their first names. Not so now, though he said hello to as many of them as he could, testing his memory every day. The clinically relevant workers who provided the direct patient care had been diluted by the ever-growing army of administrators, who now represented over half of the total work-force.

"I know and we have our flu-jabs normally in any corner or cubby hole in the hospital and are back working, before the needles out." Dan had obviously been equally frustrated with the ten-minute compulsory wait.

"I had my flu jab in the linen room on A1, even this year." Jamie agreed and remembered being in and out of the room in seconds.

"The only reaction you might get inside the ten minutes is going to be anaphylaxis and that's just as likely with the flu jab as the covid vax." Dan and Jamie were both in agreement and were just voicing their shared frustrations.

"The ten-minute policy is paying lip-service to the social media hysteria over this jab. It's just a fucking vaccine after all." Dan and Jamie shared expletives freely, when the office was quiet. Tim had finished his phone call and was turning to join the conversation.

"Did anyone spot you escaping early?" Dan clearly was intrigued that Jamie had ignored the policy.

"I left when the nurse was distracted checking a vaccine dose with another nurse. I aimed for calm nonchalance as I walked, but suspect I failed miserably!" Jamie laughed at his own inability to escape quietly. "Someone said 'that wasn't ten-minutes'." He mimicked a high-pitched voice.

"But no-one called you back?" Tim's first contribution. He had just had his own vaccine, earlier that morning.

"No, but I'm pretty sure it was a manager who called after me, so who knows if she saw my name badge, I might still get 'HIRs'd'."

"Oh c'mon, no one is going to report you for leaving the post-vax corral surely?" Dan's voice started confident, but by the end, he was already doubting his own words.

Shipman had been responsible for many changes in the NHS. Open reporting of negative events was one of the good ones, but the HIRS reporting system was now widely abused and over-used and as a result the concern for Dan and Jamie, was that you couldn't see the wood for the trees, so to speak. Real issues were buried in a mountain of trivia and individual point-scoring, brought about by the abuse of a well-intentioned system.

"Are you sure it won't happen?" Jamie asked, knowing he didn't agree with Dan's comment.

"Now you ask, no, I'm not certain. It'll teach you. Eight more minutes biding your time or an hour of mindless paperwork. It was your choice!"

Jamie grunted and wondered if Dan was right really. Even if he was, Jamie wouldn't admit it.

He recalled how he had walked faster than was actually necessary along the stark white walled corridors to the relative sanity of their shared office. He missed the patients, the wheelchairs, the anxious faces on the route. A senior doctor, smiling and saying hello to as many of them as made eye contact, had been part of his own daily routine, imagining the tiny gift of calm and reassurance, it donated.

The contrast for now, was the melee of the mask covered faces of staff. All that was left to view was their eyes, which for the most part over the last year, had just demonstrated either fear or extreme fatigue.

****

Dan was a well-built guy, but was super fit approaching fifty. He cycled to work every day unless the weather was cataclysmic. He ran for fun instead, on his days off. Although ten years younger than Jamie, Dan had slightly less hair, giving him a face of real integrity and authority.

He had an organisational skill, that was massively superior to Jamie's, which the older consultant admitted openly. Jamie's best skills were centred in the patient communication aspects of Medicine. Not that Dan wasn't skilled in that area too. Dan was also blessed with a sharp but incredibly dry sense of humour.

Both consultants despised political nonsense and frequently joked about starting together the 'Pitch-Fork Party' and turning up at the houses of parliament with their band of pitchfork carrying rebels. They differed in the way they fed their own political perspectives, however. Dan read the papers and on-line news feeds voraciously, his phone pinging repeatedly with updates.

Jamie by comparison had long ago, got bored with the futility of politics and couldn't even bring himself to vote in the Brexit referendum. He had decided months before the vote, that the campaign arguments on both sides for 'Remain' or 'Brexit', were so manifestly superficial that they weren't worthy of rational thought or debate. However, the two consultants' political interactions in the office were always playful, each of the senior consultants respecting the others cynicism.

In response to Dan's organisational skills, Jamie had encouraged him to become the departmental head in severe asthma.

Jamie had officially started the local interest in severe asthma on his appointment as a consultant, when it was still considered as a Cinderella speciality. Now the department had over thirty members of staff dedicated to their patient population. The absolute size of the department, they had to count to believe, when it came to Christmas. They had booked the number of seats needed, for the entire team to go to see 'We will rock you' at the Palace theatre, before the pandemic. Dan's idea had been a great success as a Christmas present, vastly superior to the usual round of wine, candles, scarfs, trinkets and smellies, that Jamie had bought on his own, when the team was much smaller.

Dan took to the new role as leader, with great prowess and had already progressed the legacy, that Jamie had initiated. Jamie on the other hand, knew it was time for the wind down phase of his career.

Tim, was a relatively new consultant, appointed only a couple of years before. He had the build of a rugby player, which he had done to a decent level apparently. Jamie had known Tim from as long ago as his third year as a medical student. Tim's teaching group had stood out head and shoulders above the circulating small groups that Jamie taught for seminars in pods of four or six. Jamie was delighted that one of this elite group had been inspired to do respiratory medicine as a career and then eventually come back full circle and re-join Jamie and Dan as their third full-time consultant.

Tim had been one of the expansions to the team needed, before Jamie could work towards his retirement.

'Wind down' by going part time, had been the theory at least. Jamie was over sixty and had planned to be working just three days per week by now. This working schedule, he had originally hoped to continue for two years or so, before standing aside completely.

The pandemic had scuppered that arrangement, with Jamie, ending up doing much more than full-time office hours, in the last ten months. He reckoned he had peaked back at seventy hours per week, during the height of the first wave as they did additional evening shifts in ED, to deal with the Covid related workload.

The schedule had reminded Jamie of his early days in medicine, though now his brain and body, didn't quite have the same stamina, that had developed within those early years. For the first two years as a junior, Jamie averaged eighty hours at work per week, peaking at a hundred-and-thirty-six hours in one critical week. When he recounted these events with the current junior doctors, they couldn't imagine or fathom how anyone (patients or doctors) survived at all.

Chapter 2
The House Officer Year: Day 1

Jamie was there early. It was his first working day as a doctor after all. They had all been invited to a room close to the medical wards in the hospital. Here, their bleeps and first white coats would be waiting for them, as well as keys to their on-call room in the doctor's residences. Jamie had a rented apartment with his then fiancée Diane, which was about ten miles away.

As Jamie entered the allocated meeting room, he sensed something akin to the smell of a new car about the old room. It had wood panels and the equipment was set out on a huge oak table, that filled the centre of the room. Jamie imagined the room being used for interviewing new consultants, with a panel of eight or more interviewers, sat on one side and a single chair or small stool, for the candidate on the opposite side.

Today, the table was covered in the medical paraphernalia, for the new intake of doctors. The entire junior doctor population of every hospital, changed jobs on the same day at the start of August. It was not a day to be ill!

The 'bleep' was the central part of this pile of provided equipment. Prior to mobile phones, each doctor would be contacted hundreds of times per week, using the small device, which beeped like an annoying morning alarm clock, before either speaking to them, or more commonly, flashing up a phone number to ring. The live-voice from switchboard, only followed a more strident audible tone, when it was a life-threatening emergency or a cardiac arrest.

It would be the focus and controlling item of Jamie's life for the next five years or more. He couldn't believe on that morning, that within a few weeks he would be imagining hearing it's shrill call in his sleep, his car, his home and even when he was in the cinema or theatre. When he was a student, qualified doctors told him, how the mind would play tricks and any sound with a similar pitch would make them jump and react as if it was their medical call bleep. They were depressingly accurate.

Much more so than the stethoscope, having a bleep was the marker of his progression to being an actual 'doctor'. It was of course because, now they as individuals, were actually needed, rather than just being in the way as students were largely perceived. The bleep alone signified, this change of status.

They had worn white coats as students of course, but as a doctor this new one was provided by the hospital. He would hand it back to the laundry and take a new one, every day if it was appropriate from what it had been in direct contact with. Especially which bodily fluids had stained it, that usually (but not always) came from patients.

The pristine white cotton, didn't have his name on it, but on the table was a white plastic badge, with black letters: 'Dr James Carmichael, House Officer'.

His first badge with the doctor title after six years of training. It was a huge moment, that might have given him a sense of pride. Instead, it felt strange and almost patronising after all the years as a 'student'.

He must remember to get his next badge changed to Dr *Jamie* Carmichael. Only his mum called him 'James' and then only when she was cross with him.

He started to pack his white coat. It had a slightly bleached smell to it, like the ones they had used in anatomy classes, when doing 'dissection' on real human cadavers. Jamie still couldn't eat sweetcorn, since his very first day of practical anatomy. The cold human adipose tissue, looking miraculously like sweetcorn, was entrenched in his visual memory and just wouldn't let go.

"Try it on before you fill it up, they often don't fit." The voice came from a kindly female face, framed with sandy hair and set off by smiling eyes. She stood momentarily in the door and Jamie wondered how long she had been watching him.

She was older than him by a year or two and had the air of 'done this before', about her, so he guessed she was a year or two more experienced, working maybe as a Senior House Officer. If Jamie managed without getting himself reported to the General Medical Council, he would automatically become a 'Senior' House Officer in just 12 months-time. The medical registration passing from 'provisional' to 'full'.

"Thank you." Jamie smiled back at the new arrival. He walked across the room and shook her hand, which was warm and confident unlike his clammy nervous one. She smelled of subdued floral perfume.

Jamie introduced himself, before trying the white coat on as she had advised.

Jamie was skinny at six-feet, with long lanky arms and legs, but this coat must have been made for a midget. It came half way down his arms and he couldn't have fastened it at the front even if he had wanted to.

"Oh, good advice." He smiled at the lady and they shared a chuckle at his appearance in the ultra-small white coat. Jamie stood and pushed his arms out to model the ridiculous 'look'.

The newcomer was already ignoring the tidy piles and was looking at the size labels of coats under other bleeps and badges.

"Try this one!" she said passing him one she had extracted from under a bleep and badge with the name of 'Katherine Long'.

The label said '40', which was bigger than the jacket of the one suit, he currently owned. It fitted perfectly, especially as he needed a little extra room as he had pockets to fill.

"Jemma Lawton!" she introduced herself, whilst inspecting a piece of paper. "I think you are my House Officer looking at the team allocation here. So, it is definitely in my interest to look after you. We are also both on-call today you know, so we are definitely better getting on together from the get-go."

Jamie was already silently pleased this confident experienced 'doc', was on his team. She would become his first guide and mentor and he was delighted with the fates, that put them together.

Jamie had already perused his rota, but knew it's intensity well from his student days. Nothing had change in the last 2 years.

Like most of the hospital jobs at the time, it was a one-in-three rota. This meant for most weeks, it was one night on followed by two nights off. However, if one colleague was on holiday or off sick, it got to be a one-in-two (and occasionally a one-in-one in, when one colleague was on holiday and another ill). There were no regular locum agencies, to provide last minute doctors to plug gaps. Weekends were the hardest, as they were full weekend working and still requiring the doctor to be in for a normal following week. Jamie had warned his fiancée what it meant, when he was covering as a one in two. He had even written out the actual hours for both patterns and pinned them to the fridge door.

1 in 2, with weekend on-call included:

- Mon arrive 8 a.m., work continuously until 6 p.m. on a Tuesday.
- Back Wednesday at 8 a.m. and work continuously until Thursday at 6 p.m.
- Back Friday at 8 a.m. and work continuously until 6 p.m. on the Monday.

"That will be just twenty-eight hours of being at home in a whole week, with the weekend shift accumulating eighty-two hours continuous on-call work." He explained the reality to her, just a few weeks before he started. Fortunately, she was not a doctor and worked 'normal' hours.

The rotas Jamie and colleagues worked in the 1980s, would soon become unimaginable. Whilst, it might not seem appropriate to have anyone looked after by someone, so potentially exhausted, the positive counter argument was the junior doctors, as tired as they were, knew absolutely everything that was going on with all the patients, on all the wards under their jurisdiction. Continuity of care could not have been more completely achieved.

****

"We will get on famously I'm sure, especially if you keep looking after me this well." Jamie stood modelling the new better size white coat, before asking, "What do you think I should do with the one I tried on?"

"Fold it up and put it under Katherine's badge and hope she is five-foot-nothing and as skinny as you." Jemma had a mischievous smile as she caught his eye this time.

He did as she advised, very quickly, checking the door in the hope the new owner didn't arrive, just as he was messing in her tidy pile of equipment.

The area looked untouched, when he had finished smoothing the first tried-on coat.

He started loading up the pockets again. The British National Formulary (BNF) in his left hip pocket, which contained all the medicines in current use in the UK, with doses, side effects and interactions. It was the bible of prescribing for years before and remained so for decades after.

Next, the 'Pocket Oxford Guide of Medical Emergencies' went outside the BNF in the same hip level pocket, stretching the pristine starched white garment. The stethoscope, tendon hammer and tourniquet, which they all used as standard essential equipment went in the right hip pocket. Bleep and pens and a pen torch went in the breast pocket. Badge clipped in place in front of it.

"Look at you, you almost look ready!" Jemma said smiling again.

"Are you living in the residence full time?" she asked as an afterthought.

Jamie knew that most doctors lived in hospital accommodation full time. The hospital had significant sized residences for both doctors and nurses (usually separate in physical space, though individual day and night time transit was high). The Stockport hospital doctor's residence had a mess with fully filled fridges, washing machines and the somewhat surprising fact, put into the modern era, was a mess area with a bar.

Social life revolved around the 'mess' and the bar. One of the doctors offered to be (or more likely was randomly selected) 'mess president' and order in the small kegs of beer, which were emptied most Friday and Saturday nights after the pubs shut.

Back in these times, both the 'on' and 'off duty' doctors, would often come together for a last drink and a de-brief on the day's medical events. Such a set-up is inconceivable in the modern hospital quite understandably, but with the rota patterns that doctors did in the 1980s, it was the only social life many of the junior doctors had.

"Not a hundred percent as I have a fiancée. We have a rented place in Didsbury. She is not a doctor."

"Nearly a snap. Though my house is further out into the sticks. Does your other half know how little she will see you?" Jamie was nodding but Jemma hadn't stopped. "My fella took quite a bit of getting used to it, when we both started two years ago. He spent some nights in my on-call room, mostly sleeping alone anyway." Jemma wasn't smiling for the first time since she walked in. Jamie also now knew she was a second year SHO and this explained the air of confidence she possessed. However, she was confessing the reality of a stressed personal relationship.

"Two in one of those small single beds must be a challenge anyway, even if there was time to sleep." Jamie's pragmatic thought didn't lighten the mood.

They were saved from further negativity as another gang walked in together, anxious and excited in combination and all said greetings, with highly variable levels of enthusiasm.

Jamie knew none of them well. Manchester had three teaching hospitals and he guessed the other house officers had done most of their training at the other hospitals or less likely, had come from other regions of the country.

There was quite a hubbub, as the same process Jamie had gone through was repeated on several occasions. He was however relieved to meet Katharine, who was a shy, tiny blonde, who fitted into her revised white coat perfectly. Any guilt Jamie was carrying was immediately assuaged.

The process was going well, until last in came Callum, who was ginger haired and sullen. Jamie, did vaguely recognise him from medical school. He wasn't too different a build from Jamie, but the white coat left for him turned out to be the same size as Jamie's original. Callum wasn't impressed he had the last white coat on the table and it didn't fit and was just beginning to argue, that someone had stolen his white coat, when three more senior figures walked in. Authority and confidence were written all over their demeanour, but they appeared friendly with it.

"I'm Jon, no h, Calinas", said the dark-haired slightly olive–skinned and really scarily handsome one, who took the lead role. The girls in the room were completely silent, looking at him with unabashed sexual interest. Jamie particularly noticed Katharine was staring at him, with what he felt represented unrestrained lust, despite her quiet and shy external demeanour.

Callum however, was still complaining in a strong Scottish accent under his breath.

"Can you be quiet whilst we just sort the teams out, so we can get on with some work!"

His rebuke had the effect of silencing Callum, but the girls in the room just stared even harder at Jon as if the slightly aggressive tone, had even more sexual lure for them. Jon appeared not to notice this interest, but was looking directly at Callum, a smile on just one of the sides of his mouth.

He then reeled off names of the teams. Four teams for medicine, two for geriatrics, with ward and consultant allocations. On-calls were one in three, with a first on, working all day and all-night and a second on, who would finish at midnight (allegedly). Jon said the 'second on' doctors weren't to go 'off' until the 'first on' team were up to date and happy. He added, that he would prefer 'second on' teams, to stay in the hospital accommodation overnight just in case, but that this wasn't a rule…just a recommendation. It was clear it was a recommendation Jamie and the others should not ignore.

Jon, Jemma and Jamie were allocated to base their team on both A11 and A12 wards, for the patients of a new consultant called Dr Peter Lorimer. He was a cardiologist. This was the first thing Jamie heard, that he wasn't expecting, as he thought he was working for a Dr Gokal who was a neurologist, whom he had met when he was a student. Jamie had been slightly scared of Dr Gokal, as he had a very stern resting expression, that never seemed to change.

It transpired that Dr Gokal had retired over the summer. Jamie's team would switch to work with Dr Chapman a diabetic specialist after the first three months. This was definitely good news, as he had liked this consultant, during his student placement. Dr Chapman used to smile all the time and had a great rapport with patients, Jamie recalled. He had also been kindly and had time for students, especially one like Jamie, who had worked hard and had not been frightened to 'step up' and practically support the doctors. Jamie had seen the potential benefit of practising as many of their roles as early as possible and as often as possible.

"As I think you know, I have put our team on call today, partly out of responsibility but also, Jemma and I, are both a little experienced at least in our roles. Sorry Jamie, in at the deep end though for you." He addressed Jamie and Jemma with his eyes, without having been previously introduced. Again, Jamie was instinctively happy at his first team.

Suddenly a bleep went off. The room went silent and all heads turned in Jamie's direction. He looked down to see it his bleep alright and the number showing, which meant switchboard were after him.

"Two zero, zero one, that's switchboard." He announced to the watching crowd. "And so, it starts!"

"I'd go to the doctor's office next door, on ward A12, James." Jon spoke directly at Jamie. "Once you've taken the referral, ring around the wards and see where the beds are. I've written down the ward telephone numbers on this card." Jon, gave Jamie a card as the younger doctor, walked towards the door as instructed.

Jamie did the first bit as instructed and rang the switchboard number. "Doctor Carmichael on call, Medical House Officer." He started, very formally using his 'Doctor' prefix for the first time in earnest.

"James, are you the lucky bugger who got the short straw? I've got those fuckers from ED on the phone already. Thought they would know better than to start this early, on hand over day."

Jamie was slightly taken aback by the swearing from someone he didn't know, as well as the use of his own first name. In truth, he was more put out, that it was his 'Sunday' name, rather than worrying about whether he got called 'Doctor' back.

"Jamie! If you don't mind?" he responded, turning it into a question.

"Good man, its John here, I will look after you better if you dispense with the formality nonsense. Prefer my young docs with no airs 'n' graces, if you know what I mean?"

"That's good by me, John!" Jamie was laughing openly for the first time in his medical career.

"Righto patching you through, Jamie." The line to John was cut and Jamie could hear a noisy backdrop as he waited to speak to the referring Emergency Department (ED) doctor.

Jamie's first call was to accept a new patient. It was a seventy-year-old gentleman who had suffered a stroke. Before the ED doctor had put the phone down, he said his colleague had a referral too and put another doctor on. The second doctor referred a young man in his late teens, who had 'taken' forty aspirin tablets as an overdose.

"Not acidotic though." Jamie knew this probably meant that the lad hadn't actually taken all forty, or had vomited them up, as dangerous aspirin overdoses caused acid change in the blood stream, which itself could be fatal.

"I haven't got the bed statement yet. Can I have the number to ring you back on when I have checked and know where they can go?"

"Ambulances aren't here yet, but should be in ten minutes!" Their hospital had separate sites for the Emergency Department and the medical wards, which meant all admitted patients were 'shipped' in ambulances between the hospital sites. A journey of ten minutes at best up the busy A6 trunk road, which ran from the east, through Stockport and on into central Manchester.

Jamie knew from his student days, that the ward phone could go ignored for a long time at peak nurse activity hours of 8-10 a.m. Instead, Jamie started to almost run down the corridors to each of the medical wards, which he knew were under his jurisdiction, for new admissions.

There were no ward clerks sat at the desk in the 1980s and similarly there were no 'bed managers' or as they are called in 2021 'patent flow co-ordinators' (the name for what is now a team of highly paid administrative nurses). This role of managing the beds, used to be the house officer's job in the 1980s on top of all aspects of medical treatment.

In doing this run around the wards, he managed to introduce himself (if briefly), to the nurse in charge of the five main wards. Angela was the sister and Christine her very friendly staff nurse colleague on A12, which was where the office he had been sat in was. Angela had a shock of black hair tied efficiently in a pony tail and a huge smile, with barely a trace of make-up. She gave him the free bed numbers and the expected discharges in a very efficient manner. Jamie was taken by her striking beauty, but also her statuesque stance, even in nearly-flat nursing shoes. She actually had a very small wedge heel.

"Good luck today!" she said with a great deal of enthusiasm. "We will look after you as we know this is a tough day for you. There is milky coffee available at eleven, if you get time. Our auxiliary Freda is on, and she makes a superb panful. Christine and I will be on our break then."

She gave him the full wattage smile. He checked her hand and spotted the wedding ring. Always worth knowing he thought. Christine by comparison was very slightly built with mischievous green eyes. As Jamie looked at her, she appeared to wink at him. He wasn't sure it really happened and wondered at first, if she had a nervous tic. He had never been winked at by any nurse, whilst there for many months as a student, he remembered briefly. This might be the ward to set up base-camp on, he told himself.

He then ran along the corridor and up the stairs to B3. He was even more thrilled to meet Sarah, who was stunningly beautiful, even in a nursing uniform and no make-up. She was also of a slim build, tall and elegant in her stance. She had dark brown hair tied in a bun on top. The cardboard hats they wore, were very unflattering, but the colour of and the number of stripes, told those who understood the code, the experience and training/seniority grade of each nurse as a result. Sarah wore hers slightly off horizontal and it gave a coquettish look.

Her eyes were deep brown and seemed to smile continuously, even when the mouth was speaking. He introduced himself as 'Jamie', got the news there were no beds and ran off down the stairs again.

Janice by contrast to his new 'friends' was the nurse in charge on A4 and she had more make up on, than any female Jamie had ever met before. She still looked good and more importantly gave him a piece of paper with the bed numbers, she had prepared clearly in advance of his coming. Janice's rich perfume lingered on his nostrils as he ran back down the corridor, calling in on A1, before making his way back to his base wards.

The marble flooring clicked under his new grey brogue shoes.

Finally, he met Sister Arbuthnott on A11. She was old school, short, dumpy and with a no-nonsense face, that brooked no debate. First names were not on offer.

She was treated to Jamie's most outrageous charm offensive as he introduced himself with his first and surname together. He used both, not knowing whether to risk a 'Jamie' on its' own.

"Lovely to meet you." He tried. "And thanks for the bed news, no female patients for you yet though from the calls I've had already."

He went back to the small office where he had taken the call from ED, where both Jon and Jemma were now sat chatting and apparently waiting for him. It looked like an underutilised space, with just six wooden chairs and a small wooden circular table and a metal trolley for carrying notes around.

"Wondered where you had gone," Jon said, with an open friendly tone.

"I decided to run round and get the bed-numbers in person as I thought it might be quicker, than waiting for the phones to answer. Managed to say hello to all the nurses in charge and had a chat with John on switchboard, so took a little longer than I planned!" Jamie included an explanation in his breathless reply.

"Now he *is* a character. It is definitely worth having him on your side. Good plan to introduce yourself early though." The message and tone were both positive.

Jamie was relieved he hadn't annoyed his more senior colleagues.

"Now what have you got for us from the call?" Jemma wanted to get on with business.

"Stroke and an OD, aspirin, forty or so tablets allegedly, but no acidosis." Jamie went deliberately into shorthand.

"Have they pumped him?" Jon asked. Jamie recognised he was referring to the stomach pumps which were generally used for serious adult overdose cases in the 1980s. Emetic medicines were occasionally used as a substitute.

"No, they doubted whether he has really taken that many, so were just planning repeat gases in an hour or so." Jamie was pleased to have a rationale for his new senior doctor's first clinical question.

"Have you allocated the wards yet?" Jon asked, nodding gently at Jamie's explanations.

"Not yet. I took the number to ring back, once I knew where the beds were." Jamie again ready with a plan.

"Good!" said Jon. "Give A4 or B3 the stroke. A12 is our base ward and we will keep the easy discharge or interesting cases for our favourite ward. You've probably met Angela? She is the best nurse in the hospital and lovely with it. How did you get on with 'Notty'?"

Jamie didn't doubt this nickname referred to the battle-axe sister in charge of A11.

"Used my best charm and smiles, so fixed I almost got cramp." Jamie laughed gently as he recalled his actions.

Jon half laughed. "That won't get you that far, but I bet it works better than Callum's approach is going to. He must get prizes for being miserable." Jon had sussed out Callum in five minutes and come up with the same conclusions, Jamie had acquired in a similar time augmented, with a distant memory from the odd interaction in group lectures.

Jemma finally chipped in. "Do you know him, Jamie? Does he ever actually smile?"

"I think he trained in central, so I don't know him other than to have seen his face in the lecture theatre." Jamie was quite relieved not to be tarnished, with his senior colleague's early perception of this rather sour House Officer colleague.

"I'm betting 'Notty' will give him a hard time." Jon didn't sound concerned with the prospect.

Jemma started to move before adding her thoughts. "Think I will go and have my first introduction to this lady, before Callum gets her riled. I will double back round to the other wards and show my face, as long as I've half an hour until the first cases are here?" She jumped off the table where she had been sat in her white coat and slacks. The whiff of soft floral perfume, followed her.

Jamie picked up the phone and rang the number he had kept for A&E. Then he went to get some ECG cards. These request cards had blank backs and neatly fitted into the white coat pocket alongside the BNF. He kept the list of admissions on one of these and the current bed state running tally on another. He had seen one of the junior doctor's he had shadowed last year, do this trick. It seemed to work, so no point 'reinventing the wheel'.

There wasn't really room for a notebook as well as the two essential books in the pockets and the cards seemed the most efficient option. Even running down the corridor, the books hadn't moved, such was the tight fit in the white coat pocket. The jiggling of the other contents on his right hip had been more disconcerting and he kept one hand in the pocket as he ran, slowing his pace.

Just then Angela popped her head in, her dark blue sister's outfit pristine. "Can one of you do a cannula quickly on bed three. He is on a 'doxapram' infusion and I would prefer no arrests on day one."

Jon replied first. "Right; first test for Jamie. You have five minutes on your own as you know this is urgent, I presume? I'm going to start getting the notes together for my ward round. I want to see if you can impress Angela though!"

Jamie jumped up and recognised the relative urgency, knowing that in a patient with 'type II' respiratory failure, usually seen in the late stages of COPD, the only treatment was a respiratory stimulant infusion called 'doxapram'. Jamie knew that if the infusion suddenly stopped (because a cannula blocks or falls out) and this wasn't spotted, then the patient could rapidly have a respiratory arrest and though a crash call would be put out, it was very unlikely to be effective.

"Yes. I know it's urgent!" he shouted back to John as he left the room quickly.

Angela, slipped a cannula and alcohol swab out of her pocket and gave it to Jamie. He felt her warm hand touch his as she slipped the essential medical equipment for the task ahead, into his palm. She led him to the drowsy, shaking and rambling gentleman in bed three. She immediately whispered soothing noises to the patient, whilst grasping his upper arm, in part to help keep the arm still, but also to act as a tourniquet. She used her other hand to straighten and again hold the forearm.

Jamie was shaking gently as he pulled the sheath off the cannula. Although he had done this hundreds of times as a student, this was the first event as a real doctor. There was a sense of urgency and even life-saving potential.

He controlled himself and slipped the cannula into the bend of the elbow, having already quickly cleaned this spot with a swab.

Just as the needle went in the patient thrashed and Angela was unable to keep the arm still. Jamie quickly withdrew the needle to avoid injury to the patient and just as importantly avoiding a needle stick injury to Angela, at the same time.

After calming the patient for a second time, Angela fished a second cannula out of her uniform, leaving Jamie thinking momentarily of Mary Poppins handbag.

This time, he found the vein, as Angela kept the arm still. Jamie removed the central needle, placing it for now in the plastic case it had come from. Angela now found a 5-ml syringe, and ampule of saline flush from the same pocket and past them to Jamie.

He connected all the parts quickly and efficiently to allow restoration of the flow of 'doxapram', whilst Angela taped and bandaged the canula in place. How did Angela have all the right stuff in that pocket and still look crisp and smart, he wondered?

At that moment, Jon, popped his head around the curtain, just as they were tidying up the bits of debris.

"Good job!" Jon said both as a statement and as a question. He was actually looking at Angela. She smiled back at Jon, before replying.

"Very good in fact. He has passed his first test for sure." Angela's response was said in a very matter of fact voice. No fuss, but Jamie was fully aware that an assessment event had just happened and was based on a senior nurse's response to the senior doctor. No written feedback would be received, but Jamie, fully acknowledged he had been given a positive report. Jamie was sure the event would influence in future, the way he was given responsibility, from this first task as a junior doctor.

"I will sort the sharps out for you Jamie!" Angela started to turn to pick up the two plastic cases.

"Not at all!" he said gently but firmly. "I will always do this job myself, if you don't mind." He looked at her and smiled, so she wasn't offended.

"Double points!" she said, though she looked at Jon and smiled, what Jamie took for a warm and affectionate smile. It was returned by the registrar, with interest. Jamie felt a little tinge of jealousy and wondered if there was something between the two of them, as he departed, feeling like a gooseberry.

He thought of the wedding ring and realised for the first time that Jon didn't have one. He would perhaps ask Christine at a later date as to Angela's husband's profession and Jon's status if she knew it. However, he would have to wait a while, to find out if there was any gossip about Jon and Angela, being an item.

He had already reckoned, A12 would be his favourite ward. He would make the coffee 'elevenses', if at all possible and if not today, the next time this group of nurses were on shift together.

Jamie, picked up a plastic dish referred to as a kidney dish from its' curving multi-purpose shape and put his two used needles in this before heading to the treatment room, where the one ward 'sharps' bin was located.

Sharp needle items and broken glass ampoules went in this 'sharps' bin. All other non-dangerous rubbish went in to plastic bin-bags for incineration. Before he left the treatment room, Jamie collected two fresh cannulae, two 5-ml syringes, multiple aseptic swabs and plastic saline flush ampoules and added them into his right pocket, where his stethoscope had held place of honour only an hour before. Never travel without these new items, he learnt from Angela and this first incident. He wanted to be prepared for any similar event in the future, especially if on a ward, where he might not have the same efficient provider on hand, as Angela clearly was.

Just as he was doing this, Christine came into the treatment room. She was short and slim and her light blue dress uniform fitted her hips so snugly that he was able to tell that she was wearing tights, not stockings beneath her light blue uniform dress.

This was a minor disappointment as Jamie loved the nurses in stockings fantasy.

He blushed as the thoughts came in to his head and just as he did, she came up alongside him and without hesitation nudged him with her hips and looked coyly up at him.

"Well, look who is starring on day one, Jamie Carmichael!" He wasn't sure if it was a question or a statement and he didn't reply.

"Thank you for your really warm welcome on here, it is appreciated," he changed the subject.

"You are very welcome and we are very warm," the comment was open ended, but he couldn't think of a quick rejoinder in time.

Christine, turned around and left the treatment room, without further comment. Was that an intentional wiggle he wondered as she sashayed through the door?

He hadn't been sure about the wink, but that wiggle was clearly for his benefit, he concluded.

Chapter 3
Getting Covid: Day Zero, Discussions of Virus Transmission

"Thanks for the tea, by the way!" Jamie managed in a quiet and subdued voice as he looked at the mug of tea. He was still troubled.

Jamie had not let anyone make him a cup of tea for months, preferring to look after his own cup, plate and cutlery. He had even taken the responsibility of washing his and everyone else's dirty cups at the end of the day and this had become an accepted routine in the office.

Jamie was not normally quite so obsessive with cutlery hygiene, but Covid was different. Medically, it was different from anything he had seen before in his near forty-year career and it broke all the rules and patterns of medicine, on which his personal and medical practice had previously been based.

Jamie had recounted to his office colleagues just three months into the pandemic: "if you have a logical based idea of what should happen with a virus, then it looks like you would be proved wrong on every point, when it comes to Covid-19."

An absence of logic unnerved Jamie and made him likelier to support the view that the virus was indeed created in a Chinese laboratory. The alternative option was that a nature-driven mutation of an existing strain had developed spontaneously between animal species. This natural mutation would have to suddenly include a prion protein, that had only previously been identified within a man-made virus in a Chinese laboratory. The laboratory in question was geographically very close to where the start of the pandemic had occurred. The entire team had come to believe a natural mutation was unlikely, though frustratingly, they suspected they would never know the truth.

Jamie had also suggested months before, that the early strains of Covid-19 were not predominantly an airborne virus and these little green droplets floating in the air were a fallacy of government, media and scientists' imagination, born early in the pandemic.

The premise that airborne particles were the primary transmission mechanism, had not been subject to any real challenge. More recently, the new 'delta' mutation arrived and looked like it could be different with greater and easier transmission.

Just like the whole UK population, Jamie remembered vividly the cartoons played on the national news at the start of the pandemic, when public anxiety was unencumbered by the more recent fatigue and cynicism. The images themselves, depicting green viral particle monsters drove the public fear of inhalation at the expense of other important components of reducing transmission risk. Jamie had no doubt that the 'green cartoon particles' had stuck in the imagination of at least 90% of their patients, if not the entire UK population judged on his subsequent consultations.

As a result, everyone had become addicted to the idea and the belief that masks were their saviour, even though the truth that their only real function of preventing the expulsion of particles, was repeatedly reported.

Jamie had also debated with the team, that the population had been wearing masks diligently for ten months and covid transmission had continued, without apparent abate. It was very simple to conclude therefore, that as a single method of protection and prevention, that they had about as much efficiency as a punctured condom did, at preventing pregnancy.

Jamie's belief of this fact had grown stronger as the weekly viral statistics had come into his computer in-box from September until now, confirming the absence of isolations of flu, rhinovirus (common colds), RSV (the croup virus) and the adeno virus (viral sinusitis).

Each one of these normal winter viruses, could be the final insult for any one of their team's six thousand long term severe asthma patient population.

However, this year there had been barely a single isolate of any of these normal winter viruses, that they knew were definitely transmitted through the airborne route.

Coincident to Jamie opening this weeks' email of the viral data, still looking nervously at his tea, Bushra Khalid arrived. She had the next pod in the office to Jamie, but was the one member of the team, who was not as convinced of Jamie's belief. She was barely over five feet tall, but had enormous drive, energy and passion. She was the politically connected member of the team and only did a few clinical sessions with them. The rest of her work included a role on many of the regional and some national committees and she was a particularly strong advocate for the medical BAME community.

They had discussed just yesterday, how the usual arrival of the rhinovirus in September had briefly flickered on the weekly statistics, but then disappeared and today's email confirmed, there were again zero isolates from the last week. Jamie told the team he was just forwarding them these newly updated figures.

"For a while, I honestly thought it was just the sloppy way people are using masks." He started to try and explain why Covid was circulating, but the other viruses weren't. "But, if this was true, then it would be the same for all viruses and so we would have had the same winter epidemics of these viruses, as well as Covid."

Tim joined in. "I agree. It doesn't make sense, unless something is different in how Covid-19 virus is being transmitted, compared to our normal winter viruses."

Bushra, was half-listening, whilst preparing to attend a 'Teams' meeting about 'virtual wards' for patients post discharge from hospital. She liked verbally jousting with the boys, when she had the time. She checked her watch, fifteen minutes until her meeting started and it was lunch time.

"You still do wear your mask going round the supermarket though Jamie?" It was a taunting question. She knew Jamie would dislike being called for hypocrisy. Like all of them, she knew they wore their masks diligently at work. However, the use in the clinical setting was different. They disposed of the masks, without touching the front of it and changed them after every patient contact, unlike the public domain, where a single mask was being used for several days and people repeatedly touched the front of the mask.

In previous lunch-breaks, Jamie had frequently recounted the stupidity of what he called 'mask culture'. Being the one member of the team who lived alone and not having the guarantee of being in for home-delivery, meant Jamie was the one who regaled the rest of them, with his 'supermarket experiences'.

"She shopped with her mask and disposable medical examination gloves on, so in her head she was indestructible." Jamie had responded to Bushra's trigger, by describing the retirement age lady, he had followed round Tesco this week.

"The suit of armour!" Tim chipped in.

"Indeed, so she picked up seven separate bottles of milk, looking at each one's sell by date."

"What were you doing watching her all that time? I thought you went for younger models?" Jamie had dated a much younger nurse for a few months in the years since being single, Bushra teased him mercilessly whenever she got the chance for his 'mid-life crisis' as she referred to it.

"Waiting to get a pot of cream to make a stroganoff! It was above the milk." Jamie cooked for himself most nights and continued his story undaunted, giving a factual explanation for his unusual show of patience.

"So next, she gets a hanky out of her bag, pulls the mask down holding the front of the mask, blows her nose, puts the hanky back inside her bag and moves on to the cheese section, only after she has reapplied lipstick."

"Haha, well the gloves aren't much use now," Tim again.

"She probably had done the same routine several times before she got to the milk section, I only caught up with her there. That means potentially *seven* bottles of milk were contaminated from her nose, as well as countless cheese packets being definitely contaminated."

"That's assuming she was a Covid carrier of course," Bushra chipped away.

"Just as well it wasn't lasagne you were making this week," Dan retorted from the corner.

"If it had been, I'd have changed the menu on the spot!"

"But the studies have shown that masks *do* reduce transmission," Bushra replied now irritated, by this persistent attack on masks.

"Yes, but those studies were done on hamsters not humans. Last time I looked hamsters didn't use hankies or mobile phones."

"That's why, we keep our phones in a plastic bag when we are on ICU! We can wipe the bag clean with 'alcowipes', when we've had a message," Rebecca, one of the team physiotherapists, was joining in the conversation for the first time. She had been moved from the severe asthma team, to support ICU during the peak of the first wave. She was now pregnant and therefore, off the frontline.

"Then a young lady, also holding her mobile phone while shopping, jumped in front of me and picked up one of the bottles of milk. It's now Russian roulette." Jamie knew he was being dramatic to make his point, but the team got his argument.

Dan, hummed the theme music for the film 'Deer-hunter', picking up on Jamie's analogy.

"So, the virus spreads from gloved hand to bottle, bottle to hand, hand to phone, phone to lips or mask," Jamie was moving his hands around as he spoke, mimicking the movements. He had turned to Bushra. "It really won't make much difference, whether anyone is wearing a mask or gloves, will it? Where has the messages about hand hygiene disappeared to in all this time?"

Tim Coffey sat one further desk to Bushra's right, he and Jamie had her sandwiched in.

"They can measure the amount of virus in sewage effluent, meaning live virus is in poo. If you don't wash your hands properly when you go to the loo, then it's on your hands from that source too."

"But countries who used masks early like China and Thailand, have had much smaller epidemics, than the UK," Bushra continued to defend the role of masks.

"I bet the hand hygiene in those countries is *way* better than here. It will be interesting to see what happens, when the epidemic gets to huge areas of Asia and Africa, where hygiene is much worse," Tim Coffey came back.

"It might reduce the number of people rushing for a ticket for a holiday to Spain when we are flying again, if you need an anal swab rather than a nose one, to be allowed to fly." The conversation was heading down the gutter as medical conversations often did. This time Jamie was the culprit.

"Maybe not from what I've seen of 21st century pornography," Dan added drily from his corner of the room. Nobody dared ask him, what he knew about 21st century pornography, though Tim was sorely tempted, but thought better of challenging his boss with the room nearly full!

"All of this explains why the transmission of virus only slowed down, when we went from tier three to full lockdown. My guess, is still that the bulk of transmission is occurring in pubs and restaurants, gyms and processes like hairdressing and 'beauty' salons, where close hand to hand or hand to glass or cup contact is inevitable," Jamie restored the conversation back down a medical track.

"Perhaps, the persisting level of unexplained transmission during full lockdown, is caused by contamination of take-away or home delivery packaging, cups or cartons," Tim was fully engaged with the hand transmission theory.

"No point getting overly focussed on supermarket behaviour though, Jamie, if people are going to do stupid things like going on holiday to a ski resort and then when there is an outbreak or a closure of borders imminent, running home, bringing the virus with them, or leaving it at petrol stations on the route from the Alps to Calais." Dan was referring to recent outbreaks that had occurred in ski resorts, where those who could afford the inflated prices, had gone for a quick pre lockdown ski fix. At the threat of needing ten days of quarantine on return, they had fled through every available route to beat the deadline, many hiring cars in France and leaving them at Heathrow or in Kent. Dan, Tim and Jamie had already done this discussion for a previous lunch entertainment.

"Didn't get much newspaper or television publicity that story! I bet there were plenty of politicians and media leaders in *that* exodus party!" Jamie was always quick to be critical of the media, who he believed decried everyone else publicly for any error, but yet was the only industry, that didn't have any effective self-policing or governance for its' own highly questionable moral behaviour.

The group ended their lunch time banter, when Bushra's Team meeting started and she insisted that she needed to be left in relative peace.

Jamie looked at the mug of tea, one last time. Dan was half watching from his own desk, whilst answering emails. Jamie's phone rang and his secretary was on the line wanting him to chat to one of their very anxious patients, regarding vaccines. This was one of thousands of similar conversations that were needed in an attempt to reassure their patient population, who in theory at least had the most to gain from vaccination, but many understandably still had unassuaged fear.

During the call, he sipped idly from the mug of tea and continued to do so as he cleared his emails, ignoring that niggling instinct, to have left the tea undrunk and wash the cup and his hands, before making a fresh one. Doing so, with Dan there, would have been a huge insult.

Chapter 4
The House Officer Year: Day 1
(Part II)

Jamie never got to coffee break. In fact, he barely made it back to A12 before the change of nursing shift at 2 p.m. Within his first shift, there were twenty-six new admissions in the first twenty-four-hour period, for which he was responsible. Jemma proved to be a very conscientious and supportive colleague and worked alongside him at times and independently at others. The only thing that appeared to matter to her, was how efficiently they could assess the patient, complete paperwork and establish first level treatment.

Jon came around seeing all the patients behind them, until 11 p.m., when he went to bed, leaving his two junior colleagues still at it.

Jamie made the mess, sitting room situated in the middle of the hospital for twenty minutes, to eat his lunch at approximately 4 p.m., when there was a brief lull in the flow of admissions.

He was eating the homemade ham and cheese sandwiches he had brought in, as fast as he could in case his bleep went again. He reckoned it had gone off, over fifty times already. The sandwich was tasteless and dry, but he was so hungry it made no difference.

Forster, the parrot, which had been there since Jamie was a student two years before, was eyeing his sandwich with interest, as if there was no cage between them.

The parrot looks a little unwell, Jamie thought, and then shook his head. It was probably the day of dealing with patients which was making him crazy. Although he was sure there were more feathers flying about than he remembered from the last time he was in this room, over a year ago.

Just at that moment, one of the surgical junior doctors crashed into the room. He had been there as a house officer when Jamie was a student and he recognised him and even pulled the name up, Richard Rock.

He was sporting what looked to Jamie like a vacuum cleaner attachment for soft furnishings. It was of dark grey plastic, with a round hilt, that Rich was holding, a narrower neck and then a larger oblong shape top section with brush elements.

Jamie was nonplussed, but the excitement on Rich's face was unrestrained.

"Whose got the keys, anyone know?" the young surgeon asked the near empty room.

There were only two people there before the surgeon and judging by the even more tired look of Jamie's female compatriot, he didn't imagine she would know what he was on about either. She was also having lunch at almost tea time.

Jamie had guessed that she was a paediatrician. He based this assumption on his personal observations that they worked longer hours than any doctor other than cardiothoracic surgeons, who seemed to patrol their hospitals at all hours of day and night.

This Stockport hospital didn't have cardiothoracic surgery and hence paediatrics was Jamie's first guess. Jamie looked across more closely now and saw the badge: 'paediatric registrar'. Special Care Baby Unit must have been very busy both last night and today. Her eyes were bagged, her red hair looked a little unkempt, even within a ponytail. Jamie knew that the registrars didn't always change over on the same day as the juniors and guessed she was on-call last night and covering her own new juniors today.

As the lady hadn't answered and wasn't showing interest in anything other than a green salad that looked just as tired as its owner, Jamie was forced to do the asking. "Which key?"

"The trophy cupboard, of course!" Rich (as Jamie remembered he preferred to be called) had irritation in his voice and a stare of scrutiny. Jamie expected he was disappointed by his audience. "Do you think I'm here to hoover the floor?" Jamie remained nonplussed and knew he was missing something important as Rich lifted the attachment even higher and waved it at him.

More commotion came from behind Rich in the hallway and stairs.

"Let me through. I've got the key!" Several bodies now poured into the room. One of them, a slightly chunky and senior looking male, who Jamie later knew as Mark Smith, surgical registrar and a tall Arabic looking gentleman who had both poise and a tall stance. The latter was sporting a goatee long before they were fashionable. His name was Firaz and Jamie learned later, that he had arrived a couple of years before, from Iran.

"Whoa, that is quite a big one!" Firaz's accent was unmistakably middle eastern in origin.

Last to enter was a surgical consultant, who again Jamie recognised from his student days. Jamie remembered the name easily; Paul Scotland. He had been attached to the surgical consultant as a student. He was clearly calmer than the rest, but was watching the developing scene, with much humour.

"Biggest of my career for sure!" Rich announced.

Jamie was still bemused. In the end, he was forced to ask, as it appeared they were waiting for him and the tired paediatric doctor to comment, or at least join in their excitement.

"I'm really sorry, but what is in the 'trophy cupboard'?" Jamie sounded even more sheepish than he had feared he would and instantly regretted asking.

"Oh god, you must be one of the new medical house-dogs!" Rich almost spat out the last two words. The young surgeon was perhaps two years ahead of Jamie in terms of medical seniority and yet the patronising tone appalled Jamie. Momentarily, he wasn't sure he had even heard correctly, the term 'House dog' rather than 'house doc', but Jamie learnt quickly the style of surgeons, who as self-proclaimed superior beings, put their non-surgical colleagues down with annoying regularity. There was also at this time, an unmistakable, misogynistic element to the career and Jamie, had long ago decided surgery was not the future for him.

He was trying to remember if it was Mr Scotland, whose list he had visited, and watched a leg amputation. Once the saw was going through bone, with blood-stained chippings that otherwise looked like wood sawdust emerged, Jamie had started to lose control. He was forced to leave the table and sit on the floor with his head between his legs, in preference to fainting completely at the operating-table. These embarrassing memories making him even more unsettled and fighting with new embarrassment.

It was Mr Scotland who enlightened him, perhaps taking pity on him.

"The trophy cabinet is for items, removed surgically, from the rectums of predominantly male patients." His voice was intoned as if given a speech at an erudite medical meeting. "Inserted there for some unexplainable sexual pleasure, as I understand. More unexplainable is how they ever think they can remove the said items themselves, without surgical help, when you look at the size and shape of this relatively moderate sized object. However, I concur it definitely merits its place in the trophy cabinet." Mr Scotland had turned back to face Rich for the last sentence and his voice had returned to a normal speaking tone.

"It has been washed, I hope?" Everyone turned to look at the paediatric registrar, the one lady in the room. Her female sensitivity was swamped by the male machismo and the unmistakable odour of testosterone, of this dominant surgical gathering.

"Why, of course!" Rich finally replied, sounding even more exasperated than he had been with Jamie a minute before.

Mark Smith had now got the cabinet open. It was a nearly six-foot-tall mahogany wardrobe with multiple shelves. Jamie saw for the first time, the plethora of objects of multiple colours, sizes and shapes which filled the space.

Two huge dildos fell out on the floor, bouncing before coming to rest, with their rubber latex bodies and irregular shape.

"Oh, for goodness-sake!" sighed the paediatric colleague, who although pretending to be disgusted was now sat up from her previous position slumped in a comfy chair. She was even craning her neck to get a better look at the contents.

Jamie couldn't resist standing up and getting closer.

"Fuckin' hell!" the screechy voice belonged to the parrot.

"Correct, Forster!" Mark Smith was the one to recognise the parrot's intervention.

"It was Mr Ball who taught him to swear like that, when he was just a registrar." Mr Scotland was referring to one of his newly promoted surgical colleagues. "Timing was good though, Forster!" the latter was said over his shoulder in the direction of the cage.

"I think Mr Ball taught him to say that phrase every time the cabinet was opened," Mr Scotland added.

Jamie's eyes dilated at the variety of objects. At least half looked like they were actually designed for sex, such as the dildos. However, there were glass ones, rippled ones and ones that looked even too big for the loosest of orifices of the female form, that had been designed through evolution to dilate at least during child-birth, to a wide capacity, unlike the anus.

On the higher shelves, the other half of the items, did not have primary sexual functions. There was a loofah, a water hosepipe connecter, an old milk bottle and a champagne bottle on the middle shelf. Higher still, were a variety of shapes of plastic bottles including ketchup bottles. On the top shelf, once Jamie could see it, was a variety of really unlikely objects including a kitchen tap, a toy dinosaur that resembled a triceratops and was the size of the champagne bottle and most hideously a rippled hose connector for a hoover that must have been two feet in length with nearly five inches in cross sectional diameter.

"Not the whole thing?" Lady paediatrician was getting more interested as her eyes landed on the last object that Jamie had spotted.

"It's not that big, I will show you mine later if you like?" Rich's words coming out lasciviously and of course with completely unrealistic exaggeration.

"I got that hoover pipe connector out with just sedative." Mr Scotland had turned to the paediatric registrar. "He had eaten three curries after losing it inside, the victim told me." Mr Scotland had a reminiscent quality to his voice, ignoring and indeed talking over his foolish younger colleague. "He thought if he got raging diarrhoea, he would be able to 'shit' it out. Once removed, I had to persuade CCSD to put it through the autoclave twice before I dared put it in the cabinet, it was so disgusting. Cost me a bottle of Christmas whiskey to get it done, but it was worth it, to own the biggest item here."

There was a general murmuring of approval at the story.

Mr Scotland continued, "He was as camp as they come and as soon as we gave him a touch of propofol anaesthetic, he got giddy and relaxed his arse completely. As it came out, he had a raging hard on, despite the anaesthetic." Jamie was wishing he hadn't just finished his sandwich before observing this event.

"Crazy!" said Lady paediatrician.

"Crazy cunt!" chipped in Forster who obviously recognised the first-word from many nights of medical story telling in this room.

"Have you heard of the splenic squeeze?" asked Mark, trying to get a voice loud enough that would control the hubbub.

"Not me!" said the Arabic colleague, who treated Mark with respect, despite looking older than him.

"Diana, you might not want to hear this," Mr Scotland spoke to the paediatric registrar, "I've heard him tell this story once before."

"I am not leaving whilst you misogynistic bastards have a party in here."

Jamie was astounded that she had effectively called a consultant surgeon a 'bastard'.

"Bastard, bastard," chirped the irrepressible Forster.

Mr Scotland and Diana made smiling eye contact. The fatigue leaving her face for the first time. Jamie's gossip radar twitched momentarily.

"Right, for those that haven't heard this story, it came from a medical physician friend," Mark looked pointedly at Jamie at that moment, as the only representative of the medical side of the hospital.

"You don't have many of those, do you?" a newly arrived female surgeon, that Jamie also recognised from his early student days, was the second female voice.

Sally Wise had been a surgical registrar for six years to Jamie's knowledge and still hadn't been appointed as a consultant. She was reportedly an excellent surgeon, but it was the 'XX' chromosome, that was probably stopping her getting a senior appointment. There were so few female surgeons in the early 1980s, something Jamie fervently hoped would change rapidly. He also knew she was very feisty, as she would have to be, to have survived in this environment of male machismo.

"Physician friends I mean," she clarified, but Jamie had worked out what she meant and so he guessed had the rest of the group ahead of him.

Mark had ignored her arrival and was about to continue anyway.

Sally beat him to that too. "Sorry, delete the 'Physician' as the sentence works just as well without it."

Ouch, two-nil to Sally, thought Jamie.

"Anyway!" Mark continued, ignoring the jibes. "He referred a chap from the infectious disease clinic from Guys in London, to his GI colleagues for investigation of Left Upper Quadrant pain." Mark pointed to the top of his abdomen close to his spleen for visual effect, even though he was talking to mostly surgeons.

"They did cameras up and down, ultrasound of liver spleen and kidneys, and even a CT scan. Three months later and still no explanation for the pain." There was a murmur of medical interest from the gathering and a few whispered potential diagnoses.

"Now, of course 'infectious diseases' at Guys in London, is pretty much effectively, the AIDS clinic, but this chap didn't have any active AIDS disease either. My mate saw him back in the infectious unit and the patient was still complaining of this pain. Stuck for ideas, my friend mentions the medical mystery to the specialist nurse, who was of course gay himself. 'Have you asked him if he practices the splenic squeeze?' asked the nurse quietly. 'What's that?' asks my mate. Just like you lot, he didn't know."

"What's that?" parodied Forster, the fluttering of wings accompanied with a cloud of feathers and dust.

"Anyway, apparently, what these guys do is anal fisting. They can get so good at the anatomy, they can follow the colon up to the splenic flexure, turn their partner on, blow job or whatever and at the moment of orgasm, they grab the spleen from the inside and squeeze hard. Blood rush at the moment of orgasm blows their hair off apparently. Left upper quadrant pain explained!"

Jamie felt sick. His ham and cheese sandwich sitting very heavily just to the right of his own spleen.

He was rescued by his bleep.

"Oh, that's disgusting," said Diana as Jamie fled from the room in search of a phone that wasn't in earshot of this surgical craziness.

"Beep, beep, beep!" chirped Forster after him.

****

In the remainder of his shift, Jamie got to bed at 2 a.m. for an hour. He did his IV-drug round at 5 a.m. even though it was a little early and spoke to the night shift nurses on each of the wards.

The second on-call doctor, as was the routine, had done the day time IV drug rounds until midnight. They came off duty, after this was complete and generally headed to the mess bar for a beer or two.

Jamie as 'first on' doctor was then responsible for the 6 a.m. round as well as overnight admissions.

On A11 (Sister Arbuthnott's ward) and A12 (Angela's), Jamie found all the drug prescriptions (Kardex's) with a kidney dish on top, containing the exact drug ampoules, diluting liquid ampoules, drug labels and bags of fluid for the antibiotics to be put into. These parcels were placed around the white plastic surface of the treatment room, waiting for him.

When Jamie thanked the nurse in charge for getting them ready, he was surprised by the answer. "Sister's orders for you, Dr Carmichael." The 'you' was said slightly oddly. Jamie raised an eyebrow at it, but was too tired to really worry about its' meaning on that first night.

He hadn't realised how tired he was and was grateful there was an additional primary check on which actual ampoules he was expected to make up. He tried to focus and double-check everything twice. A day one mistake on intravenous drugs would be a disaster for his reputation, even if double dose antibiotics would be pretty harmless for the average adult.

Making and giving IV infusions, was one of the most important safety events of the day and leaving it to a doctor who had already done twenty-two hours unbroken, with just one hour of sleep, was he realised not necessarily the smartest of organisational decisions. The nurses were allowed to take the filled and labelled bags and attach them to the cannula, but not do the mixing and labelling themselves.

Inevitably one or two of the patients per ward, had pulled out or lost their vein cannulas, in the period since midnight and so there were patients who needed another one inserted. During the day, Jamie was pleased, that he had over a 90% success rate at putting them in first go on his first day and this included the patient in bed three with the respiratory failure who had jerked his arm away, even when held by Angela.

Now at 6 a.m., his success rate was dipping to nearer 50%. This really frustrated Jamie. Most importantly because it added to the discomfort for each patient, who themselves had probably just been woken from heavily disturbed and uncomfortable sleep.

The morning nursing shifts came on just around the time the IV-drug round was finishing. Jamie was pleased to see Christine as he arrived on A12, which he had saved until last. Angela wasn't on duty, so he guessed she was on a late shift.

He wasn't surprised that Christine came into the treatment room, whilst he was doing his tidying up.

"Jesus, you look and smell like shit!" she said immediately, leaving Jamie crestfallen. She retreated quickly, having not let her hip get within a 'barge pole' length of him.

He finished the IV-drug round in misery. He had one more, new patient to admit, before getting to his on-call room for the second time in twenty-four hours at about 7.30 a.m. Half an hour leeway. *Sleep or a shower?* Jamie thought to himself.

He had no doubt in his head, that if it hadn't been for Christine's comment, he would have chosen the extra sleep, setting his loud wind-up metal alarm clock he had brought with him for exactly this purpose of waking him when he was most tired.

However, the 'smell like shit' comment was still burning inside him, as the worst insult he had ever experienced, so he chose the shower.

At 8.15 a.m., he was pristine, shaved, smelling of cheap deodorant (possibly 'Brut'), but completely exhausted. He went to the canteen and had his first ever morning coffee (he normally drank tea first thing, but realised the coffee might help) and had his evening meal (a bacon sandwich). It was only as he devoured it, he realised he hadn't eaten since the ham and cheese sandwich yesterday afternoon. In response to his hunger, he headed back to the counter for a second.

"Nearly came over to give you another one, you looked so hungry after downing the first in one bite," said a kindly smiling middle-aged, red-haired lady.

"Thanks! I'm earning so happy to buy it…" Jamie peered at the badge, but couldn't get his eyes to focus, clearly enough to read the name, which he had wanted to add at the end of the sentence.

"Elaine!" she laughed, "but if you can remember it tomorrow, I will give you a free bacon bap for breakfast. Your brain looks more scrambled than my eggs. Good luck getting through today." She laughed again. He told himself to remember 'Elaine', not because he was bothered about a free sandwich, but just to joust with the kindly canteen lady.

He met Jemma and Jon in the doctor's office on A12 as planned. Jemma had left him at 2 a.m. and he hadn't needed her help after that time. Jon had disappeared at 11 p.m. and Jamie assumed he had slept all night. He looked smooth and smelled of good aftershave. Jemma looked fresh, but not as full of vigour as yesterday's early encounters.

"Oh crap! You didn't get any sleep then?" Jon was first to comment.

"Maybe an hour, not too bad," Jamie responded weakly. He was going to have to learn to hide the 'no sleep' look, he convinced himself.

"Dr Lorimer has messaged me and says he will be on the ward for nine-thirty to do the consultant ward round."

As the consultant responsible for the admissions of the last twenty-four hours, Dr Lorimer would come to review all these patients, plus any patients still in hospital under their care since the last ward round. Consultant ward rounds traditionally happened twice per week and they would only come on the ward again if directly requested by the registrar or occasionally the senior sister. The consultant ward rounds could be very grand affairs with a 'royal visit', type feel.

Most of the wards Jamie had worked on during the twenty-four hours were mostly old long dormitory type areas, but with only curtains to separate beds, there was no real privacy. As the ward often went silent at ward round time, the discussions with each patient were likely to be overheard by the neighbouring patients at least and the whole ward if the consultant had a strong voice.

A12 was a more 'modern' ward design, with two areas of four beds, but also a 9-bay area at one end. The nursing station, looked into the bays on both sides as well as the ward entrance corridor, which had the kitchen, clean and dirty utility areas and a nursing and doctor office along the length. There were only two side-rooms, both behind the nurse's station.

Dr Lorimer was new and only had a few patients left allocated to him, so this meant they had thirty patients or so to see on that post-admission ward round. Jamie would do most of the jobs he created, after the ward round was done. The team would keep the notes up to date between them during the ward round. This was the plan they agreed, whilst they waited for their new boss.

****

When Dr Lorimer arrived, he was tall and had a very vertical stance like he was standing to attention. Yet, to counter the posture, he was softly spoken, but with a gravitas suited to his new status as consultant. Jamie reckoned he was mid to late 30s. The hair was fair but balding prematurely on top. There was a resemblance to a young Duke of Edinburgh.

"So, are we starting here team?" he asked after introductions. "Can we have sister in charge to go through the patients with us?"

"It's a staff nurse in charge today, I will go and see if she can join us," Jamie volunteered.

Dr Lorimer turned to Jon. Jamie caught the first half of the sentence. "Standards must be slipping up north. The sisters in London would ensure they were rostered on duty for the consultant ward-rounds. I will expect this going forward."

Jamie wondered how that conversation would go down with both Angela and more interestingly, Sister Arbuthnott.

Christine was not impressed to hear half of this sentence as Jamie retold it, as she followed him down to the Doctor's office.

"Nice bum and glad you showered!" she whispered in the empty bit of corridor, so softly, that Jamie could barely hear it and wasn't sure in his fatigued state, whether he had really heard it or whether it was wishful thinking in his state of profound sleep deprivation.

Either way, he turned round and switched on his best smile for her, before opening the door.

She went in first, but her smile faded quickly as Dr Lorimer set to berating her, expressing disappointment and again comparing standards in London, to what he was seeing for his first ward round in Stockport.

The room was awkward in silence, after he had finished.

Jon eventually broke it. "Shall we get on nonetheless? It was a pretty busy day yesterday."

"I thought the message was out there not to get ill on the first day of August, or are the great unwashed of the North not as educated as where I came from?" Dr Lorimer was in full 'South is better' patronising flow.

Jamie thought the start of this ward round could not have got worse. The three months could be a long drag, he feared on that morning.

They discussed the first two patients that belonged to them on the ward. The first was Jamie's overdose case, who had remained non-acidotic and therefore would be fit to go home today and then the COPD patient, who was on the infusion Jamie had rescued yesterday.

Jamie had felt sorry for the young man who had allegedly taken twenty-five aspirin (what he told Jamie). His life was terrible. He had come from a broken home and already spent a year in prison, after two years in foster care. His father had abused him physically and mentally before he was moved in to the foster care. He had no job and had become addicted to opiate painkillers whilst in prison.

Post prison, he had moved back to his mum's house. She was an alcoholic, chain smoker and had no money left for food. Neil had done his best to contribute, working at the local Co-op and then MacDonald's, but he was too unreliable to keep a job for long.

Jamie started to tell the reason for the 'OD', but was stopped by Dr Lorimer.

"Save me the sob story, they are all the same," Dr Lorimer silenced the junior during his first consultant ward-round presentation. Jamie had to bite his tongue such was his disappointment. Jon sensed Jamie's ire and did the signal you would use for a dog, to make it sit. Jon did it very subtly with his hands, using a set of notes to hide the movement from their new boss. Jamie watched it and kept his face passive.

"I presume he has had a 'psych' review?" was the follow up question from Dr Lorimer, when Jamie went silent.

"He has been referred. He can go home and will have a call tomorrow from the psychiatrist, as they perceived it as not a serious attempt on the basis of the absence of acidosis."

"Ok, next!"

They were on to the end stage COPD patient and Jon took the lead explaining the infusion and how it was holding the respiratory failure, although on review by Jon yesterday afternoon, the improvement had stalled somewhat.

Christine chipped in. "Seemed a bit brighter this morning and had just asked to sit out on the commode."

"Not always a good sign!" Dr Lorimer responded negatively. "In my experience, it often precedes the cardio-respiratory arrest."

"I've certainly seen that a few times," Jemma intervened for the first time. Jamie suspected she was not trying to curry favour, but did it more out of a desire to keep the mood light and avoid any dissent.

Jamie had managed to calm himself down somewhat and even though he had helped Mr Thompson getting the cannula in quickly, he also didn't think his intervention would last long. Lazarus acts were rare in reality.

Having voiced further agreement, he looked up at Christine, who had her side to the rest of the team, but was facing Jamie as they had sat in the two seats either side of the door.

She held his eye for a moment and waited until Dr Lorimer and Jon were speaking again about blood gas numbers. She then looked at her lap and gently opened her knees which had been pressed together. Jamie didn't see much, her skirt was tight after all, but it was the implication of the act, that got his blood pressure jumping. If he wasn't careful, he was going to lose concentration altogether and with a fragile ward round, that could have been disastrous at that moment.

He shook himself internally and turned pointedly towards Dr Lorimer, who was talking about the blood results and their meaning.

After a few minutes, they went to see these two patients, who were in one of the four-bedded bays before discussing any others.

The curtains were still around Mr Thompson.

"I will just find one of the auxiliaries to get Mr Thompson off the commode," Christine spoke before she hurried off, when they saw the closed curtains.

Dr Lorimer spent less than thirty seconds with young Neil and wished him well, recommending he joined a church group for support, an act that really surprised Jamie. *Young adults from Stockport, who had experienced prison and foster care, didn't hold much stock in church*, he thought. However, he held his own counsel.

Christine hadn't made it back within the thirty seconds and Dr Lorimer went to pull the curtain, that separated Mr Thompson from Neil.

"He might still be on the comm…" started Jemma. It was too late, the curtain had been pulled back far enough for Dr Lorimer, his junior team, Christine who had just returned with Freda the auxiliary and sadly even Neil, whose head was turned, to see Mr Thompson sat still on the commode, butt naked, with skin as blue as an Everton football strip. The drip containing the breathing stimulant, was leaking fluid on the floor.

Jamie noted the unmistakable smell of faeces.

A shocked Christine, spoke first. "Shall I call the team?"

Jon quickly intervened. "No! It would be futile and unkind. We wouldn't recover him!" Jamie was pleased his senior colleague had made such a logical but immediate call.

The next event really surprised Jamie.

Dr Lorimer, closed the curtain very softly, apologised quietly to Neil, that he had seen what he had seen and then went back inside the curtain, dropped to his knees and started to say a prayer, his hands pressed solemnly together.

Nobody else really knew what to say. The silence once Dr Lorimer had finished, was very awkward initially, before Jon took charge and turned to Christine. "Once Dr Lorimer is ready for us, please get Mr Thompson back on the bed. We will leave Jamie with you to certify his death and speak to the family."

"Yes Dr Calinas!" Christine sounded very close to tears herself.

Dr Lorimer, got back to his feet and confirmed he had heard Jon's suggestion and agreed with it.

Dr Lorimer, Jon and Jemma left the bay.

Jamie helped Christine, Freda and a male auxiliary Jamie later got to know as Tim, negotiate the blue lifeless form back into bed.

This was a particular challenge as Mr Thompson was partly wedged into the commode. He had clearly emptied his bowels before the passing and he was a substantial weight. There were no easily accessible hoists and manual handling training had not made its' way into the dictionary and knowledge base in 1984. Backs were probably strained, but Christine insisted they did it with as much dignity as they could muster under the circumstances.

Once Mr Thompson was in bed, Jamie did the necessary tests and procedures to officially confirm a death, which was not a job which required six years of medical school training on this occasion, but he followed all the protocols.

He then rang Mr Thompson's family to impart the sudden and sad, but perhaps not surprising news. During this latter conversation, which he was forced to do sat at the nurse's station, as he couldn't go to the doctor's office, because the ward round was there, a milky coffee suddenly appeared on the desk, courtesy of Freda. She smiled at him.

"That's especially for helping us lift Mt Thompson. It was appreciated. Not many docs would have done that bit!" she whispered later to Jamie, after he was off the phone. He did also spot her take a tray in to the ward round office too. He suspected it was an attempt to cool the troubled waters of this first ward round. Christine, he was sure had requested it.

"When we are all in the shit together…" he started, "…better if we all chip in."

It was only after he said it that the phrase 'in the shit', didn't seem quite so appropriate or sensitive at the time. Freda let it ride, without further comment.

****

The rest of the ward round took best part of four hours. Jamie had re-joined the party pretty quickly. Even with Jemma and Jon helping to keep the notes up to date and paper work jobs and blood requests done as they were going along, Jamie knew he was not going to get done by 5 p.m.

By the end of the ward round, the early nursing shifts were handing over to the later shifts. The ward-round team made their way back to A12.

Perhaps unfortunately, Angela had arrived a little early and was stood at the nurse's station in her dark blue uniform as they turned into the ward.

"Ah sister, perfect, could I have a word with you," Dr Lorimer almost barked this down the long narrow entrance corridor to the main ward.

"Oh shit," whispered Jon as Dr Lorimer turned into the doctor's office again.

Angela marched forcefully up the corridor. It looked like she had heard the stories of the morning already from Christine. Her head was high, but it looked like she was tense for the first time in Jamie's brief experience of her.

Jon touched her arm as she went past, but Angela didn't react.

Angela joined Dr Lorimer in the Doctor's office and the junior team stood outside at first. Although the door was closed, they could hear much of the conversation, quite clearly. Dr Lorimer firstly expressed his 'disappointment' at only having had a junior staff nurse on duty for his ward round and his shock at finding a patient dead behind a curtain, that the said junior staff nurse had obviously left there, for a long time on a commode.

Angela did not hold back and was clearly not intimidated. Or if she was, she wasn't going to show it.

"Dr Lorimer, our shift rota was written 3 weeks ago, when we didn't even know your name and certainly not your preferences for the days or times, that you have chosen as your ward rounds. I will do my best to ensure either Sister Mattison, who is actually on holiday this week, or myself is on duty for Tuesday mornings and Thursday afternoons going forward. Will you routinely take five hours to do it as I will have to do a long day on a Tuesday to accommodate you if so?" she didn't draw breath. "As for Staff Nurse Carter, she is our most experienced senior nurse and is applying for Sister Mattison's post, who retires in two months-time. I suspect you may find, that she will be in a darker dress, within this time period. I have spoken to her about the commode incident and she recognises she should have asked one of auxiliaries to check on the patient before joining the ward round. However, we were not even aware of what time you were coming. Shall I put nine-thirty into the ward diary for every Tuesday Dr Lorimer?"

The three juniors couldn't resist smiling to themselves as they listened, but Jon nudged Jamie off to get some jobs done, before he could hear anymore.

Christine was just preparing to leave having finished her shift and she was back to her smiling cheeky self. She again found him in the treatment room, this time she had her coat on over her uniform.

"I'm on nights for the rest of the week, so will only see you if you are on call. But I quite like you, Dr Carmichael. Next time I try my little distraction trick on you, you never know I might have put stockings on especially for you. You will have to wait and see!"

"I'm first-on call all weekend," said Jamie, blushing freely again.

"Tights on nights," she said laughing. "It's one of our nursing rules, be patient boy!" she flittered off.

Jamie was happily living with his fiancé and was due to get married in eighteen months-time. He had never experienced female attention of the sort he was getting from Christine. Whilst he loved the feeling of excitement, he had no experience of how to handle it. He had been a very shy and gauche teenager and he was not at all experienced in responding to real sexual interest. Jamie knew how to flirt to get himself liked, but he didn't know what to do, when it was returned with intention.

As Jamie thought about his first two days of experience on the wards, he assumed it was having the 'Dr' letters in front of his name, that changed things. Alternatively, he could be a little different himself. After all, he had achieved his aim of qualifying and meriting the title of 'Doctor' and had a largely successful first day and a half. Perhaps he had the first external signs of confidence and maturity on show. Physically though, he actually knew he looked younger than the twenty-four years, that he actually was.

****

Jamie finally finished his first shift at some time after 6 p.m. Having arrived at 7.30 a.m. in the morning the day before. He calculated it to be nearly thirty-five hours of continuous work, interspersed with one hours sleep and still he had the whole weekend looming ahead of him.

With his fiancé Diane, he met with a couple of friends for a beer that evening and made it until at best approximately 8.30 p.m., before doing the first of what became quite a familiar party trick.

Jamie had just finished the story of the trophy cupboard and was considering whether to progress to the 'splenic squeeze' story. Only one of this group, were actually medical, so he decided against it for a week night.

Whilst one of his male friends spoke about dildos, with rather surprising confidence, Jamie found his eyes starting to close. On-lookers watched as his neck bent and he fell forward. He took out his beer glass in a bowling ball style as his forehead met the table. Fortunately, the glass was nearly empty and was caught by his friend, who was mid-sentence. No damage was done. The table stopped the head's descent and Jamie slept like the dead. Neither moving, nor caring where he was.

His friends carried on chatting for an hour and two more beers/gins each, before they stirred Jamie and encouraged him home.

Chapter 5
Getting Covid: Day Zero
(Part III)

Telephone clinics were new to Dan, Jamie and the rest of the team. First wave lockdown resulted in a huge backlog of missed appointments. Jamie had rolled up his sleeves and set to ringing all the patients, who had their clinic appointments cancelled, well before the managers told them to do it. He knew how much anxiety and stress would be in their patient population. Especially as Severe Asthma had been labelled from the start as a high-risk group. The latter was done on the basis of logic.

The team had not seen the expected excess of their patients admitted unwell through the first wave and were already postulating that there may not be an increased risk effect of having asthma, even before the first wave was calming down.

Jamie missed the personal contact of virtual clinics. He had made a lifetime out of shaking hands with patients. His medical radar already switched on, picking up dry heat, cold clammy anxiety or tremors from the feel of the hands during the shake.

You could only do this if the connections between your hands and your brain were connected and the receptive area of the brain was in active processing mode. Jamie did this at the same time as establishing eye contact and searching the eyes of the patient for signs of nervousness, pain, fear or much more rarely, animosity or aggression. He had only got fully confident in this process as he progressed in his career and spent more time in clinic.

In his teaching sessions with medical students, he often demonstrated the skills of concentrating on lateral information at a new group of students first teaching session. The principles were simple and transmitted to other senses. You could only 'hear' if you were listening, you could only 'see' if you were looking and 'feel' if you were sensing. The best doctors could do all of this for all their senses at the same time, but it took practice, Jamie believed.

As such telephone clinics had significant limitations. No seeing the eyes of the patient or the movements of the body, no senses from the handshake. Hearing was largely unhindered, but that was it. He had learned to tune in more closely, to the hesitations or crack in the voice as fear was announced. It was subtle, though and therefore much more easily misinterpreted, with just the one sense to use.

In the next room, Shanaz Khan was working on her phone. She was the newest colleague in the severe asthma team. They had 'stolen' her from a neighbouring hospital, in large part based on her energy, and her ability to co-ordinate and run meetings. She was so enthusiastic, people found it impossible to say 'no' to her. She had the same work ethic as Jamie and was always smiling, which the patients loved (when face to face).

"God, I miss shaking hands," Jamie said. No wonder he was in the last stages of planning his retirement.

"I just want to see someone face to face," Shanaz concurred. She was like Bushra tiny physically, but Jamie would want her by his side in a battle. She would just not give up, if she went after something she really wanted.

"It's like Bake Off and MasterChef, this process," Jamie commented.

"10 million viewers can't be wrong," said Dan, knowing what was coming.

"Would you watch a programme about music, where you can see the singers singing and the guitarists plucking the strings, but there is no sound. Why watch a programme where you can see the food, listen to some self-proclaimed expert spout about it, but you can't actually taste it, which is of course the most critical part?"

Tim Coffey was behind Jamie and had heard this argument before. "Someone heard you talk about this and they have invented it. You get to see someone pretend to sing and the competition is to see if the experts can pick a real singer from a tone death numpty."

"You are joking, please tell me?" Jamie was in shock at the thought that his best argument of why Bake Off and similar programmes, should be 'outed' as mass hysteria had been turned round against him.

For a moment, Jamie wondered if and hoped that, Tim was just deliberately winding him up. He immediately realised that it would be a new and dramatic change of skill for Tim to keep a straight face if it was.

Jamie desperately didn't want to believe such a banal idea was real.

"Saturday prime time," added Shanaz, who was too straight to even attempt to wind him up and Jamie had to accept, that this inane concept for a programme must indeed be real.

"Emperor's new clothes!" Dan parodied using a vague imitation of Jamie's Manchester accent. Dan knew well, this was Jamie's explanation of how 10 million people can waste an hour watching a tv programme about cooking, when you can't taste the outcome. That hour, would be better spent being in the kitchen and experimenting with a new menu dish, or changing an old one. If someone was really interested in improving their cooking, real-life experimenting was Jamie's repeatedly spouted alternative approach.

Jamie in his own beliefs felt that the watchers of MasterChef and Bake Off were the crowds watching the emperor in the new gown. "Look how fine the silk is! They are all effectively parodying on a Monday morning. But is there any silk at all. Does the food taste of anything? You actually don't know, it's only the voice of Greg and his cronies, that, makes you think it might!"

"Don't get him on love island!" Tim chipped in, as a sign off before they restarted clinic. Moments of banter and leg-pulling was an essential part of dealing with the slightly repetitive content of an afternoon of telephone clinics.

It went as the other 121 telephone clinics had gone since they had resumed doing them after the first wave of the pandemic (Jamie was counting). Most of the work involved reassuring the patients and trying to get them to keep fit and active. Weight gain was going to be a huge long-term negative for their patients.

The team now looked after nearly six thousand severe asthma sufferers, making it possibly the biggest service in Europe. They had wondered if 'in the world' was a possible claim, until an international visitor from Denver in the USA explained that they had thirty physicians, dedicated to severe asthma at their institution, therefore being at least six times bigger, than the Manchester service.

The novel approach Dan, Jamie and the team could claim they were doing differently, was being fully inclusive with many of the very large regional network of hospitals and colleagues. This had resulted in a network involving multiple hospitals with, medical, nursing, pharmacy, physiotherapy and psychology colleagues from a huge geography all getting together and discussing the complex cases. They had additional collaboration with speech therapists for managing one of the linked conditions called ILO (inducible laryngeal obstruction). It is a condition that looks like asthma, sounds like asthma, but isn't and spending money on expensive drugs on patients for whom the best treatment would be speech therapy techniques as one example, would be a very expensive mistake as well as being bad for the patient outcomes.

The Manchester and greater regional teams had led the drive to identify the conditions and co-morbidities of conditions that mimicked asthma and therefore didn't respond to asthma therapies.

Ten years before, there were no great treatments for severe asthma other than oral steroids. The primary goal for Jamie early in his consultant career was to trade off, the short and medium-term quality of life benefit of using them, whilst minimising the long-term side effects.

In the new era, for those with genuine severe asthma, this meant instituting new but expensive therapies which were effectively life-saving. If you could prevent dangerous life-threatening attacks, you also saved lives as a proportion (small as it is) of dangerous attacks of asthma result tragically in death. Both oral steroids and these new therapies protected the patients from the worst outcomes.

For many patients, however, the condition that looked like asthma wasn't in fact asthma. Oral steroids did these patients' irreversible harm, with no benefit. The new expensive medicines if used unwisely in this group wasted huge amounts of limited NHS financial reserves.

Funds weren't limitless. Identification of the right drug to the right patient, was the key to cost-effectiveness. Jamie had sleepless nights when he thought of the total drug budget their centre alone was responsible for (several million pounds per year on these new drugs alone).

Counter-intuitively, by the time Jamie and team had, had their vaccines, the data that inhaled steroids had a protective effect against Covid was published and the evidence that asthma sufferers, were less likely to be hospitalised or die of Covid was fully established.

This data was however, not reported widely in the popular media and so their patients for the most part, hadn't heard it. Jamie knew that information and beliefs patients had acquired from the television and newspapers were hard to shake.

The team used all sorts of approaches to inform their patients of the need to exercise and keep fit, as well as reassure them regarding their individual risks as asthma sufferers.

"There was a great study done in the 1980s, when they compared the health of bus drivers and bus conductors. Bus conductors, back in the day, used to run and up and down stairs collecting the bus fares as you know. Bus drivers sat on their 'arse' and drove the bus for an 8-hour shift. They came from the same social background, smoked the same number of cigarettes and had the same diets," Jamie paused for a moment, like a comedian about to tell the audience the punch-line. "However, bus conductors on average lived 5 years longer than bus drivers."

Jamie was explaining to a 70-year-old patient, who hadn't been out of the house at all in nearly 12 months. He used the vernacular (on this occasion 'arse') sparingly but with deliberate effect. It was usually brought out, when he wanted to make the point in the strongest way possible. Most patients were initially surprised at this from a consultant, but generally smiled or accepted it, perhaps considering the consultant more like a normal human being, when they used 'swear' words.

"But if I get this damned virus, I am done for Dr Carmichael," said Marjorie Hays, who had been a patient of Jamie's for 10 years or more. She reacted as if she hadn't even noticed the choice of language.

"I know that's what all our patients have been thinking, Marjorie. However, we now know it isn't actually the case at all. We noticed quite early, that we barely had any of our patients admitted, when they have got covid. There is now proof that there is a protective effect of inhaled steroids, that is the reason." Jamie paused to see if Marjorie would interject with a question. When she didn't, he continued.

"The inhalers actually block a pathway that the virus uses to proceed from the viral phase of the illness to this second phase of pneumonia, which as you know is the dangerous bit of it."

Jamie paused again, allowing the idea to sink in a little. "We now know you personally are less at risk of dying of Covid, than your friends of the same age at church for example, or in your old rambling group." Jamie knew that, remembering facts like Marjorie being a church-goer and rambler from the past contacts was really valuable in educational terms. It meant you could personalise the arguments and helped in gaining the trust of a patient.

"I do walk in the garden, Doctor Carmichael!"

"Do you think that is safer than getting out in the park?"

"Well, the government said we should stay in our gardens." Marjorie was referring to an argument used during the first wave of lock-down, which Jamie had known was valueless even at the time and was of course now long removed as advice, though the anxious remained stuck in a time-lock.

Jamie didn't blame the government for much during the crisis. Most of the time they listened to their scientists and acted accordingly. He believed that most of the decisions were as good as they could have made at each specific moment in time. His main exception to this, would have been a theoretical option of an. international agreement to have stopped all international travel in January 2020. This was before the general population would have seen or realised the true devastating impact of such a pandemic to every individual in the country. Without experiencing the impact at a personal level, Jamie doubted that a complete flying ban was ever realistic in the UK.

However, Australia and New Zealand have shown how effective such a ban would have been, if introduced.

Jamie was predicting there would be an imminent urge for a large proportion of the population to jump back on planes as soon as travel bans were lifted. With new strains and mutations, developing as fast as they were, such behaviour would just risk the import of a new vaccine resistant strain and immediately the country would be back to square one.

How therefore, would the population have accepted a complete travel ban, before they had been shown the brutal reality of deaths and devastation that the pandemic would cause?

Jamie dragged his thought processing back to Marjorie. Of all the arguments advocated in the first wave, the advice to stay within the line of the garden fence was the most illogical.

What was the likelihood that being outside was going to result in an individual acquiring the virus particle floating in the air? Even in a busy city the millions and billions of gallons of atmospheric air that individual particles dilute within and the speed of air movement meant the likelihood of inhaling a live viral particle in the open outdoors was incredibly small. Jamie and his team, couldn't actually calculate the risk, but it was in the order of magnitude of that of being struck by lightning and it was Dan, who had originally come up with the phrase. "We don't walk around with lightening conductors on our heads, do we?"

Jamie continued to try and talk Marjorie into extending her exercise for both her physical and mental health. "What protection is a garden fence going to give you anyway Marjorie? I don't think that even if there are enough viral particles floating around in the outside air, that they will recognise your fence and avoid floating over it, do you?" Time to back off after this argument, he was getting close to being confrontational and that wouldn't do.

What Jamie and the team did know was the damage that lack of exercise did to the physical health. Multiple factors were involved, including isolation, loss of contact with friends, lack of seeing the outside world, green trees, fields, running water, the sea and most critically fear of this unseen virus. All were devastating to the mental health of their patients.

Jamie had also talked to colleagues about observing the ageing of people who were fully isolating. They had physically and perhaps mentally aged, must faster than in a normal year. "It's like watching the ageing process of a prime minister or president of the United States. Four years in office looks like ten in normal ageing terms," it was Tim, who had come up with the last analogy.

"So, Marjorie! Getting out and about is really important and now you have had your vaccine, lack of fitness is much more dangerous to you than Covid is going to be."

"Ok, Dr Carmichael! You have badgered me enough and I hear you. I promise I will try and go for a walk tomorrow." Jamie could still hear the fear and reservation in the voice.

"And the next day and the next, please. I know it will be hard, that very first time you go through your garden gate, when you have barely done it in a year."

****

"That sounded like a really hard sell, Jamie?" Dan commented more as a question than a statement as Jamie put the phone down with a loud thump.

"Coals to Newcastle! I wasn't meant to sell this hard. It wasn't what I signed up to medicine to achieve." He slid his chair back and went off to make himself another cup of tea.

Clinic was the same message patient after patient, in this strange post-Covid world. Perhaps, not much different than normal in principle, as Jamie had always believed that education of the patient was the primary target in a medical (i.e. non-surgery) speciality clinic consultation. Patients had to understand why it was in their interest to take a preventive inhaler every day, it was no good just to give it them and say 'this is the script'.

To educate a patient, you needed time and needed not to waste that time on irrelevant acts.

Jamie had long ago given up on using a stethoscope in his own clinics. His first experience of any doubt in its' value was seeded in his mind as a student observing a consultant in clinic. The elderly consultant was examining the back of the patient's chest and had the stethoscope pressed to the patients back, but the earpieces were placed on the consultant's neck, not in the ears.

The consultant had then turned his head and theatrically winked at the confused young student. When the patient had left, the consultant explained that he had a bout of 'otitis externa', the medical phrase for an ear infection.

"The patients expect you to listen to the chest as if it's the way we make the diagnosis. If you don't do it, they think you haven't done your job properly," the consultant had added to Jamie by explanation.

The experience had resounded with Jamie for a few years. Deception of a patient was in his mind, inexcusable. In addition, he later calculated, that the cumulative hours of using (legitimately or otherwise) a stethoscope, that a respiratory specialist might consume per year was perhaps a couple of hundred.

If it was valueless, the time could be better spent, talking to a patient about their concerns ('could it be cancer? Is that what you were thinking?'). Asking the right question could give great relief. Finding out what might make them not take the treatment that could improve their life dramatically was also essential ('My Auntie Joan says taking inhaled steroids will make me infertile?'). This was another time for Jamie to use the vernacular. Using this question as an example, Jamie would counter, firstly with facts. "Actually, nothing could be further from the truth. Studies have shown the better your asthma is controlled the better the potential outcomes are for a healthy pregnancy." He then would add an adjunct to reinforce the message. "So, when you see your Auntie Joan, will you tell her, that Dr Carmichael said one word in response to her theory and that word is 'bollocks'."

Understanding the patients fears and education take time. Wasting that time listening with a stethoscope, including the time taken removing the shirt or blouse, getting it back on, and calling in a chaperone all accumulates. This precious time would be much better spent exploring fears, was Jamie's powerfully held perspective.

His final word when explaining this theory to Dan one day, told a long past experience of one of his pals. "Jim, who is now a medical director at one of our local hospitals, was a registrar at the same time as me. We were doing the walk-in clinic alongside each other in neighbouring rooms. Thank God he got this chap who was about 30 and had gone to see his GP with a cough. Apparently, he had coughed up a little blood. GP sent him straight to walk-in clinic. He had his X-ray first. Jim saw him, and then asked to listen to his chest."

"Ah that was his mistake then?" Dan asked goading Jamie.

"Correct. What was listening going to tell him, when he had an X-ray in his hand. Anyway, the guy was reluctant at first and Jim, said not to worry and come behind the curtain. Anyway, when the guy reluctantly stripped off, he had full kit on. Basque, suspenders, the lot."

"What colour was it?"

"You weirdo asking that! But red of course. It's always red."

Chapter 6
The House Year: Day 2 and the First Weekend

Thursday morning, Jamie was in early enough to get to the canteen. He was convinced he was in for a free Bacon sandwich, but as yesterday, his motivation was more about forming a bond, with a member of staff, who might be very important to him.

The canteen was like a school refectory, with plastic tables and chairs laid out in rows. There was the overpowering smell of bacon or chips frying depending on the time of day. Healthy eating had not met hospitals at this time, but at least smoking had been finally banned from the staff canteen.

He joined a queue as this was prime time for the canteen, before the doctors came on duty and around first break time for the nurses who started early shifts at 6.30 a.m.

When he got to the front of the queue, his smiling redheaded friend looked up and recognised him.

"A little sleep last night then?" she opened.

"Morning Aileen!" Jamie said bright as a button. There was a momentary pause as a frown crossed her face and then she smiled.

"Close, but no cigar, young doc."

Jamie's face fell, he was sure he had remembered her name. He had even written it down on his card job list.

"Elaine," she said!! "That'll be a pound!" she said. "I'll give you your coffee free for the effort."

Despite her kindness, Jamie felt very foolish with a queue of staff behind him and felt the heat of a blush hit his face. He mustered a smile, but took his sandwich and coffee to the mess.

She was in again the next morning, when Jamie started his weekend on-call shift. He was in much earlier, because of it being his on-call day. As he entered the canteen, this time he was alone and he summoned up the cheek to shout loud enough for all the kitchen staff to here.

"Morning Aileen." She threw a serving spoon across the room at him, a baked bean narrowly missed his left ear, but that was that. Elaine became Aileen for the next 2 years. Every morning almost without fail, Jamie would wander through the canteen whether he was stopping to have breakfast and coffee or not and would shout the wrong name.

She had rolled up serviettes or even tin foil ready for him from that day on and was delighted with herself any day she managed to hit him with them.

****

"Jamie, have you heard the one about the Englishman the Irishman and the Scotsman…"

Jamie looked at the clock. 4.30 a.m.! He didn't listen to the joke. His brain wasn't really working. He had been in bed for just over half an hour.

John finished the punch-line anyway and didn't seem to mind at all, that he got no response. Switchboard teams obviously did night shift rota's just like the nurses, Jamie registered. John had rung the phone that was in Jamie's on-call room, he looked at his bleep and it hadn't gone off, which was a relief, he would have hated to know he *could* actually sleep through it, when on-call. He might never sleep again if that happened to him.

"I've got one of these locum GP wankers on the phone for you, sorry Jamie." Jamie smiled at John's outrageous political incorrectness.

What Jamie realised was that in the 20 seconds of telling the joke, which he had actually missed and listening to the politically incorrect blasphemy, that half made him smile, Jamie was actually awake and able to take in what was about to be said to him as another referral. Twenty seconds earlier, he was completely senseless.

Jamie came to realise, that John did this all intentionally. Jamie did wonder, how John had worked it out, in the first place. He guessed that years of talking to over-tired junior doctors and you would learn the patterns that worked best.

Perhaps he listens to all the conversation, thought Jamie and as a result could tell when the doctor is so asleep, he is just not with it. But that would be wrong for a switchboard operator to listen in on a medical conversation between doctors. But then again, what else would you do at 3 a.m. if you were on switchboard and having to stay awake yourself all night?

"Oh, dear Dr Jamie! I am really sorry to wake you. Dr Islam here from GP Locum service. I referred you that stroke patient earlier." It was a thick Indian accent, but the referring doctor, sounded genuinely sorry for disturbing Jamie and that was something to encourage. He might be less likely to refer rubbish in the middle of the night, if they understood the fatigue of the admitting doctor.

"I have a 45-year-old gentleman, Mr John Taylor, smoker with already some heart disease. Just came back from Greece and he appears to have meningitis. Photophobia, neck stiffness, fever of 41. I've given him a dose of IV benzyl penicillin as that's all I had with me, hope this is ok. There is no meningitis rash right now."

Jamie sensed the medical emergency and despite the fatigue, there was a surge of adrenaline.

"Ambulance is here, but I thought better coming straight to you rather than stop in A&E and get delays. Are you ok with this?"

"Dr Islam, that's perfect, red-light him to A12, where there is a bed and I will be waiting for him." Jamie only realised he had said 'red-light' rather than 'blue light' after he put the phone down.

"I wonder where my dreams were, or if that was subliminal from John's joke?" He looked around and realised he was talking to himself. "Sleep deprivation," he added to the rest of the inhabitants of the room! Two cockroaches giggled silently from behind the rickety wardrobe in which his spare white coats were hanging.

"Fuck right off," Jamie said to his audience as he put his fingers down on the phone to get a tone.

He dialled the number, that he had now remembered 2112.

"A12!" a voice replied as awake and cheery as it was on a day shift.

"Christine, it's Jamie, I've got a query-meningitis coming in. I'm getting up, so I'm ready for him. Can you prepare a lumbar puncture trolley please? I'll do it as soon as I've got IV access if the locum GP is right and it looks like meningitis."

"Yes, sweetie, we will be ready for you. I'll let radiology know you will need a portable X-ray too I presume. It's Clare my friend on duty, so she might even be here waiting too. She owes me one as I got her the phone number of that dishy surgeon yesterday."

"Ok see you in 5." Jamie was interested in the gossip, but would wait until later to ask her which surgeon. Gossip, he knew was the oil in the cogs of the hospital. It kept the workers going and kept the day (and night) alive when it was mundane. However, it had a time and a place.

As Jamie dressed hurriedly and walked outside into the balmy August air, he contemplated the needs for meningitis. It was a medical emergency. The sooner it is treated the better the outcomes, hence Jamie recognised the excellence of the locum GP giving the first dose of antibiotic. This is especially true for 'meningococcal' meningitis, which is more commonly an illness of children.

It is one of the rare situations in medicine, where you would absolutely advocate the treatment based on the suspicion of the diagnosis. The second target is to confirm the diagnosis early, identifying which organism was responsible, so then Jamie and the team could give the best possible antibiotic choice. Jamie was awake enough to smell the early morning floral scents of the garden as he past it and took in the slight orange sky of pre-dawn.

Once on the corridor, Jamie thought of the other illnesses less serious than meningitis, which can mimic it, with the symptoms of severe headache, fever and photophobia (light hurting the eyes). A lumbar puncture was the investigation of choice and needed to be done early. It was nearly a year since he last did one, so he wondered if he should wake Jemma now, or have a go first. He had first to make sure Dr Islam was correct and that sepsis was present as a brain haemorrhage was another option if the fever wasn't high. In that case, a lumbar puncture would be the wrong thing for Jamie to do.

He contemplated and was impressed with Christine's suggestion of an early X-ray, as lung conditions and brain symptoms could be linked. Getting the X-ray done quickly, was also important.

****

"I think you ought to glance at the X-ray, I will hold it up to the window." Christine was coming to the end of her shift, but was giving Jamie pretty much her undivided attention, because the urgent case merited it.

The soft August morning light was filtering through the window, casting shadows mixed with the ceiling light, whilst Jamie did the procedures. Christine had put the new patient in a side room, which had made it easier to get it done, without disturbing the ward.

Dr Islam had been correct to be worried. The symptoms were highly suggestive of meningitis, with profound headache and photophobia, along with a fever of over 40 degrees. The first job was to get IV access and indeed Jamie put in two cannulae as quickly as possible, one for the antibiotics and another to get fluids in.

Christine had sent Freda, who was the auxiliary on for the night shift, with the bloods to the lab, rather than waiting for a porter. She was panting and a little breathless on her return, but she had a coffee ready for Jamie within 2 minutes of being back. Not a milky one this time of the night, but it was still welcome.

A second dose of antibiotics had been started, following the Hospital protocol for suspected meningitis. They had put a fast bag of fluids going through, whilst waiting for the bloods.

Radiology had been, and Jamie made a point of thanking Clare himself. Even though she had the hots for the surgical wanker Rich (Jamie used John's approach, but said it only in his head…he hoped). He had written his notes and drug Kardex whilst Christine put a bladder catheter in, so they could check urine output as the kidneys could fail early in a septic illness and Jamie had started the lumbar puncture. Jamie decided to ring Jemma and apologised for waking her, but he thought he better check in with her, with this case.

She agreed that he had been right to wake her, after she listened to all the observations and data and said she would let him start the lumbar puncture as he had done several as a student doctor, but said she would be down in twenty minutes after a shower and a coffee.

Christine had helped very efficiently get the patient positioned on his side, knees tucked up and curled as much as he was able. Jamie had advanced the needle as he had been taught, but knew even then, there was a little bit of luck involved in finding the right angle and space.

Today, it happened first time.

The big surprise for Jamie, was that the first few drops of the spinal fluid (CSF), looked pristine and this wasn't what he was expecting. Meningitis often caused the CSF to be turbid or even slightly blood stained.

Christine had popped out once Jamie had 'struck oil', to see what else was going on, in the ward and had come back within a minute clutching the X-ray. This was printed on a large piece of celluloid and she held it up to the window of the side room. Normally they would view it on a designed light box, but Christine had known for herself that it was clearly abnormal.

Jamie was counting the specified number of drops for each sample bottle to give to the various labs that would process it. He had enough time to glance up at the X-ray. If he let too much fluid come out, he could leave Mr Taylor with too low a pressure in the spinal fluid, which can lead to a very profound headache of its own and the inability to sit up or stand for some time.

As Jamie glanced up, he saw immediately, that there was clear density within the lung fields.

"What does it show?" said Mr Taylor, who was fully aware, although still feeling very poorly.

"Mr Taylor, I do need to look at it properly, but it does seem to show a sort of pneumonia, from first glance. These can cause high fevers, but generally not meningitis. There are some rare pneumonia that do cause the symptoms of meningitis, without the infection being in the fluid or brain at all. I also can tell you this fluid I am collecting looks very clear to the naked eye. We will still need to have it analysed properly in the lab."

Jamie had finished counting and had reinserted the central component of the lumbar puncture needle into the main barrel. Counting drops and talking was a skill, Jamie realised he had already acquired.

"I'm just going to take the needle out and we are done. This shouldn't hurt like it did going in."

Jamie added a question, "Still no pain in your legs anywhere?"

"No, nothing in my legs. It wasn't as bad as I was expecting, just the sharp jag, where it went in and the local anaesthetic injection," the 41-year-old solicitor responded. The latter was a fact that Dr Islam had failed to report to Jamie. Whilst it would make no difference to the treatment approach, it was considered a professional courtesy, to advise colleagues of certain occupations. Other health care professionals and solicitors especially, topped this list.

"Ok, we are out. I do need you to stay lying down horizontal for a couple of hours, but you don't have to stay on your side or curled up tight as you are."

"We will also turn the lights back down now as we have finished sticking needles and tubes into you. You did really well, John," Christine had added, stroking her patient's shoulder as she did so.

As Jamie, wheeled his trolley with his kit and samples out of the room, Christine said loud enough for both the patient and Jamie to hear.

"Dr Carmichael did a pretty slick job as well, that was as smooth as I've seen it done."

"Thanks, Christine, I haven't got them all first go, I assure you."

Jemma was sat at the nursing station, reading the notes he had made, nursing her own coffee and a fresh one for Jamie, which she handed to him. Jamie gave her the X-ray. "Fluid looks clear, the X-ray not so, I may have chased a wild-goose." He was a little deflated in reality.

There was a light box as was the case on almost all the wards, behind the nurse's station and whilst they normally used the one, which was strategically placed in the doctor's office, there were no patients or relatives milling around at this hour, so she went for the nearest to hand.

"Bilateral pneumonia!" said Jemma pointing to the white cloudy shadowing on both sides of the image. "So, we know you have procedural skills, Dr Carmichael. Is it too unfair to test your knowledge base at 6 a.m.?"

She looked at him over her glasses, which she hadn't worn before. He guessed she had taken her contact lenses out and had clearly come quite quickly. Jamie had heard the more senior doctors, discussing frequently, who they would leave to do a particular procedure or manage specific cases. Jamie had really got involved in doing as many practical skills as possible in the last 2 years of his training and had done loads of procedures, that other students hadn't done and some doctors would never do, such as temporary pacing wires and even a liver biopsy. Jamie knew Jemma had given him a chance to do it himself, but had come quickly to make sure it was going smoothly. He guessed that, she might even have even peeked in the door whilst he was concentrating, without him noticing.

"There are some atypical pneumonias that can cause meningism. I think, but am not certain, that Mycoplasma is one of those and I guess we would have to say Tuberculosis." He didn't mind being tested, but wasn't sure he would drag remote knowledge from the base of his memory as tired as he was.

"Any other, bearing in mind your chap has just come back from the Mediterranean?" The latter was a big clue. It prompted Jamie, not from direct knowledge but from the clue itself.

"Legionnaire's disease?" he said with a deliberate question in his voice, so Jemma knew he was guessing.

"Correct!" Jemma sounded impressed. "I haven't seen a case, but I was reading about it for the membership exam last month. It can present as meningism or peritonism, even though the predominant pathological finding on tests is the pneumonia. Anything else going for it in the blood tests?" She passed him the results she had written down, presumably, the laboratory had rung, whilst she was sat there.

Jamie looked at them. The white cell count wasn't as high as he might have expected for the severity of the apparent sepsis. He mentioned both this and the slight renal impairment, which might have been expected in any sick sepsis case.

"The Liver tests are also a little abnormal, both ALT and Alk Phos," Jemma pointed to those numbers, letting him off the hook. Jamie felt stupid, that he hadn't spotted that.

"Not up much, but it fits," she added.

"Do you think I shouldn't have done the LP?" Jamie was now doubting his own decision-making.

"Jamie, it absolutely needed doing. Especially with fever and photophobia and meningism. I'm also impressed with your speed and technical skill to get it all done so quickly. You also knew to ring me and check, so I'm a very happy SHO." Jamie felt better for her reassurance and he could even feel a little welling of fluid in his eyes at her unreserved support.

"Any more cases referred?" she diverted, whether she spotted his fatigue-driven emotion or not.

"No! Though, I need to go and do the IV round about now." He realised he still had significant jobs to do before, they started with Saturday's cases.

"Ok, I will say hello to Mr Taylor, do any of the IV drugs on here and then I will ring micro at 8 a.m. and decide which antibiotics we will use, to cover an atypical pneumonia including Legionella, but we will give him Clarithromycin as well, whilst we are waiting. I see he has had Ben-Pen." She was in organisation mode. "If you get done by half-seven, I'll meet you in the canteen and treat you to breakfast!"

"As the GP gave IV 'Ben-Pen' at home, I gave him a dose of Ceftriaxone just before the LP, covering my bases." He said as he started to head off down the corridor leaving Jemma, with the sick patient, he could leave A12 with a clean conscience.

Even though Jamie doubted he would make it by 7.30, her offer was a real boost to him and he vowed to himself, he would do the same when he was a senior doctor and had tired and potentially demoralised juniors working with him.

He patted the pocket of his white coat and knew he needed to load back up with cannulae syringes and flush, so he was ready.

"Thank you for your help today," he said to Christine who was also in the treatment room as he went in for his supplies. She had actually just laid out the IV drugs for the rest of the patients.

"Anything for super-doc Jamie." She still looked fresh and had twinkly eyes, despite finishing her night shift. She started to walk past him to the door, but stopped, leaned up and pecked his cheek.

"That's my last night shift this weekend. See you next week, hope you get some rest."

"Can't believe Clare actually fancies that arse-hole Rich. He is so arrogant!" Jamie diverted to gossip, before she left.

"No accounting for taste. Some women like bad boys you know!" she replied packing up.

She flounced and wiggled her bottom at him. This time it was clearly deliberate. Jamie watched noticing again how pert and tight it was.

Jamie was left distracted. He collected his extra equipment and had thinking time as he set off down the corridor, in search of B3.

Chapter 7
Getting Covid: Evening Zero

"Mate, really sorry to tell you, but I started coughing about 6 p.m. and did a lateral flow test just now. It's positive." It was Dan, calling at 10 p.m. that evening.

Clang!

Jamie mustered the sympathetically correct lines: 'hope you are okay', 'that's you and your wife off work for 10 days' and 'you are super-fit, cycling to work every day and running all weekend, you will be fine'. However, Jamie missed the line crashing around in his head: 'and twelve years younger'.

The mug of tea and how he had drunk ¾ of it (as was his norm), came flooding back into Jamie's consciousness. The little green germs crawling all over the handle and onto Jamie's hands, suddenly imprinted indelibly on his brain (doctors had irrational flights of imagination too!). He tried to remember washing his hands or 'gelling' before grazing on the self-made lunch he had brought in.

He couldn't recall doing so, but his memory was not as good as it had used to be!

Jamie knew he was likely contaminated, even though he had worn his mask nearly all day. Jamie's only saving factor would be if he had, had Covid already. Perhaps he was one of the lucky few, who had mild disease and didn't really notice it. He had, a few days of breathlessness and fatigue in March at the start of the pandemic, but he knew that could have been mild neuroticism and wishful thinking at the time.

If he hadn't already had it, he was pretty certain he was going to get it now.

He rationalised to himself that he was reasonably fit and walked many hours in any given week. He was relatively lean and no one considered him overweight, even though he hid a few pounds under his shirts. But nothing would replace the fear that would now pervade his waking days and sleep disturbed nights awaiting the fifth day, when he would likely get symptoms. The irony being if his exposure had come inadvertently after 10 months of working at the hot end of the hospital treating Covid patients and ending up getting Covid, from his own cup.

Chapter 8
The House Year: First Weekend (Part II)

"Doc! Really sorry to wake you, but I am feeling more breathless."

Jamie opened his eyes.

He was exactly where he had been, an undetermined time ago. Still sat on the bed of Herbert Harper. The notes he had been writing in, were in his lap still. Where had he been for that period of time? The dawning realisation of the truth was crashing around him, but he still had to ask himself the question. Had he really just gone to sleep on the job?

"I'm really sorry, did I actually fall asleep?" Jamie checked he wasn't dribbling, by lifting his fist to his chin as he finished the sentence.

"You looked so tired, Doc. I didn't really want to wake you back up, but not sure how much longer I can stay like this," Herbert said kindly through the oxygen mask he was wearing.

Herbert had a pneumothorax, which had a degree of tension on it when Jamie had looked at the X-ray.

Herbert had been wheeled past him, as Jamie waited on B3, for this new arrival from Accident and Emergency. With the Accident and Emergency department being in a separate hospital, 3 miles down a major trunk road, if immediate life-saving treatment was required, then this should be performed in the Emergency Department itself. On a Sunday, the journey would have taken 10 minutes.

The doctor who had referred Herbert, said the pneumothorax was a 'simple' one, meaning there was no urgency for treatment.

When Jamie saw the X-ray, he disagreed with the diagnosis. The heart was definitely pushed off centre, and the wind pipe might also have been pushed to the opposite side. The pocket of air responsible for these changes of position, which was forming in the space between the lungs and the chest wall was therefore under-pressure and the degree of pressure could build up quite rapidly.

As such, this diagnosis was another relative emergency. Although Herbert's oxygen levels had been good, Jamie was beside himself with guilt as there appeared no forgivable reason why he had fallen asleep sat up, halfway through taking the medicines history in Herbert's case. He had compounded the delay, caused by a diagnostic miss in ED.

Jamie had been planning to go and check if the trolley for the chest drain was fully ready, when he finished the drug history. Sarah had started making it up as soon as Jamie saw the X-ray. Jamie had been delighted to see it was her on duty, when he went to the ward on this Sunday afternoon.

Just as Jamie started to move from his seat straight in front of his breathless patient, a head peered around the curtain.

"Just got the drain pack ready for you, Dr Carmichael, sorry for the delay! We were waiting for the drapes to come from CSSD," Sarah reported.

Jamie was confused, as he thought he had seen the drapes pack already on the trolley, but his fatigue was clearly playing tricks on him.

"Ok Herbert, what I am going to do is quickly go and take off my white coat and roll my sleeves up and wash. When I come back, I am going to slide this drain into the space where the air is collecting. Once it is in, you will be almost instantly less breathless. It does hurt a bit going in, but I will put some local anaesthetic in the skin and muscle layers. The last layer called the pleura is so thin, it is impossible to anaesthetise, so there is a sharp catch as the drain goes through that layer, but it won't last long." He said all this quickly as he wanted to catch up on the added delay.

"Which position do you prefer him in, Dr Carmichael," asked Sarah, knowing doctors had different techniques and positions in which to insert the drain.

"Edge of the bed, leaning on his table with his pillows on the table please, Sarah." This was the set-up Jamie liked best, from those he had been shown in his training.

Sarah was as efficient as Christine had been earlier in the weekend and had the patient positioned and the pack open and ready. Jamie slipped into his surgical gown, from the top of the pack, that they used for this procedure. Tapping on the chest confirmed the right side was the hyper-resonant side and this is where the drain should go.

The other side was duller to the same percussion, by comparison. Jamie was happy where he was going to place the drain.

Jamie donned his gloves quickly this Sunday.

As he did, he recalled briefly the time when he was doing his obstetrics training. In a day when he was getting multiple deliveries to meet the expected target of 10 in a 6-week attachment. The midwife had asked him to gown and glove in preparation. Whilst he was mid getting the gloves on, slightly clumsily with his lack of experience, the midwife asked the mother, who was on her seventh pregnancy to give one exploratory push. Jamie had his back turned and the second glove half on, when there was a popping and gushing sound.

Turning quickly, he saw the baby coming explosively out in one push and starting to slide towards the end of the surgical trolley they were doing the delivery on. Jamie hadn't even got the sheets in place, so the baby was sliding rapidly, slick from placental juices across the plastic surface of the bed. Jamie's one contribution to this delivery, had been to drop an arm like a train signal across the end of the bed, to arrest the baby's journey in its slide, just as it prepared to drop off the end. The amazed midwife was still standing stock still, mouth open aghast and frozen in shock. Baby was delivered safely if 'precipitously' and placed on the mother's chest as if nothing was amiss. The midwife apologised as she had never seen a baby pushed out, so quickly and admitted to both the mother and Jamie, that she should have waited until Jamie was ready, before asking her to push.

After that incident, Jamie practised getting his gloves on very slickly. He never wanted to be caught 'almost' short again. Nor in fact, did he want to have to scrub the mix of placental fluid and blood off his wrists again for that matter.

Jamie shook the memories off and set to work putting local anaesthetic into the skin on his chosen spot. He talked to Herbert explaining everything that would be done. He was working behind Herbert in part deliberately as the equipment looked quite brutal and the drains used at this time were frightening for the patient to see. He chatted during the minute or so, it took the local anaesthetic to work. Herbert was breathless but still doing ok.

Jamie felt correctly that the drain kits at the time, looked (and indeed could be used as) a form of brutal torture equipment. In his hands, the drain felt like a giant knitting needle, with a rubber hose over it. Indeed, this is essentially what it was. The knitting needle, just acted as a rigid 'introducer', just like a needle inside a venous canula.

Later in his career the drains became much smaller than Jamie was using in the 1980s unless they were being put in, during a surgical procedure.

Using a scalpel, that was part of the equipment pack, Jamie made a single deep incision in the skin where the anaesthetic was now doing its' job. Jamie was aiming just above the rib as the angle for insertion. The aim was to avoid the big blood vessels and nerves, that run at the bottom edge of each rib.

As Jamie had been taught, he put a metal clamp on the drain, 2 inches from the tip. The danger with these old-fashioned style of chest drains, was the possibility of pushing the drain in too hard and too far, so the sharp tip would reach the lung edge and puncture it, making a second and bigger hole.

Herbert's drain went in smoothly, the inner metal introducing part (the knitting needle) was then withdrawn. There was a woosh of air, that came with it, confirming the fact that the pneumothorax was under pressure and that 'a tension' pneumothorax was indeed the confirmed diagnosis.

Jamie and Sarah set to connecting the external end of the drain to the tubing, which connected to a bottle containing sterile water. This acted as a valve allowing air out, but not air or water to be sucked back in during the breath in.

Sarah had the equipment prepared correctly and was ready for the connection. She was standing close to him as Jamie took the needle out. Was the rub of her leg against his own, really necessary, as she bent down to do the connections for him? Jamie wasn't sure but, it was a warm feeling for the briefest of moments.

The drain was bubbling air in time with Herbert's breathing and the job was done, apart from taping and stitching the tube in place.

The material that they used as tape, which wrapped the stitches and fixed the first few external inches of the drain to the chest was called 'sleek'. Jamie thought it was rather an inappropriate word as though it was shiny, it was a brutally tough adhesive tape. Those with hairy chest were better shaved if time allowed, or alternatively a very painful waxing would occur as the sleek was pulled off, when the drain was ready for removal.

Jamie put in first the 'purse string' stitch, keeping within his anaesthetised field. This would be drawn closed as the drain came out. He then apologised, that there was one painful stitch, used as an additional anchor, to hold the drain. This had to be placed outside the field of local anaesthetic. As Jamie explained to Herbert the discomfort from putting a single stitch in was less than that from reinserting new local anaesthetic would be, as long as Jamie did it quickly and efficiently.

"How are you feeling?" he asked Herbert who was still leaning over the table.

"My breathing is much better doc, just as you said it would be." The relief was evident.

"Everything is done and you can now sit up straight. This drain is going to need to stay in a couple of days. It will hurt at first and Sarah has gone to get you some painkiller. However, it is mostly bruising from the muscle that is damaged as the drain goes in. You will get used to it pretty quickly and indeed the best thing to do is to keep moving around as much as the discomfort will allow you." Jamie was into his explanation mode with a script he had spoken many times already.

"You can even walk around carrying this bottle, but the bottle mustn't be lifted above the height of where the drain goes in to your side here." Jamie touched very gently around the level of where the drain went in.

"The aim is to keep the bottle to waist height or below when walking and on the floor when you are in the bed or chair. The tubing is quite heavy so I've used a giant safety pin to take some of the weight off by attaching the tubing to your pyjama top. I hope it's obvious but that pin, can only pinch the tubing, it can't go through the tubing making a hole or you recreate an extra air-leak."

The latter explanation seemed obvious to Jamie, but 2 years ago, he saw one of these pushed through the tubing. The doctor, blamed the nurse. On the contrary, she was crying, but adamantly saying that she hadn't done it and that the doctor had done it like that.

Jamie reckoned it was the doctor, who looked sheepish, whilst the nurse was distraught. The drain as a result had to be removed and reinserted. Medical training teaches you quite a lot, but common sense is not part of the curriculum and a higher proportion of doctors than you might imagine, seemed to lack it in Jamie's experience.

However, who was he to criticise, as after all today he had fallen asleep on the job?

"Thanks, Doc. My breathing is a million times better now, although it feels like I've been punched in the side by Mohammed Ali, but I presume that is to be expected."

"Absolutely, we have done more damage to muscle, than a single punch from me would manage, not sure about Mohammad Ali though, he might do more."

Jamie was trying to keep the tone light, but his internal conscience was on fire. Finally, he put his hand on Herbert's shoulder and encouraged him to straighten up.

Hebert pushed himself back from the table and straightened a little gingerly. He looked at the tubing and the bottle properly for the first time. Jamie always like to have the insertion point of the drain covered up, before the patient looked, as it would make a strong person flinch to see the entry wound itself. Jamie always described the whole procedure as one of the worst things, doctors did to a non-anaesthetised patient. Specifically, it was a much harder procedure to tolerate, than the lumbar puncture he had done on Friday, over 48 hours before.

"I'm sorry I woke you up now, you look so tired." Herbert was back to apologetic mode.

"I have had only one hour sleep in the last 2 days, but to fall asleep when you needed that doing immediately was inexcusable, so all I can do is apologise." Jamie was distraught and his emotions were threatening to get the better of him, now he had stopped concentrating on the procedure.

"Nothing was wasted time-wise as we were waiting for the pack of drapes before we could do the drain," Sarah interjected, stroking Herbert's other arm for reassurance. "No harm no foul." She moved slightly behind Herbert and winked at Jamie.

Jamie was still confused, but was now beginning to work out what she was doing.

"Last thing we will need to do Herbert is another X-ray to confirm all is in the correct place, though I'm confident it is, with the bubbling and the change in your breathing."

Jamie and Sarah tidied up together and got Herbert back into bed. Sarah gave the grateful patient some pain killers, whilst Jamie sorted the sharps from the trolley and then went into the office to write the notes.

Jemma was again waiting for him.

"Saving lives again without me Dr Carmichael. Sorry though I was on Cardiac Unit with a Ventricular arrhythmia," Jemma's tone was apologetic.

"You know I actually fell asleep sat on his bed taking his history, before I put the drain in," Jamie confessed. "The patient actually woke me." He thought it was better that he told his senior, than leave it to the patient to 'dib' him in, as Jemma was guaranteed to go and check the patient.

"Haha! Oh dear, the amazing Dr Carmichael is actually fallible." She laughed at Jamie's most embarrassing predicament. "So sorry though. I really should have given you a couple of hours sleep, last night and covered you. So, it's my fault really." Jamie was surprised that she actually sounded remorseful herself.

"I fell asleep in patients' chairs, the nurse's station and even the floor of a treatment room in my first year as a doctor," she confessed. "So, don't worry! No harm, no foul." She didn't realise she was mirroring verbatim, what Sarah had just said.

"I told him that, in front of the patient," said Sarah, from behind Jemma.

"You confused me when you said we were waiting for the drapes. I thought the trolley was ready to go?" Fatigue was really leaving Jamie, short of sharpness.

"Durrggh!" said Sarah mockingly. "You are cute, but just a little literal, Dr Carmichael. I'd actually popped my head in and seen you had dropped off and run off to get the trolley, but Herbert woke you before I was back. I said that, so he didn't think you had delayed the procedure," she paused.

"You are a numpty! You didn't have to tell Jemma either. Herbert is actually feeling so guilty he woke you. I don't think he will mention it to anyone either. He knows you saved his life after all." Jamie definitely couldn't cope with praise, when he felt so inadequate.

"So, it was fib?" queried the exhausted doctor.

"Oh, for goodness-sake!" said Sarah and turned on her heel and left the room, leaving only a trace of her perfume behind.

"You need to thank her, when you get the time. It's what we do. Cover each-others' backs. At least as long as there is no harm to the patient. You are so tired you are not getting it." Jemma paused and changed her tone to playful, "I also think she has the hots for you, just so you know, because you probably aren't getting that signal either."

Jamie's bleep went off for the hundredth time that weekend. He now felt stupid as well as guilty and Jemma's pep talk, didn't sink in for a while.

"Delivery for Dr Carmichael on A12!" it was Angela's playful voice. "It's in our staff fridge if you are busy, obviously not urgent and it is actually from Freda if you are wondering, I'm not that inventive in the kitchen, though I can do better than the stuff they leave you in the mess fridge."

This sounded like the best news of the weekend even though it was cryptic.

Jamie tidied up his paperwork and apologised to and thanked Sarah for what she had done. He still felt foolish, even after his lame attempt to regain the ground he had lost with her, through his own stupidity.

"It's ok, we like doctors who care, Jamie." This parting shot was as good a line as he could have hoped for.

****

Jamie headed to A12 and chatted with Angela. He hadn't had a referral in 90 minutes, the longest time all weekend he guessed. He asked her about her husband. He was a joiner it turned out.

"Hope you like it. It was made this morning for my family Sunday dinner who will be having theirs without me. I reckoned there was a junior doctor who could use a plate too," it was Freda, who had joined Jamie and Angela.

Jamie received a plate of Sunday lunch, with roast chicken roast potatoes, carrots and beans smothered in a rich looking gravy.

"No Yorkshires I am afraid I don't think they reheat very well."

"Oh, Freda that looks amazing. If you don't mind, I'm going up to the mess to eat it, whilst I've no cases to see." He thanked her and promised to bring the plate down as soon as he had finished and washed it.

He hot footed it to the mess, to get it reheated. The bleep went and it was a new case of a lady with poor diabetic control and a foot ulcer. He gave it to A11, but knew he had half an hour before she arrived. He sat down in the mess and ate his first real meal of the weekend. Yesterday had been milk, toast and mars bars as his diet.

He sat down with the surgical team and Forster.

"Bloody hell," said Forster as Jamie walked in. It seemed to be Forster's specific greeting for Jamie now. Forster had different phrases he said, when other specific doctors came and went.

Jamie reckoned Forster definitely looked less healthy and was losing feathers and the poo in the bottom of the cage looked unusually green. Rich, the surgical doctor who had retrieved the hoover attachment, was sat next to the cage and feeding Forster peanuts.

"That looks a better dinner than I had," Richard turned as he spoke. "Fuck! Ouch Forster," the parrot had hold of Richards thumb in which a peanut had been. Instead, there was now a trickle of blood. Richard got up and left the room without speaking another word.

"Stupid prick," commented Forster in his wake.

Jamie just had time to finish the plate, wash and clean it before Sister Arbuthnott, bleeped him to tell us the new patient had arrived. He went in to A12 and gave Freda a hug as well as her plate back.

"Don't get any ideas, Dr Carmichael, you are way too young for me," said Freda blushing for the first time he had seen.

"Freda, look at the state of me, I'm not fit for anyone to fancy," he reposted playfully.

"Not what I know!" Freda was laughing and looking at Angela as she said this.

****

Later that evening he had a call from a GP. It turned out to be Phil Knowsley, who had been the house officer on medicine, when Jamie had been a fourth-year medical student at this hospital, two years before.

Partly out of his own laziness, Phil had let Jamie do a lot of clerking of patients, especially in the middle of the night. As a result, and partly in response to Jamie's enthusiasm, the senior doctors on the team had taught Jamie so many procedures. Jamie hadn't really liked Phil, with his taciturn style. However, the attachment had worked out well for him. So, in a way he was really grateful for that period of his training, with Phil as his House Officer.

"I've got a patient for you Jamie. I heard it was you on. My girlfriend had mentioned your name and I remembered you as a student."

"Who is your girlfriend?" However, Jamie had already guessed and regretted asking and more importantly didn't want to know.

"Sarah, she works on B3. I asked if you were still skinny as a rake and have the same half a moustache. She said you have lost the latter, which I'm sure is a good call!"

Jamie guessed Phil had heard about his story today as Sarah would have finished the shift already. He was more concerned about this, than the personal comments.

"I suppose you have heard about my event with the chest drain guy today then?" Jamie said imagining the worst and his abject embarrassment that was about to be released.

"Haven't seen her today as I'm doing locum shifts to pay for a holiday. She mentioned seeing you yesterday after her early shift. She will be in the nursing home, not that I want you getting any ideas on her, as she seems to like you already." This information was better than Jamie expected and he didn't tell Phil anymore about the incident, other than to say the two of them had put a drain in together.

He didn't see them as a couple. Sarah was a tall slim and very beautiful dark-haired nurse, with large almond-shaped deep brown eyes. Jamie imagined she could have anyone she wanted. Phil was dumpy short and prematurely balding and didn't look like he looked after himself that carefully.

Jamie took the referral and sent it to A4 as it sounded like a case that might stay in for a few months, if the stroke was really as profound as Phil made it out to be. Though Jamie guessed he was exaggerating a bit and social reasons might be at the forefront of the referral.

Not surprisingly he worked out later, that the latter was indeed the case. Jamie found himself left with a feeling of disappointment that an ex-colleague, couldn't have been more honest, rather than sell him a load of old 'bull'. The patient was going to get admitted either way.

Jamie managed to get 2 hours sleep that Sunday night and managed to stay awake in the pub until 8 p.m. on Monday evening, before resting his head on the table and missing 2 hours of pub chat, as he slept hard, snoring quietly. No beer was spilled this time, as he knew the crash was coming and moved the pint glass to the side, half drunk.

His first week as a junior doctor was over and he was learning new skills all the time, including how not to spill pints during a sleep crash.

Chapter 9
Getting Covid: Day 1

As the news of Dan having Covid spread around the severe asthma team 'WhatsApp' group, the other colleagues from the multi-user office were naturally worried about how much time they had spent in the office together, how many metres apart and whether they had kept their masks on for the whole time. They had become good at wearing their masks over the months, but was it good enough when there was a potential source in their small office? Jamie didn't think his mask would protect him on this occasion. He had broken his own rule with his crockery after all.

Dan's area of the work surface became the 'contaminated corner', even though the data suggested that 12 hours was more than enough for the virus to die and it was already 15 hours since Dan had left, by the time the team filtered in the next morning.

By the time Jamie arrived, the desk circumference had been alco-wiped to within an inch of its life, by each one of the room residents as soon as they had arrived. Jamie recognised sunglasses would have been a helpful adjunct to his dress code that morning, such was the overcleaned gleam of white laminate. The smell of alcohol meant a managerial visit might have resulted in them all being drugs tested.

The laminated surface (even whiter now after the 16 packs of disinfectant wipes had been used), circled the entire room, allowing the 8 computer work stations and desk tops working in an office, that would have managed to get 4 or 5 single desks in maximum. At full capacity, there were work stations for 4 consultants, one senior nurse, one senior physiotherapist, (which was hot desked by the pharmacist), one for the consultant speech and language therapist and the last for the consultant psychologist. The days of medical consultants having individual offices had disappeared years before. Jamie recognised that television medical dramas had not kept pace with reality.

As Jamie arrived, he also sensed the anxiety in the office was almost palpable. The physiotherapist Rebecca Sanders was pregnant, Heather Horne, the psychologist had just been through a cancer scare, though wasn't on chemotherapy, so probably had the same risk as the rest of them. Two of the senior team members were of BAME origin and perhaps at the greatest risk.

Jamie was the oldest. He had to admit to this by some distance. Originally in the epidemic, he had been asked if he wanted to work on the back line, minimising the risk of exposure to patients presenting to the hospital with Covid.

Nothing would have allowed Jamie to accept this offer. This was his job and his calling. One he had given everything to over the thirty-seven years of his career to date. He knew he had been well paid for it and if he survived, he would have a very decent pension to retire on. His kids were grown and he had no dependents after a traumatic separation five years previously. He couldn't accept hiding away in a back corner somewhere and let other people face the challenge without him.

Additionally, those colleagues in the office around him had partners, one with a serious cardiac risk factor. Almost all with young children.

He was if anything the most expendable, in his own thoughts at least. For all these reasons, he formally declined the offer and requested to be on the same work rota as all the lung specialists at his hospital, when the pandemic took hold in Manchester. In some trick of roster development, he had taken the hardest series of front-door shifts at the peak of the first wave, compared to any of his colleagues. The rota had been written for 6 months, but Jamie's share of long evening shifts (when the majority of sick Covid patients had presented to hospital), seemed to all come during the first 10 weeks of the Roster, when the first wave had been most active and whilst PPE was still a little scarce.

"Which of us can work from home for the next week?" he said bringing his thoughts back to the current mini-crisis.

Shanaz Khan one of their BAME colleagues got the desk in the small annexe room, which prior to her arrival had been used as an emergency consultation room. It was no longer of any use for that purpose, being designated too small for its role during the pandemic.

Prior to its' redesignation to an emergency consultation room, it had been Jamie's office. It was also going to get white laminate soon and a second work station! She was happy to stay there as she was effectively separated off and had, had almost zero contact with Dan, in the week to date.

"Can I?" Heather spoke first, a little uncertainly at her offer.

"If you can do your clinics purely by phone from home and keep the records secure, then yes, you should go and go now. Rebecca you should too. However, in reality, the exposure was yesterday, but one of us, may have got it and infect the others in a cascade process, so the fewer in, the better." A wan smile crossed Heather's face at the reality of Jamie's words.

"Are *you* ok, Jamie?" the question came from Heather, but they all knew how Jamie would answer, though the question was all the empathy Jamie could take at that moment. It showed the realisation, that as the oldest member, he was potentially most at risk, but as Jamie would argue, he was fit and did not have the ethnic risk factors, which were so dominant within the statistics.

"You know I will be fine Heather, but thanks." They exchanged eye contact briefly, but all was said, that needed saying.

"Jenny is already working from home," Tim said slightly muffled through the ever-present mask, referring to their speech therapist. "And Liz is not in on a Thursday, so we don't have to decide what to do with her until the morning."

"She was exposed like the rest of us yesterday, so better she works in here with us than goes up to the ward office, where hopefully none of the rest of the team was exposed to Dan, during his infectious phase. I doubt Liz can work from home really." Jamie was intent on getting a plan in place. *They should have done this by zoom conversation last night*, he thought and chastised himself, for not being ahead of the game.

Liz was their specialist nurse, now perhaps the leading authority on asthma within the UK nursing community and she and the pharmacist had both taken roles on the national respiratory council. More relevantly, Liz's husband was considered vulnerable with a chronic condition, giving her real concern about getting infected and passing it on within the household.

"We will know by Monday I guess if any of us are positive from Dan, even though we all wore masks all day, pretty reliably." Jamie thought out loud something they all knew.

"Shanaz have you done a lateral flow test this morning?" Shanaz had risk factors of being Asian and had her own medical conditions, but they knew none of the latter conditions were relevant to Covid-19 in theory.

She was full of life, but a tad inclined to be a little rebellious with rules just like Jamie. She had needed persuading to start doing the twice weekly lateral flow tests, recommended from Christmas onwards, when they finally got their self-test kits. She still hadn't had her vaccine, but had agreed to have it and had an appointment after some aggressive persuasion.

"Yes of course, *Dr Carmichael*," stressing and using Jamie's surname rather than his first, as a message that he was being patronising. It was done and accepted jovially! "We are all negative, assuming you are?" she added.

"Excellent news, Dr Khan. As you know if I was positive, I wouldn't be here," Jamie retorted playfully.

"The secretaries have blockaded their door, so we can't go into them!" Tim brought the conversation back to practical issues.

"That's fine and the right thing," responded Jamie. "We don't have to go in their office at all really!" He wondered, how many times Dan had been in there in the 24 hours or so before testing positive, the time when there was most risk of transmission.

"The two who have slight risk factors were both working from home the last 2 days," said Tim, almost reading Jamie's thoughts. More relief as their 4 female secretaries all had either health concerns or lived with elderly relatives. The fifth was a male secretary, which was still something very unusual within the NHS. When he had been appointed, Jamie had wondered if it would work, but Jim had fitted in like a metaphorical glove, balancing the female hormones and preventing any escalation of temporary infighting, which would go on in any all-female office eventually. Jim had a very calm persona and clear dislike of disharmony. Jamie guessed he was a Libra star-sign, like himself, but had never had the nerve to ask directly.

The way their current secretarial team worked, reminded Jamie of his own early days in the same hospital when on leaving school, he became a filing clerk in the biochemistry and haematology offices. He had to learn fast how to chat with females, as he had been at an all-boys grammar school. Jamie had used flirting as a tool, even before he had lost his virginity. Jim the secretary on the contrary, had a steady boyfriend and was only focussed on harmony.

The team recognised their plan was set for their work for the two days up to the weekend. Jamie reckoned they would know, before 9 a.m. Monday if one of them had acquired Covid from Dan. He still imagined the mug of tea, which by now had been polished and bleached in boiling water this morning 21 hours too late he feared.

Jamie set to work. He had another telephone clinic ahead, but he had also been on ward cover earlier in the week, but was free of that task from now until the following week, which worked out well as he felt they should minimise their contacts around the hospital.

However, he still wanted to know what had been going on with the patients he had been responsible for that week. He couldn't acknowledge favourites, but they always existed in reality.

Jamie rang the ward and was pleased it was Annie, the Physician Associate who answered the phone. These new roles of Physician Associate, did the work of junior doctors. Or at least, the sort of work Jamie did as a junior doctor, including bloods, cannula insertion, writing notes and ordering tests. They could do pretty much everything, except prescribing drugs. They were paid less, but were invaluable. The biggest bonus to Jamie was that they didn't rotate every few months, nor did they do night shifts. As a result, they provided the day-to-day continuity to the ward, which had long been lost in the working hours limitation and the fast-rotating rotas, that the juniors now did.

"How is the ward, Annie? Things calm overnight?" Jamie started with an open-ended question.

"Sorry, Dr Carmichael. Mrs Dobson died in the early hours." Annie was smart and knew exactly why Jamie was ringing so early in the day.

"Peacefully I hope?" Jamie said it as a question, knowing Annie and himself had worked really hard to make sure this was the case. Mrs Dobson had been dying of rapidly progressive lung fibrosis and all treatments had been tried and failed. She had been part of the national network of patient experts in the field, having joined the day she was diagnosed. She talked openly about dying and talking about palliation with her was easy.

However, when Jamie had taken over the ward that week, he was left in the invidious position of organising her discharge for palliation at home. Whilst very much the vogue, and right for many patients, dying of lung fibrosis, needed the provision of very high concentration oxygen and aggressive sedative agents, or the death could be distressing with intense breathlessness which would drive fear until very late in the dying process.

Whilst home care could provide drugs at home, particularly using pump-based treatments, the doses couldn't be changed quickly or augmented. Additional oxygen at home, whilst available, was not of the same strength or concentration that could be given in hospital. Oxygen concentrators were being set up, but they had significantly less oxygen output, than the piped oxygen in hospital.

"Why do you want to go home to die, Sylvia?" Jamie had asked. He was blunt, but his gloved hand was on her arm and he was crouching down at the side of her, head at her head height, his eyes exploring hers as he asked the question.

Mrs Dobson, swallowed hard and looked away.

"Really?" it was a question from her, not a statement.

"Yes really!" Jamie said, not missing a beat.

"I want to see Max one last time. Max is my dog." She turned and looked at a picture of a white bundle of fluff on her bedside cupboard. Jamie didn't know her very well, but had met her earlier in her stay, when they were still hoping for an elongation of her life by a few months. He didn't know she had a dog.

"I understand. Isla my cocker spaniel would be my biggest issue, if I was where you are. What sort of dog is he?" Jamie found it easy to empathise in this situation.

"He is a border terrier, perhaps with a bit of Heinz thrown in." She was leaking tears silently, but still had a strong voice, despite the breathlessness.

"You know that I don't think dying at home would be easy, don't you? I know we talked about it once before?" Jamie had to choose his words carefully. Other colleagues, would have been much more in favour of assisted discharge and he didn't want to leave conflict.

"I know you have explained before about the oxygen. They have arranged for three concentrators to be put in, but I know you said this won't be as effective as what I'm getting here on the high-flow circuit."

Jamie looked up at Annie, who was welling up listening to the conversation. She turned away slightly. She couldn't meet Jamie's gaze.

"Annie has guessed, what I am going to say, I think." Jamie paused a moment and took a deep breath for himself, knowing he needed it. "If I can make it happen that we get Max in to your room for a visit, would you stay here instead of going home?"

"But you can't, can you? The rules due to this damned virus don't allow it," Mrs Dobson's voice showed emotion for the first time, bordering on anger.

Annie, gave out a little supressed laugh and cry mixed together. Jamie looked up and smiled.

"Annie knows, Dr Carmichael breaks rules when it's the right thing to do."

"And this would be the right thing to do," Annie's voice cracked a little as she joined in.

"How?" This time, there was hope in Mrs Dobson voice. Jamie had stood up and gone to look at the window. He opened it fully. Whilst a human wouldn't get out of it easily, they would fit a small dog through.

"We will go through the official channels first and ask for special dispensation. It should really be given, but I'm not promising that, as the managers are a bit crazy at times and especially right now. If not, could someone in the family come to this window with Max tomorrow at five in the evening and pass him through. I would stay with you to deal with any flak, if anyone else finds out. We are blessed you are on the ground floor."

Mrs Dobson was now crying openly, but didn't answer Jamie. Instead, she looked up at Annie.

"Is he being serious, would he really do this?" she asked fixing her eyes on Annie's.

"Oh god yes, he is deadly serious. A little crazy." Annie laughed at the moment and took a breath to steady herself. "But deadly serious. If he says he will do it, he will be good to his word."

"As long as you do your bit and hang around until tomorrow evening!" Jamie added, crouching back down next to his patient.

"Ok, Dr Carmichael. I will trust you. You have until 5 p.m. tomorrow. I could get my sister to come to the window if needed."

"Deal!" Jamie responded, taking her hand in his own gloved one. "But our secret for now. No one other than us three and your sister, to know about the 5 p.m. option."

Jamie genuinely had no idea how the Matrons would react. It was hard enough getting permission to get relatives in to patients dying of Covid. If they said no, he would do the illegal act and take the hit if he got in trouble. Annie was right, he believed rules were meant for breaking, when it was clearly the right thing to do for the well-being of the patient.

To Jamie's amazement, half an hour later it was all fixed. Jamie and Annie had gone together to see Matron, who was in a very positive mood and understood Jamie's concerns over the experience of dying that Mrs Dobson might suffer at home. Jamie had been honest and told Matron, what he would do if she said 'no'. He missed the timing details.

"If we don't get permission and you go and do it yourself, I would have to report you, you do realise?"

Jamie had sighed, but knew that she would have no choice. "Understood! And it would just be me, not Annie involved if so."

"Which Annie?" Matron had said, not moving her eyes off Jamie.

"Exactly!"

However, special dispensation for Max was granted from the higher managers, with Matrons supportive and positive request.

Max had arrived on Monday afternoon, 24 hours ahead of the deal expiry. Jamie had popped in to meet him, taking Annie with him again. Jamie had lots of support from the ward nurses before this incident, but he went up in their standing even further. Annie had to deal with a little jealousy, for her active involvement.

Mrs Dobson was good to her word and managed comfortably to see Max, still in full awareness.

****

"Very peacefully from what the night team said," Annie brought him back from his reverie.

"Well done, Annie. You were brilliant!" Jamie loved giving the juniors praise.

"Dr Carmichael, Mrs Dobson asked me to tell you something, but only to tell you after she died. So, I hadn't told you." Jamie could tell Annie was struggling to get this out, her voice cracking and if he was with her, he knew he would have seen tears. "She said you were 'fucking awesome'. Her exact words."

"Couldn't have done it without you, Annie," Jamie was blubbing before he finished the sentence.

Jamie hung up quickly and looked to the sky. 'Go dance with the angels Sylvia, now you can breathe'. The words this time certainly said inside his head.

Chapter 10
The 'House' Year: Disasters and Dreams

25 August 1985. A very sad day in Manchester!

Jamie was on-call again, waking at 5.45 a.m. with his alarm to do his IV-drug round. He had, just had his longest undisturbed on-call sleep, since starting as a doctor, possibly approaching 3 hours.

It was not all positive. He had woken to a nightmare, so vivid that it disturbed him.

Sister Mattison was on night duty and he hadn't really bonded with her, but Freda had already come in for the early shift, though Angela and Christine were not there.

"Just woke from a horrendous dream of a plane catching fire and crashing on a runway. Not sure this sleeping whilst on duty is such a good idea. Scared me senseless it was so real!" he explained to Freda and Pippa another of the nurses on duty, who were in the treatment room together.

He repeated the exercise on A11 where Sister Arbuthnott and an auxiliary called Maggie were on duty for morning handover, by the time he made it there. Finally, on A4, Janice listened to his story, again painted and impeccable for the start of a 6 a.m.-2 p.m. shift.

Jamie was spared B3 as there were no patients prescribed IV antibiotics at 6 a.m. that day.

He was done quickly and decided to take that extra hour option, resetting his old metallic bell alarm for 8.15 a.m.

Splashing on copious deodorant and shaving quickly he even had time to pick up a coffee and a bacon sandwich from 'Aileen', before heading to meet the team on A12 at 8.45 a.m. as planned, to prepare for the day ahead.

As he walked on Freda was walking down the corridor to meet him. Sister Mattison was still there, staring at him quite oddly.

"Jamie, have you heard the news?"

"News about what, Freda?" Something in her tone made him wary and not be his usual joking self.

"Hospital is on red alert as there is a major incident at Manchester Airport. Plane burst in to flames on the runway apparently."

Jamie's blood ran cold.

"What time?" Jamie stammered his question out.

"Just heard now when they called the major incident, but it's just been on the news. Sounds bad, there are survivors though." She was about to walk away, but turned and added, "Matty has gone really weird about it. Doesn't want us to spend time with you. I'll take no notice of course… Have you ever had premonitions like it before?"

Jamie regretted he had told so many people already. He had never had anything happen like this, but first there was a potential medical crisis for lots of people. The issue that everyone was going to think he was a witch…or rather, a warlock, was secondary and could be shelved for now.

He was desperate to know what time the event happened, but any chance to investigate by listening to the news, was quickly curtailed.

"Jamie, action stations! We need to identify patients for discharge to free up beds. Major incident alert. Jon is already on ICU and CCU looking to identify patients to move off ICU if possible. Then the registrars and consultants, will be there on standby."

We've to sort the ward patients on A12 and discharge as many as possible and then sort the rest. Callum and Fraser are doing the same on A11.

****

The Manchester Air Disaster:

As it happened, none of the patients who survived the 1985 Manchester Air Disaster, came to Stockport's ICU or wards. The cardiothoracic ICU and wards at South Manchester had been on a week's shut-down, for a deep clean and all the critical patients of which there were only a modest number were managed there.

The disaster survivors who got off the plane early were predominantly walking well. Those who didn't survive (55) including 2 crew, largely died of smoke inhalation and suffocation. Only one of those who got off the plane, died after arrival at hospital. A handful of those who got off after suffering significant smoke inhalation, suffered long term damage to their lungs with major limitation of breathing thereafter, developing a form of asthma, which was poorly responsive to any treatment.

However, the difference between surviving and not, was measurable in the seconds/minutes it took to clear the planes seating area, with the non survivors further away or obstructed from reaching the escape routes.

The incident clearly had a major impact on all those directly involved in the loss of life or the seriously injured. Our thoughts are still with them.

The events changed culture at airports regarding safety, crew training and simulated incident training.

Specialist teams were set up who would be first responders at any major incidents in the future. These teams also developed into international responders, travelling to foreign disasters such as the Tsunami in the far east.

The original thoughts were, that these teams would be major life-savers, but such catastrophic events are fortunately so rare, that their really good work, was more frequently associated with clean-up operations, managing the aftermath of mass death. Arguably, their most important work may have been doing the difficult work of internationally retrieving and returning the bodies of non survivors to their families for proper grieving and burial or other forms of commemoration of life.

Sadly, when subsequent disasters in the Manchester area of such a scale (The Arndale centre and Manchester Arena bombings), occurred, such a locally developed major response team no longer existed in the form for which it was designed.

Whilst not involved directly in the Manchester air disaster, I (the author of this book) was fortunate enough to be mentored for a large part of my career by one of Physicians who was involved. I also had the rare privilege of looking after some of the long-term survivors and learning therefore first hand of some of the physical and psychological scars and perhaps most interestingly but powerfully, the guilt that some of the survivors experienced.

Whilst in the rest of the book, I will not declare where fact meets fiction, Jamie's story is as close to 'my' truth of this day as I can remember it, whilst not identifying colleagues.

It had a profound effect on me personally and opened my eyes to the concept, that we cannot and should not try and explain every one of our personal experiences scientifically.

Chapter 11
Getting Covid: Night 2 and Other Stories

Jamie woke up Thursday night, sweating, rising up from a bad dream where he was drowning.

His faithful spaniel lifted her head wearily and looked at him in half annoyance, half excitement at the thought of getting up and chasing the rabbits and squirrels out in the back garden area.

Her tail momentarily thrummed a beat on the bed, it slowed before stopping and she let out a sigh.

There was a feel of hot sweat on Jamie's back, but he didn't feel shivery, he may just have been overheating in his dream.

"Too early, Isla, back to sleep!" Isla sighed a second time.

Jamie contemplated whether this was just a dream or was actually driven by anxiety. It could possibly even be the start of covid itself making him breathless. His covid swab, which he had done just before he went to bed was again negative.

They had all decided they would do one every morning, but Jamie couldn't resist doing an extra one. He was getting through the 12-week supply a little quicker than intended, but he only had a few weeks left before his retirement date and if he used them all up early, he would make do the last couple of weeks. In part, because he would have had his second vaccine by then anyway.

He took a deep breath in, to see if there was any sense of restriction or heaviness, which was likely to be the first sign. Or he postulated, that it might trigger a desire to cough. Jamie was relieved there was neither.

Sensing nothing amiss physically, he rolled on his side and attempted to return to sleep, but he already knew, it would be elusive.

Since getting Isla, he now mostly slept well. She gave him the comfort he had not had since his separation, six years or so before. For the first three years alone, he barely slept for more than three hours at bedtime, before waking in the early hours and ruminating about the events leading up to him finally giving up and moving out. Eventually he would doze off after a couple of hours of tossing and turning. It would feel like less than an hour from returning to sleep, when the alarm would go.

Despite these nocturnal disturbances, most of his colleagues only knew of his troubles, nearly a year or so after his separation. For all his outgoing nature with patients, he kept his inner personal feelings and events well hidden from most people.

He was well aware gossip flew around hospitals at a rate of knots, implausible in any other work setting.

In his sleepless state and trying to avoid bad memories linked to his separation, he tried pulling up funny memories as a distraction. He recalled the evening, he had slipped on a down slope whilst playing a 9-hole evening round of golf, with his good friend Jack Smithson and the then 'Mr Captain' of his club, making a 3-ball.

There was a sharp pain as he landed on his right buttock, slipping a few feet down the slope in the process. Partly due to the embarrassment, Jamie promptly jumped back to his feet.

He had been scoring well and was in position to win this relatively inconsequential, 9-hole, evening, roll up competition. However, Jamie was fiercely competitive at sports. So, he made his way down to the 7th tee, trying to refocus on the next shot and keeping the scoring run going.

In these evening competitions, time was precious so there were no practice swings for Jamie. He teed up first having come off the last with a birdie '2'. He was again aware of the soreness still coming from his buttock area as he bent over. He had his driver in use and in the middle of the swing, Jamie became aware that this discomfort was more severe than was conceivable from just a bruise from landing. Pain shot through his buttock at the moment of impact.

The ball duck hooked and landed seventy yards away amongst the trees, his chance of winning perhaps already gone and if not, certainly floundering.

He slid his hand into his back right pocket to rub the area, where he had landed. The variety of tees he used, were there, where he always kept them. Most of them moved under his touch, but one was still. He nudged it again, experiencing the dawning realisation of what had caused the intense pain.

The golf tee that wouldn't move was buried through his trousers and boxers and was deep in the muscle and fat of his right buttock.

Golfers amongst you would understand Jamie's, next thought. Those who don't golf, nor know the materials used for making golf tees might not understand this. However, the thought was 'which sort of tee was it that had got itself buried'? Was it one of the short plastic ones used for taking iron shots off the tee? Or, perhaps more sinisterly, was it a wooden one, which were 1 and ¾ inches in Jamie's preferred length for using the driver.

He gently felt the top of the tee and realised with mounting anxiety, that it was the latter. They had a flatter top, whilst the plastic ones had a cave effect on top.

By now, Jack had taken his shot and Jamie, quietly explained the scenario to his medical colleague friend. Almost before Mr Captain had played his shot, Jamie's trousers and pants were down and Jack, was exploring the puncture wound in Jamie's buttock as best he could in the external environment and circumstances.

The careful exploration of the entry site was being done with Jamie's trousers down, still stood on the 7th tee in the middle of the golf course.

Jack was a doctor, but like Jamie, not a surgeon.

"What do you want me to do, Jamie, I can have an exploratory pull, but if it is broken inside, it could act like a barb on a fish hook. It will hurt like hell and need a surgical removal anyway?"

"What are you two up to?" Mr Captain had turned and was now sounding a little queasy. He started looking around the course, hoping no-one else was in sight. He thought of throwing himself in a bunker as the ground would more easily swallow him up that way.

The doctors were blissfully unaware, having gone into medical mode and had little care for the embarrassment factor.

Jack and Jamie both knew medical crises were not moments for worrying about social etiquette.

"Let's go for a pull!" said Jamie. "Are you happy to do it, or shall I do it myself?"

"Stay still!" said Jack in a brief response, *no point wasting time*, he thought.

There was a comforting 'splot' sound as the tee, came quickly out.

"It's in one piece!" said Jack with a degree of incredulity in his voice… And perhaps disappointment Jamie wondered. Doctors are lovers of drama after all by nature.

"Any bleeding?" asked Jamie hoping to be able to pull his pants back up.

"Just a dribble, do you have any tissues?"

Jamie at least, was relieved there was no arterial spurting and that the intruding inch and a half of wood had missed any major vessels! He carried a pack of tissues because of his hay fever and fished out a couple of clean ones, pressed them on the wound, pulled his tight boxers up. He was glad he preferred them tight, rather than loose, as it applied some pressure to the wound site. With this minor pressure in place, Jamie pulled his golf trousers back up.

Mr Captain let out a relieved sigh at the covering of all the embarrassing features, that had been on show.

Jamie nonchalantly strode on up the fairway, leading his two slightly bemused partners.

"Are you playing on Jamie?" asked Jack not attempting to hide the surprise in his voice? "Do you want your tee back?" as an afterthought. "There isn't much blood on it."

Mr Captain audibly groaned. He was already a pale fellow, but was now ashen.

"Damn right I am, I've a score going and oh yes, let's just check there are no cracks, so I can be sure there are no splinters left behind." The tee he had used, was one painted white and apart from the blood stains the inspection found no source of likely splinters. Jamie was relieved again. Even now looking back, Jamie realised how crazy his behaviour must have appeared to a non-medical golf captain.

Needless to say, although the round of golf was completed, concentration for all three was damaged beyond repair. Jamie had acquired 14 points from his first 6 holes, but these were only supplemented by a single point in the last 3 holes. His playing partners fared no better and Jamie had to settle for 4th place after such a good start, but no prize.

Jack didn't seem to mind being worse off in the scoring. Mr Captain had been silent through the rest of the round and the post-match, '10th hole' awards. The exploits of Jamie and his medical colleague went unreported to the other golfers. The medical pair, never knew whether Mr Captain was just plain furious or might have been suffering from the first signs of post-traumatic stress disorder.

Jamie lay in his bed interested at the detail of memory, he had for this incident, even down to knowing exactly which holes he had got his 14 points at, in the preceding 6 holes. Memory is a strange beast.

It was the next day, that really influenced his desire for secrecy in his personal life.

He called in at pharmacy and wrote a script for himself for a tetanus booster, something Jamie laughed to himself about. "Fancy trying that on now, you would be sacked on the spot." Isla sighed again, this time at the sound of her Master talking to himself. It was the middle of the night, after all.

Jamie recalled picking up the vaccine ampoule and heading to chest clinic.

He was saving the NHS hours of time by not registering in A&E, like he should have, if being politically correct. Whilst going through such official channels, he would naturally extend the waiting time for the generally unwell. Additionally, and most importantly to Jamie, his own time wasn't being wasted either, skipping some steps of the process.

Jamie decided a self-injection into his buttock or shoulder, was beyond his slightly squeamish skills for that morning. The next issue was who to ask. Of his various contacts who he might have asked to do the deed he chose Jackie, the chest clinic nurse he knew very well.

He asked her quietly for a moment of her time and they retreated into one of the clinic rooms, before they were in use for the morning clinics. Jamie entertained her with the story and exaggerating the tale in terms of the noise of the tee coming out of the muscle and the response of Mr Captain. In this iteration of the story, the captain had to be revived on the ground after a profound vaso-vagal attack at the sight of what was going on, on the 7th tee. Such are the way doctors' medical stories get embellished.

Five minutes later, Jackie was the last person in this sorry tale to see Jamie's pale buttocks and had inserted a second, smaller puncture wound. Jamie was immediately raring to go again and start his ward round for the day.

As was his routine, he chose to start at the furthest away point and rang the juniors to meet him on F7. Ten minutes later he walked on to the ward. He liked the sister (Nina) here, but it was a difficult ward for him to go to as his own mother had died in one of the side rooms on F7, many years before. His mother had suffered a long and frustrating illness, that neither party would have wanted for her. Nina had been there all those years ago he recalled, and he liked her empathy and efficient care of his sick mother most of all.

"How's the golf game coming on, Dr Carmichael," asked the cheery Nina. The use of the surname again a testament to the fact that his leg was being pulled.

"We hear you have been terrorising Mr Captain again." She laughed light heartedly, her eyes twinkling and her bosom gently heaving. Jamie knew many of the male doctors (and a few of the females perhaps too), craved a sight of the unencumbered and generously proportioned breasts of sister Nina Smith, which were likely a sight to behold, if you were a breast man. Jamie wasn't, but unusually he didn't know of anyone who had boasted or even reported achieving this sought-after prize.

"Crikey, I know news travels fast, but I only told one person and that can't have been more than 10 minutes ago." Jamie was half amused, but actually shocked at not only the distance, but the speed at which his personal gossip had travelled.

"You should know better than that Jamie, news goes through the ether of a hospital like a scalpel through lard." Both parties knew Nina's analogy, was referring to medical 'lard', specifically meaning, the adipose tissue on an obese patient, not the refrigerated cooking variety.

Jamie learnt fast from this amusing story and added it to a similar experience from his time as a junior, recalling a premonition of the air disaster. From the tee story on, Jamie only reported stories or gossip or dreams, if he wanted the news spread around the hospital. Occasionally he would play a trick on a colleague, by inventing false news, but he was careful to ensure no real harm could come from such inventions of the imagination, after an early learning experience of a trick gone wrong.

****

In his waking dreams, it was inevitable that his mind would drift to the Xmas party many years later, bringing with it the unwanted recollection of his separation.

Prior to the specific party, he had gone nearly 12 months, since his separation, with only one person knowing.

He couldn't recall whether he had pre-planned releasing the news at the Xmas party. It was perhaps as he had been asked too many times how Heather (his by then ex) was. He was being forced to make up more nonsense replies. The timing of nearly a year seemed about right for Jamie and his personal secrecy. However, it was possible that Jamie chose that day, he accepted, on the off chance that he might be offered a sympathy shag, by one of the attractive and single members of the attendees if the news was out.

As such he whispered the news to Jackie again that night and five minutes later one other specifically selected predictable loose lipped colleague.

Jamie was able to watch the train of Chinese whispers travel across the room, with the odd craned neck in his direction. The news had certainly stopped anyone asking him how Heather was again, but instead he did suffer, several "really sorry to hear your news comments." He also failed in his ambition for the 'sympathy shag'.

Liz, his senior specialist nurse was at the party, that night too. Liz was the one colleague Jamie had confided in, at the time of his separation. Jamie acknowledged that he needed someone to know, choosing wisely one close to him work-wise, who actually could be trusted to keep the news to themself.

Halfway through the evening, Liz had sidled up to him.

"I presume you decided to let everyone know of your separation tonight or was it a 'wine' mistake?" Jamie knew she meant had he already planned to do it, or was he so pissed he was making irrational decisions on the spur of the moment.

"No, I decided it was time after being asked 'how Heather was' too many times. I also chose my carrier pigeon victims specifically and carefully!" He smiled back at her.

"It certainly worked! You will be pleased to know, that you are the talk of the dance floor."

"I was hoping that was for my pert bottom and sassy dance moves."

"Sadly not!" She laughed and floated back into the dance crowd.

Having relived the party scene and the golfing event and tetanus story in his head, Jamie, finally rolled over. Isla huffed again at the new disturbance, but sleep finally returned to both.

Chapter 12
The House Year: Dealing with Infamy

Jamie was struggling with the aftermath of the events surrounding his premonition even though its personal importance to him, paled into insignificance compared to the events of the day itself.

However, he was finding that all the effort he had put in to be liked by the ward teams in the first few weeks, was largely undone, as mistrust and venomous gossip worked its evil.

Jamie's plight, wasn't helped by the fact, that he was working for the consultant who got down on his knees and prayed with patients, who were actively dying. Dr Lorimer's first demonstration of his style of praying, at the times of death, was a forerunner for lot's more episodes, largely at the time of imparting bad news.

Although Jamie didn't like using a specifically Christian or religious approach in general, what he observed was the fact, that patients who had been prayed for (with), by Dr Lorimer, understood their fate and in the most part could accept and be better prepared for it. They dealt with the fear more positively and could discuss wishes and plans with their family much better than those patients of the more traditionalist consultants, who would not normally mention the 'death' or 'dying' words in 1980s communication. They skirted over, the inevitable outcome, until the patient themselves was past communication ability and then talked only with the family in closed rooms.

Jamie, confirmed to himself, his wish to be much more open than was currently the practice about death, with patients, when he was a senior doctor. However, he would not invoke a Christian model as Dr Lorimer used. He was sure it could be done successfully in open communication, without the need for a religious symbology.

In the 1980s, there were no dedicated palliative care teams. Individual doctors broke bad news and gave individual and often non-expert support. Only much later did the skills of breaking bad news, become part of medical school and junior doctors learning curricula.

In 2021, it is expected that every patient with capacity, will have a discussion about their wishes, if the doctors considered it futile to attempt cardio-respiratory resuscitation in those actively dying or for whom long term conditions would render attempts guaranteed to fail.

This 'routine' approach, is for the majority of patients massively beneficial for all concerned. It puts the patient at the centre of knowledge and decision making. Indeed, it is often not understood, that relatives themselves, have no role or responsibility in the decision making over 'not for resus' decisions. Terminology has changed (currently to 'Respect forms'), but the former is the phrase, that most of the readers will understand. The doctor's make decisions in the 'patient's best interest', if the patient doesn't have capacity to make it themselves.

Dr Lorimer's style, gave Jamie more license and opportunity to practice being more open with patients, even in these early junior doctor months.

He would occasionally prepare some patients for what Dr Lorimer might do or say, by talking to the patients himself ahead of ward rounds. His relationship with Dr Lorimer improved through this process, even though it was never formally discussed. The level of improvement from the senior's perspective was such, that Jamie had to decline an invite to come to one of the 'services' at the specific church that Dr Lorimer attended.

****

In relation to the premonition and its impact, Jamie found most of the close bonds he had made with the ward nurses were negatively impacted in the short term. Rather to his surprise it was 'Notty', who continued to insist, he was 'looked after' on her ward and one day asked him in a quiet moment how he was coping with it.

"Do you think yourself, that it was just a coincidence mixed with your naturally open and effervescent approach of telling everybody everything?" She continued without waiting for a reply, though Jamie's mouth was open. Perhaps in surprise at the question. "What I mean by that is, not many of us would actually tell the rest of the staff what our dreams had been that night." She had caught him alone at the nurse's station, whilst the junior nurses, were doing a nursing handover.

"Haha! I do keep what I consider the more interesting dreams to myself, Sister Arbuthnott!" he initially brought the tone down and not surprisingly got a frown for his troubles.

However, Jamie was relieved to have an opportunity to talk to someone about the dream, so he continued through her disapproval. "Though really, I don't believe that it was a coincidence. The clarity of the dream and the pictures, I saw later on the news, were so closely aligned and I don't normally remember dreams that clearly, if at all."

Sister Arbuthnott was listening intently and using the skill of saying nothing.

"If I hadn't done the 'IV' round and as a result told enough people of the dream, before the event actually happened, I would have later imagined I'd heard about it subliminally and got the timing of the memory of my dream and the actual events the wrong way round. I would have rationalised it, as due to my tiredness."

This was as much as he had talked to 'Notty' about anything other than patients.

"I'm going to tell you something, Jamie Carmichael." She paused a moment, listening to a patient call bell, but one of the auxiliary nurses shouted out that she was on her way, so she turned back to Jamie.

"My sister is a clairvoyant. I haven't told anyone here as they would turn their noses up. If you go telling anyone, you will be sorry by the way. Callum doesn't get anything like the looking after and support you do."

"Why do you do that, Sister? I appreciate my bonuses, and Callum is a numpty and his own worst enemy, but what is the rationale?"

"Well! It's like looking after children and animals. I reward good behaviour and ignore or withdraw benefits for bad behaviour." This was the obvious explanation, that Jamie had assumed, but did want to have clarified.

"Anyway, I believe it was a premonition, that's all I was going to say. You will have to wait and see if you have any more in your life." Jamie had come to this conclusion, but it was good to hear someone talking rationally about it.

"How are you coping without being quite so popular on the other wards as a result?" She wasn't being distracted from her line of questioning.

"It's a shame as I intentionally worked hard to get liked, it isn't all, natural personality! I do have to work at it. Now I'm not sure what to do to get it back." Jamie even sounded wistful to himself. There was a real sense of loss in his voice.

"I couldn't work out what they all saw in you at first. You are a bit of a skinny runt after all." She laughed too vigorously for Jamie's complete comfort. "It's the beefy boys who are normally the popular ones in the first few months and I would have been after that lot myself in my young days."

Jamie was staggered, she had been so blunt. She was right of course, at 6-foot, he had always been slim. However, he had actually lost weight and was already down to substantially less than 10 stone. He hadn't been particularly popular with the opposite sex before becoming a doctor. In those first few weeks, he had been subjected to lots of attention from student and trained nurses alike.

"Anyway!" Sister continued, "The right answer is it's because of how you put patients first and carry on being supportive and kind with staff of all levels. I mean you keep chatting to me and I'm 'Nasty Notty' after all." She was smiling kindly and Jamie had often wondered if she knew her nickname. He had never used the 'Nasty' pronoun himself, as she never merited it, but Callum called her it all the time in the doctor's mess.

"But..." he started, however, 'Notty' clearly had something to say first and wasn't going to let it go.

"I'd get back to flirting hard if I were you. That Christine next door, really had it bad for you and Sarah on B3 fancies you I'm told and she is, or was, going out with one of our old junior doctors, who made Callum look sweet." Notty's view of Phil, clearly matched Jamie's own view.

"Just keep being interested in the rest of us too and most importantly first and foremost just keep focussing on the patients." Her advice and pep talk came to an end abruptly. "On that note, Sally in bed 15 needs a new cannula and one of your chats before Dr Lorimer comes round and gets on his bloody knees again tomorrow."

Jamie was staggered by all the revelations regarding Notty's knowledge and her use of the 'b' word. He had never heard her swear before, or say anything vaguely disrespectful of a consultant at any time.

Jamie realised however, that speaking as she just did and asking him to have 'the chat' with the patient in bed 15, meant that she knew and approved of the joint style that had quietly developed for Dr Lorimer's patients in the first month and a half.

"Oh, and if you don't know, Jon, has worked out and discussed with me, what you do with patients who Dr Lorimer is going to pray with. He approves too or he would have stopped you." She was almost reading his mind now and he wondered if perhaps clairvoyance ran in the whole of Notty's family.

"Thanks, Notty, for all of that, it really has helped." He had called her 'Notty' without realising it.

"Sister Arbuthnott to you!" she admonished. "You are good but not that good!" This time she did finally walk off into the bays to see a patient and Jamie went off to canulate and have a chat with Sally Jepson. She had been admitted jaundiced and had just been diagnosed with having metastases from a pancreas primary cancer on her scan. Though she didn't know it yet. Her life expectancy would be short.

He had just finished chatting to Sally, finishing about her worrying about who might look after her dog 'Sasha' a King Charles spaniel, if Dr Lorimer did bring news as bad as Jamie feared.

Jamie asked about family and friends as Sally lived alone. She told him that, she had been on her own for 15 years, since her children that she had brought up alone, had left home. One daughter lived in Australia, the other in London. Neither were dog friendly. Her younger sister was however, nearby and her own Labrador, was getting old. She might take the spaniel if necessary.

Jamie was content, that he had got Sally thinking in the right direction and planning for the worst, even though Dr Lorimer would want to give the scan results and therefore the confirmed diagnosis himself. As such, Sally had 24 hours to prepare herself for potentially bad news. Then Jamie knew that Dr Lorimer would drop to his knees and would pray for her.

****

Jamie was bleeped from A12, pretty much at the moment that he had done all he needed to do on A11. Jamie looked across from the nurse's station, where he had just finished writing in Sally Jepson's notes. He could see straight across the corridor from one ward's, nurse's station to the other nearly fifty yards away. Angela had half started to walk towards him and was waving him over to come quickly. This was not normal behaviour, Jamie knew.

They were expecting a young unconscious man, that A&E thought might have had a stroke. He was only 35 and Jamie had his doubts about the referring doctor's diagnosis, even before he arrived.

Jamie, didn't run as fast as he would for a cardiac arrest call, but Angela waving was so unusual, he scooted across at a respectable sprint.

"David Hampton has arrived, he looks really flat, barely breathing and looks a bit blue."

When Jamie got to David Hampton, the ambulance crew were still standing by, one holding an 'ambu' bag, just in case some supportive ventilation was required before an anaesthetist came. An airway was in place, which he was tolerating, even though this plastic tube was resting on the back of his tongue, to pull it forward. This meant the gag reflex was completely absent.

Christine was doing observations and checking the 'IV' infusion, which had been started. Another lady was standing by looking very nervous.

"Respiratory rate is 6," said Christine reading Jamie's mind as Jamie was making a very quick assessment of the situation. "BP is good, heart rate 70," she followed up. Pulse oximeters weren't routinely available in 1985 and only intensive care units had them at this time. Jamie would need to take an arterial blood sample and send it to the lab, to confirm David Hampton was as cyanosed as he looked.

"Is he on any medications?" Jamie asked the nervous bystander, without even introducing himself, such was the apparent emergency of the situation. David looked cyanosed but was still breathing, but only just.

"Nothing, he is normally fit and well," the voice was squeaky with fear.

"Anything unusual happen this morning or last night?" He was quick with this follow-up question.

"He went to the dentist, he has had tooth ache this morning," the anxious lady replied. She was almost crying openly in front of the gathered crowd.

"Angela, can you get me a blood gas syringe, call Jemma and Jon as I might need them."

"I've already done Jon," she said as she headed off.

Jamie pulled the patient's eyes open. The pupils were very constricted. "Angela, some Narcan too!" he half shouted wondering how far she had gone.

"What's that?" said the lady who Jamie had assumed was Mr Hampton's wife.

"Can I just check you are family?" asked Jamie, now he thought he had the answer and the next steps planned in his head.

"Yes, I'm his wife, Doctor."

"Jamie Carmichael, I'm the receiving doctor today," he replied, "I am wondering if your husband has reacted to some pain killer, the dentist might have given him. Do you know if he had taken anything?"

"Not that I know of, he was fine just a little tired when he came home. He just went to bed and when I went to check on him an hour or so later, he didn't respond," was her explanation.

"Some people get a really big reaction to first dose of a strong pain killer. Like other people do if they have an overdose. I'm going to give him an antidote to such a pain killer and see what happens. The reason I think this might be the case is that his eyes are really pinpoint closed, which also happens with these medicines."

For the first time in 2 weeks, Christine made eye contact as he moved his gaze from Mrs Hampton to her.

"We noticed the pinpoint pupils, but as there was no history of any medicines or drug taking behaviour, we didn't call it. We've been with him both from home to ED and then on to here," this was the female member of the ambulance crew team.

"It *is* possible that the dentist gave him something though," Jamie reinforced, perhaps hoping to convince himself, that he was right.

"We didn't even know he had been to the dentist," murmured the other ambulance crew, by way of explanation. "Mrs Hampton, just joined us."

Just then Angela was back with an ampoule in a kidney dish, syringe drawn up. In the other hand, she held a blood gas syringe. Jamie held his hand out, slightly leaning towards the blood gas syringe, but the move was indecisive. Angela thrust the dish with the ampoule at him and held back the blood gas syringe.

Angela and Jamie briefly smiled at each other as despite a moments hesitancy the decision was influenced by the senior nurse.

Jamie picked up the glass ampule now empty. Narcan was the specific antidote to morphine-based pain killer. He checked the dose and expiry date quickly.

"It might not be necessary to do the gases," he spoke, thinking out loud. Angela already knew this and that Jamie was just reinforcing 'their' decision.

As was the style with medical equipment in use in the 1980s, he used the cannula port to attach the syringe to. Satisfied he had checked everything, he squeezed the syringe, having pinched the tubing on the infusion and then released it again, letting the flow of fluid take the antidote drug through into the blood stream. Christine momentarily opened the flow control, letting a short flush of saline take the drug through into the veins more quickly.

"How long before we know if this works?" asked a pensive and anxious wife.

"A minute or so," answered Jamie cautiously, realising he had rather gone all in on this explanation. He was about to reach for the blood gas syringe, so as not to waste time, when two things happened.

Firstly, a breathless Jon came around the corner of the curtain.

Before he could speak, there was a second answer to Mrs Hampton's question.

"Hello Darling. Where are we?" came a slightly slurry voice.

Everyone looked at David Hampton. His eyes were a little cloudy but open and looking around at the gathered crowd around him.

"You are in hospital and my name is Jamie Carmichael. We just gave you a blocker to a pain killer, as you were rather deeply asleep. Did the dentist give you a pain killer to take?" Jamie was the first to respond.

"Err yes, just 2 tablets though," Mr Hampton replied, his eyes now almost clear.

"Narcan?" interrupted the breathless Jon.

"Yes, he had pinpoint pupils with a resp-rate of 6." Jamie looked up at Jon for the first time. "Dental treatment this morning, nothing else made sense."

"I presume I can go back to Dr Lorimers clinic." Jon was smiling benevolently.

"No worries from me. History and paperwork, has to be done. He might need more 'Narcan' of course, but we will see."

"Hourly neuro and resp-obs!" said Jon as his last contribution, looking at Angela as he left and then bumping into Jemma who had also just arrived. "It's ok! Jamie has it all in hand."

Jemma looked in at the crowd of patient, 2 senior nurses, a relative and Jamie on his knees at the bedside. "Narcan?" she asked mirroring Jon's question of a few seconds before.

However, she added as the in-joke that patient, wife and ambulance crew would not understand, "Or is Dr Lorimer rubbing off a little too much on Jamie?"

Jon raised an eyebrow that from the angle they were all standing, only Jemma and Angela could see.

"I will go back to Coronary Care. I'm there if you need me. We have someone who looks like they need a pacing wire if you are interested Jamie?"

"I did half a dozen as a student, so only if it's not urgent as I might stay here for a while and make sure he doesn't go backwards and need an infusion," Jamie answered, still on his knees by the patient.

"That's fine I will get it done. Good job again!" she said with almost a hint of irritation in her voice.

Jamie returned his attention to Mr Hampton, "Do you know what the tablets were called or their strength?"

"Letters and a number if I remember, but can't for the life of me think what they are." His voice was already strong and almost normal. "How did I get here?" he had turned to his wife.

"DF118?" it was Christine who spoke, the ambulance crew were packing up and retreating. The wife had her mouth open, planning a response to her husband's question.

All eyes turned to Christine. Jamie took the opportunity to look at her himself and winked, when she returned the look at him.

"I think it might have been. They are in my coat pocket." David Hampton was looking to his wife, still a little non-plussed.

"I've left it at home darling, I'm sorry, I will ring the ward as soon as I have checked it, if that's alright?" Her voice was now stronger as her husband had miraculously returned.

"It is of course alright. It won't change what we do for now." Jamie said before turning back to the patient. "Can I just confirm that you are sure you only took 2? Not more?"

"Yes definitely. I even wondered about only taking one, but the pain was so bad, just as it is again. Can I actually have something now, for the pain?" Mr Hampton of course had not been through the panic and anxiety. He had just been asleep.

"Oh darling of course not," said Mrs Hampton who was clearly now relieved and taking back charge of the situation, but still actively crying.

"Well actually!" Jamie interrupted, "We could give you both Paracetamol and Ibuprofen, neither have any sedative effect, but we aren't giving you anything in the 'opiate' range. Going forward you will need to know you are unusually susceptible to opiate style pain-killers, assuming this has all come from just 2 DF118 tablets," Jamie took back charge. "Can you take aspirin and ibuprofen type drugs normally, Mr Hampton?"

"On it!" Christine's response as she disappeared from the dwindling huddle.

The excitement was over and the ambulance crew left, thanking the team and apologising for not trying 'Narcan' themselves, as they left.

"Totally understandable with the story," Jamie reassured them. He was however, slightly disappointed with ED for not picking up and reporting the pinpoint pupils at least. He had accepted the patient over the phone, without asking this question though. Jamie was a little annoyed with himself for not doing so, but he was sold a totally different story and the dentist appointment was of course missing information, until the wife arrived.

Jamie looked at the transfer notes and realised it was the same ED doctor who referred Mr Hampton, who had missed the tension pneumothorax of a few weeks before.

****

"I'm sorry I've not been nice to you over, these last few weeks. The air disaster and your dream, wasn't really a reason. 'Matty' has been non-stop in our ears, saying you are trouble and weird." Christine had her head down as she made her apologises, but was standing at his side at the nurse's station whilst he tried to write up his notes.

"Don't worry, everyone has been the same. I totally understand. I struggle with it myself of course. Never had anything like it happen previously and of course it could just have been coincidence."

"Freda is the one who tried to stick up for you the most, but Matty has been really horrid to her because of it. She made you a coffee one day and Matty took it off her, before it got to you."

"She is a good egg, I know, that Freda"

"Something else you might need to do, is to do something to make Jemma feel wanted and needed. You are taking all the credit right now. She is lovely too, you know, and doesn't get the female attention you get." This time it was Angela talking, who had joined them during the last half of Christine's conversation. Christine hadn't moved and indeed leaned in and nudged his thigh as he sat.

"Angela's right as always," Christine said, moving off to do the observations another time.

Jamie took this cue and said, "Angela, thank you, you are always steering me in the right direction. Calling Jon was absolutely the right thing to do, even before I asked you and I loved that you passed me the Narcan, instead of the blood gas syringe before."

Angela actually blushed. Jamie was amazed, but pleased. The thoughts, he had spoken tumbled out as a genuine compliment. The response was the best he could imagine.

"Christine has a fella she lives with, just so you know." Angela completely steered the conversation away from herself, with the least amount of subtlety. Like Jamie, although she might like compliments, she didn't handle them well, either.

"I am married too, just in case you wondered." Angela added, "And a bit old for you!"

"I know about your man. Freda and Jemma told me how happy you are. I was spying on you I am afraid. Not because I am after you for me. I do really like you though." Honesty was working, so Jamie followed the theme.

Angela changed the subject again. "Christine is right about Matty really stirring it up. I decided to stay quiet. All that's needed is another bit of gossip or another odd event about someone else and then your premonition will just be boring history. Making a fuss over it with Matty, I thought might do more harm than good. My personal view hasn't changed. Next Friday's mess party should do the trick as long as you aren't the one making the headlines at that too."

Angela knew that each mess party, tended to create a whole new package of gossip for the teams to feast on.

"I'm second on call, so I won't make it until the end, so I should be safe," Jamie retorted. This was the second mess party during his 6 weeks placement to date. He deliberately didn't go to the first. They were strictly staff only and he was spending so much time at the hospital. His fiancée was still being very supportive because she knew how tired he was and how hard he was working.

The 'second-on' meant he could go once he finished his responsibility for the 10 p.m. 'IV' drug round as long as the wards were all under control for Callum, who was going to be first-on. As per Jon's first day instructions Jamie stayed in his on-call room overnight when second-on call.

"Well, if all is good, we can get back to making you a coffee or two after then. Matty retires soon too," Angela added, making to move away and get. On herself.

"Thanks again, Angela."

Jamie went off in search of Jemma, but only after he had finished the paperwork. He had also checked on and said hello to Mr Hampton again, who was now effusive in his thanks.

The pacemaker was already in and clearly working, when Jamie arrived on Coronary Care Unit.

"When shall we three meet again? In lightning, in thunder or in rain?" It was Orla one of the Coronary Care Unit staff nurses. She was tall and lithe and as her name suggested looked like she had Scandinavian blood. She had put on a 'cackling' quality to her voice, which helped Jamie who had little knowledge of the classics. He worked out that this was a reference to the witches of MacBeth. She had a huge mischievous smile and Jamie knew this was good hearted teasing.

"Break a leg!" was his tame reply. "Preferably a frog's." He tried to recover, failing by some distance.

"I thought the witches' quote was quite clever, Orla," said Jemma, helping Jamie out of his hole.

"All sorted here! I presume our 'Narcan' man is ok?" Jemma turned to Jamie himself, getting back to business.

"Fancy a bite to eat in the mess then? Forster's office?" Jamie offered.

"No Sunday lunch this Wednesday then?" Jemma was now digging him.

"It's witch's broth for outcasts like me," he replied, loud enough for Orla to hear, who was still loitering nearby.

"Think you are back on the way up." Jemma was referring to the events on A12.

"Only because I have the best senior team any House Officer could wish for." He went in hard, with his metaphorical hug, prompted by his advisors.

She leaned back in her chair and stared at him for a brief moment. "Who told you I need soft soaping?" she said, incredulity laced heavily in her voice.

"Haha! More than one person actually and I do as I'm told most of the time. Ask my mum!" His response was honest.

"What about your other half, shall I ask her too?" she was teasing him now.

"Perhaps not if you want a consistent reply!"

"Right! I will follow you. Black coffee, one sugar as you know."

"Anything from the vending machine?" Jamie offered.

"No, I've brought my own dinner as 'ordinary' doctors need to do!" She was smiling again, but there was probably only partial irony, Jamie realised.

****

"Bloody hell!" said Forster as Jamie walked in. He looked less well, with fewer feathers was Jamie's initial medical assessment and he was now convinced Forster was suffering with some unknown veterinary illness. He wondered if he should be doing something.

"Hello Darling!" was Forster's next line as Jemma followed him in.

"You get a better reception than me, though, I don't think Forster looks very well," Jamie was talking to Jemma.

"What the Fuck would you Physicians know about a Parrot?" Richard, the surgeon, was being objectionable again. Jamie did his best to ignore him most of the time, but riled on this occasion.

"What the fuck?" mimicked the ailing Psittaciformes creating more dust as he ruffled his wings.

"Those who have work to do, keep their brains sharp and have some observation skills." Jamie couldn't help himself rising to the surgeons' jibes.

"We've done 2 appendixes and a Cholecystectomy today I'll have you know. Watch you lip as well young 'Dog'. You might be working on my team in February." Every word in Richard's voice felt like the shriek of a blackboard rubber, screeched along the board, to Jamie.

Jamie erred initially on discretion and didn't escalate the banter any further. He wasn't really looking forward to his 6 months on surgery as it was and he didn't need to make it worse by alienating his future colleagues completely, before he got there.

Richard started coughing.

"Talking of sharp brains, you don't look too good yourself. The best house officer in this hospital is on-call today, you might want him to listen to your chest." This time Jemma had joined in.

"Please don't offer my services without checking with me first," Jamie said directly back to Jemma, but his voice was projected. "My stethoscope has standards." Jamie immediately considered his capitulation into sarcasm, might ultimately be regretted, even though he and Jemma had the surgeon temporarily outnumbered.

"Alright, alright you two, I'm not going to be the butt of medical humour. Anyway, if you want your services offered, try floozie Suzy, the new staff nurse on B5, she has the tightest but wettest little snatch, I've ever had the pleasure to pleasure."

"Oh, Richard you can be such a conceited asshole." This time it was, Sally, the female surgical registrar. Jamie hadn't noticed her as she was sat silently, behind the door. They didn't have him outnumbered after all.

"Anyway, Jamie has enough attention right now, he doesn't need your cast-offs." Jemma had decided to support her junior from this lower form of life as she perceived him.

"Witches and ghosts I suspect, would be favourite, from what I hear."

"Let's go and eat in the kitchen, we need more intellectual conversation, there are a couple of fridges and a microwave down stairs," Jemma turned on her heel.

Richard had the grace to laugh, but went straight into a coughing fit.

"Piss off!" but it was Forster joining in as Jemma and Jamie left.

Chapter 13
The House Year: Doctors Get Sick Too (Pre-Covid)

The following week, Jamie joined Jemma and John in the doctor's office on A12 before Dr Lorimers ward round. Jamie had a coffee and a bacon sandwich in his hand recently acquired from Elaine/Aileen. Both his colleagues looked jealously at his prize. The smell of cooked bacon, pervading the room.

"Heard about that arsehole Richard, your best mate Jamie?" Jemma was straight in, before even a hello, so this sounded important.

"Let me guess!" Jamie paused for dramatic effect. "Has he invaded our territory and shagged Notty?" Jamie went straight for gutter zone humour.

"Yuk! Your mind is a sewer at times Jamie! Anyway, she would chew him up and spit him out." Jon joined in, helping Jamie keep the tone low. He finished by making a spit and ping sound as if a piece of chewing gum had hit a bell.

"No, he is actually on ICU." Jemma pressed on ignoring her male colleagues attempting to de-rail the exciting news she had in store for them.

Jamie and Jon were stopped in their tracks.

"What, we only chatted to him a few days ago, what's wrong with him?" Jamie now feeling guilty, for his jibes.

"Probably some nasty infectious disease! Has he got syphilis or systemic herpes or something equally terminal?" *Jon wasn't normally this disparaging,* thought Jamie. There must have been a history, between Richard and Jon as well, he decided. "I'm surprised they considered him fit for ICU. Lower life-forms aren't normally deemed suitable for level 3 care."

"Jon!!" Jemma looked shocked at his outburst. "I know he can be a prick at times, but he is one of our colleagues. Anyway, Jamie might guess closer to the truth as we saw him together last week." This was a challenge to a diagnosis, which Jamie recognised and got his competitive head on and dragged himself out of the gutter for a few minutes.

"He was coughing like crazy, has he got a pneumonia?" Jemma had an eyebrow raised at him. "Something atypical?" Jamie added with a big query in his voice.

"Woah! Double points to Dr Carmichael. You need to catch up Dr Calinas. It does look atypical, from what I have heard."

"Not another, legionella?" Jamie added.

Christine joined them at that moment for the ward round, she sat across from Jamie.

"Not likely really. He has no underlying heart or lung disease that we know of and no travel history, unlike our meningitis guy. Mycoplasma is the most likely. As you know for your membership I hope, it comes around in epidemics every 4 or 5 years." Jemma was in teaching mode and Jamie was glad she hadn't quizzed him on this fact as he had forgotten it.

"What is 'Psittacosis'?" asked Jon looking at both Jemma and Jamie in turn.

"Jamie first!" Jemma declared, her face turning over the thought.

"Oh god, is that the allergic reaction you get in the lung on exposure to birds?" Jamie was hesitant with uncertainty, embarrassed as Christine was there to see him struggle.

"Sorry Jamie, you are thinking of 'bird fancier's lung'. That is an extrinsic allergic alveolitis, you get from allergically reacting to bird plume, most commonly seen in those who breed pigeons for racing I believe. Psittacosis on the other hand is an atypical pneumonia, you get from certain birds and parrots especially, hence the name for it. 'Psittacus' is the genus of birds, that parrots are a member of. It is a chlamydia-bacteria, however, I think." Jemma still in teaching mode corrected him.

"Perfect answer Dr Lawton," it was Dr Lorimer, who had just joined them. "It is a strain not related to the chlamydia that causes venereal disease of course. The strain that causes psittacosis is called *chlamydia psittaci*. There is another chlamydia strain that causes atypical pneumonia, which is called *chlamydia pneumoniae,* but that is not acquired from birds. Chest physicians or microbiologists don't have much imagination in my view, judging by all these stupid names." Dr Lorimer was enjoying his entrance.

He then added after a slight pause. "Is this the surgical doctor on ICU you are talking about. The consultants were talking about him in the morning consultants meeting. I'm not sure the admitting team had thought about the damned parrot. Jon, will you just nip to ICU and make sure they add chlamydia antibodies on to the bloods they are sending off this morning, so there is no delay. Who had this idea?" the latter question was added after a brief pause. Jon had only just got up and was about to try extricating himself from the tight space.

"Jon, of course!" Jemma was first to respond.

"Just another thought?" Jamie interjected. "I've been saying for weeks Forster doesn't look well. Losing feathers, diarrhoea and red eyes and perhaps a bit scrawnier than I remembered from two years ago."

"Do Parrots get ill with *chlamydia psittaci*? Is what you are asking or do you know this?" This time Jon was following up on the thought process, Jamie had started.

Jamie confessed to knowing nothing.

"How about the pre and post membership pair?" Dr Lorimer's turn to look at Jemma and Jon, switching his gaze between the two.

"Sorry no idea," said Jon the most likely to know minutiae of fact.

"Not likely to find the answer in the medical library either!" said Jemma. (*Mr Google didn't exist in the 1980s. Research had to be done from textbooks usually*).

Christine had sat in silence, but then spoke up. "You could ring the vet, I've the number in my purse for my vet. I have a cat." Her voice was laced with uncertainty as she rarely spoke spontaneously in Dr Lorimer's presence since their first run-in.

There was momentary silence as Dr Lorimer still standing perused the suggestion.

"Jamie, your job! Let's get that information now. I'd love to have it and pass it on to Dr Firman's team. As well as Angela Downing, the ICU consultant, before they think of it. Christine, firstly well done for your great idea. Secondly, is it ok if Jemma and I make coffee for 5 of us and we delay the ward round for a few minutes?"

Christine and Jamie's mouths dropped open in unison. Firstly, from the compliment to Christine herself and then the thought of Dr Lorimer making coffee and as a result they couldn't help laughing momentarily.

Christine recovered herself first, "Of course, Dr Lorimer, do you need me to show you where the kitchen is?"

Jamie thought she was pushing her luck. However, Jemma chipped in quickly to diffuse any chance of a reaction.

"I know where it is and what you all like."

"Reconvene in 15 minutes. Jon, no mention of Forster's symptoms until we have an answer on Jamie's question. Just the blood test," he spoke to the room initially and then turned to Jemma. "Lead me and tell me what to do Jemma. We are on the most important job."

Christine, took the lead for Jamie and went to get her handbag in which she would find the vet's number, amongst the chaos.

15 minutes later they were all back in the office.

"Judging by the smug look on your face, Dr Carmichael, you might have an interesting answer for us?" Dr Lorimer was in incredibly engaging form. Jamie knew that this was because his boss was sensing the opportunity to get some points scored on his colleagues.

"Parrots with active *Chlamydia Psittaci* disease have diarrhoea, feather loss and conjunctivitis. They excrete the bacteria in their droppings at least. The first vet I spoke to, didn't know, but she asked a colleague and she checked it in a text book for me. I will buy a box of biscuits and drop it off for them one day this week as a thank you, as they went out of their way to get the answer for us." Jamie spoke with some pride, but also looked across the room to where Christine sat, in their usual position, opposite each other nearest the door. He smiled at her as he mentioned the biscuits.

"Great work, team. Jon, you came up with the potential diagnosis, make sure you speak to Dr Firman and Angela Downing directly. I'll catch up with them after the ward round. We will start without you, but do find the consultants personally before you tell anyone, what we know. Thank you, Christine too. Great idea! This is an example of great success from team brain-storming!" Dr Lorimer actually turned to his right to look at Christine, with a benevolent smile. It was the closest, she would get to a full apology.

Jon had to squeeze past Jamie and Christine to get to the door. As the door closed, Christine kicked Jamie, inadvertently perhaps. He looked at her and she just dropped her eyes and crossed her legs slowly, patting her dress down on the side next to which Dr Lorimer was sat. On the other side, her dress had ridden slightly up and there was a gap between Christine's slim but muscly thighs and her skirt. Jamie could see the change of colour/texture mid-way up the hosiery. He worked out that Christine had fulfilled her promise to wear stockings and show him. The fact she had chosen to demonstrate this, in the ward round with Dr Lorimer, was flagrant teasing and provocation. It added to Jamie's feeling of huge achievement at only 09.50 a.m.

"Right, who is first Jemma?" Dr Lorimer wanted to get started on the ward round proper, whilst Jamie briefly held Christie's gaze, with a very gentle smile on this face, but a degree of discomfiture elsewhere.

****

Dr Lorimer's team's suggested diagnosis and the potential role of Forster spread through the hospital at incredible speed, as all gossip did.

Like Chinese whispers it got distorted along the way.

When Jamie came in to the hospital early the next day, he first went up to have a look at Forster. He did this primarily to look at the eyes again, as the conjunctivitis was the symptom/sign he was least sure of.

As he walked in, he waited for the customary blasphemous welcome.

Silence.

He looked over to the part of the room from which the silence was most deafening. Forster was lying face to the base of the cage. Legs pointing straight up as if rigor mortis was in full flow. It looked like something from a cartoon strip. The position was so abnormal as if it was staged at Jamie's first look.

Jamie didn't know if rigour mortis, happened to Parrots, it wasn't one of the questions he had asked the vets, the day before, funnily enough.

Jamie approached and looked in the cage more closely, at the unusual position of the neck and head. He decided someone had been in before him and twisted Forster's neck.

Jamie was amazed by his reaction as he was half pleased. The vet had told him, that not only was the Parrot untreatable for Psittacosis, but that his life expectancy was only weeks. Also, he might suffer as the illness progressed.

Perhaps one of his colleagues had done the same research, or maybe one of Richard's colleagues had reaped revenge for the illness of their friend. The surgeon's diagnosis was not confirmed yet as the bloods took a few days to come back, but everything pointed to this as the explanation. Jamie knew that if it wasn't Psittacosis, there was a very unlikely coincidence at play here.

Jamie thought about how Forster had died. It would need someone with a strong character and little remorse, to act so quickly. Jamie's mind went around the faces of all the colleagues he liked least. He realised it was an impossible task. After all, he spent his days off, with mostly non-medics for a reason.

He picked up phone that was on the table next to the bird cage and asked John his friendly switchboard operator who answered, to get him the mess president. Jamie didn't know what to do, but thought he should start with the mess president.

"Jim Dewar, is doing it now, the surgical registrar. He probably won't answer or be in the building before nine. He isn't as keen as you Jamie!" John's response was informative. "I can bleep him at nine and ask him to bleep you," he added.

"You can tell him, that I've come in to find Forster is dead." Jamie had decided letting John know was the best and quickest way, to break the news to all his colleagues as John, would get the ball rolling very effectively. John, just like all the staff in the hospital, medical or otherwise, was familiar with the presence of Forster in the doctor's mess. They probably all knew the story of Richard's pneumonia as well by now, he realised.

"Can I pass that message on more widely Jamie?" John probably realised his responsibility.

"Might as well John. It's a statement of fact." Although Jamie was only a doctor and not a vet, he felt satisfactorily positioned to confirm that Forster was indeed dead and not just sleeping with a cricked neck.

Jamie decided he should get a towel or a sheet from somewhere to cover the cage, just as Firaz the Arabic surgical colleague, came in with a sheet in his hands.

"Just came to put this over the cage after finding Forster dead!" Firaz was not normally known for his early starts, but Jamie realised he could have been on call overnight. Firaz was on Jamie's hit list, although only because all the surgeons, from his first day and the trophy cabinet incident were on it, with the exception of Mr Scotland. The latter was exempted in Jamie's mind, because he had taken pity on him that day.

In reality, if Firaz had been the deed-doer, Jamie wouldn't have known whether to thank or despise him. He was more convinced, that whoever it was, had definitely put Forster out of misery and a painful death.

"Sad to find him silent. No more 'bastard' or 'piss off'. This common room will never feel the same." Jamie felt some words were needed.

"Not as sad as for poor Richard," Firaz replied sharply.

"Think he will be fine, his numbers looked good last night," responded Jamie, who had taken a little look in on ICU, just before he left for the night and met Angela Downing the ICU anaesthetist, doing the same.

Jamie hadn't personally met her before, though she had a reputation for being tough. She asked Jamie if he was a friend of Richard's and Jamie admitted not particularly, but he was worried about him and explained his own role in the Psittacosis theory. Dr Downing had been kind to Jamie anyway and had taken the trouble to explain the ventilation settings and the signs that Richard was responding to treatment.

"We will see!" The reply from Firaz in response, was even harsher and drew Jamie back from his recollection of the night before.

"Anyway, thanks for getting the sheet I was just off to do the same. I've asked 'switchboard John' to let the mess president know as soon as he is responding to his bleep. I'm off to the wards."

Jamie didn't wait for a reply from Firaz, who was now setting the sheet in place. Instead, he dropped down the stairs and went through to the canteen.

"Hi, Aileen, not up for food this morning, just found Forster dead in his cage. Can you pass the news on, if you see any of my colleagues?"

"Oh no, that's so sad, was it this illness he has given Richard? Poor Forster."

"Not sure to be honest, but I'm off my breakfast," was all Jamie could manage. He didn't want to start a rumour about a possible Parrott murder going on. He turned on his heels and headed for the door. Before he got there, he couldn't resist adding largely to himself inside the large echoey room: "Poor Fucking Forster!" mimicking a Parrot-style voice for good measure.

No one heard other than Elaine/Aileen. She didn't laugh. Jamie wiped away his tears as he left the canteen, not letting her see his movements.

Chapter 14
Getting Covid: Day 2

"Dad, how are you coping with all these non-believers? The ones who think Covid is all a government-manufactured story to control their lives?" Jamie hadn't told either of his children that he had likely been exposed. He would wait until he had it.

"Why are you asking?" Siobhan was 33 and only phoned when she needed something.

"One of the people I know at the health club is posting all sorts of shit, saying we shouldn't be in lockdown and that vaccination is mind control. I just can't let her get away with it without responding. She even reckons the vaccination includes a micro-chip, so they can monitor our movements!"

"They wouldn't need a micro-chip. The mobile phone you all use does that just beautifully, especially if you leave your location app on all the time!" Jamie started with the obvious, but it was just to give him a little thinking time.

He knew he would have to give Siobhan something to work with, but he couldn't give medically confidential information away, that might identify a patient or a family member.

He thought back over the last few weeks and landed on a story. He changed the detail enough to make it fiction over fact, but the message would be the same!

"Please tell your friend to talk to any doctor, nurse or any healthcare worker on the front line before they spout their bullshit! It would be better if it were someone working on intensive care unit, as they are having the worst of it."

"I've said that stuff, Dad. They won't listen." Siobhan's answer was what Jamie had expected.

"So, if you want a vaguely real story from my recent experiences, then last week I had to tell a mother, that her 40-year-old, Downs syndrome daughter was dying of Covid. ICU had been and said they couldn't take her, as they didn't think she had a chance of coming off a ventilator. The daughter had awful covid pneumonia on top of multiple complex physical disease and learning disability associated with her Downs. She was just going downhill despite all the treatments we have. The mother was so scared of catching Covid herself, that she couldn't bring herself to come to the hospital and see her dying daughter to say goodbye. Even if I could have got her dispensation to visit. She had brought her disabled daughter up single-handed for 40 years. I was on the phone for an hour with her and we cried together. Imagine how you cope with that grief, especially when guilt catches up with you after you have buried her, because you didn't visit."

Siobhan was a tough cookie who had surprised Jamie with the success of her own business in the beauty industry. Even before he had finished his half factual, half fictional story, he could hear the catch in her breath and knew he had given her the sort of real story she wanted to hear, to use in debate with her 'friend'. Jamie's own experience didn't fill him with confidence, that the 'truth' scratched the surface of the ultimate conspiracy theorists. Not the ones who wondered if the virus was man-made as that was eminently plausible, but the ones who spouted rhetoric on social media about the pandemic being all fake. He knew also that anti-vaccine 'bollocks' was just round the corner.

Chapter 15
The House Year: First Mess Party

Jamie met up with Callum on Friday evening around 9 p.m. to see how things were going and to make sure Jamie had passed over any outstanding issues from the wards, to his overnight on-call colleague.

Jamie had worked hard and checked all the wards, for issues with ongoing inpatients and was going to start the IV-drug round at 9 p.m. and hopefully be done by 10 p.m. and then head to the mess party.

"I've had 3 feckin' overdoses referred in last 20 minutes," the deep Scottish brogue accentuating the misery in the voice.

"Do you want me to see one for you?" said Jamie regretting the weakness as soon as he had shown it.

"Aye if you don't mind, that will get me straight and I might make the last half hour as well."

Jamie set off to do the drug rounds and to see one of the overdoses. He took the patient who had taken the Librium and an antidepressant combination.

He started on the over-dose patient after doing two of the wards' IV drugs by 9.30 p.m.

It became instantly clear that it wasn't going to be a simple case. There were lots of psycho-social issues with an abusive father that the female 17-year-old spoke about, for the first time to anyone that night. She chose Jamie.

Additionally, Jamie needed to transfer the patient to coronary care unit (CCU) to be on a cardiac monitor as the anti-depressant could induce cardiac arrhythmias in the doses the teenager had taken.

It was no surprise to Jamie, that it was yet again the same ED doctor, who had missed the tension pneumothorax case and the respiratory failure from the dental abscess pain killer, who had also referred this overdose case and transferred her without a cardiac monitor requested or planned for the correct destination ward, for such a case.

Jamie grumbled to himself that the patient should have been accepted directly to CCU by Callum as well, when he took the handover.

He asked for an ICU review as well, as the patient had taken a large dose of sedative and could become unresponsive or respiratory suppressed. There were no known reversal agents for this type of benzodiazepine drugs in the 1980s and ventilation would be needed if respiratory failure ensued after a benzodiazepine overdose. He also had to do blood gases before asking for the anaesthetic review.

The possible parental abuse issues meant Jamie wanted a psychiatric review early in this case, especially because she might now become more agitated and want to take her own discharge. Jamie thought it likely that she would need to be put under a 'section' in this eventuality and he wanted to speak to the Psychiatrists that evening to ensure an agreed plan was documented.

Psychiatrists were not familiar with the concept of an 'urgent' opinion in Jamie's experience, nor indeed even a rapid response. It took nearly 45 minutes for them to answer the call. By then, Jamie had given up and gone to finish off the 'IV' drugs on the remaining wards.

He finally managed to speak to the consultant psychiatrist, who said they would come first thing in the morning and that she should be 'sectioned' under the emergency act, which allowed them 24 hours, if she tried to self-discharge in the interim.

Rob Bolton was the senior house officer on duty and Jamie found him and discussed the case and where they were at.

"Thanks, Jamie, for doing all this especially on mess party night. You should be dancing by now."

"Yeah maybe," said Jamie a little despondent. He knew he had done a good job and that he wasn't really officially off duty until midnight. However, he had been looking forward to a little serious if harmless flirting.

Christine had whispered in his ear after finishing the early shift, that she would be there. "Who knows might be your lucky night."

Jamie didn't know what he would do if she came on to him. His fiancée had been his first real girlfriend and he hadn't been unfaithful to her at all. He was finding all the attention he was getting and especially Christine's, rather tricky to deal with, especially when he had time to reflect on it.

He cleared Rob Bolton at 11.25 p.m. and went straight to the mess via his room, just dropping his white coat and splashing on some after shave.

Eighties electronic rhythm greeted him at high decibels. The mess room was dark and sweaty. Thankfully smoking was not allowed inside, a local rule only at the time, but one Jamie fully approved of.

He walked to the bar and poured himself a lager as was the protocol, slipping cash into the 'honesty box'.

He peered through the gloom. The first person he saw was Jon, who was dancing very closely with a statuesque blond, who Jamie recognised only as one of the sisters from one of the surgical wards.

He looked past them, making note to keep an eye on that liaison for the night.

The next couple he saw riled him beyond belief. Callum was there ahead of him, when he was first on-call and Jamie had helped him out. To make it worse he was slow dancing with Christine, who had her eyes closed in his embrace.

As they rotated slowly, Jamie could see Callum had his right hand very firmly placed on her fine bottom, resplendent in 'spray-on' satin trousers. She wasn't protesting even as it became clear Callum had his middle finger pressed down the crease in her buttocks. If he wasn't actually doing it, he was trying hard to press it onto her anus, Jamie imagined.

Callum smiled, even though he wasn't looking at Jamie. Jamie thought it was meant for him, as he guessed Callum would have seen Jamie arrive.

His pulse thundered in his head. He thought about going over and confronting the pair of them, but everyone in the room knew him pretty much. Another part of his brain told him it was good, that nothing would happen. So, no guilt for himself.

"She is so pissed! she won't remember it in the morning." Jamie turned, startled by the proximity of the voice and the fact that he hadn't sensed anyone close.

He stared immediately into those deep brown eyes, that now looked almost completely black in the dark lights of the disco. Sarah was statuesque, standing right next to him. He inhaled an exotic perfume she didn't wear for work.

"Who?" he managed lamely.

"Oh c'mon, everyone knows she has had the open 'hots' for you. Even when you were persona non-grata." Sarah's voice seemed an octave lower in the noise of the mess and she hadn't taken her eyes off his.

"Fancy some fresh air?" She slipped her hand in his and coaxed him away from the dance floor edge, not waiting for an answer. He put his barely touched pint down and his pulse skipped.

They slipped outside into the cool night. Her hand was warm and dry and soft.

The night had the fresh evening scent of autumn.

Once outside, Jamie looked both ways, not out of embarrassment, but to decide where to walk as he liked the idea of time alone with Sarah. One direction, went past the boiler room and round the back of outpatients. The other led immediately to the path to the nurse residence and maternity. He felt the former was safer and would give him a longer walk, without having to break the hand contact. He turned that way. Sarah accepted the choice, keeping hold of his hand.

"Your fella threatened me to keep away from you, you know?" It was a comment more than a question, but he followed it with one. "He isn't going to turn up, is he? That's the last sort of gossip I would need following me right now. Getting punched by Sarah's boy-friend."

"Haha! Firstly, he isn't my 'fella' or perhaps more accurately, I'm not his girl. He comes by, hoping for a casual shag every now and then. He rarely gets it, by the way. Though, he tries hard, at least until he has got my clothes off. Secondly, if he did come by, I suspect you could handle him, he is less agile than you presumably are and he is much shorter."

She was smiling at him, her dark eyes twinkling in the street lights as Jamie turned to look at her and realised, that they were eye to eye height-wise. He looked down to see the height of her heels, giving the statuesque effect. Sarah worked out what he was up to and showed him the spikey heels she was walking on. She looked elegant and comfortable in them, despite wearing flat shoes all day for work.

He also noticed she had a shortish black leather skirt on and shiny hosiery in the orange hew of the hospital street lights.

Sarah shivered and lent into him, squashing their hands between their hips.

"Cuddle me please, I'm cold in this blouse. Then tell me about yourself, Dr Carmichael, I want to know it all!" her voice was confident, yet quiet. There was no pleading or whine.

So, he did. He didn't think it that interesting, except the story about why he became a doctor, which was where he started.

"Mum was a bit of a racist and she had this thing for our two GP's Dr King and Dr Capper. They were old school, like off that old TV show Dr Finlay's casebook."

"Oh yeah, my mum liked that too," she encouraged him, looking into his eyes again, squeezing herself against him. He liked the feel of the soft mound of her breast pressing against his chest.

"Anyway, one day Mum had cellulitis in her leg, we called the doctor out and they promised to do a home visit. When the bell rang, it was me who went to answer the door. Standing there was a young Asian GP. We didn't even know there was one at the practice."

Jamie looked at Sarah. "Am I boring you?" he asked concerned.

"Not at all." She leant across and gave Jamie a brush on his cheek with her lips. He loved the dark lipstick she was wearing, it almost looked black in the dark light, but glistened slightly.

He carried on despite his distraction. "I didn't think it was going to go well and indeed Mum was downright rude at first and even said, she was disappointed it wasn't Dr King. Anyway, over the next fifteen minutes, Dr Rahimi, chatted to my mum, even flirted with her a little. He talked about antibiotics and creams, that her mother would have used, like a poultice. Within the fifteen minutes, he had my racist mum, eating out of his hand. He gave her a prescription with three different treatments and she took every-one."

"And he was your first role model?" Sarah turned slightly towards him and stopped walking as she said it.

Jamie knew she wanted him to kiss her. They were almost back in front of the main entrance. He was embarrassed and unsure.

He leant forward and kissed her very gently and lightly, feeling the slight stickiness of her lipstick. He went searching for the taste and was surprised as it tasted more like cherry.

He pulled back. "Yes, he was, but I must tell you more, before I kiss you again. I have told that story to quite a few people, but you are the first to use the 'role model' word. Which of course was spot on. I wanted to be able to do what he did. He sensed a problem, captured it, controlled it and sorted it all in the space of a few minutes. One day, I would love to meet him again and tell him the role he had in my life!" Jamie surprised himself being so forthright with his feelings and thoughts.

He had to tell her more and so he forced them to walk on. He told her about his long-term fiancée and she surprised him, by asking for more detail.

When the circular route brought them round to the residences where Jamie had his room, she rather nudged him towards the door and just said, "Make me a coffee, but don't expect anything more." He was thrilled by her decisiveness, which prevented an awkward moment.

Jamie obliged and led her to the door. He could still hear the slight thud of the base coming from the disco a couple of hundred yards away, as they had done a full circuit.

Once inside his barren on-call room, which had a single bed and white walls, he made coffee.

They sat cuddled on the single bed and it was Jamie's turn to ask Sarah about her life.

She had a brother, who was a GP and Jamie bluntly asked, whether it bothered her, having her brother as a doctor and her as a nurse.

"Not at all. I won't always do this job even though I love it. Unlike you, who will be a doctor forever." She leant up and kissed him again, gently at first, but her hot breath and the feel of her soft skin made Jamie respond and returned the kiss with gradually increasing intensity. She groaned softly and wrapped one of her legs around his and pulled him back onto the bed alongside her.

****

Jamie's alarm was set, as he routinely left it, for 8.15 a.m. on the days when he was second-on (though when first on, he had it set for 5.30 a.m. for the IV-drug round). The loud metallic ringing made him jump and he knew that he hadn't been asleep for long. His body was now already programmed to recognise the time of day and how long he had been asleep.

Sarah stirred next to him as he moved to switch it off.

His memory came back very quickly in the absence of alcohol. They had talked most of the night, interspersed with periods of protracted kisses.

He looked down and saw that he was fully dressed, as was she. Both were more than a little dishevelled. She had controlled the whole evening. "That's far enough for tonight, Dr Carmichael!" she had said firmly, but playfully as he started exploring her silky blouse and let his hands run over the outside of her hips and thighs. The soft rebuke came when he had pressed on a little too firmly, perhaps. He recalled her doing it, when he had started to head for her glorious alabaster neck and ears. She had pulled away to break the intensity and then settled back into his arms to continue the cuddle and to start a fresh line of chat.

"Don't think I'm not liking it," she had said, through slightly gritted teeth on one of the occasions. "However, I'm not risking being seen leaving with you last night and coming out of the doctor's residence the next morning dressed like this, just to be a one-night shag and a notch on your bedpost."

Her directness was so refreshing and like nothing Jamie had imagined. He looked at her legs, which were still covered in her stockings.

"What time is it?" she mumbled, as she curled into him, pressing a thigh between his as best as you can do in a tight black leather skirt. Her black hair was mussed all over her face.

"You, Sarah Thomas are something else," he said after telling her the time.

"You, Dr Carmichael are rather cute and hot all rolled into one. Well-done, for controlling yourself by the way!" She pulled her head back to look at him as she told him this, patting his chest for good measure.

"I didn't, you did it. Very effectively as it happens." Jamie smiled knowing his choice of words were spot on.

"You would be so lucky! I just controlled myself...'just' in both meanings of the word."

"We better get cracking. You've got your hockey game and I've got my football team to play for." They had discussed their shared interest in team sports and competitive edges.

"Do you have and surgical scrubs in this room?" she asked, "And perhaps a pair of soft shoes or trainers? I don't really want to wander out there at 9 a.m. in my party gear."

"I've no scrubs, but I'll run across and get some. I'll be 2 minutes." He was 3 and a half!

She dressed in scrubs asking him to turn his back as she stripped to her underwear, before donning the scruffier clothes. Then she slipped into his spare trainers he kept for the middle of the night. He had a plastic bag, in which she put her skirt, heels and blouse.

The hold-up stockings she had been wearing she gave him. "Something to remember me by. Don't you dare put them on, I might need to wear them for bed, the next time I come here. If I get that invite that is." The smile was warm and genuine. Jamie felt a crumbling inside him as he sensed a huge change of direction, was potentially coming.

"I do need you to have a think about what you want to do with me. However, I'm not playing games if you are going ahead with your wedding plans."

"I understand that." His reply was cautious. "I have some thinking to do."

She kissed him lightly, pulling back a few inches to speak. "I had a lovely evening whatever and I will always be your friend, as long as you don't start to get arrogant or 'arsy' with me."

She slipped out of the doctor's residence, not knowingly seen. Jamie watched her from his window a gentle aching empty feeling inside his chest.

They both set off on their sporting adventures, that morning with an excited tingle. Jamie was playing Saturday league football.

He knew, making team sport work as a junior doctor was hard when you were working every third week or so. He had to miss one game in every three. The week after being on-call he tended to be on the bench and then made the starting line-up the week after. Even if he played well enough from the bench and were starting the following week, it was just in time to miss the following game as you were back on-call again. Jamie thought it must be even harder on nursing shifts.

****

Despite the closeness of that night, they didn't see each other again for 8 weeks as Sarah broke her arm in her hockey game. Fate had chosen their path, though neither knew it at the time.

The next four words Jamie got to speak to Sarah were to confess: "I'm sorry, she's pregnant."

Chapter 16
Getting Covid: Day 3

Jamie's lateral flow test was still negative as he had his breakfast.

They had dealt with the anxiety of yesterday and gotten through. The telephone clinic was not an issue and Jamie had changed his student teaching session to a fully online tutorial.

He loved teaching and it had been scheduled to be his lung function teaching session. This was only the second time he had done this specific session via Zoom. The latter brought new challenges for Jamie, though he saw both advantages as well as disadvantages.

In this session, he was explaining the use of one of the lung function machines called a 'body box' to measure total lung capacity. Jamie knew understanding this measure of lung function was complicated as it involved both the air that was breathed in and out, but also the air that was left in the lungs at the end of expiration.

The 'body box' is one of two ways of doing it and uses the physics' principle of 'Boyle's law', which basically means that if pressure of a gas changes so does volume.

Jamie started the explanation, every session by asking the females and male members of the group, what specific clothes they wear, when they go on a plane. Jamie estimated, that over the years, ninety percent of the female students, say that they prefer 'loose clothing', whilst almost all the boys will say 'normal', 'jeans' or 'just shorts'.

Jamie would counter: "but with a normal belt?" Jamie had to be careful in the current 'PC' world, that he didn't completely alienate one of the students before they understood, why he was making this point.

"On a plane, the pressure around us goes down as the plane goes up. The pressure inside a plane at cruising altitude is set to the equivalent pressure of that at 8 thousand feet altitude."

The students all recognise that their ears pop when they go up hill in a car or during an aeroplane take-off and this is caused by the reduction of pressure around the body, leading to the gas in the ear expanding.

"If you don't swallow or do that little trick with your ears at this time, the volume gets so great, that the eardrum stretches and it hurts like hell. All babies cry on planes at take-off and landing right?"

"Yes, it's because they are scared!" Claire one of the engaging students in the group, gave the typical response.

"Not the case actually, but great for commenting," countered Jamie. "Under the age of four at the very best a child can NOT open its 'Eustacian tube' as we adults can, to equalise the pressure. As a result, during take-off and landing, the young children's eardrums stretch. I have heard it estimated that the pain a child experiences during these times is equivalent to the pain of a lit cigarette being applied to the skin. We can't truly measure the intensity of this pain, but they are as you recognise inconsolable during take-off and landing." Jamie was in full flow of this explanation, which sounded to the students like a random diversion.

"If you think about it in the 'politically correct' society we are now in, we are no longer allowed to smack a child, even a tap on the hand as it's 'child abuse'. However, the same people who support the concept that smacking is child abuse, do want for themselves the personal and social freedom to fly when and where they want, even since the pandemic."

Jamie paused and surveyed the eyes of the students, to ensure they are listening at least, hopefully hearing as well.

"They take their young children with them, to put them in a cot and fry themselves in the sun somewhere. On every flight, both during take-off and landing, imagine those parents are putting the equivalent of a lighted cigarette on the skin of their child and holding it there for 10 minutes. The baby screams to tell you the agony. But this isn't classed as child abuse, because it is about their (the parents I mean) freedom of choice." Jamie, used the inflexion in his voice to stress the concept of 'their freedom of choice'.

For a long time, Jamie's strongly held, but hugely unpopular medical view was that a child flying on a plane, was a huge abuse event and should have been banned many years before.

"Now let me get back to why I am telling you all this in a lung function teaching session. It is because the body box uses the principles of Boyle' law. If the pressure is changed, so is volume. The pressure changes and the volume of air required to exert that change inside the 'box' indirectly measures Total Lung Capacity (TLC)." He continued to explain the science, but uses a simple blood syringe to allow them to visualise the concept.

"Twenty ml of air inside this syringe. If I put my finger over the tip, then apply a little more pressure, the volume goes down to fifteen or ten ml depending on how much pressure I apply." He had the syringe up to the camera and pressed the plunger, changing the volume. Then, he let go of the plunger and the volume slowly returned to 20ml on the scale on the side of the syringe.

As always, he now had the students captured. He could always sense it on all, but except perhaps the one disinterested or lazy student in a group. Today all six of them were fully engaged.

"Sadly, despite the intricacy of the 'body box' test, it does also have, its built-in inaccuracies. As well as measuring the total lung capacity, it also measures two other volumes of 'compressible' gas within the body."

Jamie paused and waited to see if the students were following the train of thought.

"Middle ear gas," said the brightest, an Asian girl, but not always the one to be first to offer an answer.

"Yes Karina, and the other?" Jamie again used silence to encourage one of them to have a go. He had realised this technique takes longer over zoom for the pause to be effective enough to make one of them try. Silence is more awkward, when a group is sat around in a room all together.

Jamie encouraged the students to try and answer these lateral thought questions. The more they do, the easier he can work out, which of them is concentrating and who is sharp in their thinking.

"Stomach or bowel gas?" he asked it as a question. The images of the six students are up and Jamie's screen and he can see they are now starting to follow his train of direction. This wasn't just a mad ramble after all.

"So, what happens to stomach and bowel gas when you go up in a plane?" he asked, seeing the full realisation start to cross the minds of four of the group. Two pairs of eyes are still not quite there yet.

"It dilates presumably," the response this time from Rory, the one white male student. He is openly confident and not wary to have a guess.

"So why did the boys and girls answer differently about clothing?" Jamie asked, continuing to watch the eyes. He realises looking at six sets of eyes on the screen, is at least in part easier and quicker than scanning them around a room.

Rory has got it and Jamie can tell he is about to speak. Jamie thinks that Karina has too, but she looks a little embarrassed. He is not sure about the rest.

"Guys decompress their gas, like the middle ear!" Rory continued, not at all embarrassed.

"Exactly Rory!" Jamie was pleased, he didn't have to give the answer himself first. "Boys fart on planes! It is socially acceptable for them to do so. They equalise the pressure and the stomach and bowel doesn't dilate. For females, it is socially unacceptable to fart in public."

They are all getting it now, the opening question explained. This way he hopes the complex principle of the body box measurement and its' inaccuracy will be remembered for longer.

"Actually, the volume of gas in the stomach and bowel almost doubles during those first ten to fifteen minutes of take-off. If you've ever taken a packet of crisps or a half empty plastic bottle of water, you will see this effect for yourself." More of the eyes, show their understanding.

He asked them to guess what the average volume of air, we all have in our stomachs and bowels at any given time. He wanted it contextualised so he compared the volumes to that of mini bottles of water or 1 litre plastic bottles of coke or lemonade.

Again, he paused as he wants them all to make their internal guess. With a recalcitrant group, he would get them to write their response on a piece of paper before putting them out of their misery.

This group all had a go, with widely different answers, some completely unrealistic.

"The average adult has about half a litre (one standard plastic bottle of water, or a half of the full litre bottles of coke) volume of gas in their digestive system at any one time. This doubles to one litre if it is not vented out of the body during take-off." He stops, wanting them to have a visual memory of why the body-box test, important as it is, has this in-built inaccuracy.

Jamie continued by recounting the day, when one of the students of a group challenged him and said that her sister was a flight attendant and would have told her (the student), if this was true. Jamie had challenged her to ring her sister in the week and ask her what the sister knew and bring the answer back to the next teaching session.

The student did her homework and at the next meeting confessed, that her sister knew all about this medical effect. So much so, she said the flight attendants were 'taught' or encouraged to learn to fart on demand at an early stage of their training. If they couldn't do so, an irritable bowel type syndrome would develop, because of the recurrent dilating and shrinking of the gas in their bellies, which could be so bad, they wouldn't be able to work in this career. Jamie hadn't known this detail before, this student's intervention. However, he used it as reinforcement at every subsequent teaching session.

Jamie hoped now, the complex methodology of the Body Box to measure lung volume, would at least in part stick.

****

Jamie had anecdotes and stories for all parts of his teaching sessions. Most were acquired long ago, learning which ones he could get away with without offending anyone and which ones were 'too close to the bone'. He had never had a complaint in under-graduate education, but he joked with Tim and Shanaz about it after the session.

"I love hearing your teaching sessions. I've learnt so much listening to you, since you have had to do them on Zoom." Shanaz was always so enthusiastic with her infectious positivity.

"You're right Shanaz. I've heard that session two or three times now and I'm not bored of listening to it. You must get bored of doing it eventually though Jamie?" Tim Coffey, replied and quizzed Jamie about the repetitiveness of the sessions.

"I concentrate on their reaction, that is what keeps it different for me. The words are just a script, but I play it differently every time, depending on how they are responding as a group." He explained how he doesn't get bored, doing the session every 6 weeks each year. He kept to himself the fact that he knew the three-month summer break, genuinely refreshes his enthusiasm.

"Have you ever had a student complain?" Shanaz again, "I mean with the child abuse stuff. They might get upset."

"No and my teaching scores and comments are almost always good." Jamie didn't like being positive about himself, so countered with a negative story.

"Thought I'd blown my chairing career at the National Lung conference, a few years back, have I bored you with this story?"

"No go on!" Shanaz was delighted with the break from checking and signing her letters.

"I was chairing a spoken session with Gary Conroy, from Montreal. I did some of the 'Thermoplasty' work with him, so I knew him well. An Australian group were presenting a paper on CT scans of the larynx during attacks of Inducible Laryngeal Obstruction. As you know, we make the diagnosis, by looking down with the scope, but this Aussie group had done CT scans during attacks."

Jamie paused to take a sip of his tea.

"Gary had heard the talk at another conference and passed a note over to me as we sat on stage in front of the five hundred or so colleagues listening to this talk."

"The note said and I quote: 'Wait 'til you see the images. They look just like fannies'. I did actually manage to keep a straight face, when I read it."

Jamie paused again, but his colleagues were listening with interest.

"Sure enough, two minutes later, the CT images of the larynx were shown on the giant screen. I'd not seen them before and they looked just like the female anatomy. I scanned the room and there were a few smiles and nudges going on. So, when it came to question time, I waited until all the serious ones had been asked and answered. I took chairs privilege to ask the last question of the day. The question was of course: 'how had they managed to get the images of a larynx, to look so exactly like a vagina?' I at least used the politically correct medical term. Anyway, the room just fell apart with laughter, that muggins here, had actually asked the question. Almost everyone in the room was howling, except one dour lady on the front row. She was stern and furious and started making notes in her pad, whilst everyone else was laughing. I waited months to see if I was getting the letter from the faculty telling me, that my services as a chair, were no longer needed. After two months, I stopped worrying and it never came."

"Did you chair the next year?" Shanaz asked grinning wildly.

"Yes, in the main auditorium, so she either didn't put the complaint in, or whoever read it was actually in the room at the time and got the moment!"

"You fly by the seat of your pants, Jamie," this time it was Tim, but he was smiling.

They all needed a diversion from the anxiety of that day. Jamie however, encouraged them back to their tasks of phone calls and admin. He was keen to finish on time this Friday.

Chapter 17
The House Year: Trouble on Board

"Is there a doctor on-board? If so, please attend the purser's office immediately!" The first 6 words are usually either a doctor's dream or nightmare, depending how you feel about being the centre of attention, or how drunk you are when you heard it. The latter most often on a plane of course.

When Jamie heard it for the first time in his career, he was on a ferry from Felixstowe to Amsterdam for a long weekend. The first days off since starting work. He and his fiancée had travelled down by train overnight to London, then a further train out to the port for the first ferry out on a Friday.

He had only received a couple of wage packets, when they booked it as a last-minute break. It all had to be done on a low budget. They had travelled in their really scruffy clothes and would change and smarten once they had checked in to their hotel in Amsterdam. Jamie had on corduroy trousers with a knee patch, that he would otherwise, only have worn for doing painting or gardening.

"I can't go looking like this!" he whispered to Diane, hoping no-one overheard. "I will wait and see if the call gets put out again."

Sure enough 5 minutes later, this time with a plead in the voice of the purser, the same request came over the tannoy. Jamie lifted his tired body, with a sigh and headed following the signs to the purser's office.

The man in front of Jamie was approaching 50, with greying hair and was dressed in a white shirt and black suit, with shiny lapels. It reminded Jamie of a very tired dinner jacket.

"You might not believe this," started Jamie, looking down at himself. "But I am actually a junior doctor."

Jamie felt stupid, for the apologetic tone, which he could even hear himself. He knew that he looked young for his actual age at any-time, but with a night of half a face of stubble and little sleep again, he imagined himself looking the least like a doctor of any of the passengers on-board. At least of those that weren't stowed away in the freight section or currently playing in the free on-board creche.

The purser stood upright and peered at Jamie along a hooked nose. It was clear to Jamie, that he wasn't convinced that Jamie's approach was genuine. The purser remained silent for what to Jamie was an uncomfortably long time, whilst he very slowly looked Jamie up and down. He was taking his time appraising his obviously limited options.

Jamie read the thoughts of this officious and unkindly senior crewman. 'You look like you are twelve and you are telling me you are a doctor'. Jamie wondered if this was his second surreal moment of a sixth sense and maybe he was actually hearing this troubled man's thoughts.

The purser finally made his decision and almost reluctantly spoke, "Come with me."

The 'patient' was lying on his back in the bar area, which had been cleared and there had a been a large group of people outside as Jamie was led through the glass doors. There was a large bar to Jamie's left. The floor felt sticky underfoot and there was the smell of stale beer and cigarettes.

"Hello, my name is Jamie Carmichael and although I don't look it, I am a junior doctor out of Stockport in Cheshire and I appear to be the only doctor on-board. Do you mind if I ask your name?" Jamie got down on the floor and knelt on his knees next to the stricken man. In this position, Jamie was hoping to hide the patch.

"Harold," said a strained voice. "Call me Harry if you can make this pain better."

"You look in heap of pain there, Harry, but can you tell me what happened?"

"I was at the front of the queue at the door waiting for the bar to open, as I came in there was a bit of a scramble and I slipped and twisted and my back went before I even landed on the floor." He was gritting his teeth even to speak.

"Has it given you trouble before?"

"I've had sciatica, Doc, especially in my left leg." It amazed Jamie, that this stranger accepted him as a doctor so quickly, just from the nature of the questions he was asking.

"And where does it hurt?"

"Excuse me!" interrupted the purser who had been hopping from one leg to another. "Is this going to take long. If I can't move Harold, I can't open the bar and that will cost us thousands in revenue and we will have angry travellers. There are hen parties and stag parties galore on board."

"Bear with me a minute, Harry," Jamie spoke firstly to his new 'patient'. He then turned to the purser and youthful appearance aside, Jamie had no intention of being jerked around.

"You have asked me to come and help. You can and will give me the courtesy of enough time to do the right thing here. At this moment, I have someone with a back injury, you might be responsible for because of slippery floors. We will be taking no chances with Harry. You can either turn this vessel round and go back to port and get a paramedic ambulance to meet us, get an air ambulance on-board or give me time to do what needs to be done here."

The purser looked shocked and as surprised as Jamie felt, by the assertive tone, the younger man had adopted. Jamie knew he wouldn't have managed this strength, prior to his experiences of the last 3 months.

"If you want to get the captain down, I am very happy to say the same to him. Good or bad, until you get a more senior medical person here, it is my responsibility. Please also remember you asked me here."

The purser visibly paled at the continued monologue.

"Also, you need to know I won't be moving Harry alone. One option might be to see if there are any nurses on-board with another tannoy call. You might find some who might be able to help me move him safely, if I decide that is an option." Jamie's confidence grew as the purser, who had appraised him so aggressively just a few moments before, was now quivering at Jamie's option appraisal.

"I...I...I'll go and put a call out and go and speak to the captain," the purser was almost stuttering as he spoke, before turning on his heel.

"Nice one, Doc!" Harry had clearly chosen sides in the conflict. "Don't fuck with the Stockport milky bar kid."

"Haha! Nice line, Harry. I'm very shy and placid normally, but you are now my priority, so we will do the best we can for you."

"Don't turn the boat round though, kid, I would hate to be responsible for that."

"We will see, Harry," Jamie's tone for Harry was much softer, but he also needed to do the right thing here. Jamie silently acknowledged that he did of course have his medical defence union insurance to think about too.

Amazingly, whilst Jamie was still examining Harry, using a beer bottle as a makeshift tendon hammer, three ladies and one man, all dressed in yellow Tutu dresses and yellow and pink striped leggings appeared, escorted by a gentleman, Jamie took to be the ship's captain. The purser followed behind the unlikely troupe.

"Hi, Doc, we are 4 nurses from Arrowe Park Hospital A&E department on the Wirral. We are on my hen weekend, only one drink in. Can we help?" Jamie looked at her with a huge grateful smile. He wanted to hug her for coming to the rescue, whilst at the same time look her up and down as her physique looked amazing even in the 'poor taste' fancy dress. He decided it wasn't the time and the place to ogle, so he kept his gaze fixed on her eyes as she spoke to him.

"Well, who would have believed that stroke of luck." Jamie turned back to his stricken patient. "These are the perfect team mates for me, to get you moved safely from here. What do you reckon, Harry? Do you want to put your back in the trust of the Milky bar kid and the Wirral Ballet Society?"

"I'm happy to do so, if that's your call." Harold was either very brave or equally stupid, Jamie considered, but he kept his personal answer to himself.

Jamie explained the situation to the nurses and the likely slipped disc. Harry had normal sensation, reflexes (Jamie lifted the Heineken bottle and demonstrated its' use as his tendon hammer) and power in the muscles that Jamie could test in this position. However, Harry was suffering agonising spasms on any back movement and there was no way Jamie could exclude impending spinal cord compression without a scan.

The male nurse, was the first to talk to the captain, who had been waiting patiently but silently. "Do you have a stretcher board for evacuation?" Jamie felt out of his depth for the first time as he hadn't even thought about asking this question. "If so, we could move him for you to a private area."

"We have a berth available on this level. We are now well over an hour out to sea. Just to turn the ship around would be 25 mins for the turn and an hour and a half back, or we can go straight on for another two and a half hours. An ambulance can be ready at either end? We don't have a helicopter landing pad for an air ambulance." *The captain interestingly chose to talk to the nurses despite their costumes, looking even less professional than Jamie's own attire,* Jamie thought briefly. He perhaps was misguided in this personal opinion, however.

"I suppose the key question is, if forty-five minutes is critical for the management of this gentleman's problem?" The captain, had done the maths quicker than Jamie's tired brain could muster.

The response came from the floor, before anyone else got to speak. "Don't turn around under any circumstances."

It was Harry, who made the call and was broking no argument. The milky bar kid and the Wirral Ballet society were quietly all relieved as they got their much-needed break in Amsterdam (Jamie) and the Hen party (with the honorary male) got their alcohol fuelled riotous party weekend.

The Emergency Department nurses, efficiently and safely moved the patient, with Jamie effectively watching on, once the emergency rigid evacuation board was delivered.

Jamie wrote a long letter for the Dutch hospital, which would take Harry in and hopefully do the needed scan. Jamie was thanked by the captain, whilst the still desultory purser took his details and promised Jamie a thank you gift from the ferry company.

Nothing ever came!

Apart in fact for his first daughter, who was conceived in a hotel in Amsterdam a day or two later, as far as Jamie could work out later from the dates.

****

On his return from Amsterdam, Jamie was troubled with uncertainty and doubt over whether he had actually done the right thing for Harry. He wished he had taken the stricken gentleman's telephone number to check up on the outcome. Instead, he ended up asking many of his colleagues what they would have done.

Half of his colleagues admitted they wouldn't have answered the call at all. This depressed Jamie, but made him feel better for trying.

The other half, all gave different answers. The most popular option was getting the air ambulance on board and insist on escorting the patient in the helicopter. This answer of course was based on the selfish desire to go in an air ambulance for the excitement, not because it was the correct medical call. It made no difference to Jamie's colleagues, that the captain had said this was impossible. There was general disbelief about this statement.

As he explained to Jemma, "It is relatively easy doing things quickly and confidently in the ward environment, but here I know I've always got your and Jon's back-up to bail me out, if things start to go wrong. Additionally, everything you might need is at your finger-tips."

It had been the first and certainly not the last time, Jamie would make a call, with no medical colleagues to offer immediate support.

Jamie finally realised, that the biggest issue for himself, was not knowing the outcome. Despite the excitement that could come from it, Jamie realised a career in an Emergency Department, would not be for him, as ultimately, you send the walking well home, or admit the sick patients under someone else's care and never see them again.

It was only much later, that the events and happenings of this fateful first short holiday break, decided issues around his personal future as well as the impact on choosing his medical career.

Chapter 18
The House Year: All Change

On return from Amsterdam, it was time for Jamie's first team switch over. He stayed with the same junior/middle grade team, but they all switched to work for Dr Chapman the endocrinology consultant. Callum, Rob Bolton and their registrar went to work for Dr Lorimer.

The new consultant lead was more of a natural fit for Jamie, as Dr Chapman was very much a patient orientated consultant, who sat on the end of the bed and chatted to the patient about medicine. However, he also had the skill of remembering so much detail about every patient. He could see a patient and talk about their family and pets, who he might have last chatted about months before. He could even remember the names of their wives, daughters, cats etc. without any prompting. Jamie noticed how this made the patients feel especially important, in the subsequent interactions. The memory for linked family names was a skill Jamie never mastered, it clearly took a very special memory, that he wished he had.

The more serious the illness the patient was suffering, the more time Dr Chapman invested on ward rounds. Jamie found this also to his approval. As a leader of a team, he was also visibly a team player. He looked after all the members of his team and was always took interest, in their personal stories and especially weekend experiences.

The whole team's base moved to A11 and Sister Arbuthnott became their key nurse contact. She was always rostered on for Dr Chapman's ward rounds with the exception of her week's holidays, though it was clear this was her personal choice, not because it was demanded.

Whilst Jamie remained in her good books, the ward was still considered the least welcoming ward for junior doctors. Jamie found he missed the natural banter and friendliness of A12.

Before he moved wards, Jamie and Christine had spoken briefly about the mess party. She confessed to being really drunk by the time she arrived and not remembering much apart from Callum getting 'too fresh' with her and she said she eventually slapped him.

She was sorry that he had only turned up briefly. To counter this Jamie told her about his pre-party evening and how he had done work for Callum and was 'so pissed off', that Callum actually got there before him and was dancing with her. He didn't confess about seeing where Callum's hand was or his subsequent night with Sarah, naturally.

It appeared that Christine didn't even know he had made it for a 'quick lager'.

"You see I was so pissed, that I didn't even see you arrive. I would have come over to dance with you, if I had known you were there," her voice sounded genuinely contrite and disappointed.

From this conversation, it was also clear his rapid departure with Sarah and her morning escape from the doctor's residence had happened, without it reaching the gossip round, if anyone had even noticed at all.

"Oh god, I am sorry!" she said. "I think if you had been there before Callum, I might have had my wicked way with you. Though I might have vomited on you, before or after any physical activity, I was so drunk. We will have to wait for another day…or night."

For Jamie, the spell however was at least partially broken and although they carried on flirting, it was less often and not as natural as it had been before the party. Christine also got the dark blue uniform as 'Matty' retired and perhaps became a little less adventurous with her flirting in response to the newly senior status.

Richard survived psittacosis, though he needed to be put on a life support machine for 3 days and nights, before recovering completely and being back in work, six-weeks later.

The mystery of who killed Forster was never solved, although his story is written into the hospital's folklore.

Jamie found out his fiancée was expecting just before Christmas. The previously set, wedding plans were brought forward, to a date half way through his surgical placement.

Around the same time Jamie applied for and got the medical SHO rotation to stay at Stockport for another year, effectively taking Jemma's job, when she moved on.

****

Dr Chapman held a dinner at his house for the medical juniors, just before Christmas. Both teams, who had worked for him since August with their partners were invited. Jemma, had a regular partner, that Jamie had met just once. They seemed very suited to each other and he thought this was why she never flirted with anyone at work, nor was involved in any hospital gossip at all. Jon kept his 'partner' status secret and never spoke about who he spent his weekends and time off with, even under Dr Chapman's post weekend inquisitions.

Callum was another, who never talked about his private life, not that anyone really asked him much. Jemma and Jamie had a running debate about who he would or might bring to Dr Chapman's Christmas party. Oddly, they didn't have the same debate about Jon, perhaps because it felt disrespectful.

Their best money was on him coming alone. Jemma had decided in her wisdom, that Callum might be gay, but Jamie assumed otherwise. He hadn't told Jemma his observations of the mess party and interestingly Christine and Callum's dance hadn't rated highly enough as meriting status in the hospital gossip top ten. Jamie didn't want to add to any embarrassment for Christine. As a result, he didn't give Jemma evidence against her gay theory. It did cross Jamie's mind, that he himself, might get a surprise if Christine did indeed show up with Callum, if there had been any post party follow-up rendezvous between the two.

Dr Chapman's house was a big old Edwardian detached house, not far from the hospital. His wife was as charming and gregarious as they had guessed she would be, a retired nurse herself. The smells of fresh baking were lingering in the hall, as Diane and Jamie were ushered through the hall, by both the hosts.

"Callum and Jemma are here already," said Dr Chapman, with the hint of mischief in his voice. Jamie passed over what he thought then was a decent bottle of wine. If asked about his choice years later, he would blanch at the thought of his naivety on what constituted 'decent' wine. Jamie introduced Diane to Dr Chapman and his wife in the hall, before heading into the sitting room, where the early arrivals were clustered.

Only a handful of times in his life did Jamie have a physical reaction to meeting a female. The second time was much later on, when he met a film-star after she had become famous. The fact this later 'icon' was in jeans and a jumper at a charity event meant the reaction surprised himself even more. The star wasn't even wearing any discernible make-up. Jamie later rationalised, that his reaction was in part because she was already famous.

At Dr Chapman's party, however, the dark-haired beauty, with intense black eyes and dark swirling hair was sitting comfortably on the settee next to Callum holding his hand. Although her beauty was known only to a few on that day, it wasn't going to stay that way for long.

Jamie recovered from the punch to his guts, hoping he had achieved it without obvious outward demonstration of this internal reaction.

Joe Jackson's song: 'is she really going out with him?', crashed into Jamie's head and almost filled his consciousness with its' full lyrics. In fact, it took him a great deal of effort to avoid starting to hum the tune out loud. As Jamie turned to put his focus on Callum, introducing Diane, the world lost reality for a further moment. The settee moved and swayed. It seemed as if Jamie was in a dream, where truth and fantasy had rolled into one.

There was just no other rational explanation for the sight of the normally sullen, ginger Glaswegian who never smiled at work, sitting composed with a natural smile now, almost making his face look radiant. It felt like the girl-friends electricity was passing through their joint hands and was lighting Callum up into a happy likable doppelganger of the sulky doctor.

Jamie composed himself enough to say hello and shook the beauty's hand and introduced himself. Her hand was warm and tingling, leaving his fingers alive with sensation as he withdrew them a little too quickly.

Jamie turned to Jemma and her husband. Jemma raised an eyebrow as Jamie came close enough, waiting until even with his slim physique, he would obscure anyone else's view of the eye-level interchange. Jamie raised both of his in response, as he hadn't quite mastered the skill of raising a quizzical single eyebrow on demand.

Just to add to the excitement, Jon arrived with the tall leggy blond, he was dancing with at the mess party, but this time she was sporting an engagement ring.

Bubbles were called for by Mrs Chapman and a bottle retrieved from the fridge. Cheerful congratulations, were shared with bonhomie.

Callum and his guest were charming throughout Dr Chapman's event. They were informed, that she was leaving the North to star, in a TV series. Jemma and Jamie, would follow her career with great interest. She moved to Hollywood and married and divorced a Hollywood superstar, but had Hollywood status of her own for a series of roles. Interestingly she later rather lived her life, predominantly out of the media or social media spotlight. Jamie liked her even more after hearing this latter fact.

Immediately after the party, Callum went back to being his normal sullen and grumpy self in the work place and for the rest of their placements together.

Jamie often wondered if Callum stayed in touch with his famous girl-friend, whilst acknowledging in himself, what was undeniably, an all-pervading jealousy.

Chapter 19
Getting Covid: Day 3
Anxious Patients

The rest of Friday, came and went without too much concern. All the team had done their lateral flow tests. All were negative, no one had symptoms. The 3 doctors were the only ones left in the office, the rest were all working from home, with the exception of their head nurse, who had, had to do biologic injection clinics. The nurse team were depleted in numbers. As she had been in the same room as Dan on his infectious days, it would have been better if she had worked from home too, but it was impossible.

Cups and crockery were only handled by the individual using them and they all kept as big a distance from each other as possible and kept the 'damned' masks on all day, without complaint.

Jamie had actually done a bronchoscopy list, but as they were wearing space-suit type PPE, for their own protection, Jamie was not worried about the risk of transmitting virus to one of the patients that day, even if he were to be in the prodrome infectious phase.

One of his last acts of the day was to field a question about masks from an anxious patient.

Jamie knew the name well, when his secretary had phoned him to tell him she had been on to her in tears. Jamie knew her as an anxious and sometimes neurotic individual even before the pandemic and it looked like no-one had spoken to her in the last 9 months. Certainly, there was no letter documenting a conversation on the computer record.

He decided, just as his secretary had known he would, that he should ring her back, even though it was late on a Friday.

"Oh, Dr Carmichael, thank you for ringing me back." Michelle Crump had a slightly squeaky voice and Jamie always wondered if she had a little, or possibly even a lot of ILO, superimposed on her asthma. She never consented to a camera procedure however.

"Can I have some of those masks, you wear in hospital, the FFP ones? I'm so scared to go outside without a really good mask on." She finished and waited.

Jamie thought for a second or two about how to handle this with Michelle. Once she had a thought in her head like this, she would be very fixed in her mind. He needed an argument that would take her off in another direction. For one thing, there was no way he could deliver supplies of key medical equipment to an individual patient. So, the answer was going to be 'no' whatever. How to deliver this news, without doing damage to their relationship was important.

"Two questions, Michelle, before I answer. Do you use a mobile phone?"

"Yes of course, Dr Carmichael, but I…" He cut her off before she asked the obvious.

"The second is even more left field. Have you ever used a tea strainer, like the old-fashioned ones you used with real tea leaves?"

"Well yes, of course, but a very long time ago," she answered, but was now clearly non-plussed.

"Next is a rhetorical question. How would a mask work to protect you?"

"Well to stop me breathing in viral particles of course." The answer was what he expected.

"We know someone else wearing a mask means they don't cough out or explode out droplets on sneezing. Any material will do pretty much do for that. However, if you wear a mask to protect yourself, it has to have certain properties and to be used in a very specific way." Jamie paused for a second, part for effect part to see if she was still following.

"So, for a mask to work to protect the wearer, it has to act as a tea strainer. That means, that particles of all sorts of course will collect on the front of the mask. If you wear one for even a short time, without changing it, you get a build-up of all these particles including any virus particles on the surface of the mask. That is assuming virus particles are floating in the air."

Another pause, but it appeared she was listening intently, though Jamie missed being able to see the face, to tell if she was following.

"Most people out there wearing coverings will take their hand up to their mask and pull the front of it down. I bet you do that?" the last few words were said as a question.

"Err, probably sometimes," Michelle answered honestly.

"Or use your mobile phone, with your mask still on or do you pull the mask down to answer the phone?" Jamie wanted Michelle to work it out for herself. The impact would be stronger.

"Ok, so I see what you are getting at, those particles filtered by the mask are now on your phone and hands." Her slightly high-pitched voice, had changed in tone ever so slightly.

"But in the TV and papers, it says this is airborne spread, they've done research," she added.

"Correct Michelle! but their original research was on hamsters and last time I looked they hadn't got long enough front legs, to pull the mask down or use their mobile phone." Michelle even had the good grace to laugh at Jamie's diversion.

"Doctors and nurses using masks in hospital, never touch the front of their mask, for example, they take their mask off using the side straps so as not to contaminate their hands. Personally, I never use my mobile phone with my hands whilst I have a mask on. Finally, of course, I need to wash or gel my hands after every phone call." Jamie felt slightly sheepish as he had let his guard down, with his tea cup, just 2 days ago, but he wanted Michelle to understand that a better mask wasn't the important part of self-protection.

"So, Michelle, if you want to do something to help yourself, just be really careful what you do with your hands and also bear in mind that outside of high exposure environments and small enclosed spaces, that at least 99% of the use of masks is to stop particles being expelled."

"I do 'gel' my hands a lot, Dr Carmichael, so much so my eczema is really bad."

"The gel is really tough when you have eczema, I know, Michelle," Jamie genuinely sympathised with this allergy-driven combination. He reinforced, hydrating skin creams after gelling.

"I think the last thing to say is we as doctors and nurses, don't even wear those FFP3 masks you were referring to, unless we are in a closed space with a patient, known to have Covid and they are coughing, or are using equipment that create particles. Otherwise, we just wear a simple surgeons mask, that you can get from the supermarket. I've been working on the front line for 10 months and I've not got it yet from inhaling particles." Jamie knew he was tempting fate, with the last line.

"Aww! Dr Carmichael, you always make me feel better, when I've spoken to you. Thanks for calling me back." Jamie had achieved something for the day, indeed for the weekend. She was anxious by personality and the reassurance would only last so long, Jamie knew, but she sounded so much calmer, he could be happy with the outcome.

Having written a letter to the GP to document the call, Jamie tidied his desk for the weekend.

Just before leaving, he sent the senior team a message on their 'WhatsApp' group. Shanaz and Tim were still in the offices.

'If I am right with the timing, maybe Tuesday and definitely Wednesday would have been Dan's infectious stage to us. That means Sunday or Monday is the most likely if we are going to start with symptoms or test positive. Therefore, Saturday and Sunday could be our highest silent transmissible risk days. Low profile weekend for everyone and keep in touch if anyone has a hint of cough or breathlessness and daily lateral flows over weekend and early next week I reckon'.

Jamie had calculated backwards and reckoned Dan's exposure from which he acquired it, would have been most likely to have occurred on the Saturday. Dan had messaged saying he thought he got it at work, as he had been covering one of the wards at the end of the week before. It was a yellow ward and so had only 'unlikely-Covid' cases on it. They knew that about one of the patients on a yellow ward per week turned out to be covid and had to be moved onto a red ward. It was possible that Dan had got it on the Friday at work, but after 10 months of working in ED and the red wards and Jamie knew Dan's hand hygiene and use of PPE was exemplary, Jamie somehow doubted it.

"I've been thinking about how Dan got his exposure." Jamie had started talking out loud that morning, when both Shanaz and Tim were listening.

"More likely he got it when he had a coffee from a take-away. Dan likes his coffee and I bet he had one when he went out walking on Saturday," Jamie postulated to Tim and Shanaz.

"He did. I asked him in one of my messages." Tim was in agreement with Jamie regarding the commonest mechanism of transmission. This didn't make Jamie feel any better for himself right now.

They frequently talked about transmission and their own risks and behaviour. They gently took the 'piss' out of one of their colleagues, who had already had 8 weeks off work, in 4 separate events of either him or his family having COVID or symptoms, but each time tested negative. Tim meanwhile had children of the same age and had barely missed 5 days of work all year. Jamie, living alone and keeping a low profile outside work, had not had a single day off in 10 months.

On the opposite end of the spectrum, one of their same hospital lung specialist colleagues was really ill with 'long' COVID, that did sound like it was acquired at work.

"You know about the cluster on the Jones ward?"

"5 nurses all swab positive on the same day!" Tim said.

"Yes, and one junior doctor." Jamie was off again. "When I was on there on Tuesday, the infection control team were there all clutching notepads, wandering round. I stopped one of them and asked them what they were up to. She said, 'well 6 cases on here, standards of hand hygiene and PPE use must have slipped'."

Jamie paused for effect. "Really, is that the sharpness of mind of infection control? Another enemy made I fear." Tim was shaking his head in disbelief at Jamie's ability to be so blunt.

"Anyway, I dragged a couple of the infection team to the nurse's station and said to the nurse." He paused again and changed his voice quality, to make it clear he was talking about the words as he used them last week.

"So, I asked, 'Maggie! When you all got COVID the other week, what had happened five days before you all got symptoms'. Maggie did look a bit sheepish and I wasn't sure she was going to tell the truth. 'Maggie, the infection control team are wasting a whole load of time here', I told her. So then, she just said. 'Actually, it was my birthday'. So, I said to her and the infection control team 'and you all had pizza and cake brought in, which you all ate I am guessing?' 'All six of us were on the ward that day, so probably', Maggie said. I then turned to the infection control nurse, who was speechless. 'I think you can put your notepads away. Six staff all getting it on the same day, all to do with poor hygiene suddenly after ten months and this ward and these staff being red ward for eight of those months. I don't think that is really likely. Do you?' Needless to say, she didn't respond."

"Wow, I knew there was a cluster, but I didn't realise they all got it on the same day," Shanaz enthusiastic again.

"Same shift!" Jamie reinforced.

"Heard about the two tigers that have been found to have Covid at New York Zoo?" Tim continuing the argument about the mode of transmission.

"No keeper got close enough to them to transfer it from inside one or two metre social-distancing, did they? It had to have been transmitted on their food." Tim finished his additional information to the argument. Jamie logged it as another piece of his ammunition.

On his way home and shortly after getting there, Jamie rang his daughters, friends and neighbour, who he bumped into from time to time walking their dogs in the fields around the properties and said he was going to keep a very low profile this weekend.

At least he had his dog, who that night like every night, ran to him from his friend's front door and straight into his car, when he went to collect her. They would keep each other company (Jamie and Isla), during this long weekend, with an anxious wait.

Jamie did some sit-ups to see if he could tell any difference in breathlessness compared to normal. His 'pathetic core' however, gave up on the exercise, before he worked out if there was any new breathlessness or not.

He guessed that was a good sign. At least relating to him having Covid or not, rather than the fact his core was pathetic.

Chapter 20
The 'House' Year: Surgical House 'Dog'

Jamie found himself attached to Paul Scotland, which pleased him. In his senior team was Firaz, whom he still considered as the culprit of 'Psitaccide' (a word Jamie had made up, for killing parrots…or Forster at least). The third member was Mark Smith, the portly and somewhat dour surgical registrar.

At least, he had avoided Richard, Jamie was relieved by this at least. Jamie's appointment for the following year as medical SHO, had been announced officially. As such he had already announced himself as a 'Physician', with no interest in surgery, which Jamie thought might play against him.

His first day on surgery turned out to be free of on-call, so he had all day to see the post-operative patients, clerk the new ones admitted for routine surgery and chat to the nurses.

He had this all sorted, including a problem list to present at the ward round the next day, by 2 p.m. The rest of his surgical team were in an all-day routine theatre list and he was happy on his own.

He only had 2 wards with any patients, B5 and B6, (two wards along the corridor from Sarah's ward, who was now back at work, following her broken arm).

Jamie and Sarah had stayed friends after he broke his news of impending fatherhood. Other than a long chat one evening in her room in the nurse residence over a coffee, when he was second on-call, close to Christmas, there been no hint of a repeat of the mess party evening.

His first afternoon on surgery, with the unusual experience of having no work to do, he went along the ward corridor and showed his face on B3, but Sarah wasn't on duty.

He already missed his team of Jemma and Jon. They were both still in the hospital, looking after a new house officer 'Simon', who had done his surgery job first. He knew they would be busy today and didn't want to disturb them.

Jamie even tried popping in to see if John was in the switchboard room. Jamie had taken John a bottle of wine and the rest of the team a box of chocolates on Christmas day. The visit on Christmas day, was his first physical visit, to the switchboard room. It was a windowless square room in the basement of the main hospital block. It felt dark, with its' low ceilings. A musty smell, laced with stale coffee pervaded the air.

"How come he gets the wine and we get boring chocolates?" teased Margaret, one of the other operators and the only other one in on Xmas day. She was in her mid-fifties with greying hair, but the smile and eyes were twinkling.

"He tells us the rude jokes whilst we are coming round when we are asleep." Jamie decided on straight honesty in his response. "It makes a hell of a difference to how much you process the referral, but I think you know that, John?" Jamie twisted his head, so that he could talk to both of them as they were in their booths. It wasn't flat out in switchboard, being Christmas day.

John just laughed in reply. Jamie was surprised when he physically met John, the first time. It turned out he had a bit of cerebral palsy and walked with a profound limp. Amazing what you could misinterpret from a frequently heard voice. It was strong deep and resonant and Jamie thought he sounded a little like Brian Blessed. The voice certainly gave no hint of a physical weakness. Jamie liked him all the more for it and doubted that John would accept the physical anomaly, was actually a disability.

"Well, I don't know any!" said Margaret after her next call. "Jokes that is."

John got out a book from his desk and threw it on the table 'Bernard Manning's 100 best jokes'. He read out unnecessarily after his next call finished. "Fuck knows how many times I've told you the same joke at 3 a.m., but I bet you barely remember one of them," he said, simply. His wisdom was matched by the practicality of the book, Jamie realised.

"Margaret, it's Christmas and I think an Irish coffee is called for, can I unplug and make?"

"Excellent idea!" she said, though John was already detached from the headset and extricated a whiskey bottle from the bottom drawer. This draw one below, the one that housed Bernard Manning.

No wonder the jokes John told, were all politically incorrect, thought Jamie, as he flicked through the book.

He let John go about the business of putting a kettle on and gathering 3 cups. He felt if he offered to help, John, might think it was because of the limp. That wouldn't do.

Jemma had warned Jamie about Christmas day and being careful. Every ward had a sherry or an Irish coffee moment, for all the staff who were interested. It was just something that happened on Christmas day. Perhaps, New-Year's eve too, Jamie guessed. However, it happened once on each shift of those days and between Jemma and Jamie, they had 5 wards as well as CCU to visit. Self-control was needed!

Jamie had already had one Irish coffee on A12 with Angela and Freda, who were on the morning shift. He had judiciously declined them on all the other wards, so John's one was going to be his last.

He was also amazed how quiet the hospital became on Xmas day. He had 56 empty beds to play with for the day. No additional work needed, chasing beds today.

"Tiny drop of Irish for me John, I've lots of wards to visit!" Jamie was using the truth thinly as his mechanism for minimising alcohol intake. He was managing to tolerate a bit more alcohol as the years went by, but in part due to minimal experience in teenage years and his lack of fat on his frame, 2 beers used to make him legless when he was a medical student.

Jamie reckoned he was probably the only student who made a profit from his student grant in his first three years at university, whilst he didn't have a girlfriend. Jamie reckoned the saving was mostly to do with the minimal alcohol he required. He estimated, that his weekly tab at 'Andy's chippie' on Market Street in St. Andrews, must have been higher than his weekly alcohol costs back then.

"I knew you were smart from day 1, young Jamie!" John passed him his made coffee. Jamie added his own sugar.

"Better than that cunt Callum, hey Margaret?" It was really a statement and his swearing came out of the blue. Jamie often wondered if he had a degree of Tourette's syndrome.

Jamie decided to veer off Callum, who clearly had his enemies in all corners of the hospital and Jamie now felt a little guilty having met the human side of him. "Do you know I was saying to Jemma, if you wanted to close a hospital, the one way you could bring it to its' knees, would be to shutdown switchboard." John and Margaret, both smiled knowingly at his comment.

"Nurses could do all the jobs of doctors for at least a day or two, we or the students could move patients around instead of porters, we could keep patients alive without X-rays. However, nobody would have a clue how to do this job and communication would fall apart."

"You tell the managers of the hospital we need a rise!" Margaret was first to respond to Jamie's explanation.

"Close the fucking manager's offices, then the hospital would run more smoothly." John was years ahead of his time.

Jamie had enjoyed a further half hour chewing the cud, with the switchboard team, before Jemma had rung switchboard to find out where Jamie was. John always seemed to know, where he was. That Christmas morning, there was no prize for knowing.

****

On his first day of surgery, when Jamie descended into the basement, neither John nor Margaret, were in the busy switchboard, when he popped his head in, so he just waved at the gang who were there and who were all working looking flat out anyway.

He picked up a coffee, but Elaine/Aileen wasn't in the canteen either, so he resorted to getting a newspaper and heading to the doctor's mess. He never normally read the paper apart from the sports page, but the crossword would pass an hour with a bit of luck.

He still missed the vernacular welcome and it was strange going into a silent doctor's mess sitting room even months later.

Jamie knew he had to stay at the hospital, until after the team were out of theatre and any post-op jobs had been dealt with. The honest truth was he was already bored on day 1 in surgery, compared to the non-stop buzz of medicine. He had chatted to the kindly Sister Jones, who had silver hair, was slim and fit, but he knew she would take no prisoners if challenged. She was easy for him to get on with, however. Karen, the tall, slim staff nurse with soft red hair, was also lovely and had a little flirting potential, but she wasn't really Jamie's type, so he had not even tried.

The tiny 'student' nurse who Richard had referred to as 'floozie Suzy', had qualified and stayed on B5 and was now in, as she was on the late shift. She was tiny, with an incredibly narrow waist and hips that only flared slightly. If she didn't have beautiful pert female features, Jamie might have wondered if Richard was into young boys really, such was the boyish bottom shape. Jamie knew he was being unfair however, just because he despised the surgeon, who called him 'dog'.

The term 'floozie Suzy' and the alleged physical and mathematical dimensions of her internal anatomy, had gone round the doctor's mess and seemed to be talked about whenever Jamie was on-call. Perhaps she didn't know what the misogynist had said of her, though this seemed unlikely, unless she was the only one who didn't seem to have heard.

Alternatively, she may have liked the accolade, but Jamie, couldn't bring himself to be anything other than benignly pleasant to her.

On B6, Sister Roberts was a large middle-aged lady with rosy cheeks and bright red lipstick. Again, Jamie knew he would be able to get on with her. Molly was the staff nurse here today and she was nearly 6 foot tall and the same build as Jamie. She talked about religion at any given opportunity and Jamie had already had a lecture of disapproval from her.

How was he going to fill his time and cope with life in surgery?

He had returned despondently to the wards just as the team came up from theatres. There were only bloods to request, painkillers to prescribe and fluids for overnight and Jamie would manage that in 20 minutes.

The surgeons were all tired from the rigours of all day theatre and the only interaction was regarding one of the patients, who was day two, post-surgery. She had gone into atrial fibrillation, for the first time. Jamie explained what he had done, as he had done a hundred times in the last 6 months, for patients presenting to medical admission.

"Medical opinion please." Mark Smith, the Registrar, spoke flatly.

"They will only say, what I have done, I've worked with them the last 6 months." Jamie was clipped, perhaps too clipped he feared.

"I said medical opinion, tonight!" the tone broached no redress. Jamie blushed with a combination of embarrassment and anger, but he kept silent, other than a quiet "Ok." He wanted to say, that he would be the medical opinion in 6 months and the only experience he would have different is 6 months of surgery.

This experience wouldn't change his management of atrial fibrillation, but logic didn't sound like it was going to have any success.

Mr Scotland crossed his legs and looked a little uncomfortable with the irritable exchange.

The team dispersed quickly after this. Sister Jones was left to commiserate with Jamie.

"They are like that with everyone. Don't let it worry you. The medical SHO's are on our wards almost every day, saying the same thing over and over. The surgical registrars are just covering their own backs. I kind of understand them."

It was Jemma who was on-call for medicine. Jamie wasn't sure if that made it easier or harder for him to ring her and ask her to come and document that his treatment was the right call. She told him not worry and that she would come and write something before bed, but she wasn't rushing.

Jamie went home completely flat for almost the first time since he started working as a doctor.

****

The simple answer to 'how was he going to fill his time' came to Jamie the following week, when 4 medical students were attached to the surgical firms. Two on his two wards and the same on the urology two wards on the corridor above.

Jamie set about organising the teaching sessions and even managed to persuade the SHO and Registrar of each firm to do an hour per week of teaching. The consultants only wanted to teach in theatre, so each student was allocated a minimum of 2 lists per week. Each student was attached to a ward, to do the 'House-dog' jobs as Richard called it, for the rest of the week.

Jamie took charge and gave them their ward duties and expected each student to present two patients on each of the consultant ward rounds which happened twice per week.

The latter worked the least well of his ideas, as surgical ward rounds were short and to the point and the surgeons impatient when the students took a little too long with their presentations.

To Jamie's surprise, the teaching sessions were particularly successful, when done by the SHO's and registrars and he had to acknowledge that Richard and Firaz, were both particularly good at it and had enthusiasm for it.

Jamie worked out, that the teaching role played to their egotistical personalities. Sally the female surgeon was the hardest to manage as she was very aggressive in her style of teaching and had two of the students in tears after her first session. One was a shy female and the other one a pushy male called Damien, who was of Jewish descent.

Jamie thought Damien himself, had the perfect surgical personality. The other surgeons really seemed to like him of all the students, probably largely as he knew all his anatomy. Like Jamie, he had done his training at St Andrews where anatomy was much stronger element to the curriculum, when compared Manchester.

"Watch him! He is trouble." Sally took Jamie into her confidence, after the teaching session. This was the first time the female surgeon had actually spoken to him as a colleague, but Jamie wasn't sure what to make of the comment. The very next day Jamie learnt the hard way, that Sally had a better radar, than he had.

****

Damien was on ward attachment with Jamie the next day. Jamie had asked Damien to go and take blood from one of the patients 'to check the kidney and liver function 24 hours post op' on a lovely lady following a gall bladder removal. Jamie was teaching one of the other students and was not keeping an eye on the clock. Karen, the red-haired nurse, finally asked him if the bloods had gone.

It was only then that Jamie realised Damien had been half an hour and hadn't returned. He got up and went down the long ward, with beds on either side. It was old fashioned with no bays and only a couple of side rooms. 22 beds, pretty much with patients on either side of a large central space running down the long length of the ward. Lunch had been and gone and the ward smelled of cabbage.

The patient and Damien were behind the curtain, when Jamie slipped his head inside.

"Stop!" was the very loud and forceful command. Jamie was staggered by what he saw.

The bed was littered with syringes and needles, some with traces of blood. At the moment Jamie had entered, Damien was approaching a very scared looking patient, with yet another needle. She had both arms rolled up on her pyjamas and there were, multiple stab-marks all the way up both forearms. She looked like a junkie.

The thing that made Jamie shout 'stop' so vehemently was that in Damien's hand was a cannula needle, normally used for attaching fluid drips. With the large needle, Damien had been approaching the terrified patient's neck. Jamie had arrived just in the nick of time.

"Mrs Thornton, I am really sorry. I will come and get these bloods myself. Damien should have come and got me after a couple of missed attempts."

Jamie turned calmly to Damien. "Please tidy up the mess, making sure **every** one of the sharps ends up in the sharps bin. We will go for a coffee when I've sorted out these bloods." Jamie tried to be matter of fact.

"Can I ask the nurse to tidy up for me?" the young student said. Jamie could not believe his ears.

As quietly but with as much force as he could Jamie replied. "Not today, not ever. We take responsibility for every sharp hazard we use. Nobody, does that job for you."

"But…"

"Go and get a large tray to get started." After the final firm line, Damien stalked off with a clearly sulking demeanour.

Jamie started to clean up, the mess on Mrs Thornton's arms and looked carefully at the neck, to make sure there hadn't been any attempts at getting the blood here, prior to his arrival. He asked her whether Damien had tried anywhere else other than the arms already.

"He asked me if I would prefer if he tried the groin or the neck. I said the neck, but I am so glad you arrived, Dr Carmichael. I didn't know how to stop him." Damien arrived back at that moment, blushing but still acting in a surly manner. He picked up all the needles, of which Jamie counted 12, including the unused cannula. Jamie checked the bed, sheets and even the floor to make sure none were left behind, to cause a needle stick injury to one of the nurses or cleaners.

Once Damien had gone to take the offending objects to the utility room and sharps bin, Jamie set to apologising in full force. He explained he would talk to Damien. He would also speak to the medical school dean and Mrs Thornton's consultant about what had happened.

He then apologised profusely for himself, for being so long coming to check. Jamie then asked her if she wanted to put in an official complaint, especially as what Damien was just about to do was probably enough to be considered as assault.

To Jamie's surprise Mrs Thornton declined the suggestion, saying that she was so grateful for the care she had received since her admission. She was especially grateful to him, Dr Carmichael, and told him all the patients say 'how lovely you are'.

Jamie was completely embarrassed, knowing that he had let her down badly, in not checking on Damien before. He thought of all the times he was doing complex procedures and how Jemma and Jon always appeared when he was due to finish. This was the first lesson he learned the hard way, rather than from listening to or copying his role models.

Whilst the attachment students were in their 5th year and should all have been competent to take blood by now, Jamie knew this wasn't a good enough excuse.

However, the knowledge and insight of when to call for help, was something all students had drummed into them from day 1 on the wards and should undoubtedly have been acquired by now. The latter was the main reason, Jamie wanted to talk to the dean, so that some note was made, if this was a recurring theme, for this particular student.

Most importantly for Jamie he had learnt a lesson for himself in adequate supervision. He would reflect personally on this. It would happen in the way all reflection was done in the 1980s. Over a beer one day that week with colleagues and peers, probably on his next on-call shift.

Once the bloods were taken properly, the damaged arms were plastered up and the bloods were run to the lab, Jamie took Damien for a coffee. They had a long, frank, but difficult 'discussion'. Jamie explained what he thought Damien had done wrong. The greatest concern for Jamie, was that Damen was still not in any way remorseful, nor accepting that he had done anything wrong.

"If you had tried to do an invasive procedure, that you have never done before without supervision, then that would have been enough for the patient to make a charge of common assault, even if you got the sample with no complications." Jamie thought he had to strongly express the seriousness of the situation.

"I have never done a jugular vein puncture to get blood in my career. You should never try to do anything for the first time, unless you are supervised." He was increasingly frustrated that he wasn't getting any apologetic response, just indignation in return.

Jamie had asked Damien what his career aspirations were. Damien was very forceful in wanting to be a plastic surgeon even commenting on the financial benefits of this career.

Jamie personally supervised every practical procedure Damien did for the rest of the placement and barely let the student out of his sight. The dean was grateful and impressed that he received such specific feedback, stating it was uncommon to get this type of specific detail from clinical firms.

On the day of her discharge, Mrs Thornton, gave a bag to Jamie, containing the biggest supply of biscuits and chocolate, Jamie had seen as a patient gift.

"Thank you so much, Dr Carmichael, for your fantastic care. This is just a little something to feed you up, as I think you need it." She even took his hand to her cheek and gave it a little squeeze, that Jamie referred to as a 'chuck'.

Jamie thanked her outwardly. Inwardly, he shook his head and learnt for the first of many times, that the most grateful patients are sometimes the ones you do the least for.

He gave the entire bag of goodies to Sister Jones with the simple explanation, that Jamie thought the nurses deserved it more.

Jamie did get to meet Damien again many years later and to his unfathomable surprise, Damien had become a consultant psychiatrist!

Chapter 21
The House Year: Crisis, What Crisis?

Jamie was settling in to his life as a surgical house officer. His accelerated wedding was only a few weeks away as his fiancée was now 4 and a half months pregnant and starting to show. Not that any of the family or friends were in any doubt what the reason was for the accelerated wedding plans.

The quieter days had allowed him serious time at looking at new houses as their 3rd floor rented apartment with one bedroom was now woefully inadequate.

He was on-call and having a quiet day, but had just accepted an admission of an acute abdomen in a 13-year-old boy, direct from a GP.

The boy had apparently come off his bicycle and was complaining of severe abdominal pain. He had been referred by the GP who the family had taken him to, so he by-passed the Emergency Department and so was coming straight to the surgical ward. Jamie was waiting for him on B5. His team, who were on-call that day, were all operating on the elective lists.

The rubber doors to the ward made a resounding crashing noise both on the sudden opening and then the rapid closing. This sound was matched by urgent voices from the ambulance crew.

"We need immediate assistance," the voice was authoritative, but held a note of panic.

Sister Jones jumped up from her desk, with reflexes more finely tuned than Jamie's. He followed her out the door, right on her heels.

"Low BP, 'tachy' of 150 after coming off a bike. Something major internally going on," the high-pitched voice was from the more senior of the two male paramedics.

"Side room 1 first door on the left!" Sister Jones went into no nonsense mode.

"Venous access?" asked Jamie still on the corridor, such was the pallid look of the boy even from a few steps behind.

The boy was supposed to be 13, but he was tiny and looked more like 8 in Jamie's view. The pale skin from blood loss perhaps accentuating the young features.

"Been trying for the whole journey and just can't get anything. Veins are tiny."

Jamie contemplated what to do. He was tuned to recognise trouble and danger and knew he was out of his depth alone here. However, which 'friend to phone first' was the key question.

It was clear to Jamie that he needed friends and the first priority was to find anyone who could get IV access the quickest. If this experienced paramedic, couldn't get it, Jamie didn't bank on himself to be able to, however skilled he had become in the last 8 months. Even assessing the boy's clinical state from three yards and hearing the 'obs', meant IV access was the absolute priority.

After that, he would need a senior surgeon and quickly.

He considered in the space of a few seconds, 3 options.

1. Ring ICU and get an anaesthetist here 'asap'. However, he might be on the phone for a couple of minutes waiting for them to answer and he didn't want to waste 2 minutes.
2. Get a paediatric specialist here, used to getting cannulae in small children's veins.
3. Put a crash call out, but this wasn't quite an arrest and all the wrong people would come first and might clutter the scene.

The deciding factor for Jamie, was the realisation, that the paediatric ward was on A5, immediately below where Jamie stood. He chose option 2, hoping he wouldn't waste thirty seconds at most on this gamble. He ran off leaving Sister Jones initially surprised, but not arguing. Taking the stairs three at a time he was in the office immediately below where had been sat (calmly half a minute before), in just 6 seconds from his decision moment.

The paediatric registrar Diana, with whom he had shared the views of the trophy cabinet, was sat writing in notes and looked up in shock, but alert at the sweating but focussed face of Jamie.

"Diana, I need you and need you now, tiny 13-year-old lad, come off his bike, no blood pressure, ambulance crew haven't been able to get IV access. B5." Jamie was as concise but as clear as he could be.

Diana didn't respond with words. Jamie could see the recognition of urgency, the specific needs and why Jamie was here, in that setting.

"Spleen or Liver I suspect, but haven't been near him yet."

As they left the office Diana shouted to him, "Picking up paediatric cannulae, I will be just behind you. Ring ICU next, then the surgeons." The sound of the last words was tailing off as Diana was running to the treatment room, which was a few doors down on A5.

"B5 room 1!" Jamie shouted, probably scaring half the ward, such was the volume he used.

Jamie ran straight upstairs and was back within the thirty seconds he had allocated. He ran into side room 1, skidding to a stop. The paramedic was trying to cannulate the right arm using a tourniquet, whilst Sister Jones was taking the blood pressure on the left.

"60 systolic, 150 and thready," she said to Jamie as he came back in.

"Paed reg coming!" he said in reply. "Can you leave the BP cuff on." He moved in alongside Sister Jones and gently eased her to one side.

Jamie spoke to the patient for the first time, who was both obviously in shock as well as terrified. "I'm just pumping the cuff back up, but not as high so it won't go as tight." He listened with his stethoscope until he heard a pulse, knowing arterial blood was getting in to the arm, with the certainty, which you couldn't do with a normal venous tourniquet. Jamie had been taught that it was possible to pull a tourniquet too tight and stop arterial blood supply getting in to the arm when blood pressure was low, therefore, the veins wouldn't fill with blood at all. If that was the case, it was impossible to find a vein.

Jamie had seen Angela Downing do this once, when he was on his medical attachment, with a patient with sepsis, who sadly didn't survive, such was the severity of the illness.

Diana came in to the side room at speed and also almost skidded to a stop. She assessed the situation and came round Jamie's side asking for confirmation, rather than uncertainty. "You are below systolic?"

"Yes, audible," he answered.

"Go! ICU, surgeons!" She almost pushed him out the door.

Jamie ran to the office. He was sweating and his heart rate was at least three quarters that of his patient, but he rang the urgent number for switch. Hearing John's dulcet tones, he said.

"ICU reg, urgent bleep B5, now John…please!"

Jamie heard the fingers working on the switchboard over the telephone ear piece long before he got to the 'please'. He knew it was an unnecessary addition and John would have got the urgency in his voice.

"Done!" was the one-word response. Perhaps it was the only time Jamie had a conversation with John, without a single swear word being uttered in the entire 2 years he worked in Stockport.

Fortuitously, as Jamie put the phone down from John, one of the theatre recovery nurses came through the door with one of the patients returning after surgery.

"Woah, one second!" Jamie recognised his second stroke of luck. "What is the best number to get someone to respond in theatres. I need one of my team, desperate emergency!"

"Oh, I see!" said the nurse, who had been cut off asking which bed, their patient was in.

"2793, it's the reception number, almost always manned."

"Thanks," said Jamie with the number already dialled.

The reception staff answered on the third ring, Jamie counted 30 heartbeats in his head in that time.

"I need a message please to Mr Scotland's theatre. We have a young boy on B5 probable ruptured spleen, no blood pressure. I need one of my senior team immediately."

"Understood. I will run in with that message and prepare the emergency theatre just in case for you Dr…"

"Carmichael…and thanks!" Jamie was relieved by the sense of urgency he heard in the voice at the other end, despite the request for the name.

Jamie ran out of the office with the aim of getting back into the side room. Instead, he nearly crashed directly into 2 very worried parents, who had just arrived and opened the door and walked onto the ward.

"We are the parents of Stephen Markham, young boy just come off his bike," said the mother clearly in charge, her voice was shaking though.

"He has just arrived and is not well. I have one of the paediatric senior doctors getting IV access. ICU and surgeons are on their way. Can I take you to the relatives' room and come back, as soon as I have some more information and we have control of the situation?"

Jamie was unhappy giving this information on the corridor, but he felt there was no option.

"I need to be with him, please doctor let me in!" she was almost screaming. Suzy was the junior staff nurse on duty and had been standing outside the side-room, looking in, taking in the events. She stopped and came to Jamie's aide.

"Mrs Markham, we really do need a few minutes on our own initially. You will just get in the way of the doctors in there if you try to go in now." Jamie was keen not to let the parents, delay the process worried that hysteria might ensue, especially if the boy did have a cardiac arrest.

"Come with me, Mrs Markham, I will make you some tea," Suzy tried. Mrs Markham initially made to push past the pair of them. Jamie noticed Suzy was gripping her arm, quite forcefully and had put her body directly in Mrs Markham's way. She looked ready to lift the frightened relative up and carry her over her shoulder to the relatives' room. Like Jamie, she knew well, that the last thing Diana needed was the boy moving around in response to a terrified parent.

Jamie was surprised by Suzy's strength physically and in terms of resilience. The relative's room was just off the ward at the top of the stairs, which had its' good and bad aspects. Right now, it felt like they were taking the parents further away from the scene and Mrs Markham started to resist again, once they tried to go through the rubber flapping doors.

"I promise I will be back as soon as I can, but I do need to go and help the team with your son." This line finally broke the resistance and Mr Markham's silence and patience.

"Deirdre, let them do what they need to do." The grieving mother fell into her husband as he said this and with Suzy taking much of the weight in her tiny frame, she managed to steer, the now crying family, into the relative's room.

Jamie immediately left and re-joined the team in the side room.

The first sight to greet him was the heart-warming view of seeing an IV-fluid bag running freely on the left side where Jamie had been a few minutes before with the 'sphyg'. Diana was now on the other side, with the 'sphyg' on that arm and had a second cannula in. Blood ampoules with blood collected were in a plastic kidney dish.

"I will go and ring the 'lab', we need some O-neg and group and cross-match 4 units straight off. They might do it quicker for me Jamie. Any luck with senior surgeons?"

Sister was retaking the blood pressure. She spoke before Jamie had time to reply. "75 systolic, rate 145: slightly better than pre fluids."

"They are coming." Jamie said after listening to the new 'obs'. "Family here and are distraught not surprisingly, sorry that is what took my time up," he added.

Before he had finished his sentence, three figures appeared simultaneously in the doorway, all breathless. The seriousness of the emergency had not been lost on anyone. Angela Downing had escorted her registrar. Mark Smith, who was not the slimmest of the expanding group, looked the sweatier of the trio.

"Thanks, Jane," Diana said, acknowledging the blood pressure for the first time. It was the first and only time Jamie heard Sister Jones' first name used. Diana seemed to know everyone.

"So, we have a 13-year-old, who looks much younger, fell of his bike, handlebar to abdomen. Arrived here straight from GP with blue light. Paramedics, couldn't get access, not surprised, took all my skills with a 'sphyg' tourniquet. Veins like a neonate. Epigastric pain, haven't laid a hand on, but it's ruptured spleen or liver until proved otherwise. I'll request 2 bags of O-neg and 4-unit cross-match. That is if you let me out of the room?" Diana had taken charge and was slick. Jamie was in awe. She almost pushed her way through the new arrivals.

"Theatre is prepped, we can take him down now if you like." Mark Smith had never agreed to anything without discussion and thinking about it before.

Angela Downing had appraised the situation and realised all was in hand for now. "Sorry we were a few minutes behind. We had our hands on a bleeding femoral artery aneurysm, literally when the call came. We knew it must be super urgent, when it was the 'milky bar super-doc' calling us."

Jamie had not had that nick-name said in the hospital before, though he had told Dr Downing the story of the incident on-board the ferry, when Dr Downing was on-call on Christmas day too. He had included the tail of Harry calling him the Stockport Milky-Bar kid. She had remembered the detail 3 months later.

"I'm missing something who is super-doc?" Mark was back to sullen.

"Jamie here, best house officer we have had for ages, and he has contacts with higher authorities."

"Jamie?" Mark's voice was incredulous. "He is just a surgical house-dog!" he responded, mirroring Rich's view.

"You mark my words, he will go far! You be nice to him. He might be your boss one day!" The ICU anaesthetist was not going to be ignored by the surgical reg.

Sister Jones was first to get the gaggle back on track, "Can we get back to our sick boy, once you lot have had your chin-wag." She had already attached a second bag of 'Jelofusin' to the other cannula and was preparing a third, for the first arm accessed.

Jamie was so embarrassed by the complimentary interlude, that he didn't know where to stand.

"Can I go and tell the parents where we are at and bring them in for a minute or two. Is that ok with you Stephen?" Jamie had turned to get the patient back as centre of the power struggle and took the hand of the young lad.

"If you want us to take him post-op, we will," Angela had her final say. "David will stay with you for now and help resuscitation and be the anaesthetist, in case you have any trouble with emergency anaesthetist availability. Clearly this boy needs surgery as soon as possible." Dr Downing left as quickly as she arrived.

"Yes please," whispered a terrified 13-year-old to Jamie, who squeezed his hand in response.

Jamie got up and headed past the cluster of medics, nurses and the 2 paramedics, who were almost ready to leave the scene as well.

"I'll come and consent them in 5 minutes," this was Mark, giving Jamie final instructions as he headed still blushing from the room.

Sister Jones sighed and said in an exasperated tone, "Is anyone other than Jamie going to talk to the patient?"

Jamie heard this and cringed some more. Dr Downing had probably made his life even harder for the next 4 months, with her praise and now Sister was joining in on the act.

As he entered the relative's room, Mr and Mrs Markham were drinking tea and Suzy was holding Mrs Markham's hand still.

"Firstly, my name is Dr Carmichael and I have just been co-ordinating everyone today in the emergency situation. I apologise for not introducing myself before, but things were very hectic at first. However, I am going to take you in to see Stephen in just a moment."

Mrs Markham started to move as if this was the cue for her to go. Jamie reached a hand across the space and placed it kindly, but with a degree of strength on her other forearm, to make sure the message was clear.

Jamie wanted them prepared and with as much information as possible.

"Firstly, he is not surprisingly terrified and in a lot of pain, but the biggest problem when he arrived was that he was in shock, with a very low blood pressure. We think he is bleeding internally. Likely a ruptured spleen from where the handlebar hit him in the stomach as I believe is what happened."

He paused intentionally, but there was no reaction from either parent and so it seemed the story of the bike was what they understood.

"The biggest issue when he arrived, just a few minutes before you, was to get fluid in to replace the lost blood from the circulation. The ambulance crew hadn't been able to get into a vein. Fortunately, one of the paediatric doctors, came running up to help and we now have two drips running giving him blood substitute for now. We will change that to blood soon. He is still in a fair amount of danger and we need him in theatre very soon. If it is the spleen that is ruptured, it might need removing," Jamie finished the sentence even though Mrs Markham was speaking already.

"Oh my god, what does that mean for his future." Mrs Markham was leaping on the bad news, Jamie realised.

"Well, it's a good question, but actually it isn't that big an issue to live without a spleen. It does play a part in fighting infection and we usually leave people who have lost their spleen on antibiotics life-long, but they can live a healthy and full life expectancy, this aside."

"If it is a ruptured spleen and we don't take it out?" this was Mr Markham.

"I am not the surgeon, Mr Markham, so please do ask him that question, but very simply, Stephen would probably die of blood loss, would be my expectation. At this time, he certainly isn't out of danger." Jamie wanted them to know how serious the situation was and was intentionally, being very clear in his communication about the severity of the situation.

The parents were crying, but the husband was consoling his wife and making as reassuring gestures as he could.

"Shall we see if we can now pop in and see Stephen, there are lots of doctors around I just warn you. We may need to come back here after a few minutes as the surgeon will need to get consent from you to do the surgery."

****

Just ten minutes later, Stephen Markham left the ward, with his mum still holding his hand as he was wheeled down the corridor to theatre. Within forty-five minutes from arrival, he was in theatre, having the life-saving surgery.

However, without the IV access and fluid resuscitation, Stephen would probably have arrested and died within minutes of his arrival and never have got near getting into theatre. Jamie knew, that this was a very near miss.

Jamie was in the office and gave Sister Jones the good news from theatres.

"I will go and tell Suzy the good news, she did very well today too. By the way, 'Notty' told me you were good, she was spot-on!" Sister finished her sentence as she started walking out of the room.

"Thank you. Can I just mention about Suzy? She did such a great job with Stephen's mother. I was in a jam there, before she came to help. I thought the mother might go hysterical on us. Let her know I told you how good she was, please," Sister Jones had waited in the door way to listen to him finish.

"Thank you, I will. Though do bear in mind she has a crush on Richard." Jamie sighed at this comment.

"I'm saying it, because I mean how well she did and she isn't actually my type, however gorgeous." Jamie tailed off and knew Sister wasn't listening anymore as she was off clipping down the ward.

A few hours later, Jamie called into ICU to find Stephen awake after surgery, both parents sat by the bed. Apart from being pale, scared and in pain and with a blood transfusion running, Stephen didn't look too bad for his brush with death.

"Hello, Stephen, just came to see how you are doing," Jamie spoke to the patient first as always.

Stephen started to speak, but his mum cut over him. "He is doing ok considering he has half his liver cut out, it was this that was ruptured, not the spleen!" She spat out the last few words.

"I heard," Jamie replied calmly. "That wouldn't have changed the immediate management, we just needed to stabilise him with fluids and then get him to theatre. I was amazed how quickly we achieved that. The NHS is an amazing place in a crisis you know. So many of the pieces of the system working so well together," Jamie genuinely meant this.

He had actually felt like he was privileged to be effectively an observer. Once he got Diana from the paediatric ward, he was superfluous. However, he genuinely believed that to get Stephen fluid resuscitated and get him in theatre and protected in less than 45 minutes from arrival, was just incredible. He was proud not of himself, but the oiled machine the NHS was when it was most needed.

"I wish we had gone to a private hospital as I asked the GP, when we took him, at least we would have been able to be with him at the most frightening time for him, poor baby!" after this comment, Mrs Markham wept noisily.

"Oh darling, please don't say that, these doctors saved Stephen's life." Mr Markham clearly, rarely spoke it seemed to Jamie. However, when he did, he whipped his wife in terms of sense and insight. He mouthed 'sorry' to Jamie, who decided there was no point agreeing with Mr Markham with words, however true it was.

Stephen didn't need to hear, that he was a matter minutes from death, his trauma had been enough for one day. Jamie knew that if the GP had succumbed to any pressure Mrs Markham had him under and sent Stephen to a private hospital, there would never have been enough of the right people at the right time in one place to have saved Stephen. Jamie knew this, without a shadow of any doubt. Stephen would have died, but Mrs Markham, would never understand this fact.

Jamie contemplated what to say, but left it at talking to the one that mattered. "Stephen, well done today. I am really proud of how brave you were in those bad minutes and hope you get a little sleep tonight." Jamie sensed he would not call by to Stephen again, though Stephen should come back to B5 from ICU. Jamie didn't know why, but he suddenly thought it was the last time he would speak to Stephen Markham.

He was walking away, in another despondent reverie, heading to the exit of ICU, when Angela Downing intercepted his departure. "The parents aren't as enamoured with 'super-doc' as the rest of us," she said missing out the 'milky bar' pronoun.

"No, I can tell," Jamie said audibly saddened. "It's funny how you get thanks from the ones you haven't helped and when you do something really important, then you get no thanks at all."

"Welcome to the real world of medicine. We see that anomaly all the time working on ICU. But you know in here you saved that boy's life by making the right calls in a crisis." She put her fist into his chest over his heart and Jamie had to wipe away a tear. "His haemoglobin was 3 when we took blood in theatre you know, before we gassed him." Jamie was relieved she carried on doing the talking as he didn't think he could have got any words out.

"I reckon he had 5 minutes max, when he arrived on the ward with no BP. If you had wasted time trying to be the hero with a cannula yourself, it might have been too late," Dr Downing was telling Jamie, what he really already knew, but was relieved to have it reinforced after his brush with Mrs Markham.

However, he still couldn't work out what instinct drove him downstairs to get a paediatric doctor, but whatever it was it served him and most importantly Stephen very well.

"Thanks, Angela." He realised it was the first time he had called any consultant by their first name, but it just felt right in the moment.

"Go rest, you did good. Even if you do look like the milky bar kid. Oh, and I should say sorry for saying that to Mr Smith. I realised later it wasn't my smartest move. Surgeons are arses generally."

"It's okay, I will get over that. Thanks for coming as quickly as you could today and for the pep talk. It's appreciated." He remembered his manners and his voice came back strong.

"Mutual appreciation society closed, I have work to do. But thank you too!" She turned on her heels.

Jamie decided he would try and search out Diana, if she was still on duty and both thank her as well as give her an update. He went to A5 and was told she was probably on paediatric ICU, as they had a sick new-born. He wandered across the car parks and past the nurse's home to maternity, where the neonatal part of ICU was. He recalled, when he had been a student and had actually wanted to do paediatrics at the time. One day he met one of his brother's friends (Mike), who was then a qualified doctor. Jamie's brother and his friends were 4 years older than Jamie, but Jamie got to play football with his brother and his friends. Jamie didn't know Mike was doing paediatrics at the hospital, Jamie was attached to as a 4th year student. When Jamie bumped into Mike, he found the shell of a figure that he knew from the football pitch. Mike was thin and drawn, with huge bags under his eyes and looked as if he was prematurely ageing.

"Whatever you do, Jamie, don't do paediatrics," were the words Jamie remembered from that chance meeting. Jamie never found out what had made him so drawn and changed as 3 months later, the young doctor was found by friends drowned in a bath having taken an overdose of alcohol, diazepam and apparently insulin. Such a waste, but the pressures are not born by some people.

Jamie shed more tears on his walk as he recalled the sad story. The events of the day had drained his resilience and made him emotional.

By the time he made it to the neonatal ICU, he had just about dried his tears. He only got to speak to Diana briefly as she was knee deep in a jaundiced prem baby.

"Thanks for coming over and letting me know, that's really kind of you."

"Had to, you saved my boy, but I will leave you to this one." Jamie smiled as he turned tail, realising he never could have dealt with such fragile things. His parents were wrong that he was too sensitive to do medicine, but to do paediatrics, they were definitely spot-on.

Making his way across the car park, he started to veer over to the nurse's residence. He had a desperate urge to talk to Sarah and tell her of his day. He didn't even know if she was in, whether she wanted to see him or not. At the last minute, he turned away from the door. He had never walked up unannounced and didn't know what would happen if he rang the bell.

He never saw her in her room window, looking out at him.

She was desperately wanting him to ring the bell and when she saw him turn away across the grass, she cursed under her breath, and got a tissue for her own tears.

Later in the evening, Jamie got invited to join Firaz and Mark for a drink in the mess bar. It was positive to be included in their little huddle for the first time. They talked about the surgery on Stephen and how they were glad he was on ICU on not on their wards. They talked of how sick he had been at induction and all the time until Mr Scotland found and clipped the bleeding vessel, with impressive speed.

Jamie thanked Mark for coming so quickly after he had rung the theatre reception, but there was no reciprocity in thanks or support. Jamie did however, guess that the invite to join them for a drink was message enough. Jamie, had a half of lager, as he did when on-call. He left Mark and Firaz having a whiskey.

"Drip and suck 'til morning, Jamie." Mark called after him as he walked off, meaning Jamie was to manage anything else that came in conservatively, unless it had similar seriousness to the day's events, just gone.

****

Jamie never saw Stephen after his evening trip to ICU. The next afternoon, when Jamie checked by phone to see how the boy was progressing, he learnt that the parents had moved their son from ICU to a private hospital.

When he told Sister Jones, clearly not keeping the irritation out of his voice, she kept the response very simple.

"Their prerogative, young Dr Carmichael. Don't take it personally."

"It is odd isn't it! I got such a lot of thanks and boxes of stuff from that lady the student butchered with cannulae, when she should have been making a formal complaint and these parents whose child, we undoubtedly saved the life of, didn't even have the grace to 'say' thank you, let alone leave the ward some biscuits or chocolates."

"They don't see what you see or feel what you feel though, young Jamie. They just have fear and they are out of control." Sister Jones words of wisdom struck a chord with Jamie and never left him.

Jamie decided it was time to change the subject, he wanted time to digest the previous conversation.

"The other odd experience I have had since I have been on surgery is that patients always wish for the consultants to do their operations. For me, actually watching who does what, if you had a simple problem like an appendix, you would want the registrar doing it, because they've done 20 in the last month. The consultant probably hasn't done one for years. I totally get wanting the consultant doing the complex stuff that juniors may never have done before unsupervised."

Sister Jones sighed.

"Dr Carmichael, you definitely aren't a surgeon. You think too much!!" She laughed at her own joke and started to head off. She paused. "Suzy said she was grateful for your comments by the way. She said it was her first feedback since qualifying. At least of the professional kind." Sister Jones actually winked at him, before she went back down the ward.

Chapter 22
The House Year: On the Receiving End and Life's Little Crises

"Count from 10 back to zero!" Angela Downing's dulcet tones were doing the talking. Jamie was in the minor injuries' theatre at the Emergency Department up the road from where he worked. The metallic smell of piped oxygen and the rubber mask placed on his face was filling his nostrils. Fear was being replaced by sleep.

"10, 9, 8…" he started, experiencing, being on the receiving end of a general anaesthetic for the first time, since dental extractions under gas.

He thought about how the day had gone so wrong. The lump that had developed on his left wrist only 3 days before had become increasingly painful, slowly redder and significantly bigger as those three days had progressed.

He reckoned it started in one of the few hair follicles he had on his wrist. It was like a spot at first, but by Friday he knew it was an abscess and he even experienced, full blown fevers during Friday night.

There was no choice. He had to go in driving himself to ED as early as possible, as he knew it would still be quiet in ED early on a Saturday morning.

The walking well, were still in bed sleeping off a hangover, before heading to ED about the ankle they sprained 3 days ago. More important things on their mind.

Like vomiting.

Too early for the rush of sporting injuries that would come in the two waves as morning and afternoon weekend sports, would create a mix of genuine fractures, shoulder and other dislocations and a few hyperventilating wimps to deal with.

Less chance of RTA's *(road traffic accidents)* taking up time as there was no rush hour on a Saturday, so he had hoped, he had a good chance of being seen quickly and especially when they heard his name. As he walked in to be a patient for the first time, he felt strangely out of place. He was however relieved to see the waiting room almost bare, before 9 a.m. on that Saturday morning.

Jamie hadn't worked in ED since being a student. He had loved the Douglas Campbell novel 'Bleeders Come First'. It was part of a trilogy of books, that had made Jamie guffaw, pretty much from start to finish. Yet they were so true to the life he was already experiencing.

Jamie was also slightly anxious, as he neither wanted to meet, nor come face to face with the ED doctor, who missed the tension pneumothorax and the DF118 sedation, amongst other events, where Jamie recognised poor skills.

As it happened, Colin Mitchell was on duty, who Jamie recognised as one of the SHO's on a GP rotation, who had done elderly care at the same time as Jamie was on his medical House Officer 6 months. Jamie knew he was very good.

The bad news came when Colin told Jamie, that it would need a general anaesthetic.

"No chance of doing that under local, it is too big and needs packing. It is also a really painful place and would be hard to get really numb with lignocaine. When did you last eat?"

"Last night just in case," Jamie replied despondently as he had been hoping to get done in time to go and watch Man City play. The football team he played for had no match that weekend and he hadn't been to watch a City game for a couple of months due to the clashing of home games with on-calls. He had already decided he would switch his playing from Saturday to Sunday League, even though the standard was not as good, as he would have more chances to go to see City.

"Good. I will call an anaesthetist and my senior to do you as you are staff. You will have to go and sit in the waiting room though." He was business-like and decisive. Jamie appreciated it.

"I don't mind who does it, Colin, really!" Jamie had said this not wondering if he believed his views expressed to Sister Jones just a few weeks before, now he was actually the patient.

Jamie sat for the best part of 2 hours, knowing that even if he recovered quickly, he wouldn't be able to get to the game now. He had been hoping one of his mates would pick him up from ED and take him in their car straight to the game.

Terry Greenwood was the Emergency Medicine consultant and was setting up and leading the emergency response team for the North West, after the Manchester air disaster. Jamie recognised him as he walked by the back of the waiting room and peered inside. Jamie had never met him, but his reputation was phenomenal and Jamie recognised him easily, with his beard and slightly gingery hair, from a lecture he had attended in the post graduate department.

Just a few minutes behind, to his surprise and embarrassment, Angela Downing came through the waiting area and waved warmly at him.

Jamie hoped sincerely that Colin hadn't troubled her to come and do his minor op. anaesthetic, unless she was genuinely covering here on her rota.

Sure enough, 10 minutes later he was on his back on the theatre table in minor ops, with these 2 heavy weight doctors (in seniority terms, they were both lithe individuals).

"Had to get the big boys in for staff, especially you, super-doc!" it was Angela Downing, smiling at him.

"I'm only a junior first year surgical house-dog, allegedly," Jamie protested.

"Even I know Jamie's name and reputation, though we have never met, previously." Dr Greenwood was also in a friendly and convivial mood for a Saturday morning on-call.

"You two really didn't need to come and do this for me, but thank you." Jamie was trying to remember his manners again, despite his embarrassment.

"Right let's get cracking, you should be all done inside fifteen mins and home in an hour, if you've someone to pick you up," Terry taking the lead.

Angela Downing, set to putting a tourniquet on Jamie, her anaesthetic propofol solution already drawn up.

"Enjoying surgery, Jamie?" Terry was distracting him effectively as Angela set to finding a vein. Jamie knew he had big juicy veins as they practised on each other as students for taking blood. He was a popular candidate, for those who weren't 'getting it'. It was something he hadn't enjoyed, but knew it was a necessary evil of learning.

"I'm a physician at heart," Jamie's was polite in reply.

"Done any cutting yourself?"

"They let me do an appendix last week, but I suspect it will be the last. Got the appendix out fine," Jamie chatted, happy not to have to think about the next few minutes.

"Sharp jag!" interrupted Angela.

"It appears I am rubbish at tying stitches, hadn't practised since my obstetrics and it took me nearly an hour to tie the poor lad back up. The anaesthetist was hopping mad. I was delaying his lunch." Jamie was distracting them as much as himself, with the story.

The discomfort in Jamie's elbow had gone on a little longer than he hoped or expected and eventually Angela Downing, admitted defeat.

"First cannula I have missed in 6 months," she said, apologetically.

"Shall I do it for you, Dr Downing?" Dr Greenwood was playful, but on dangerous ground.

"No, thank you, Dr Greenwood!" was the curt reply.

The second attempt was done quickly.

"I heard about the delayed list from the anaesthetist himself, you know. You must ignore the functioning gasmen though. They are such creatures of timing and habit and you made him think on his feet to keep the kid asleep." Dr Downing was talking as she prepared and started her infusions.

****

"7, 6, 5…" Jamie was starting to get very sleepy and couldn't be bothered saying 4, he knew he was nearly gone.

"Do you know, Angela, I haven't done one of these for about 5 years…" Dr Greenwood's voice filtered into Jamie's brain, just as he went completely under. The internal scream of 'Nooooo…' was never heard, as he went into his dreams.

****

Jamie, had already had, too many life events, in the last few weeks. He had plenty he could dream about, during his brief enforced sleep.

The wedding had gone ahead, but the plans had all been made even more complicated as the week before the wedding, the night of Jamie's stag do, his father had, had a severe stroke. Jamie's parents were older than the average, with his father being 60 and his mother 40 when Jamie was born. His dad was Scottish and had been married before, meaning Jamie had a half-family, who were between 30 and 40 years older than him. His full brother, who had a striking resemblance to Doc Brown from back to the future, was 4 years older. His half-brother 37 years older than Jamie.

Jamie had known he would have to deal with his parents' ill health and possible mortality early in his life. His father was 85 already, but had been pretty fit, walking to and going to the football matches every week, in his kilt. Until Jamie had started working, he had always gone with his dad to the games, all the way from being 5 years old until he went to University in St Andrews.

Jamie had put up with the away team fans and especially the scousers, who always seemed to target Jamie rather than his dad. "Hey whack! Why is your grand-dad wearing a skirt?"

His father had always insisted on wearing his kilt in full dress and therefore carried his skean dhu in his sock. The item had a very sharp blade, with a black leather handle and was adorned with a stone at the top of the hilt. Even during the football violence days of the late 70s and early 80s, Jamie's dad had never been challenged about the knife, to Jamie's complete surprise.

That was until a few weeks before the stroke. Jamie's last match and he and his dad had gone together again and Jamie was stood chatting with his father outside the ground, before separating to go to their own seats.

"Sir, what is that in your sock?" It was a deep authoritarian voice that distracted their discussion about the potential team selection. The policeman who Jamie turned to see was six foot six inches tall and looked down on the odd couple of gangly Jamie at six-foot and nine-stone wet through and his father in his 80s at five-foot six.

Jamie's father had prepared his response, ready for this challenge, having expected it for many years. Indeed he, couldn't wait to get out his prepared lines for the first time, all practised and silvery.

"It is part of my national dress and you cannot stop me wearing it." Jamie always wondered how you could 'wear' a knife, rather than carry it, but he was keeping quiet in this moment of potential conflict.

The policemen drew himself up to his full height, looked his father up and down very slowly (just like the purser had done thought Jamie). With all the authority of his uniform and height, the policemen first turned to look at Jamie, making the young doctor think it was all his fault for not persuading his father to not bring it (as if). Finally, the policemen looked back down at the white-haired gentleman, he started to move forwards and bent very slightly.

Stopping half way into the gap, he said very quietly, but forcefully: "Sir," there was a pause. "At your age…" he paused a second time for what seemed like an age. "You should know better."

In these simple few words, his father had been crushed, by the giant of a policeman. Jamie held himself together unable to believe how the policeman had so completely disarmed his father's confidence in his national dress.

Nothing changed following the incident, except Jamie's humour at going to the games. He never spoke of it to his father, immediately or after, but Jamie loved regaling his brother and friends with the story. It was one of the last happy memories of his father that he had.

A few weeks later his father was in hospital after his dense stroke and looked like being there for months. Jamie's mother had, had a stroke herself 2 years before when Jamie was still a student, but had made a near complete recovery and was certainly independent.

The stroke coincidentally happened on the day of the stag do. Jamie, his best man (Andy) and 2 other friends were to be staying over at Andy's house. They had played sport all day, had dinner and then very unusually for Jamie, they had all gone clubbing. They arrived back to the house at two in the morning by taxi. They were well-oiled as should be the case, only to find Andy's wife and Diane on the doorstep, with the devastating news.

For Jamie, things could have been so much worse. He had suppressed these thoughts and the potential implications of what might have happened, but the full potential horror came out in his anaesthetic fuelled dream. Worse for wear, Jamie had been dancing with a very attractive (as far as he could remember) brunette, who seemed to be interested in the doctor's stag night. As Jamie prepared to leave with his pals, she and one of her friends, invited Jamie and Andy back to her house for a 'party', in honour of his stag night. He declined hesitantly, although whilst the group were all stood in the taxi queue, she was encouraging his manhood through his trouser pocket, where she was pretending to 'warm her hand'!

She even tried to drag Jamie into their taxi as the two girls were allowed to get the one ahead of him and his pals.

Jamie dreamt fitfully of the events that might have occurred, if two or three of his mates had gone back to find the bearers of the tragic news and Jamie had only returned alone several hours later.

In the end, despite the trauma of the news, at least his honour was intact after the resistance he had shown. The ultimate decision being made on the back of a skinful of alcohol and a huge slice of good fortune.

The wedding they decided would go ahead, despite his father's hospitalisation. There wasn't much choice, with the evident progression of the pregnancy. The evening 'celebrations' were cancelled however. They considered it would be in bad taste after some deliberation.

Instead, the wedding couple, travelled from the venue to one of the Manchester hospitals, making quite a scene as they went on the ward in full wedding attire. The dress and bride were stunning in a cream coloured traditionally shaped dress, adorned with touches of pale peach.

Jamie wasn't sure his father really recognised them on their arrival, let alone was taking anything in. However, Jamie felt they had made the best of a difficult situation, before heading off for 3 days of honeymoon at an upmarket hotel in the Lake District, as it was all the time he could get off at short notice.

****

The dream of events had transformed into a gruesome scene of recrimination, when the sliding doors of actual events and potential ones, twisted into a volcano of psychedelic images. Voices were added to the silent scene and Jamie came gratefully back to consciousness.

The pain in his wrist had changed from a burning fiery continuous one, to a throbbing deep ache, but the pressure sensation, which had transformed the pain from bearable to outrageous in the last 24 hours, was thankfully gone.

When he was fully awake, Dr Greenwood showed him, the pack, that was inside the wound and the need to pull the wick very gently out over the next 2 weeks, so it slowly healed from below. If he could self-manage it, this would stop the need for him coming daily to the dressing clinic.

"Am I allowed to work?" Jamie asked. He knew for himself, even then (as it remained throughout his career), a state of doing nothing was the worst Chinese water torture Jamie could bear.

"You will be fine on the wards, as long as it is bandaged and covered, wear gloves if you have any procedures to do. No theatre work, though that doesn't sound like it is a problem for you or anyone else!" *Angela was gently removing the foundations of his super-doc status, piece by piece*, he thought.

"Do you think it was my watch strap that caused it?" Jamie asked Dr Greenwood, just before he left.

"Not sure, hadn't thought about it." Dr Greenwood, sounded neither interested nor bothered about the question.

Jamie however spent the next 2 weeks after his surgery, researching skin bacteria, bacteria on watches and even persuaded the microbiologist to do a few plates of swabs taken from the underside of his watch strap, some colleagues' rings and even cuff links.

The results of this investigation, turned out to be his first dip into practical clinical research and were incredibly enlightening to Jamie, who never wore a wrist-watch again. Similarly, he never wore a ring of any sort and only cuff links for 'going out' wear. To Jamie's investigation, metal, more so than leather had an excellent propensity to acquire and support the survival of pathogenic skin bacteria, though both types of strap were bad.

Later in his career, Jamie felt guilty that he never published any of these findings in the medical literature. However, he had considered it rightly to be 'Mickey Mouse'. Medical practice changed about fifteen years later, but only after MRSA had become a major medical problem and jewellery, inadequately washed white coats and additionally ties were all implicated as transmitting vectors of bacteria like MRSA and Clostridium.

Jamie of course, was not surprised by any of these later findings, but realised he should have encouraged the changes in practice of all his colleagues, long before it actually happened. However, as he rationalised to himself, who after all, would have listened to a junior doctor, who suffered a minor skin abscess and looked like the milky bar kid?

Perhaps the greater lesson to influence his career on that day, was something that also later became widely accepted and became part of clinical practice. Jamie had personally learnt how hearing was the last sense to leave the brain in the semi-conscious state, long after sight, smell and physical touch sense (including pain) had all left.

Jamie put this experience into clinical practice, long before it was widely known, explaining to patients' relatives, about hearing. He wasn't so worried if dying patients heard they were dying, as long as the words used were sensitive. If conversations between medical staff and relatives were going on in the room of an apparently incoherent or unconscious patient, Jamie believed you should have the conversation, as if doing it with the patient themselves.

Additionally, Jamie became a strong advocate of the comforting role of hearing familiar voices.

"Don't talk directly to them and ask them questions or ask them not to go, especially if you are crying. That might cause distress as they fight to respond but can't. Just let them hear your voice. The voice they know. Comforting words are fine, telling them everything is fine and it is 'ok for them to let go'. Some people might fight hard to cling on, which could just add to their distress." Jamie had this conversation with countless relatives of dying patients.

"The alternative and probably just as good option, is to just talk 'nonsense' or irrelevant stuff. For example, talk about the weather or how the grandkids are doing. Anything like this would be fine too. If you are stuck for ideas, because of the emotion, maybe read out loud from a newspaper or from a book or even poetry." These were examples of some of the lines Jamie used continuously throughout his career.

Naturally, he changed the detail depending on the individual families he was dealing with, but the message for the relatives of a dying patient remained the same in principle. Let them hear you and give them **'permission to go'**. Who knows what unnecessary suffering we can individually cause, by over expressing our own emotional grief and distress at these moments in time?

Jamie found this could be particularly difficult in some cultural settings, with some religions having a much greater natural and 'expected' emotional outpouring at these most difficult of times. However, Jamie always felt the priority was for the patient themselves and he would do his best, to focus everyone on the dying patient and to think of the dying process as an event to be carefully managed. If Jamie himself was unconscious and dying, the words he would want to hear would be words such as: 'The grandkids are fine and will miss him. But it's time to let go. We will look after your dog and give her the best life possible'. What he knew very clearly, was hearing words like, "please don't go, don't leave us," with lots of crying and wailing, would be the last thing, he himself wanted to hear, when he had no control over the process.

Jamie knew his strong held views in this regard, were made possible, by his personal experience. Counter intuitively, the 'bad' experience from hearing Dr Greenwoods words, were one of the most positive contributors, to Jamie's communication skills learning.

Chapter 23
The House Year: Switchboard to the Rescue

It was mid-June and Jamie was coming to the end of his surgical career. He had made peace with his time in surgery, realising it was good to do something he enjoyed less, as everything in the future could be measured against this 6-months. He hadn't attempted any more surgical procedures, it didn't feel right wasting other people's time, when he had no future of doing them.

His father was out of hospital recently, but life at their home was not easy. His mother's health had suffered with the extra burden of first hospital visiting and then the physical strain of having a partially disabled partner back at home. His father's mental function was much improved and he was walking with a frame. However, he seemed more, irritable and angry, than before the stroke. He had always had an irascible edge.

Work progressed as a rather dull routine for the most part.

Jamie was on-call again. Mark, the registrar was on holiday and there were 2 different arrangements in place for the surgical cover. Jim the surgical registrar and mess president was covering from 5 p.m.; after Sally had done the day time.

All was going smoothly. Jamie had just admitted a teenager at 6 p.m., with what seemed like clear-cut appendicitis and who therefore needed theatre that evening (the routine approach at that time).

Jamie had bleeped Jim and had already let theatres know about the likely case. Ten minutes had gone by and rather unusually there was no reply. Final approval for theatre slots, could only be made by the registrar was the rule. Firaz, despite his surgical skills could offer no solution.

"You will have to find him Jamie!" was all he offered.

In response, Jamie went around the wards failing to find him on any of the four surgical wards. He tried the mess and finally went back to B6. As he was paging Jim again from the office, a bleep went off behind Jamie. He turned, to see who was there, but the room was empty apart from himself. The bleep came from within the room though, the piercing noise still reverberating in Jamie's head every time he heard it.

Jamie looked around himself at the very lonely room. There was a white coat hanging on a hook and it seemed to be a likely source of the bleep. Jamie investigated, already fearing the worst.

The bleep device in the front pocket of the hanging white coat, still had the telephone number on it, that Jamie had just inputted, via switchboard. Above the bleep on the white coat was a standard name-badge with the title Surgical Registrar—Mr Jim Dewar.

"Oh crikey, he has forgotten he is on-call!"

Jamie only knew he was thinking out loud again when a voice replied.

"Who?" it was Angela, one of the new staff nurses. Angela was the sister of one of Janice's colleagues on A4 and in Jamie's view was the rather more attractive sibling. He had been flirting with her earlier in the shift. Legs that looked great in a pair of flat black shoes were rare and imagination of them in better shoes was often needed. Some of the nurses, pushed the boundaries and Jamie thought of Janice, in this regard, who always had shoes with a slight wedge heel, even though they were probably outside of accepted limits. Janice's calves as an example, were ever so slightly chunky and the inch or so, made all the difference. Angela, on the other hand, had fabulous legs, even in the fully flat shoes she had on today.

She must have walked in behind him, when he had gone across the room to look at the white coat.

"Jim! I think he has forgotten that he is on-call covering Mark." Jamie dragged his thoughts back to the pressing matter in hand and Angela's question of 'who?' But most importantly, the need to find the 'missing in action' (MIA) registrar.

"I suspect he has, as I heard him arranging to meet Rich for a beer later." Angela's knowledge was helpful in that it sealed the concern, that they had a registrar MIA.

"Hare and Hounds at 930 in fact." She had even recalled the unnecessary detail.

"Hmm great recall, were you thinking of joining them?" Jamie continued his teasing from earlier.

"God, not either of those 2 please. Rich, is such a sleaze bag," she sounded genuinely offended.

"Listen I need to work out what to do here, if I ring the consultant, Jim will be in trouble. Not sure whether to ask Sally, but I know those two don't get on." Jamie was sharing his troubles, hoping for inspiration.

"Sally doesn't get on with any of her male colleagues. She is nice to us though," Angela was telling Jamie, stuff he knew well already, from the last few months of observation.

"I'm going to ring switchboard. They may have some idea," Jamie was already dialling as he spoke. Angela, picked up the notes she was looking for and left him to it, leaving a gentle cloud of what seemed to Jamie as if it were fresh perfume as she turned and left him.

John answered on the first ring and Jamie was delighted it was him. He set about explaining the situation and his plight.

"You don't happen to have a home number for him?" Jamie finished.

"We only have the home numbers for the consultants, not for any of you lot," his voice was unusually flat.

"Any other ideas?" Jamie responded.

There was a long silence, that took Jamie by surprise, he even started to ask John if he was still there, before John spoke again. When he spoke, John's voice was quiet and sounded unusually cautious.

"I think I know where he will be, but you won't be able to say that it was me who gave you the information. Do you understand Jamie?"

"Of course, John. I can tell that you are worried about this." Jamie was cautious as he had never known John be anxious before and it was so alien to the usual political incorrectness.

"Ok, I am pretty sure he will be in room B8 in the nurses' residence. I think he is banging, that pretty nurse Suzy, who has that room." John was still nervous.

Jim was married and interestingly was meeting Rich for a beer later, who had obviously been in the same room at some time. Jamie was contemplating this, but needed to concentrate, on what John was saying.

"Six-seven-two-two is the direct number for the communal phone for the second floor. If you ring that number and ask whoever answers to knock on room eight and see if he is there, but I can't do it for you, you shit. I'm only doing this because it's you and you came in and saw us at Christmas." John had never called Jamie a bad name, directly. Jamie had flinched at the insult. "It didn't fucking come from me, have you got that as clear as I can make it?" Jamie was even more shocked, that John even sounded genuinely angry with him for having asked.

"John, I really appreciate this. I will say one of the other nurses suggested it, and that she doesn't want me to say who it is. Will that be good enough? Everyone knows other people's business, so it would be very believable!" John had been so good to Jamie, that he wanted to reassure him.

"Best you can do Jamie. Will you tell me how it goes, otherwise I might be coming for you, you fucker!"

Jamie looked around and was relieved, he was alone. To his surprise, he saw a piece of paper on the desk, where Angela had collected the notes from a few minutes before. 'You on the other hand, I would meet for a drink!'

Jamie shook his head. Too many life events were going on to get in more trouble. He told himself off, for flirting too much. He also knew she lived with her boyfriend.

He rang the nurses' residence number as given to him by John. It rang for an indeterminable time, at least 20 or possibly even 30 rings before it was answered. Jamie was shocked to hear Sarah's voice answer.

When Jamie heard her voice, he nearly hung up out of shock as she said, "B floor." He wasn't prepared for this conversation to be had with her of all people.

"Sarah, it's Jamie."

"Oh, I was just thinking about you funnily enough, never thought it would be you on the phone or I would have answered it quicker." She started, by sounding genuinely pleased to hear him. "You are taking a bit of a risk though aren't you, anyone could have answered?" The excitement started to give way as she sensed the call might not be for the reasons, that she had clearly been hoping for.

"Sarah, I'm sorry it wasn't you I was after, but I'm glad it is you that answered." Jamie realised he was potentially digging himself a hole that could become a cavern, very quickly. "Oh shit, this sounds so lame, please don't hang up, I wasn't after any of the other nurses." Jamie was in full panic mode and knew he wasn't making sense and rather surfing a wave, just before the tide broke and he crashed on to the rocky shores.

"You have ten seconds, Jamie, then I'm hanging up," Sarah sounded suddenly close to tears.

"It's Jim Dewar I need. He is on call and I think he has forgotten. I'm told he might be in room eight." Jamie crashed the words out, knowing that Sarah thought he was ringing for another nurse for his own purpose.

"Oh. I see!" she paused and was obviously taking it in. "Yes, he is there. I think they have finished." Her voice was even again, having been strained a moment before. "The wall was almost coming through ten minutes ago and I heard his voice, well his grunts I should say. He doesn't continue for long though, not sure why she bothers."

She could have spared Jamie the detail. He would have been much happier not to know it.

"I would hope that you would be at least more considerate," she added, slightly playfully, which was equally painful for Jamie.

Jamie didn't know what to say, so didn't say anything. The pause seemed to go on a long time.

"Do you want me to knock and explain, or do you want to give me a number to ring back on or do you want to hold?" Sarah, got the message, that he didn't have time for a chat and gave in to his inability to find any words.

"I'll hold if I can?" Jamie responded grateful for her decisive intervention.

Jamie heard a clunk as the phone was put down. He imagined the long, coiled extension bouncing up and down, with the heavy hand-set perhaps, even bouncing off the floor, from the continued thumps and bangs, he heard. Either that, or Sarah had taken the phone into the room where the athletics had continued, longer than Sarah had thought likely.

"He is on his way, will meet you on B6 ward, unless you tell me otherwise." She was business-like as if at work.

"That's perfect, thanks for picking up." Jamie was genuinely stuck for words.

"Next time, make sure you are ringing for me, I miss you!" Sarah put the phone down as soon as she had finished the line, not giving Jamie a chance to say anything good or bad, positive or negative in response. He wasn't sure what he would have said, even if he had been given the time.

He did write down the number for the second floor of the nurse's home in the front cover of his pocket book of medicine, which he slipped back into his white coat.

Jim appeared breathless and sheepish, 5 minutes after Jamie had put the phone down.

Their interaction was brisk and business like, until everything was done from a handover perspective. Jim came back to the hunt. "Thanks for finding me and not ringing, Mr Scotland, you never know who will be interviewing you for jobs down the line and I don't need any black marks."

That was it. No one ever asked, Jamie how he knew, it was just accepted as general knowledge. Jamie waited until he was alone and rang the switch number. John answered and Jamie explained the events. John was grateful and back to his normal self in response.

"Anything for milky bar, fucking super-doc," John finished the exchange. Jamie sat and wondered, how he had known where Jim was.

****

The next time Jamie heard John's dulcet tones, it was in his last week as a House Officer. He and Imran (one of the urology surgical house officers), had been doing a 1 in 2 as Simon Gasli, who Jamie had become friendly with, was off work having some surgical procedure done on his sinuses.

Surgery on-call, was so much quieter than medicine, that they were coping well, from a sleep deprivation point of view, but social life was nearly absent.

He was in bed as he had been since his half a lager at 11.30 p.m.

The room phone had rung and Jamie answered it on the second ring, it was 4 a.m.

"Right, no jokes tonight Jamie, just compose yourself and listen. Everything is sorted. Imran knows and is covering you. I've let Firaz know the situation. So, get yourself up and get dressed." Jamie couldn't rationalise John's words and wasn't ready for the next line. It was Jamie's time to be the blasphemous one.

"What the fuck are you going on about John?"

"Your wife is in labour and she said 'get your arse in gear' and head to the maternity ward."

****

They were intentionally booked into the maternity unit to a different hospital, close to where they lived. Jamie headed there and went through a long but uncomplicated process of labour with his wife. He was amazed with the 'husband' experience.

His abiding memory was his wife clawing at him and screaming with the pain.

"You bastard, you got me into this pain. I'm never doing this again!"

Half an hour later, with the baby lying wrapped in towels on her belly, she was calm and saying. "Oh darling, she is so beautiful. I'm so pleased we had her unplanned. Can we wait 3 years before having a second."

In that moment, Jamie realised first hand, the complex hormonal function of the brain. Clearly one of the chemicals produced in the delivery moments, was a hypnotic amnesic agent, which made the female forget most of the events and all of the conversation of the last 12 hours. The male memory on the other hand, was indelibly scarred for life with the events. However, it was the female, who had experienced the unrelenting pain. Survival of the species clearly relied on the power and effectiveness of the automatic release of this incredible hormonal surge, which wiped the female memory, like the wiping of dreams.

****

Jamie's did go on to have his own serious amnesic moment, but this happened a couple of days after that of his wife's.

Mum and baby came out of hospital on the Thursday afternoon. The in-laws and a couple of friends were popping round to see the new Baby Carmichael (Siobhan). Jamie was on-call again for the last 3-day weekend of his year and had already had to do Imran's Tuesday and Wednesday nights as a swap for the emergency call up.

Jamie was driving to work at 8 a.m. on Friday morning. His bleep started going off with a switchboard number pretty much as soon as he came in to bleep range. Jamie hadn't yet invested in a mobile-phone and he decided to drive into the hospital, rather than stop at a public phone box, which was the only other option. Ten minutes later he parked outside the doctor's mess on double yellow lines, recognising some unexpected emergency as the bleep had gone off a further 8 times in the remnants of the journey. He ran inside, knowing this was his quickest route to a phone.

It was Margaret who was chasing him. "Oh, Dr Carmichael! I am so sorry to have bleeped you so many times, but did you stop for petrol on the way home last night?"

Jamie was perplexed, but confirmed he had as he was low on fuel, without enough to manage in and out for the weekend on call.

"Well, the police say they won't press charges against you…" Jamie's world opened up momentarily and his imagination crashed unerringly to the thought of how he would look in prison uniform, rather than his white coat. He had to force himself to focus on the last part of what Margaret was saying, "…if you can get to the petrol station by 9 and pay the bill for the petrol. Apparently, you drove off without paying. I told them you had been doing 1 in 2 on-calls and had just had a baby. I hope you didn't mind? I said I was sure it was just a mistake as you were so tired." Margaret was almost breathless as she sounded like she said all this without taking a breath.

Jamie had already played his memory back in his head before Margaret had finished and indeed, he could not remember going in to the kiosk to pay for his petrol.

He checked his phone. It wasn't 8.30 yet! The petrol station was only 5 minutes away. His heart was racing at a phenomenal rate.

"Margaret, you were amazing and I am so sorry to have caused you stress. I will be back before 9, please tell Firaz what has happened if I'm not. I don't mind him knowing, he will just laugh." Jamie realised that the latter was probably a futile comment as half the hospital probably knew, before he did.

Jamie got to the petrol station in time. The attendant looked bored and not at all troubled by the events, but Jamie was effusively apologetic, requesting a receipt several times before he got it.

****

Jamie's eventful first year culminated in this story and whilst he never heard from the police or the petrol station further, the story preceded him into his second year as it was the best gossip of the week. At least, it was before the new juniors started. After this, for a few days, he was known as 'the milky bar drive-away doc'.

It was a bonus to Jamie that it was too much of a mouthful to last for long.

Chapter 24
Getting Covid: Days 3 and 4

Jamie's weekend was like so many in lockdown for someone living alone. Quiet, uneventful and could have been depressingly lonely. However, his dog, a cocker spaniel called Isla, who had been his saviour over the last 3 years, since he moved apartments, kept him company.

She was never so important as she was this weekend.

Jamie had a complex mix of doggie day-care and friend coverage for Isla whilst he was at work. It had been especially complex in the last year as the pandemic had resulted in changes to their consultant rota, with evening shifts until midnight to cover, which would never have been the case pre-pandemic.

Rebecca, his really good friend, was the one who was prepared to take in Isla at pretty much no notice. The preparation and planning for all eventualities were established, including the worst case of what might happen if he was hospitalised.

Rebecca knew about the situation at work and Jamie's concern, that he was likely to start with symptoms on Sunday or Monday.

Jamie's incredible secretary also did her fair share of Isla cover. The daughter of his secretary was only 12, but was completely devoted to Isla. The spaniel having the sweetest of temperaments, was such a bonus for Jamie as she was hard not to love, meaning having her was something his friends and his secretary, could not get enough of.

Since having her as an 8-week-old puppy, Jamie had learnt to be happy and sleep again.

Heather who Jamie lived with for 10 years, had been having an affair and Jamie had known this for quite some time in his heart of hearts. He confirmed his own expectations by choosing a moment to come home in the middle of the day and finding her in bed with one of her clients at the sports club.

Jamie didn't see them in the actual act, which he is now very grateful of, but he had come home when his intermittently functioning sixth sense had told him to. When he drove into the cul-de-sac, there was a van outside his door to compliment Heather's car. Jamie knew the van and its' owner. He tried his key in the front door of his house, but it wouldn't go in as there was a key in the lock on the inside. He saw Jura, their springer spaniel, in the living room, lying on the settee. She was normally left in the kitchen.

Jamie went round the back and was not surprised to find the backdoor locked, though the door into the garage was wide open. There was no direct link between garage and house since their extension.

Looking up he saw that the curtains to the spare room were closed, whilst all the others were open.

There was no other explanation. Jamie lost control and hammered on the doors until he was let in to his own house. The rest of the day was a blur of distraught emotions.

The next day, Heather tried what at first Jamie considered a disconnected approach. "None of what you imagined yesterday, actually ever happened you know. He was here looking at the children's fish and we weren't even in the bedroom. The door wasn't locked and the curtains weren't even closed."

Jamie didn't know the term 'gas-lamping' at the time, but he looked it all up later.

Eventually he left the house they had shared with her two now teenage children, having been together for 10 years.

He moved into a flat alone overlooking a canal for 2 and a half years, but never slept between 2 a.m. and 4 a.m. as memories and thoughts of the last 12 months of the time with Heather, flooded back as unwelcome reminders of his failure.

Eventually he knew something had to change. The completion of the financial separation, was followed by the purchase of a house in the Scottish islands, the purchase of a (then) 2-week-old puppy and the move into a new apartment where the landlord would let him have a 'small well-behaved dog'. All of these occurred within a mind blowing 7-day period.

6 weeks later Isla came to stay with him. With the puppy's arrival, contentment returned, as well as 'through the night sleep' (admittedly a few puppy-weeks later).

Isla's temperament was incredible. The spaniel had a substantial degree of her own separation anxiety from Jamie, but this just made training easier. She never soiled the house and only failed to wait until the back door was open to do a wee on 3 occasions in the first week and never thereafter. By 12 months, she was walking almost everywhere off a lead and life was good again, outside of work, as well as in it.

After Jamie's exposure to his Covid friend, Jamie and Isla had a full weekend of one-on-one walks in the countryside around the barn conversion, seeing no one and not even going to the shops.

Jamie got a joint of meat out of the freezer, knowing he would turn it into a casserole and it would feed him for most of the week. He also packed emergency bags for himself and Isla, just in case he was one of the 5 percent of the population who got seriously ill.

Even though he was over 60, he was slim in build and physically fit, with none of the additional health or ethnic risk factors. The only additional risk, was being male.

Realism told him, statistically his chances of survival were very good, even if he got Covid pneumonia. Having the vaccine should also help, even though, day of exposure and vaccination would have occurred almost synchronously and Jamie wasn't sure there would be much benefit, with that timing.

The statistic, Jamie wanted to see going forward, was not overall infections or overall deaths. It was the number of deaths or number of people who got admitted, per thousand of patients having covid unvaccinated, after one vaccine and after two. If strongly supportive as Jamie expected, this statistic would be much more meaningful to use for the vaccine resistant population.

As newspaper editors, were only invested in how many copies of newspaper they sold and the government were still invested in keeping people scared, so they didn't start being irresponsible, this particular statistic Jamie was hoping for might not be readily accessible in the near future. Or when it was, it might not be reported meaningfully.

Jamie and colleagues also knew however, that they had recently admitted several patients, severely unwell, who had already had one dose of vaccine (but not the second), before becoming infected.

On balance, he knew he couldn't take anything for granted personally, especially as he lived alone.

During the weekend, Jamie started to leave the back door unlocked and the prepared overnight hospital bag, with toiletries, underwear, shorts and T-shirts, spare computer and chargers for it and his phone. The bag was left easily accessible, but he had packed the bags, without the dog actually seeing him do it (waiting until she was asleep). If Isla had seen the bags, she would have got excited, thinking they were off to their island paradise.

All weekend Jamie kept trying the slow but full, deep breath in to see if there was any restriction. As he was putting in the roast potatoes for his Sunday dinner, he thought he sensed a tightness that wasn't there before.

He did a lateral flow test.

"Stop panicking, Jamie!" He gave himself a severe talking to, talking out loud as he did whenever he was annoying himself. The last time he had to do this, when he felt he was stuck on a challenging walk, over a ridge, aptly named 'the saddle'. He didn't do heights well at any time and as fit as he was, the young nurse he dated for a while since being single, had taken him on a couple of walks that had seriously challenged his fitness and nerve.

15 minutes of serious self-talking to later, Jamie got over the ridge without fuss and he managed his Sunday dinner in the same way.

He repeated his lateral flow test before bed, so he could plan to be going to work the next day.

Resoundingly negative!

"You see, you were just being a tit!" he spoke out loud again. Isla was wagging her tail, wondering what this new word that sounded like a command was. She was hoping for a treat and got one because of the good mood, Jamie felt.

He had a couple of glasses of wine most nights and did this night as usual, as the treat to himself. He went to bed, calm and fell rapidly to sleep.

Chapter 25
The SHO Years: Life with Wayne

Wayne Vetch was a Geordie with a profoundly deep broad accent. He had ginger hair with the odd bit of grey sprinkled into it. He obviously had bad acne at some stage as his face was marked with crevices, but he balanced all this with a really thick bristly moustache and what were clearly, twinkly eyes.

Jamie was already in the room at 7.30 a.m. to welcome Wayne there, even though Jamie's daughter was just a week old. It was change over day and the first day of being a doctor for the new intake. Jamie wanted to be there early to look after Wayne, just as Jemma had looked after him, the year before. Jamie would have a junior for the first time in his career.

Jamie knew Wayne from their St. Andrews days. Wayne had actually started medical school a year before Jamie, but had failed end of year exams on two occasions, ending up a year behind.

As a result, the young looking, skinny Jamie, with the smooth skin and baby face, was senior to and supervising, this new doctor, who physically looked at least 10 years older than Jamie himself.

Jamie and Wayne, were also from completely different social sets at their university. If such things happened at Medical School, Wayne was in the fashionable 'A-set', who kicked sand in the face of the preppie boys like Jamie. Wayne wasn't good enough looking to be the leader 'John Travolta/Danny Zuko' type character, but now Jamie thought about it, there was more than, a moderate resemblance in Wayne, to Kenickie.

When Jamie heard that he had been given Wayne as his junior, he knew it might not always be easy, but was determined to be a good senior and be very supportive.

They were to be attached to Dr Firman, who had a great reputation as a kind, funny and smart boss. Surprisingly though, they had been allocated as a registrar-free team. That meant there were no middle to senior grade doctors, between Jamie and the consultant. As a first year Senior House Officer, this was a real surprise as there were other SHO grades in the department, with more years of experience than Jamie, but they all had been allocated a registrar. Jamie didn't believe this decision was logical and as a result was uncomfortable with the plan at first.

Dr Firman, however, had contacted Jamie, whilst he was on his last day of surgery and explained the situation of their team and no registrar.

"Don't worry, I will look after you. If you have any interest in being a respiratory doctor, I can teach you how to do bronchoscopy procedures, for example," the voice was calm and oozed reassurance.

"Wow, I would love to learn to do it, though my confession is at this point in time I am swaying very slightly to cardiology, but that isn't set. It might be because I've done loads of temporary pacing wires, for example, more than to do with the career itself."

"Well, I might try and change your mind, but one thing we might need to do, if those are your short-listed specialties, is to work on you going next year to Baguley Hospital to do the Heart and Lung SHO rotation there. I know some of the lung doctors there well and one of the cardiologists too, so I'll put in a good word for you." Jamie noted, this offer, came before Jamie had even started working for Dr Firman.

Jamie wondered if the positive reputation, he had gained from the previous year, had resulted in both this attachment to Dr Firman and the 'no registrar' firm. Jamie had, had very little exposure to Dr Firman directly during the year just gone, however.

He did know from discussion with those who worked for him, that his new boss had a pro-active role in post-graduate education at the University, as well as within the hospital.

Either way Jamie recognised he must not look at this gift horse and count its' teeth. Take all the positives and not let his over-analytical mind get in the way.

He was decidedly, much more concerned about the practicalities of handling his relationship with Wayne.

Their wards were to be B3 and A1. The latter was a new base ward for Jamie. Sadly, Jamie wasn't going to see much of Sarah, who had decided to do a maternity cover for a colleague on ICU, 'for a new challenge'. This change coincided with the start of the new year. Jamie wondered if it was intentional on

Sarah's side, but he couldn't pretend to understand the motivation, especially as he hadn't tried to ring that number, even though he had opened the book he had it stored in half a dozen times.

Sister White was in charge of A1. Jamie wasn't as confident of getting along with her, by relying on his normal style. She gave little away, although she smiled a lot. Her grey hair gave her a gravitas of age, but Jamie guessed she was a little younger than the part she played, but he didn't know this for sure.

Even though she did smile, her face didn't give much away. Jamie decided he definitely wouldn't play her at poker, not that he thought he would ever get an invite for it anyway!

Jon was still a registrar at Stockport and did the greeting in almost exactly the same style as the previous year. Jamie and Wayne had escaped being on-call for the first day and Jamie knew Dr Firman was going to do a ward round with them straight away after the junior doctor meeting.

As Jamie, walked with Wayne on to A1 ward to meet Dr Firman, they met a young female blonde nurse, Jamie didn't know, but who was pretty. She smiled at Wayne, but ignored Jamie, even when he said a friendly 'good morning'.

"Fancy dinner with me on Friday, little lady?" Wayne's opening gambit, knocked Jamie off-guard. The nurse blushed profoundly but didn't take her eyes off Wayne, until she had walked past the two doctors. Wayne openly turned round to follow her with his overtly lewd gaze.

"Cute tush!" he added, clearly loud enough for her to hear.

Jamie thought this was going to go very badly and was waiting for some retort from the nurse.

"Yes!" a strong and calm voice came back from the tiny nurse. "To dinner Friday, that is."

"Excellent, you can sit that little tush on my lap after we've eaten." Wayne's Geordie accent seemed in some way to dilute the offensive nature of his comments.

"I'm not agreeing to that," said the nurse, they later knew as Lisa. "Yet!"

Wayne nudged Jamie, as if he was a pal and co-conspirator in the exchange, which Jamie thought had been bordering on sexual harassment. Or perhaps he was just jealous?

Jamie did consider momentarily, that Wayne had, however, easily gotten away with the banter in the corridor. It was just the start of 6 months of cringing on a daily basis, that Jamie had to learn to tolerate.

"Would you temper the language you use with my staff," it was Sister White speaking. Her face was a blank canvas, but the words were tough. She said it as soon as the pair entered the office door. Fortunately, Dr Firman had not arrived yet. Jamie blushed uncontrollably for the first time in a long time, feeling the guilt that Wayne clearly did not.

"Yes Sister, sorry Sister," the tone was playful from Wayne, but it certainly wasn't contrite, as Jamie interpreted it.

"Sister White to you, Dr…" she held a pause.

"Vetch"

"So 'Vetch the letch' and the 'milky bar kid'! What have we done to deserve this combination Dr Firman?" Jamie hadn't realised Dr Firman had followed in behind and now wondered if he had also heard Wayne's sexually provocative conversation with Lisa.

"I think everything is going to be just fine and dandy Sister White. Don't you worry yourself." Dr Firman's tone was definitely playful, but Sister White's face remained unreadable, in response to the consultant's arrival.

Jamie had been impressed that Sister Whites had come up with Wayne's rhyming nickname, within a heartbeat. It stayed with the Geordie for the rest of year in Stockport.

"I believe the baby face is the senior of these two?" Sister White's combined statement and question, was referring to Jamie, almost as if he wasn't in the room.

"Yes indeed!" Dr Firman said, not giving Jamie the chance to respond for himself.

"Well good luck with that one," Sister White was addressing Jamie for the first time. The dryness of her humour was now starting to become more evident to Jamie.

"Jamie has skills!" Dr Firman retorted without allowing a space.

"I've heard. Don't go trying any of that weird stuff on my ward!" she warned Jamie directly this time. In response, he could tell she was actually playing with him, even though her face was unmoved. Did he see a little sparkle in the eye, that could be a 'tell'?

"I'm sure anyone scared of a few ghosts or the like, wouldn't choose a hospital to work in." Jamie's first words. Wayne had the good grace to giggle, but Sister White gave the comment a degree of credence as she responded, "Quite!"

"Nothing scares, Sister White! Though on the other-hand, she scares almost all of my consultant colleagues, is that not right Pamela?" Dr Firman, using the first name as a challenge was in Jamie's best guess, the hearing of another first name, he would never utter.

"Just because I tolerate you, Dr Firman, doesn't mean you are going to get away with taking liberties." Jamie noticed Dr Firman's eyes were definitely twinkling and he was using the sort of skills Jamie was aiming for, just in a senior and more cultured and practised style.

"I am honoured you 'tolerate' me, and as you know Sister White, I have repeatedly promised to leave your liberties completely untouched." The jousting between the senior pair was unabated.

"That promise is reciprocated. Now, Dr Firman, shall we get on with your ward round. The new boys have heard enough 'tattle' for one day."

The interchange though over, had been entertaining for Jamie. Whilst for some people gossip, was the oil in the cogs of the hospital, for Jamie 'tattle' as Sister White had called it was much preferred to gossip, as it was generally harmless. *Especially, when done with skill and at the sort of intellectual level Dr Firman, had managed*, thought Jamie.

He considered Wayne's banter with the female nurse, was too close to the acceptable, unacceptable border, but as long as Wayne didn't really offend anyone, then he guessed there was no harm done. He realised he was probably just being a snob!

Jamie, knew he had found a new teacher of the skills of life needed to get the most out of a career in hospitals. Dr Firman that was of course, not Vetch the letch.

Once they started, the morning felt to Jamie like a supervised ward round at the highest level. Dr Firman, used his twinkly eyes, with the female patients and his dry humour with the male ones. The patients clearly all appreciated his style of communication. Dr Firman, could change to very gentle and compassionately sensitive when talking to the very sick and those who might not recover. However, he continued to keep a hint of humour in interactions, whenever it was an option.

As a team, they had coffee mid ward-round sat in the office. During this 10-minutes, Lisa came in to get some notes for a patient. She was behind Dr Firman and Sister White at one point and as a result she risked a lewd wiggle of her bottom for Wayne to see.

"Thank you, Lisa. Now go and leave us and especially Dr Vetch alone please." Jamie looked around to see what mirror or metal she had used to see the hidden movements of the young nurse. Jamie couldn't see anything to work out, how Sister White had seen Lisa's actions without moving her head at all.

"Just leaving Sister White," Lisa replied, almost running out the door. From his angle, Jamie could see the blush on the young nurse's face.

"You aren't the only one with 'skills', Dr Carmichael," Sister said in response to Jamie's craning neck, looking straight at him and accentuating the 'skills' word. Again, her face didn't show her humour even though Jamie smiled and gently shook his head straight back at her.

"I am quietly impressed with your skills, Sister," Jamie responded, stressing the 'am', when no one else spoke.

The exchange signified the coffee-break being over. The next important observation for Jamie was that Dr Firman made arrangements with sister and three separate patients, to have conversations with their relatives and the patient together for that afternoon.

"I will need the relatives' room, during these times he said," Sister White acknowledged Dr Firman's request as if it was 'taken as read'. Jamie assumed this was for Wayne and his own knowledge.

The consultant also insisted that Jamie would join him today for these meetings. Jamie realised he was being shown the style that his new boss expected him to adopt, for at least the duration of his attachment. Jamie already knew before lunch, that he had found his first true role model. Much of what he learnt in the next 6 months would stick with him throughout his career.

At the end of the day, Dr Firman, turned back up on the ward to check how the two junior doctors were doing.

"All jobs are nearly done. We should be away by 6 p.m. Not bad for a first day," Jamie answered for them both.

"On Fridays, if we can be as efficient as today, the normal plan on my team, is that we go to the pub for fish and chips together. My shout," Dr Firman started. "Hope this works for you both. All patients will have to be seen however before we can go. I expect you to do the paperwork after lunch and still be finished by 5 p.m. most Fridays, of course except when we are on-call. Wayne has a date with a lovely Tush this Friday after all!" Jamie laughed out loud having relaxed completely in the day. However, the interaction confirmed that they had been followed down the ward by their consultant, at least close enough to be within ear shot of Wayne's booming Geordie tones this morning.

The combination of the demonstrated patient centred-compassion, humour and the team centred approach, made this first day one of Jamie's favourite days in his career to date.

Jamie, noted this had happened without much direct contribution from himself. This alone, he knew meant the days would just get better and better as his role grew and expanded. He was already much happier than during his surgical placement and it was just day one.

****

"Wahay darlin', why don't you come and sit on my face," the accent as rich as if it was the 'Likely Lads' or from 'when the boat comes in'!

Jamie cringed, inwardly for the hundredth time already. Wayne's inappropriate language to the nurses, seemed to trouble Jamie, much more than it outwardly appeared to upset the opposite sex.

Jamie wasn't sure if they found it an interesting distraction from the stresses of work, tolerated it with a smile or were inwardly totally insulted, by the open and explicit sexual overtone.

Clearly some of them, quite liked Wayne's overtures. Jamie and Wayne shared neighbouring on-call rooms. On more than one occasion over the 6 months, Jamie had heard Wayne in protracted and vocal sexual interaction.

Jamie had never caught the perpetrators of the humouring of Wayne's behaviour entering or leaving. It hadn't seemed like the same voice (or wail) each time. Jamie was left to assume that a percentage of the female nursing population actually liked 'Vetch the letch's' style.

To Wayne's credit, the vocal disturbance, Jamie was forced to endure, was not of the same short-lived duration described by Sarah in attributing similar activity to the surgical registrar a few weeks before. The appreciative groaning and moaning of apparent pleasure, seemed to go on for a long time and the bouncing of the fragile on-call bed against the wall was done with languid and gentle rhythm. Jamie never heard a sound from Wayne himself, during the banging, thumping and female wailing. Before and after he could hear the tones of his Geordie accent, but always spoken so low, that Jamie couldn't make out the words. He realised of course that if they entered Wayne's on-call room willingly, after his sexually explicit opening gambits, they weren't going to need talking out of their knickers. Jamie imagined, that anyone who walked in quietly and without duress, must have fully accepted, what they were there for.

Additionally, he openly admitted to himself, that he was more than a little jealous of Wayne's success, but with a daughter just a few months old, Jamie had more than his hands full, keeping himself alive, coping with sleepless nights at home and at work.

It was always late into a weekend on-call when Wayne's behaviour became the most volatile with the nurses and by Jamie's standards even further over the dangerous line of acceptability.

Jamie also had to keep a closer eye on his medical decisions and accuracy of his prescribing and note-keeping at that time. Fatigue, seemed to leave Wayne less inhibited and less conscientious, in equal measure.

Correcting Wayne's decisions, when they did fall short, wasn't always easy and Jamie had, had to change the treatment, only to find himself challenged by the patients themselves. On more than one occasions, a patient would say that they had already seen the 'consultant' or the 'senior doctor', when the still youthful looking Jamie turned up after Wayne, to correct the diagnosis and management plan.

As a result, Jamie had to spend a lot of time explaining the medicine and why Wayne might have thought one answer was correct, but why it might not have been the right one.

These lengthy medical explanations, helped Jamie learn the skill of explaining medicine to the patient using lay terms.

One Sunday evening, he was explaining 'heart failure' to a 50-year-old alcoholic plumber, who was probably in the early stages of an alcoholic cardiomyopathy. The mechanism and cause of the weakened heart muscle (cardiomyopathy), would need further tests beyond those which Jamie had available to him on a Sunday night. However, Jamie was able to explain the principles of the breathlessness to his patient and its' mechanism.

"I've seen the consultant already. I don't need to see a student now!" Mr Benson had started when Jamie appeared. Jamie explained politely who he was and explained his badge and the difference between a house officer and a senior house officer. Once, he had done this, he then had to explain, how he was changing the likely diagnosis that Wayne had given the patient just an hour earlier. Mr Benson's eyes were not just dubious to start with, but clearly completely disbelieving, as Jamie started.

"What your X-ray actually shows Mr Benson, is an excess of fluid. This is building up in the lung tissues and in the spaces around the lungs. Later I am going to take a sample of that fluid, hopefully to confirm it is the heart causing the excess build up, as I believe. Getting the sample is a little like taking a blood test, but we have to pop the needle in a bit deeper and so it does hurt briefly, just a little more than the blood sample," Jamie was into a now, practised explanation.

"Is the senior doctor going to do that, the one I already saw?" said Mr Benson, not yet convinced.

"Dr Vetch hasn't learned that skill yet, Mr Benson. I could use you as a teaching example for him and supervise him doing it for the first time. Though I am not sure Sunday evening, when he has been up all last night is the best time to do this though. I've probably done between 50 and 100 of these procedures, even though I know I look younger than him, he just qualified after me."

Jamie used a little intentional negative dissuasion in this persuasion of the way forward. He deliberately accentuated the relative procedural experience as further leverage for Mr Benson, to go along with him as he changed the treatment plan.

"Ok, Doc, I will let you do it. Why has the fluid got there?" the tone was still not warm and bordering on belligerent.

"Good question, Mr Benson." Jamie had learnt, that telling patients, that their questions were 'good', was also a positive reinforcement technique. Even when they were inane (questions). This one from Mr Benson was genuinely good however, so there was no temptation to blink or scratch the chin as Jamie said it.

"We will need a scan called an echocardiogram, which uses sound waves to look at the function of the heart. It is the same way we look at babies in 'mum's tums'. This scan isn't available to us tonight and will be done in the next day or two. However, I think something has weakened the pump of your heart. What then happens, is that that the fluid isn't pumped through the lungs properly and a bit like a blocked drainpipe, the fluid builds up behind the blockage, filling up the gutters first, which makes the lungs wet, then spilling over the edges of the gutters as it were, letting the fluid fill up the spaces between the lungs and the chest wall."

Jamie used analogies whenever he could and by watching the patient's face, he worked out whether this analogy was making sense to this individual. If not, he would make the descriptions, more, simple in technical elements.

"How does that make me so breathless, especially when I lie down, Doc?" Mr Benson again asking pertinent questions.

"You are right to ask that and I will try and make this make sense too!" Jamie again reinforcing the good question. "Your lungs are kind of like 2 giant bath sponges. Same shape almost, stood up with their long length being upright. Can you imagine that?"

"Think so, Doc."

"So, when these bath sponges are dry, they are nice and light and fluffy and if you squeezed it with your hand muscles there is no resistance in the sponge. Now try and imagine the same sponges, placed in a washing-up bowl with 3 inches of water in it. The bottom 3 inches of the sponge gets full of fluid. Even the bit above the water level, soaks up some water, whilst the top stays dry. Now if you try and squeeze it, the sponge is heavy and more solid, so it takes more muscle power to do it, especially in the bottom half. What actually makes you feel breathless is how hard the breathing muscles have to work on the lungs, to squeeze them."

"So…" Mr Benson was starting to understand, "…my lungs are heavy and the muscles can't move the air in and out as much?"

"Absolutely correct. Now imagine, pushing the sponge over from upright to lying down in the water. Much more of the sponge is in the water and therefore more of the sponge is heavy and difficult to squeeze. Bingo, you are more breathless lying down. It's not a perfect analogy of what is really happening, but it is pretty close for you to get the idea. For what it is worth, this pattern is what we docs call 'orthopnoea'. It means more breathless when horizontal. I might bring the students tomorrow and use your description of it, as a good teaching example for them, if you don't mind?" This was a question, but Jamie was hoping this would make Mr Benson, feel a little more special as well.

"Thanks, Doc, that now does make sense to me. So, what do we do?" Mr Benson was ignoring the student question, but was coming around to all of Jamie's plans.

"Well, first I am going to treat you with these drugs called 'diuretics', also known as 'water medicine'. Because you have so much fluid on board, I will start them in intra-venous form. That means, into the vein. Using that cannula there." Jamie pointed to the cannula that had been inserted into Mr Benson's arm, close to his elbow.

"Tomorrow or later in the week, we will change them to tablets. You will need to be in hospital for a few days." Jamie was watching carefully for Mr Benson's reactions and all was going well.

"The nurse is going to put a bladder-catheter in though I am afraid. We need this in place so we can measure how much urine is coming out, so we can be sure we are squeezing the fluid out of the lungs without over-doing it and making you too dry. Blood tests will also be done every day to make sure the kidneys are coping with the amount of water medicine we give you."

"I presume this will make the breathlessness go away?" Jamie thought this question was perhaps the unnecessary one. 'Why would I be doing it if I wasn't trying to make you better?' the thought that crossed Jamie's mind, was parked and left unsaid.

"Yes, as the diuretics work and squeeze fluid out through the kidneys, then the lungs dry out. However, you will need to stay on that oxygen mask for the first day or two, to ease the breathlessness until your do lungs get dry."

"Thanks for explaining so much, Dr Carmichael. I am sorry I doubted you. What did Dr Vetch think was wrong with me again?" Jamie heard this question and thought it might have more than one motive. He was going to have to proceed with care.

"The appearances of a disease you can get from asbestos exposure, can look a little like this on the X-ray." Jamie was being kind about Wayne as the tumour called mesothelioma, was only normally seen in one lung. He wasn't going to say anything more negative about his colleague, to this inquisitive patient. "As you are a plumber, you may have had a little asbestos exposure, but there is nothing on the X-ray, which makes *me* think there is any disease in your lungs that is attributable to asbestos exposure."

"Does the fluid you are going to take off with the syringe help sort it out?" Jamie considered, the question had at least 2 possible meanings. He decided to answer both.

"Well, I won't take enough fluid off for you to notice any difference to your breathing, but if the drugs don't work, then we can take more off, which then would help. To do this latter approach, is a bigger procedure and is more painful and I hope it won't be necessary." Jamie was referring to the same chest drains they used to treat the pneumothorax, which could be used to drain more fluid off.

"However, they are much more uncomfortable than the procedure needed to just get the sample." Assuming Jamie was right, then nothing else would be needed. Mr Benson was breathless, but not in any danger right now, so there was time for the drugs to work, unlike the patient with the tension pneumothorax the previous year.

Jamie continued his explanation, "With regard to confirming, it's the heart, then assuming it is the heart causing it, then we should see a syringe full of almost clear fluid, looking like very dilute piss."

Jamie slipped into the use of a more vernacular word as he felt he had Mr Benson won over.

"And if Dr Vetch's diagnosis was correct?" asked Mr Benson, slightly embarrassed even to ask this question now.

"The sample of fluid would be thick and probably bloody," Jamie answered without skipping a beat, but knowing he was setting himself up for a fall if he actually turned out to be wrong.

"Let's get it done then, hey Doc?" Mr Benson was much calmer than he had been 20 minutes ago.

Five minutes later, Jamie was showing Mr Benson a 30ml syringe full of very pale fluid, that was medically referred to as 'straw coloured'.

"Just as we hoped," Jamie said, including Mr Benson in the 'we', to reaffirm, they were working together here. He chose 'hoped', though he could have used 'expected'. Jamie decided the latter option might have sounded, like he was implying: 'I told you so'.

"It didn't hurt as much as getting this damn thing in, either," Mr Benson pointed towards his cannula, which awaited the first dose of diuretic, that Jamie would do next.

Before that, he was busy putting the pale liquid he had withdrawn into sample bottles, to test it for infection, but more importantly today, the protein content, which should be lower than normal and finally nail down the diagnosis.

"Only thing I'm worried about now is having the catheter in," Mr Benson added as Jamie was concentrating on his task. Jamie guessed where this conversation was going now, but he had 3 more patients to review that Wayne had or was seeing.

"It's not that bad a procedure really, though I know none of us blokes like the idea," started Jamie.

"It's not that pretty little nurse putting it in, is it? I was a bit rude to her when I came in. I mean I flirted with her, but maybe a bit too much." Mr Benson was almost blushing at this confession. Christine hadn't said anything to Jamie.

"I'm afraid I've got loads of other patients to check up on, so I can't do it. I could send Dr Vetch back if you prefer, but Christine will have done hundreds of them." Jamie didn't want a protracted discussion as he had used his available time, getting Mr Benson on his side.

"How many has Dr Vetch done?"

"A few!" Jamie was deliberately non-committal.

Mr Benson went quiet.

"Last hint, but it is your choice. Christine will have had a good night sleep last night whilst Dr Vetch was almost certainly up all night one way or another." Jamie's face was straight, but he knew Wayne had made his on-call room, but hadn't focussed on the much-needed sleep around midnight. Even though work had gone quiet for a couple of hours.

Internally, Jamie was smiling and he knew he would prefer, the professional and gentle, refreshed and very skilled nurse doing the procedure. The alternative was Wayne, who was slightly heavy handed, with procedures as Jamie had witnessed, several times during his supervision and teaching of practical skills already. Wayne had also squandered the 2 hours he had as an option for sleep, by entertaining one of the receptive nurses for at least half that time, keeping Jamie awake alongside him.

"Ok, Doc. Message understood." Mr Benson was growing on Jamie, as he was sharp at picking up cues and his questions had for the most part been really good.

Jamie tidied up. Christine was close by the curtain as he came out from behind it.

She followed him to the treatment room, something she hadn't done for some time.

"Are you making more work for me, Dr Carmichael?" she was teasing him, from the tone of voice.

"Maybe!" Jamie allowed himself to sound a little sheepish. "I was just looking after him, I know which of you, I would rather have, putting in my catheter."

"Finally, I know your sexual fetish, Jamie." This time she had a full-on playful smile. She had switched names too.

"Haha! I can assure you it's not mine, but who knows Mr Benson, might be that way inclined."

"Have you tried it?" she wasn't giving up her playfulness of Jamie.

"As it happens I haven't…you?" Jamie took an opportunity to tease back.

"The trust couldn't afford to keep me in female catheters." Christine was clearly trying to wind Jamie up and he was sure she was just teasing.

"Whilst I love the banter, I've got to go and chase up around after Wayne, he didn't sleep at all last night."

"I thought you said it wasn't too bad overnight?" Christine had asked him how bad the night is.

"He gave up sleep in the interest of entertaining." Jamie started to leave.

"At least, someone is interested in providing for us needy nurses. I'll have to take out my sexual frustration on Mr Benson's lascivious willy." Jamie just heard the latter words as he set off down the corridor.

His next patient (Roger Walsh) was a 40-year-old with breathlessness and a single patch of what looked like pneumonia. The fever was only a low grade one, but Wayne had diagnosed pneumonia.

Jamie was about to get a lesson in how medicine can play tricks on you. On this occasion, he tended to agree with Wayne, even though the markers of infection were also only mildly elevated. Jamie decided it could be an atypical form of pneumonia. He did call the registrar covering their on-call work, as there was enough doubt, to require a senior review.

Imtiaz Khan, who was a care of the elderly registrar normally, agreed with the diagnosis and Jamie treated the patient with 2 different antibiotics to cover both 'normal' pneumonia and 'atypical' pneumonia. Unlike their surgical colleague who got pneumonia, there was nothing to suggest bird exposure, nor were there any suggestions of Legionnaires disease.

Although Jamie's radar was hinting to him, there was something wrong, he didn't chase the unease, late on this Sunday.

The weekend was almost over. Dr Firman, normally came round on a Monday after a weekend on-call, but Jamie knew he was away for the first time of the placement, as he was at a national conference, and wasn't in the hospital until Wednesday. Jamie was confident he could handle the patients admitted so far and had Dr Chapman as the allocated 'cover' consultant if he needed a senior review.

Before the end of the nursing late-shift, Jamie had made it back to see Mr Benson, who was already feeling less breathless.

Mr Benson was slightly sheepish, when Jamie asked about the catheter. In terms of the planned effect of the diuretic treatment on his condition, there was a good early response, with well over a litre of urine already in the catheter bag and more actively draining.

"Thanks for that!" said Christine as she was about to go.

"For what?" asked Jamie, unsure what he had done.

"Mr Benson had the biggest cock I have ever seen. He went stiff as a poker as soon as I touched him and approached with the catheter. I had to ram it in to the hilt, to get the urine flowing and I was really worried the balloon was going to expand still inside his urethra or prostate, when I inflated it, it was so long." She sounded genuinely concerned.

"Hope you have kept his telephone number? You and he could run the hospital out of all catheters if you get together." Jamie was in full retaliation mode now.

"Haha. I promise you it is so big, it would split me in two and certainly wouldn't be a pleasure, though clearly I could turn him on with just my hands, a few latex gloves and a catheter or two." Christine sounded genuinely troubled by her experiences. However, just as she was leaving, she tried again. "Sleep well later! Unless a more moderately sized doc wants to fulfil my more reasonable demands." She turned and headed up the ward corridor towards the exit.

Jamie caught up with her and checked if anyone was watching. He led her into the treatment room. He kissed her gently, there was no time for anything else unless he wanted to risk being seen.

"You know I really fancy you, but I have a young daughter at home, it's not the thing."

"So why did you kiss me?" Christine was flushing gently.

"Only so you know that I would love to, if things were different." Jamie decided honesty was the best policy.

"I don't want to marry you, Jamie. But I understand you are either paralysed by guilt, or fear of failure. Your loss though, I'm a great lay!" Jamie dropped his mouth open at her bluntness.

Christine cocked her head slightly awaiting a response. Jamie was speechless.

"Night, Jamie. See you tomorrow. You are cute you know?" Christine turned on her heel and started to leave. She let the palm of her hand, run across the front of his trousers. "Yep more my size, just as I imagined," was her parting shot.

Jamie desperately wanted to stop her but couldn't. Part of him wondered if he really just wanted an excuse, to get his own back on Wayne. In the end, he stayed silent and the moment had passed, before he even turned around to watch her wiggling ass walk around the corner of the ward entrance.

Chapter 26
Getting Covid: Night 4, Night Sweats

At bed time, sleep came quickly, but he again woke with nightmares of the past. He felt his head. Was that a fever? He was certainly sweating and had thrashed around the bed, so much that Isla was sat on the floor looking up at him.

"Sorry baby, hope I didn't squash you?" She had yelped the one time he had rolled over and squashed her with his leg, when she was a younger dog. More recently she jumped up every time he rolled over, but she almost always came back on the bed.

He got up, made a cup of tea, took an ibuprofen as he found them so much more effective than paracetamol. Normally, after doing this on the rare occasions he did have a fitful night he would get back off to sleep quickly. In the early hours of this Monday morning, sleep was elusive for a long time.

When the time came and Jamie finally rose, he went about his pre-work routine as usual. He got in the habit of doing his lateral flow test whilst making tea and toast and feeding Isla. Leaving the test to 'cook', whilst he was in the shower.

Feeling much better for having had the shower and breakfast, he was shaved and ready. The only adverse sensation was the familiar feeling of sleep deprivation, that he knew he would manage. He had learnt easily how to do so, for the last 36 years of his 37-year long career. He wandered back into the kitchen, just to double check the test strip, which was negative as he went to the shower.

Two lines, where there had only been one. "Shit pregnant!" Not everyone got his humour and this time he didn't get it himself.

"You knew it all along." He spoke out loud again, but his head was remembering that cup of tea, with those little green viral particles, crawling all over the cup.

"The next challenge is dealing with having Covid!"

Jamie accepted the negative aspects of life as a series of challenges. His parents' deaths, divorce, Heather's infidelity: all periods of time when life was tougher. The task for each of his past challenges, was to accept the challenge and get to the point where the hurt was part of history, whilst allowing the experience to influence the person you became. 'Older and wiser', for most of these events.

He didn't imagine that Covid would take 3 years to get over, as the Heather separation had.

Chapter 27
The SHO Years: Learning Lessons

During the two days after their on-call week-end, all the patients were either improving as expected, had been discharged, or those expected to, had passed away peacefully.

Except Roger Walsh.

He remained breathless and couldn't tolerate being off oxygen for more than a few seconds. Jamie repeated the X-ray on Tuesday and the appearances were pretty much unchanged.

The bloods were about the same apart from Liver function tests which had deteriorated slightly.

"Mr Walsh. My boss is back tomorrow morning and I will bring him to see you first thing, as I am not sure why you are not getting any better. The good thing is, you aren't getting any worse. The X-ray is exactly the same. So, waiting another day I think is ok." Jamie wanted to be honest, but also wanted to admit he was a little unsure of what to do next.

"Ok, Doc, that is fine by me as long as I get better in the long run." Jamie's radar was twitching and he knew he needed his boss back as a third opinion.

Jamie had already checked in, on an unchanged Mr Walsh, the next morning prior to Dr Firman coming to the ward. It was not a usual ward round day, so Jamie had left a message with Dr Firman's secretary, asking him if he would come especially, to see this one patient.

Dr Firman was in good humour after his conference trip. They sat in the ward office and looked at the X-rays together.

"It is a bit more 'ground glass' like, rather than consolidation you know Jamie," he was pointing at the abnormal area on the X-ray. Jamie knew this opened up diagnoses for which he had not treated Mr Walsh, such as atypical heart failure or a rare condition called eosinophilic pneumonia.

Dr Firman, then looked at the ECG, the electrical recording of the heart. Jamie only had the one from admission. "It isn't normal, is it? The chest leads don't show any 'r' wave progression and look at those lateral leads, the 't' waves are subtly inverted." Jamie acknowledged this. Jamie realised the changes were subtle and whilst he had noted them, he had put it down to the strain of sepsis. Imtiaz, the registrar had said the same.

They then went off to see Mr Walsh and Dr Firman, was in full charm mode.

After the usual initial questions, Dr Firman asked, "What happens if you try and lie down flat, Mr Walsh?"

"I can't lie flat. It feels like I'm drowning!" said Mr Walsh.

Jamie suddenly did too, feel like he was drowning that is. He hadn't asked this question, even though he had seen Mr Walsh, just an hour after seeing and sorting out Mr Benson.

"I've had to sleep sat up, the last few nights." Mr Walsh was giving the perfect answers for 'orthopnoea', just the same as Mr Benson had done.

Why had Jamie or even Dr Khan not asked this question? Jamie was embarrassed, but he knew the changes on just one side on the X-ray made him think pneumonia. Heart failure almost always showed up as changes on both sides.

However, Dr Firman had already worked out, that the answer here was a form of cardiac failure, just like Mr Benson. He had also opened the clues up to Jamie who was almost blushing with embarrassment. Jamie knew the appearances of fluid within the lungs gave changes sometimes referred to as 'bats wing'. This description is given as the fluffy white changes on the X-ray either side of the centre of the chest, that take the shape of a bat's wing, just like the image of batman. The trick in Mr Walsh's case, is that the bat only had one wing!

Jamie had heard that occasionally though rarely, this occurs in heart failure, with the medical term of 'unilateral pulmonary oedema'. The unilateral, just meant 'one-sided'. Jamie had never had an explanation of why, very rarely it could happen and he had never seen it before, but such was the trap he had fallen into.

"We think this is perhaps a rare form of heart disease, with the heart muscle being weak. Usually the X-ray shows, the appearances we see on both lungs at the same time, and this is what has fooled us." Dr Firman was deep into his explanation as Jamie surfaced from his immediate embarrassment. He was very relieved Dr Firman, was using the 'us' and 'we' terms. He was doing this to show the team support and include the probably blushing Jamie in the team.

"It is very, very rare to have an X-ray like yours, but if I am right, you will feel better if we stop the antibiotics and give you some diuretics. These are also called 'water medicine'. To make them work more quickly I am going to give you them direct into the blood stream for the first couple of days..." Dr Firman's explanation was parallel to those Jamie had spoken to Mr Benson.

"Also, we might need to get our cardiology colleague here, straight away as you need a scan of your heart, to see what the pattern of weakness is. I wonder if it could be a viral infection that has affected your heart. This would also explain why some of the signals of infection were here from the start, just adding to the difficulty of getting this diagnosis right. If it is a virus, you might even need to be transferred to our heart specialist colleagues, at South Manchester."

Fifteen minutes later, they were in the office. Jamie had already given the first dose of intravenous diuretics, just as he had to Mr Benson a few days before.

Jamie was devastated to have missed the correct diagnosis. He understood why he had missed it and saw there were lots of reasons, but in front of the new boss he admired so much and who had already taught him so much, he felt particularly disturbed and sensed he was close to tears. He couldn't however, show Dr Firman, that level of vulnerability, so Jamie bit them back.

"Jamie, don't worry. It is a classic trap and I personally last saw unilateral pulmonary oedema, nearly 10 years ago. Reading your notes, I can tell you knew something was wrong. You asked your registrar, which you don't do often and you brought me here first moment back."

"I should have got Dr Chapman up Monday though, or at least Tuesday when he wasn't responding." Jamie was particularly cross with himself, for not asking advice. Dr Firman and he, had talked about this in the last ward round, when they knew Dr Firman was not going to be around after the weekend take.

"None of us are flawless, Jamie, you will learn this many times over, in your career. One thing I know for sure, is you will spot unilateral oedema, the next time it crops up. I know you are upset, but that is also the right response. I would only be worried now, if you didn't look like it had upset you at all." Dr Firman was working hard to reassure Jamie. "Of course, it's my fault for being away, just when the first googly gets bowled at us." Dr Firman often used cricketing terms in his analogies and was back to using the 'us' team word.

"We must also tell Imtiaz, as he has missed this too and he is much more experienced than you," Dr Firman added.

"Shall I present it at one of the clinical meetings as a learning case?" Jamie suggested.

"I think that would be a great idea, if you don't mind doing it," Dr Firman added.

Three hours later, Jamie had called back on Mr Walsh, who was already starting to feel better and was noticeably less breathless.

Dr Lorimer came and agreed that viral myocarditis *(the term used for a virus that attacks and damages the heart muscle)*, was the most likely explanation and he reiterated this was why the low-grade temperature and the blood results were in keeping with an important component of infection.

Although Mr Walsh improved, he was indeed referred on to the specialist hospital and there was talk, that ultimately Mr Walsh might even need to be referred on to the heart transplant team in London, if the heart muscle function didn't improve on its' own.

Jamie reflected long and hard and the case remained very important to him throughout his career in terms of 'listening to', not just 'hearing' the medical radar in his head. The radar had told him something was wrong, but on this occasion, he hadn't followed it up hard enough. Nor had he 'phoned enough friends' he concluded. He had allowed himself to be reassured by a single senior review. But that senior was not as sharp as Jamie wanted or needed it to be.

He would never forget this lesson, the first major one he had learnt, in what he considered as the wrong way.

****

Nothing changed in the relationship between Dr Firman and Jamie after this case. Dr Firman had completely taken Jamie under his wing and within 6 months Jamie was a semi-skilled bronchoscopist.

Jamie reckoned there were very few first year SHO doctors, who could do these procedures half way through their second year as a doctor. Dr Firman supervised all these procedures, for 6 months, but more and more so, just as a political presence. Dr Firman, took a lot of time reassuring the patients, that this youthful looking doctor was more than capable of doing the procedures.

Dr Firman, did the procedures himself, without using any sedation. Almost everywhere Jamie worked subsequently, sedation was standard practice. However, learning from the outset, to be able to do it routinely without sedation taught Jamie to be very gentle, calm and reassuring. It was needed to be like this in order to get the procedure completed, with patients who were understandably anxious about having a long tube into their lungs.

Dr Firman's joking, calm and sometimes flirtatious behaviour with the patients, had an incredibly profound calming effect too, Jamie noticed. His boss only used flirtation with patients, in those old enough so that it was accepted as light hearted banter. It was never inappropriate. The line could be fine, but Jamie never felt it was crossed. Jamie went on to copy this style and used it on his patients as long as they were at least a generation older than himself!

Jamie wondered if this was why he found doing bronchoscopy procedures on women, was easier than with men. Men overall seemed more likely to get agitated and the ability to use flirtation as distraction was absent. Jamie didn't like the 'women can take more pain than men' argument, though having watched it, he didn't fancy testing the theory himself with a trial of labour, that was for certain!

****

Fridays were the teams' favourite day except for those when they were on call.

Wayne and Jamie had learnt that to get the most out of the day, they needed to come in especially early, at least by 7 a.m. and get all the patients and notes prepped for the ward round. The latter would start by 9.15 a.m., and was complete by 12.30 p.m., however many patients they had. It was always done thoroughly and Dr Firman insisted on giving enough time for careful communication with all the patients.

If there was an important discussion to be had with relatives, then these were invited in for 12 and Dr Firman would almost always do this himself, with one of Wayne or Jamie, keeping notes.

At 1 p.m. promptly, Dr Firman led Jamie and Wayne off the ward to the Wagon and Horses, just up the road, where they had fish and chips and a pint of lager. They never had 2, switching to soft drinks if the food was slow, then coffee and back to do the remaining administration and preparation of tests for the weekend team or Monday morning.

Dr Firman always checked back to ensure all was complete and the two junior doctors were going to get finished by 5 p.m. on a Friday. He openly appreciated the junior's early starts', which they had both committed to, to ensure the day went according to plan.

Chapter 28
The SHO Years: Success Out of Disaster

Towards the end of his 6-month placement with Dr Firman, it was time for Jamie to make plans for the following year. He was still vacillating between cardiology and respiratory, but the time with Dr Firman, was swinging him towards the latter. However, Jamie's last six months in Stockport, would be with the second cardiologist Dr Murray.

Jamie had applied for the Heart and Lung SHO rotation as Dr Firman had encouraged him to do right at the start. This would mean, he could keep both options open and would involve working at the specialist centre for heart and lung in Manchester, based at Baguley Hospital.

Dr Firman, had called up a few favours, with his contacts as promised and Jamie had an afternoon booked on a Friday to go and visit the potential new hospital and had three appointments scheduled to meet consultants. The first was with Dr Coleman, starting at 2 p.m.

Friday lunch was forgone, but the ward round was done and dusted by 12.30 p.m.

"Get yourself off, Jamie, these meetings are probably more important than the official interview and you can't be late."

Dr Firman's command would prove to be famous last words for Jamie. He set off immediately taking his rat runs from the back of the hospital, via Davenport and Cheadle Heath so as to avoid the lottery of the A6, which could snarl up and cause delays at the drop of a hat.

Jamie had recently moved into a house half way between these two hospitals and the route would take him close to home. He might even have time to call in to see his 7-month-old daughter (Siobhan). He had made it to Davenport in good time and was heading to the roundabout at Adswood.

He was driving behind an Audi and had already noticed it was driving a little recklessly through the narrow areas, where cars were parked. It also did an emergency stop just prior to the zebra crossing, having failed to see the pensioner with her shopping trolley, very slowly making her way across.

Jamie had kept a respectful distance, but was not impressed as he closed up behind at the crossing. The Audi driver, was revving, as the old lady made her final steps and cleared the crossing.

There was wheel spin as the Audi pulled off and Jamie was convinced it was a boy racer. A hundred yards beyond the zebra-crossing, was a roundabout.

Jamie could see the accident coming, before it happened. It was a small motorcycle, not quite a moped, but not much more. It was coming around the roundabout from the Edgeley direction. Quietly minding his own business, was a 32-year-old on his way back from an early shift working at a central Stockport supermarket (Jamie got this story later).

The Audi driver didn't appear to see the small motorbike at all, though Jamie did from 40 yards behind. At the last minute as the Audi started to enter the roundabout and looked like wiping out the cyclist completely, the car slewed to the left, rubber smoke emanating as the back-wheels locked and skidded. The Audi sideswiped the motorcycle, sending it sliding into the centre of the roundabout, the bike and rider, wedged together came to a stop, right in the middle of the roundabout.

Jamie accelerated to the scene, put his hazard lights on and jumped out of his car, almost before it had stopped at the entrance to the roundabout.

"Ambulance and police please, I'm a doctor!" Jamie almost screamed at the shopkeeper who had jumped out of the nearby shop, at the sound of screeching tyres and scraping metal.

The driver of the Audi was opening the car door and looking back and Jamie went to meet the eyes briefly, he was expecting a male in their teens or twenties.

To his surprise it was a 40-ish-year-old lady, who from the distance Jamie had, bore a remarkable resemblance to Mrs Markham, the mother of the cyclist with the ruptured liver from his time in surgery.

She looked back at the scene and briefly back at Jamie, who was running to the stricken motor cyclist. Whether she heard the 'police' word or perhaps it was on seeing Jamie's face, but to Jamie's abject horror, the female driver pulled the door back closed and sped off.

The next hour was a blur as Jamie looked after the unfortunate Peter, who had a seriously damaged leg, with what was clearly a compound fracture. Jamie had no doubt of this from the twisted shape, even though it was fortunately hidden inside motorcycle leathers. Jamie just gently removed the motorcycle, which was dripping petrol and asked a bystander to put it somewhere out of the way.

There were no obvious head injuries, Peter had already removed his own helmet, by the time Jamie had made it over. The helmet was not in a great shape and Jamie was not taking any chances with Peter's neck and back, so opted for keeping Peter in the same position as he was conscious, with a good airway and whilst his pulse was not surprisingly going quite fast, the pulse pressure felt as good as it might under these circumstances.

Jamie had nothing else, he could do other than, sitting on the tarmac in his best suit and keeping Peter as calm and still as possible. Other passers-by, gave Jamie coats to support Peter's head, in a neutral position and to cover him to keep him warm. One of these Jamie put over the twisted looking leg so if Peter did look in that direction, he wouldn't be able to see the extent of the disfigurement. Jamie half did it for his own comfort too, as he was feeling more than a little nauseous himself.

A few minutes before the ambulance and police arrived, Jamie looked around the bystanders and saw at least 3 of them smoking cigarettes.

"There has been petrol spilled here, please go away with those cigarettes. As far as possible!" It was said in a commanding voice, but he couldn't keep the incredulity out of it and it came across more of a whine.

Two of the miscreants, did the dutiful thing and walked away from the cluster of people around Jamie and Peter. The third dropped the almost finished cigarette on the floor and stamped on the burning ember. Jamie was expecting a flash, followed by fire, as the man had done it very close to where the stricken bike had rested, dripping contents of its' petrol tank on to the tarmac.

"You are a fuckwit!" Jamie said the words that, came in to his head, something that later became an established pattern of his behaviour, in his career, when working with NHS management. He always managed to avoid criticising patients or relatives, however stupid their actions, just not everyone else. Fortunately, he managed to filter out blasphemy at work.

On this occasion with the stress of being delayed from his appointments, Jamie couldn't withhold saying what had flashed in his head, especially as he expected a flash of flame to engulf his patient and himself.

"What's wrong with you, dickhead, it's out, isn't it?" The offended passer-by, flexed his shoulders and looked like he was ready to fight Jamie.

Another of the bystanders came to Jamie's aid, stepping in between Jamie and the surly gentleman. In rather more measured tones, the bystander explained what might have happened, when the cigarette was dropped. Jamie realised his instructions hadn't been explicit enough and he learned another lesson. 'Never over-estimate the intelligence of people you haven't had a conversation with'. The addendum, 'whatever their alleged profession', he added after contemplating some of the crazy things he saw doctors doing, over the years.

Just then, the sirens finally came into earshot, which settled most of the crowd down. Jamie asked those in cars to try and clear a passage, so the ambulance could get there without delay and with the most direct of access. He pointed in the direction of Stockport Infirmary, the most likely destination for Peter, as it was both the Emergency Department and housed the orthopaedic services at the time.

****

By the time Jamie had been given the go ahead to leave, by both Peter, (who was by then in a leg brace and on a head and spinal board, and being stretchered into the ambulance), but also the police (who wanted an immediate statement), it was almost 2 p.m.

Jamie looked at his suit, which was creased and filthy from sitting on the floor. He made his way to his car, which was still blocking one entrance to the roundabout, but he was given priority to escape, by the officers in the second panda car to arrive, who had taken on the duty of traffic control.

Jamie had given his details and asked the police officer to ring if they wanted a further report later that day, having explained why he was in a rush…referring to his appointments as an 'interview', not a 'pre-interview, chat'.

Jamie briefly contemplated heading back to Stockport, knowing he was going to be at least half an hour late, for the first appointment, but there were two others, he would still be in time for.

****

"Oh, I don't think Dr Coleman will see you now, whatever the explanation." The secretary was probably only a year older than Jamie, he reckoned. She was Irish with jet black hair and piercing eyes, but she rarely kept eye contact with him, despite his best efforts. Under other circumstances, Jamie might have found her attractive, but he at least wanted her to explain to Dr Coleman, the unusual reasons, he was late even if he was now booked up.

Jamie was hoping, that seeing his damaged suit, would actually confirm the veracity of his story with the consultant behind the secretary's office. That was, if he got a chance to say at least an apology, personally. Jamie wasn't confident the secretary was going to give Jamie's full story to Dr Coleman, from her hard and frosty demeanour to him.

Jamie had arrived with plenty of time to meet Dr Carey for whom the appointment was scheduled at 2.45 p.m. and whose office was directly next door to Dr Coleman's.

Dr Carey's secretary was a mature and smiling redhead, who couldn't have contrasted more. She sympathised with Jamie's plight and got paper towels and tried to dust him down.

Jamie got the scent of perfume and stale cigarettes in his nostrils as she bent down and even wiped his trousers for him.

When Jamie was invited into Dr Carey's room, there was nothing more forthcoming from Dr Coleman's secretary.

Dr Carey was sat in a huge office with a large single desk made of solid looking wood and there was room enough for a round table with 6 chairs to act as a meeting area.

The consultant had a very austere posture, having clearly been in the army. His neck was straight as a rod and it made it seem as if he was looking down his nose. As Jamie was still covered in dust and dirt and was creased as if the trousers had just come out of the washing machine, he imagined Dr Carey may have been looking with complete disdain. However, the eyes had a twinkle of mischief and were smiling as Jamie recounted the reason his delay.

"Just what you want when you are coming to meet prospective new consultants." Dr Carey was smiling broadly, reassuring Jamie, that his appearance wasn't important. The voice was rich and layered with wisdom. "Why do you want to do this job, by the way. We normally take first year SHO's as there is only one House Officer between all the SHO's, so you end up working alone, quite a lot, with no junior?"

Jamie had prepared for this question as he knew it was the weakness in his application. He recounted the perspective, that he wasn't shy of hard work and had experienced both above his level of years in the role (bronchoscopy), but also his willingness to get his hands dirty. He took the bleep overnight for one of the 3 nights of a weekend, so his House Officer, could get a block of sleep to survive the weekend (he didn't add about Wayne's proneness for shagging rather than sleeping). Getting to know Dr Carey later in his career, if he had actually told the addendum to the story, then Dr Carey would just have laughed resoundingly.

Jamie also told, Dr Carey how he had first come to Baguley Hospital straight from school when he was eighteen, doing six months' work as a filing clerk in the pathology laboratories. He had even managed to secure a few months' work the following summer, before such casual work in hospitals became impossible. Jamie told Dr Carey, that he felt a close connection with the hospital, that had been so friendly to him, right from his first days, back then 6 years or more before.

When asked about his possible interest in respiratory medicine, it was then easy for Jamie to talk with genuine passion about how Dr Firman had inspired him, with his approach to medicine and how Jamie had also loved the team centred approach to leadership, this respiratory consultant had inspired within him. Finally, almost as an afterthought, Jamie said that Dr Firman had recommended the job to him.

"Roger is a great colleague of ours and I have to say has given you a very good early reference." Dr Carey surprised Jamie, by telling him this. Dr Firman had told Jamie, that he had rung each of the 3 consultants, Jamie was meeting with, but Jamie didn't think this would have been acknowledged by these strangers to him.

The first meeting felt like a success. The ginger haired secretary, smiled at him warmly and winked at him as he came out from Dr Carey. He wandered across the old hospital in better humour. The place was a mix of redbrick old Victorian style wards, some barrack type accommodation where the respiratory department was housed and the newest 1960s grey concrete design, which was the new hub of the hospital.

The barrack block ward complex was where his father had been after his stroke. Cardiology on the other hand was in the newer concrete bit of the hospital. He found the relevant secretary with ease and he was immediately admitted to see the cardiologist Dr Wallace, who was equally kind and positive.

Finally, but without much hope, he called back to Mary Maloney, the secretary to Dr Coleman on his way back to his car.

"Dr Coleman will in fact see you." Mary said it with a tone and with a look at his suit, which made it very clear, that she, the secretary, was actually disappointed with her boss's decision and certainly didn't agree with it.

Dr Keith Coleman was a white-haired consultant, despite being perhaps being only in his mid-forties. His voice oozed compassion with a very English lilt to it. There was a huge sense of wisdom in Dr Coleman, that Jamie felt, even at first meeting. In fact, Jamie described the experience to Diane that evening as getting the impression that, "he was talking to the wisest owl in all of Christendom, if such an owl existed."

Jamie used the story of his journey, as it had been a great ice-breaker with the other two consultants. When he got to the part about the cigarette butt being stamped out, Dr Coleman replied.

"It never ceases to amaze me how incredibly fucking stupid some people can be."

Jamie was taken aback, by this distinguished consultant, slipping into the vernacular so quickly with him. He tried not to skip a beat in agreeing and confessing that he had told the individual, pretty much that principle, even confessing the words he had used. This admission, was despite the fact, that Jamie had told himself very strongly on the way over, *not* to relay the part where he got frustrated with a bystander.

Dr Coleman however, just genuinely laughed.

On his way out, he popped back to thank the friendly secretary as Mary looked like she had left already.

"I asked Dr Carey to speak to Dr Coleman for you. He kindly did! Frosty knickers next door, was trying her best to stop you getting in. Best she never knows it was me though." She placed a finger to the side of her nose in a conspiratorial gesture.

This confession explained her earlier wink. Jamie thanked her again and asked her to thank her boss also.

****

After the success of his pre interview meetings, Jamie was buoyed by his chances and it came as no surprise that 3 weeks later he was appointed as one of the SHO's to the heart and lung rotation for the following year.

He was the only second year SHO appointed and so he didn't know the other interview candidates well, particularly any of those who were appointed, as they weren't in his academic year of more than two hundred students per year at Manchester University.

Whilst waiting in the communal waiting-room, he did get on well with Duncan Fulwell and was delighted, when they were both pulled into the interview room together at the end and formally offered the job . Alongside them, Jamie recalled a tall chap called Bill and Gemima, who Jamie had found a touch brash when talking to all the other candidates. She had hair so blond it was almost albino like. The fifth member of the appointees on that day was a very buxom and effervescent doctor (Emilia), with the most extreme of television accents Jamie had listened to. It was so contrary to Jamie's Manchester one, it grated on him, in the few hours they were sat in a room together.

****

Jamie had completed his 6 months with Roger Firman, between the meetings and the formal interviews. Jamie thanked him for being such an 'amazing boss' as well as after the interviews, for what he must have done to help Jamie get appointed.

"Don't thank me, just go and make the most of your opportunities," Dr Firman had said. Jamie didn't need many words in a rallying speech, but these were all he needed.

Wayne and Jamie barely crossed paths again after their 6 months together. When Jamie did find out what had happened to Wayne's career, he was perhaps not surprised that his former colleague went on to be a successful obstetrician and gynaecologist.

Jamie just hoped that Wayne, never got so tired during the rest of his career as he did in his House year at Stockport, that the fatigue induced lack of filter, would get the better of him. If it had, Jamie worried he may have had a brush with the General Medical Council, especially as more political correctness became the norm.

Chapter 29
The SHO Years: More Accidents and Incidents

Two more events transpired in the first year of Jamie's SHO career, which influenced his future. The first and biggest of these again happened outside of the work environment, but perhaps was the most important individual event to decide Jamie's future career.

He was on a day off at home. His daughter Siobhan was nearly eleven months old and Jamie and his wife had decided to try, some boiled egg, for the first time in Siobhan's diet.

Siobhan gobbled the first mouthful gleefully. By the time the second or third spoon went on, Siobhan wasn't looked so excited by the taste and her tongue protruded out through the lips.

At first, the couple thought this was just the rejection of the taste, but the tongue didn't recede, even when no further egg was offered.

Then Jamie realised Siobhan's lips were swelling. Fear clutched at him as her eyes started to go puffy. In seconds, they were closing and Siobhan was clearly starting to struggle to breathe.

"What's wrong Jamie? Do something!" Only a few seconds had passed. However, dread and panic crossed Jamie's consciousness, almost freezing him.

"999, say anaphylaxis in an infant," Jamie's voice was pure panic, there was nothing he could do to hide it. Diane fled to the phone as Jamie watched his beloved daughter go blue. Jamie ran to the kitchen and got a sharp knife out of the kitchen draw, then he collected a biro and took the ink cartridge out.

Jamie had perhaps seen done on television programmes, what he might have to do, but had never seen it done first hand even in the hospital setting. Certainly, he had never seen it done on an infant, and doing it on his own felt inconceivable.

If anaphylaxis occurred in the hospital setting, then drugs and other equipment were on hand. Jamie had dealt with hospital and drug related anaphylaxis before. To work, they needed giving quickly and Jamie obviously had none in the house.

Diane had finished on the phone, to the ambulance control.

"Coming, category A!" she told Jamie.

"Try the GP, they might even get here quicker." The GP surgery was only half a mile away. Jamie wondered if he was doing this more to give Diane a purpose.

The only other option Jamie considered he had, was picking Siobhan up and driving her to ED, but the nearest one was fifteen minutes away on clear roads. Jamie knew the life (or death) of their baby would be decided in less time than that.

He watched the laboured breathing, seeing the indrawing of the tummy as those tiny muscles tried to pull the air in through the swollen tiny orifice left at the throat. Jamie knew the same swelling of the tissues in the face eyes and tongue, was occurring around the throat and probably down the windpipe. The reaction was created by the release of an avalanche of toxic chemicals, triggered by the allergic reaction between Siobhan and egg protein.

He didn't know if he could even attempt the emergency tracheotomy on his own child, nor if the biro was small enough to get in to a baby's windpipe. He cursed leaving his white coat at work. If he had it, at least he would have a cannula in his pocket, which might have worked better.

The crying had stopped. Jamie knew this wasn't good news as Siobhan couldn't get enough air in to make the noise. The only sound was the rasp of the breath in. Something known medically as 'stridor'.

Helplessness flooded him.

His instincts were to wait and not try anything reckless, until it was absolutely necessary. But he knew he could leave it too late if Siobhan became so short of oxygen, that the brain started to shut down.

Jamie was overwhelmed, by the fear on not making the right call, at the right time, in this critical moment?

Seconds felt like hours as he prayed to hear the ambulance siren, before he was forced to try something horrific.

Jamie watched as Siobhan became even more cyanosed and he wondered if some of the life was starting to disappear from those beautiful eyes.

"Dr Hunter is on his way." Jamie couldn't believe Diane had managed to get through so quickly and get a response.

"Go and stand by the door and look out for them."

In retrospect, Jamie couldn't recall, whether he said this so Diane wasn't watching him make the call on if or when, to assault their baby with a kitchen knife. Alternatively, he may have genuinely wondered whether the few seconds of time, in saving the ambulance or Dr Hunter finding the right house quickly, was really what he meant or hoped would make a positive difference.

To his surprise, Diane followed his suggestion and didn't stay with him and the distressed infant. It gave Jamie, more thinking time, whilst she had a purpose.

He tried to switch off his emotional brain and focus on what mattered.

First, she was still breathing, she was blue tinged, but she was still holding in there.

Was that tongue already slightly smaller? He wanted to say yes.

He also wanted to touch where he would put the knife if he decided he had to try, but he knew any pressure there now could tip the balance against Siobhan, whilst she was managing to get enough air in and out of what Jamie imagined to be an airway, the size of an 'eye of a needle'.

He was glad she was in a high chair and he hadn't needed to move her.

Would he be able to find the windpipe? It sounded easy in theory, but he had heard that in a crisis, it was anything but that. Open the front membrane don't go through the back. Splint the airway open to the front.

Was that a cry? He wasn't sure, but there was a noise.

Noise was good, it meant there was at least some air was getting in. If Siobhan made the noise with her voice box, then it was better news. The swelling may already be settling.

On the third breath after that, it was clearly a cry.

It was loud enough to bring Diane back in.

"Have you done it?" she was sobbing openly.

"So far I've not needed to. She is fighting hard and I think the cry means that she is getting more air in."

Jamie looked and was now convinced that the protrusion of the tongue was definitely less.

****

Dr Hunter arrived first, but by then Jamie was certain the crisis was over, the peak had passed and he had prevented himself from doing any damage, either through paralysis or good judgement. He would never know which.

Dr Hunter was breathless. It was not in the normal role of a GP to attend emergencies, but the practice knew Siobhan and Jamie from visits and talking about a career in medicine.

"How is she?" Dr Hunter was looking at the knife and biro in Jamie's hand.

"Just starting to get better," Jamie explained.

"I'll hold off adrenaline then! Shall we give her some hydrocortisone and antihistamine though?"

Jamie was impressed these were both present in his emergency bag. Dr Hunter drew up the drugs. Jamie saw even his hand was shaking. Adrenaline was in full force in both doctors' bodies. It was ironic, that the drug that Siobhan really needed was flowing in abundance through the adults around her.

Only as the second needle went in to the now fully crying Siobhan, did they hear the sirens, implying the arrival of the blue light ambulance. It was completely clear to Jamie, that they would have been too late, if the anaphylaxis had progressed to complete occlusion of the airway. It would have been down to him alone.

Half an hour later, Siobhan was settled and the crying had stopped in the comforting arms of mum. Breathing was already back to normal.

Between them, they all accepted, that going to hospital now was going to be irrelevant. Dr Hunter promised to call back in a few hours to double check. Jamie suggested he rang and only came if Jamie was worried, as he didn't want to waste anymore time of a very busy GP.

"It clearly wasn't wasted Jamie. I'm glad you hadn't needed to try anything. I've no idea how I would have felt, if that had been me, making that call." Dr Hunter had been very empathic, when the adrenaline had started to settle in everyone.

Jamie was glad in a way that Dr Hunter had seen Siobhan, whilst the anaphylaxis was in near full flow still. He wouldn't have wanted anyone to doubt whether it was a real anaphylaxis or not.

From the next day onwards, Jamie ensured there was always a couple of sterile large bore venous canulae in the house as well as an ampoule of adrenaline and some paediatric insulin syringes. He never again wanted to be helpless with no equipment.

He hid them in a part of the house, that Diane wouldn't search. Jamie didn't want her to know they were there. He wouldn't want to put pressure on his wife to make her think she would have to try to do, what Jamie wasn't sure he could have done himself.

The impact of this event was far reaching for Jamie. His increasing interest in Respiratory Medicine was nailed in this moment, not just focussing on respiratory medicine, but specifically focussing on allergy.

Siobhan was referred to a paediatric public health allergist. In part to determine if she could have the Measles vaccine, which was due imminently and it was questioned whether it could have egg contamination.

Siobhan eventually went on to have the vaccine, as a staged process, starting with a diluted dose, giving a tiny volume onto the skin. Before building up to a full dose. It went without mishap.

The energy and trouble Diane and Jamie put into to having a full vaccination strategy only left Jamie more exasperated, when patients and the media, talked about the adverse effects of vaccination and then gave associated campaigns any credibility.

Jamie had seen first-hand, the devastating impact of Measles, Mumps and Chicken-pox, when these illnesses were acquired in severe state, especially in adults.

Around the time of Siobhan's event, he was involved in a case of a mother, who was 6 months pregnant, who eventually died on the Intensive Care Unit of chicken pox, the baby dying with her, despite attempts to deliver the infant, at the moment of cardio-pulmonary arrest of the 35-year-old mother-to-be.

Chapter 30
Getting Covid: Having Covid
Day 1—The Perils of Doing Nothing

Jamie hated doing nothing. Although he could walk Isla in the fields, the concept of ten days of staying in the house and being forced to watch daytime television was a devastatingly depressing thought.

The first followers of the anti-vaccine campaign were being talked about in the media. It was being flamed by some clear and potentially genuine concern over thrombotic events post vaccine. Whilst it looked like these were going to be frighteningly rare, Jamie knew it might seriously hamper uptake.

Jamie recalled his fury and frustration over the reporting of the MMR vaccine in the 1990s. By some obscure feat of coincidental timing, the current anti-Covid-vaccine lobby was announced the same day that a prominent news and TV reporter was going to receive a royal honour.

Jamie remembered vividly this individual reporter's role in the MMR vaccine scandal.

It was in the mid-nineties, when Dr Andrew Wakefield had published twelve cases of autism diagnosed in children who had, had the MMR vaccine. There was no comparison group, just a list of 12 cases of autism and the fact that all had, had the vaccine at some stage in their childhood. At that time, the vast majority of children in the UK had the vaccination. As such a study that could even hint of a causal association, between the vaccine and autism, would have needed to be enormous, involving thousands of vaccinated and unvaccinated children, matched for age. A difference in the percentage of children with autism, between the two populations was the obvious scientific finding, which would have supported the claim.

No such data existed at the time.

Dr Wakefield fuelled by support from media reporters from the Daily Mail and BBC particularly, created a crisis of public confidence, which in the years since the first reports 31 years ago has probably resulted indirectly in the deaths of hundreds of children from measles and mumps, and many more with child deformity from maternal rubella in pregnancy all due to non-vaccination.

Dr Andrew Wakefield was later disgraced, for his role in potentially over-reporting a scientifically unsupported medical observation. His co-authors on the publication were also investigated by the GMC, though more leniently as they had not got involved in the media frenzy surrounding Dr Wakefield.

The major scientific journal 'The Lancet', which published the original case series, 'in good faith' later withdrew the article from publication, with a full unreserved apology.

The Daily Mail and the BBC never offered any substantial apology for their role in this scandal.

To Jamie's and many of his colleagues' surprise, the High Court overruled the GMC judgement and Dr Wakefield had his medical licence reissued.

Jamie found himself infuriated, this Monday morning lying on his settee, to hear that one of the key media reporters of the findings, massively over publishing trivial data was then announced recipient of such a prestigious award, coincidental with the start of anti-covid vaccine campaigning.

Jamie was in no doubt, that the seeds for the anti-covid-vaccine group, had their origins based in the events surrounding MMR.

In his anger, Jamie threw his TV control across the room, hitting the TV and narrowly missing Isla.

"Sorry babe! We will stick to music from now on!" He was additionally frustrated by his own inability to control his temper, so early in his 10 days of confinement. His irascibility would only increase over time, he knew.

Chapter 31
The SHO Years: More Life Events

Surprisingly it was not Sarah or Christine who finally took him over the edge of infidelity, but it was the surgical nurse, Angela.

Jamie had never responded after she had left her note the previous year. He had seen her intermittently since, when doing the numerous surgical consults for post-operative chest infections, blood clots and cardiac arrhythmias.

It was one of these visits, that triggered them meeting for a walk in the park one late afternoon, after flirting gently after the patient was sorted. Jamie amazed himself, by suggesting the walk. She was wearing the same perfume, he remembered from his time in surgery.

She had arrived at the park on a small yellow scooter. They wandered around the park three times talking of nothing and everything. Jamie took her hand half way around the second loop. She held it tightly. The weather was balmy, the birds were chirping gently in the trees and although the A6 was only a few hundred yards away, if felt like they were the only two alive.

After the third loop, he walked her back to her scooter. It was just as she moved to put her helmet back on before leaving, that Jamie took the opportunity to kiss her. She responded warmly.

After they broke the kiss, Angela took the reins in terms of organisation.

"Let me know what days you are on-call next week and I will come to your room after my shift, if you want me to?"

****

"Do you mind if I keep my stockings on in bed? I have veins and blemishes that I'm embarrassed about?" Jamie's long acknowledged weakness was being fuelled. She had come over as promised after her shift, still in her uniform and clutching her helmet and a bag with clothes to change into. Craig wasn't in the next-door room, as his shift pattern didn't match Jamie's, now they weren't working together.

There was no awkward embarrassed or difficult conversation. Angela took it as an assumed agreement that they were going to have sex in his single on-call bed. She started to undress as soon as she had declined a coffee he offered and had kissed him even more passionately than their kiss in the park. Her perfume encircled his brain and intoxicated him as her black curls fell around him.

Despite the risk of Jamie's bleep going off, especially his arrest team one, they made love slowly and gently at first, building up a passionate heat, but never spilling over into frenetic.

"I must go home, it's getting beyond reality for a late surgical crisis finish." She whispered into his ear, as they cuddled on top of the covers, entwined in post-coital relaxed reverie.

It was only later, that the pain came for Jamie. Not a physical pain, but just one of guilt and remorse racking his body and mind, preventing sleep.

Angela appeared to be able to enjoy the sex without carrying the sense of guilt after she went home to her partner, judging by their subsequent communication.

Jamie struggled to dissociate himself from the guilt, but never confessed to anyone of his infidelity, not even his best friend. His sex life with his wife had been good, even after their first baby, but the enthusiasm and openness that Angela brought to their shared moments was the biggest novelty. She also responded, when Jamie asked her what he could do better or more of, to increase her pleasure.

She taught a rather inexperienced but enthusiastic student a lot in just a couple of months. He would never forget her, even though they both agreed, it was best to 'stop, before it got too complicated'.

Chapter 32
The SHO Years: Wind-Ups Failing

Dr Coleman rang Jamie at a very inopportune moment to ask him to cover coronary care unit (CCU). He explained to Jamie that Bill, who Jamie and Duncan had met at the interviews, had gone off work sick and might be off for a few weeks, possibly months. Bill had been allocated CCU cover for the first six weeks of the year and was due to be on the CCU shift that day.

They had just done their first month at the heart and lung unit and were largely enjoying the experience. Jamie was back to giving intra-venous antibiotics at 6 a.m. during his on-calls as there were no house officers routinely on-call with them, as Dr Carey had warned him. However, just as Jamie had argued in his interview, he was coping with this relatively minor negative, but he and indeed all of the juniors appeared to be enjoying themselves.

Jamie had started with a ward team covering two consultants (Dr Brierley and Dr Coleman). He was revelling in the specialist unit feel of the place. It was already clear the difference between a general hospital where all the basic work was done, compared to a specialist unit, where at least half the work was of a truly expert nature. He had learnt so much respiratory medicine in just a few weeks.

Bill on the other hand, had been one of two juniors working on the CCU. They did a very unusual shift pattern of 48 hours on, then 48 hours off, meaning 3 and a half days off in a week. Jamie couldn't wait to do this shift pattern, but it appeared it hadn't suited Bill. Jamie felt guilty as he hadn't spent anytime chatting to Bill or finding out how he was coping with the novelty of the work and shift pattern, in those first few weeks.

Nothing was openly said, but Jamie worked out that this was his first experience of an actual colleague he was working with, suffering from the stress of the career and the life around it. It certainly wouldn't be the last. In the 1980s, however, medical professionals didn't 'accept' having stress at work. Life events maybe, but not just through work!

The reason it was such 'bad timing' for Jamie, was the trivial fact that he and the house officer 'Raj' had literally just set up a prank on Duncan. The three of them, Duncan, Raj and Jamie had become as thick as thieves in their first month together.

Duncan was good looking and had a boyish charm, but was currently single having just split up with his previous girlfriend. She was a secretary at the hospital Duncan had come to Baguley from and had not dealt well with Duncan moving hospitals. She had changed and become very 'possessive, needy and jealous' in his words. Duncan described it as a personality change and was clearly a 'red flag'. He did the only thing that was logical and broke the relationship off.

The consultants were generally excellent and supportive in Respiratory, whilst Jamie hadn't really had any dealings, with the cardiology ones yet, Dr Wallace excepted. The reports from his colleagues were that they were a little more aloof or distant. Dr Beardsall was a small in stature consultant with a ferocious temper, but already a worldwide reputation for novel approaches in 'electrophysiology'; the diagnosis and management of the electrics of the heart.

Jamie had already spent time in the early weeks making pals in switchboard again. Roger the chief switchboard operator was the friendliest, but they were all fun. Roger told Jamie of the day that the switchboard went on strike.

"Surely the hospital fell apart?" Jamie had asked, recalling his previous conversations with John and Margaret on the subject.

"Almost, and we were feeling so guilty, that we had decided we were only doing a day. We were actually in the switchboard room and we were doing the arrest bleeps, but nothing else." Roger had started the story. "However, a certain doctor decided to use the arrest call line to try and get a junior doctor to come to his ward."

"What did he do?" Jamie guessed this would be a male consultant.

"Rang the '222' number and asked me to call one of the junior doctors to the ward as there was a patient 'peri-arrest' apparently." He paused for breath. "So having done the bleep, I then went up to the ward and found the consultant and the junior, preparing to start the ward round. No emergency!"

"Bet that went down well with you," Jamie said, more to keep Roger talking.

"Thing is, we could put out a message like the arrest bleep one with sound. So, we did." He now imitated an electronic bleep voice. "Due to Dr Beardsall's abuse of the emergency bleep today, the switchboard strike has been officially extended to *forty eight* hours." Roger laughed to himself.

"Every doctor with a bleep heard that message."

"Hey, I'm only 2 years in and I know the line 'Don't fuck with switchboard'. It's obvious you are the ones we couldn't manage without. Did he ever apologise.?" Jamie was laughing now and cementing his good guy status.

"Nah did he fuck! Arsehole!" He used the swear words, much less freely than John, but he didn't hold back in his opinion.

"Small man syndrome!" were the final words on the subject as he turned back to get on with work. As Jamie looked around the room, one of the female switchboard operators first winked at him and then rolled her eyes. Keeping to his rules Jamie neither commented to Roger or the other operator.

****

Jamie hadn't worked on coronary care, but he guessed that Dr Coleman had chosen him as the one to fill in, as he was the most experienced and probably the only one, who had already done all the procedures, that might be required on a specialist Coronary Unit. He was hoping it wasn't Dr Beardsall as consultant in charge.

The timing of the bleep from Dr Coleman was uncanny. Jamie, who was sat with Raj over a coffee had just ordered a bunch of red roses through 'Interflora'. Raj paid for it on his credit card as if it was seen on Jamie's bill he might be in the sort of trouble, he had worked hard to avoid, during his short fling with Angela.

Jamie didn't let on to Raj about the past, just the fact of being married made him a little more vulnerable if a flower shop, showed up on a credit card bill.

Jamie did give Raj his share in cash. The roses were destined for Sally.

Duncan had talked non-stop about fancying the CCU nurse, since going to coronary care unit on his first on-call day, with an ED transfer. However, Duncan had not asked her out on a date, in the interim. Raj and Jamie had decided four weeks was enough and thought, perhaps foolishly that taking matters into their own hands was now a good idea.

Duncan had a mobile phone. Jamie was thinking about getting his first one, but they were so big and clunky, he wasn't quite convinced yet.

Duncan's ownership of a phone however gave Jamie and Raj the opportunity to put 'with love from a mystery admirer' and just the telephone number on the card.

****

"Just 'til five Jamie, then the on-call doctor will cover CCU overnight until we can get a more formal plan, perhaps with a locum in place." Jamie couldn't argue, with these instructions from Dr Coleman and was stuck on CCU until 5 p.m., prime time for the flower arrival.

Was life playing a trick on him Jamie wondered, for his bad behaviour of the last few months? He deserved it and much more of course.

As Jamie trudged reluctantly towards CCU, he realised he didn't know what Sally looked like and his next hope was that she wasn't actually there. Raj and he hadn't thought of checking to see which day she was on duty, unless of course, Raj was ahead of him.

April was the first nurse who Jamie met. He introduced himself. She had tight curly hair and clear blue eyes. Her waist was tiny Jamie noticed and she looked fabulous in her tight uniform. She didn't respond at all, to his smile and flirty eyes, when Jamie explained why he was there.

She gave him a list of jobs to do and he had to scribble fast even in his own code and learnt form of medical shorthand, to keep up.

Behind her came up another beauty, but this one was smiling.

"Give him a chance, April, or that pen is going to melt, or combust." Her voice was calm, but laced with humour and a deeper richness, despite her small frame.

Jamie looked into Sally's eyes and saw why Duncan fancied her. She was pretty, but had an aura about her. A blond version of Sarah, he decided. The patients would love her to be their nurse, he immediately recognised. Male or female, it wouldn't matter. Jamie flicked his eyes down to her left lapel, to check he was right with the assumption of her identity, but it was not a difficult conclusion.

These thoughts made him feel worse. She was going to be the collateral in their trick on Duncan.

Jamie had little experience with 'Interflora', but he knew they were planned for delivery that same day. Now he just prayed they came after 5 p.m. and he could have escaped before they arrived.

"Thank you for rescuing me, Jamie managed, trying to keep to his 'normal' script for meeting new nursing colleagues."

"Julie is in charge today. You better say hello to her too." Sally like April seemed impervious to Jamie's charm and had already broken eye contact and headed down to the nurse's station, which sat in the middle of the ten beds.

There were two bays of four beds each and two single side rooms. They were set out in an 'T' shaped fashion with a nursing station on the vertical arm. The side rooms directly behind the station. The entrance corridor went off beyond the base of the vertical 'T' connecting the nursing station to the main hospital corridor. Opposite the station, the CCU had its' own X-ray screening room, for doing pacemaker insertions. This was a major step up in technology from Stockport. However, there was no doctor's office as a separate space for Jamie to hide in. He was going to be stuck between patient beds and the nursing station as his only work portal. He even checked the screening room, to see if there was any usable desk to work on.

"We like you here, so we know where you are." Julie pointed at a chair at the end of the nurse's station, reading his mind. "We have three new admissions, the reg is already seeing one, but she will want you to get cracking on the other two, so she can get to clinic!" Julie was tall and a red head. Her voice, telling him what to do, was matter-of-fact. She was not as stunning as the other two, but 'business first' appeared to be their motto, even though they smiled continuously.

Jamie learnt almost immediately, that these specialist ward nurses knew 'their business' very well. They also were the first nurses Jamie learnt, that knew way more about their speciality than Jamie or most other junior doctors did. Coronary Care Unit at Stockport had a similar vibe, but the knowledge here at the specialist unit was massively advanced on what even the most experienced nurse at Stockport knew and yet the ones on duty were all mid-twenties at tops.

The day went quite quickly as Jamie was busy, but every movement on the entrance corridor had him snapping his head up, to see who was coming.

Jamie had already spoken to Raj at lunch, to see if they could postpone the delivery until a day when he wasn't personally there on CCU. Raj had laughed at Jamie's anxiety. "Come on it is great news. You can report on the nurses' reaction. What is the worst that can happen?"

Raj wasn't suffering from the anxiety of a wind up, that Jamie sensed was going to back fire on him personally.

He started to get optimistic as the afternoon went by. 4.30 p.m. came and went. Jamie was preparing to leave. He rang Gemima, who was on-call for the evening and night and told her the state of play, as she was taking responsibility from 5 p.m. At 4.45 p.m., the ward had gone 'quiet' and Jamie had done all the active jobs. He had just turned to the lead nurse Julie to ask permission.

"I might just head back to the respiratory wards and see if they are coping without me?" His voice was questioning and hopeful.

"Yes, of course! That seems fine. We can bleep you until five I presume, then it's Dr King?" Julie asked in return.

"Flowers for Sally Statham," the female voice spoke from the edge of the nurse's station.

'Interflora' lady had arrived, like a stealth bomber, clutching the largest bunch of red roses, Jamie had ever seen. Jamie's mouth was stuck in the open position trying to say 'yes' to Julie's question. Though Julie had lost complete interest in getting a response from Jamie at that moment.

Jamie hadn't even heard the door to the ward open, such was the silent entry of 'Interflora' lady. It didn't stay that way for long.

April squealed, having shown a quiet and professional demeanour all day.

Julie shouted, "Oh wow, how gorgeous are they!" Both leapt around the nurse's station to have a personal sniff.

Sally was nowhere to be seen.

"Oh my god, Sally, huge bouquet for you! It must be from Kostas," Julie shouted out loud, assuming Sally was somewhere near and would hear.

The name 'Kostas', was the first implication to Jamie, that Sally had a regular boyfriend. Nothing had been said during the day, that implied anything one way or another.

"Where is she?" followed on April, when there was no response to her loud-hailer powered voice.

"Oh, she took bed two, to the catheter lab!" Julie this time, with a disappointed voice, once she had recalled the reason for Sally's lack of response.

Relief flooded Jamie. He thought he could get up and slide out.

"Hey, Sally, looks like you are Miss Popular!" April had seen Sally walking towards them down the ward, wheeling the empty bed back with her.

"What's going on?" Sally sounded suspicious and cautious. She eyed the flowers with no enthusiasm, not knowing yet who they were sent for, let alone from.

"These are for you!" April was back in full enthusiasm mode. "They must be from Kostas."

'Interflora' lady decided perhaps unwisely to intervene.

"If he is an 'unknown admirer'?" her voice was positive. Her face changed at the silent response.

The silence was broken by April, with a rather newly subdued tone.

"Oh!" was the only word. She now seemed to be regretting her initial enthusiasm.

"Let's see the card, though the flowers are lovely!" said a hugely underwhelmed Sally. She took the flowers off the 'Interflora' lady, who clearly wasn't enjoying this delivery as much as she expected to.

The three nurses, then walked away from Jamie who was stranded, desperate to go, but leaving in a rush might look like a signal of involvement and responsibility. Instead, he pretended to have administrative jobs to do. He would have to walk straight through the trio, if he did make a break for it.

He eyed the nurses huddle, which fleetingly made him think of the witches' coven in MacBeth. He recalled his day on CCU, shortly after his premonition, not because in anyway, the three of them looked like witches, nothing could have been further from the truth. It was just the hushed babble, that Jamie could just about hear. It might as well as have been in a foreign language though, as he couldn't make out the words.

After a few minutes of chat, it was April who was sent back alone to speak to Jamie. She was sheepish. A tone Jamie had not heard all day.

"Jamie?" It was already a question. "Do you recognise this number?" Jamie's heart sank.

"Why?" he tried to keep his tone light, but realised this wasn't the best of reactions. He changed tack and met the challenge face on. "Perhaps it is mine! I would love to send flowers like that to a beautiful woman. I must try it one day! But then I don't have a mobile phone as it happens."

"This one, see!" April was now leaning towards him and showing the card. Despite his predicament, Jamie noticed a sweet intoxicating perfume, even subtly present at the end of a long shift. It reminded him of Angela's.

Hand-written, not in his writing, but it was his words and numbers, that Raj had spoken on the phone to 'Interflora' approximately seven hours ago. Duncan's number clear and obvious.

April looked at him. Jamie felt her eyes burn into him. He forced himself to lift his head and look her back, straight back, even forcing a smile.

"Though if I sent them here, they would be for you April of course." He tried his usual flirting approach.

"Is it Duncan Fulwell's number?" She was direct and ignoring all his tangential blocking of answering the obvious question.

Jamie twisted his mouth and eyes and forced his hands to stay still and not leap into his face.

"If it is, I've not rung it!" was the best he could come up with. Had he left enough time between the question and the answer he internally computed. It was likely to have been too quick.

Finally, he thought about his best reaction. Attack the best form of defence.

"I am really surprised Sally isn't excited to receive a bunch of flowers like that. What is the problem?"

"Oh, sorry! She is going out with Kostas, the son of Mr Dermapolous. Things have been a bit strained recently. I think she knew they weren't from him, but wished they were."

Jamie was crest fallen. Mr Dermapolous was one of the cardiothoracic surgeons. So much had gone wrong and now it transpired, they had sent flowers to Sally, when she was emotionally fragile. Jamie added guilt to the thick sludge of embarrassment, he was wallowing in, like an inebriated hippopotamus.

"Are you sure you don't know the number? Are you sure it's not Duncan Fulwell's?" This time Julie had come to join the inquisition.

"Not sure I know his telephone number. I know his bleep number if you want to ask him?"

The first half was clearly a lie and Jamie had finally started to lift his hand, with the destination being originally, to scratch his chin. He caught himself and managed to get it to his ear instead. But he sensed he had been fully rumbled with his poor body language.

Sally, didn't join in the discussion, but just eyed him from a distance.

Jamie cleared CCU as soon as he could and went off in search of Raj, partly to see if there was any work to do, but mostly to share his misery.

Jamie never found out if the three nurses, had actually gone as far a ringing Duncan's number, which had been Raj and Jamie's original expectation of what would happen. Then they hoped a bemused Duncan, would be stuck saying yes, but that he hadn't sent them.

How badly that plan had failed. Of course, throughout the day, Duncan had remained completely oblivious to what had transpired, though Raj spilled the truth to him the next day. Jamie didn't agree with that decision, but after the disaster of the previous day, nothing was going to redress the ineptly failed plan.

****

Bill never returned to work as a junior doctor on the heart and lung rotation. Next time Jamie heard about him, he was doing Psychiatry!

Sally ultimately married Kostas, but she barely spoke to Jamie again. Jamie acknowledged the blame was firmly placed on his shoulders. He resolved, that any future tricks needed, much more thought and preparation. He definitely, didn't want to hurt the innocent.

Chapter 33
The SHO Years:
Inappropriate Resuscitation

The arrest call had gone off and Jamie was staggered when it was for the ward he was on, currently behind a curtain with a patient. He came out from behind the curtains where he was talking to the giant retired policeman with emphysema.

Jamie had recently measured his chest diameter, a measure they sometimes used as a marker of damage. He had needed Olivia, the delightful and highly competent blonde staff nurse to help him. Mr Rigson, the giant policeman had the largest barrel chest, Jamie had ever seen. 'Liv' had needed to hold the tape measure twice, as Jamie took it around the outer circumference of Mr Rigson's chest.

They already had lung function test results. These had suggested that the volume of Mr Rigson's lungs in terms of total capacity (TLC) were equivalent to 14 and a half, one litre bottles of lemonade/cola in total volume. The tests could also work out, how much of that volume was actually working spongy lung tissue, that connected with the windpipe. This measure was only 2 litres (2 bottles). The rest of the volume within the space enveloped by the ribs, muscles and skin of the outer chest, was made up of what were called 'bullae' which are essentially pockets of air, wrapped in a bubble of lung tissue. Moving air into these areas, doesn't result in getting any of the oxygen into the body. The space didn't have the tiny air sacks, with a single blood vessel that need to be there, to allow the transfer of oxygen from the air to the blood. Instead, there was just the hole created by smoking cigarettes of tobacco or cannabis.

Later in his career, Jamie would explain this to patients, by saying that 'healthy lungs are a bit like a 'wispa' bar, where the air and chocolate were blended smoothly throughout the space. Emphysema was more like an 'aero' bar, where you were paying good money for a bubble full of nothing.

Emphysema was like a giant aero bar. It was just that Mr Rigson had 12 litres of these 'aero' bubbles and only 2 of 'wispa' bar.

Jamie had even asked Mr Rigson if he smoked cannabis. It was not well recognised that the type of damage in Mr Rigson's lung was much more likely to occur in cannabis smokers, compared to just tobacco smokers. It is roughly estimated that a single spliff does as much damage as somewhere between five hundred and a thousand conventional cigarettes. The surprising impact is believed to be caused by the temperature at which cannabis burns, compared to tobacco. Each high temperature particle effectively burning a hole wherever it lands.

Mr Rigson as a policeman was initially offended by the question, until Jamie explained why he had asked it. However, he then confessed to smoking up to a hundred conventional cigarettes per day for twenty years or so, during his career, which was enough of an explanation as Jamie needed.

Sadly, there was nothing Jamie or the consultants he worked for, could do to help Mr Rigson, other than support him through the chest infections, he got as a complication of having lungs which were so badly damaged. (Lung transplantation had not become an option at this time).

Mr Rigson wasn't even going to be a candidate for oxygen therapy.

When the arrest bleep had gone, Jamie had just finished his explanation to Mr Rigson, of why oxygen would make him feel better at the time, but over a longer period, it would weaken the breathing muscles and would statistically shorten his life expectancy, if they gave it to him.

"So, I'm buggered basically?" Mr Rigson had just said.

"I wish I could say something that disagreed with the choice of words, but actually, the one positive is that you aren't necessarily going to have a short life expectancy. Some people with lungs damaged like yours can carry on for many years. Especially if you quit the fags, completely."

Six rapid beeps (the cardiac arrest signal) were followed by 'cardiac arrest on B5 south'.

"You better go, Doc, hope that's not Frank." Jamie had already pulled the curtain right back. One of the auxiliaries was pulling the arrest trolley into the side room.

It wasn't Frank, who was another gentleman with Emphysema. Jamie had, had a similar chat with Frank, to the one he had just finished with Mr Rigson, just the day before. Frank's numbers just weren't quite as impressive and record breaking in the negative direction as Mr Rigson's. Frank had decided he would stop smoking and wanted help. Clearly Frank and Mr Rigson had become as thick as thieves themselves. Jamie would try and use this to persuade Mr Rigson to stop too.

"In there, Doc Jamie!" Frank shouted, helpfully. Clearly the information was redundant, from the direction of travel of staff and trolleys. Jamie had already closed the distance, to the side room where the commotion was already in good flow.

Liv already had the metal frame at the head of the bed detached and as Jamie skidded into the room, Liv jumped onto the bed and straddled the blue figure of the dying man.

Jamie knew from earlier in the day, that Mr Jamieson had been diagnosed with a severe pneumonia on the background of severe Parkinson's disease. His swallowing was inefficient and it was likely that the pneumonia was caused by food going down into the lungs instead of the stomach. A condition that they called aspiration pneumonia.

Jamie was momentarily distracted by the sight of Liv's thighs, encased in white stockings either side of the chest of the stricken patient. Her pink suspender belt and even white knickers were on full show to Jamie who had gone to the head end of the bed, to work on airway and breathing.

Although, Liv's position was not the recommended textbook position for delivering cardiac compressions, it was clearly effective at allowing cardiac output as by the time Jamie had retrieved his composure, he felt the pulse generated in the neck as Liv compressed, but at no other point. Jamie got the airway in that kept the mouth and palate apart, from the tongue to the larynx. This allowed him to start respiratory support using an 'Ambu' bag, timed to the cardiac compressions.

Jamie had performed intubation at many 'arrests' and considered himself reasonably efficient. Once he had started some adequate ventilation, he could attempt this, whilst waiting for the anaesthetist to arrive.

A detached part of Jamie's brain, was still relaying the movements of Liv in her chosen position and was perceiving them as lewdly sexual.

She was tiny in stature and he guessed she could not have affected efficient cardiac compression from a standing position without a bed, that lowered substantially more than this old frame did.

"Should we really be doing this?" Jamie started.

Immediately he regretted his loose choice of words, which his head replayed as being a little too sexual for his own comfort. What he really meant was the actual active resuscitation. "I mean it's futile," he added to be clear at least to himself what he meant.

"His wife wanted him resuscitated." Liv managed through panted breaths.

Jamie thought about this issue for perhaps the first time in a conscious way. Whilst it wasn't really time for an in-depth consideration, he realised it was a ludicrous concept, that a wife who wasn't anywhere near the scene, should decide, whether her husband died in this state of complete indignity, or was left to pass peacefully with some dignity maintained. It just didn't feel right to Jamie. He recalled the first death at Stockport and how Jon had dealt with it, when they had found the patient dead sat on the commode.

Other doctors were about to arrive and their job would be to start sticking needles in this patient's neck. He was going to have to suffer cardioversion, just in case he had gone into an electrical abnormal rhythm as the mode of arrest.

Jamie knew that even if they reversed the heart output, that the patient had zero chance of surviving the event, as there was no respiratory reserve or physical strength, to combat the impact of the arrest itself.

Jamie fully believed in resuscitating people with reversible illness. Examples he thought of were electrocutions, drownings, cardiac arrhythmias in people with otherwise fit bodies, allergic reactions and even treatable blood clots, but Mr Jamieson, was dying of Parkinson's disease.

When Jamie got old and frail, he would have 'do not resuscitate me' tattooed on his own chest. For himself, he didn't want any of his family members or even an over-zealous doctor putting him through the humiliation of this, in the foolish and ridiculous hope that a younger and fitter version of their dying relative/patient was miraculously going to appear from the aftermath.

The paradox was that visually speaking, Mr Jamieson was being given the ride of his life by Liv of course. This however didn't negate the absolute futility of what was being done.

For Jamie, the thought was even worse, if you considered it possible to perfuse and oxygenate the brain enough, that the dying patient had some awareness of the pain of the needles to come or worse of the electrocution that would also follow.

Even hearing the frantic voices of the doctors and nurses, talking of the next steps of the pathway or when to stop, was a sickening wasteful option of how to manage a dignified passing.

Jamie thought about his own father who had died at home just a few months before of a pulmonary embolism. His death was peaceful. No one resuscitated him. The only shock was for his mother who came into the room in the morning, from the spare room she had slept in recently, to see him long dead in his sleep.

Jamie was glad he personally hadn't even had to witness the death or even the body of his dead father, as the ambulance had already collected the body before Jamie had made it to his mother's side. The cause of death came from a post-mortem, as it was 'an unexpected death at home'. This Jamie also considered of dubious value.

All these musings crossed Jamie's thoughts as he went through the customary and practiced, but entirely futile last acts, for poor Mr Jamieson.

****

Fifteen minutes later, Jamie was talking to a tearful Mrs Jamieson, who had made it to the hospital in twelve minutes from when the auxiliary rang her. On the phone, she had been told that her husband had 'taken a turn for the worse', which was the medical standard code for 'cardiac arrest' or a similar catastrophic event.

"I'm really sorry, Mrs Jamieson, we did try to resuscitate him, but with the pneumonia and Parkinson's disease and his 88 years, he was never going to have the strength to come back." Jamie told her the facts, as straight as they needed to be.

"I'm so glad you tried at least. Now I can rest with the thoughts that everything was done to try and bring him back." In those words, spoken quite innocently, were the reason, so many resuscitation attempts were performed for no justifiable reason. Jamie knew it was being done to assuage the guilt of the living, not the dignity of the dying.

However, he knew this wasn't the time for anything other than condolences, with the dead man's widow.

When he had time to reflect on it, Jamie did wish that television medical programmes would show the brutal truth of a cardiac arrest. Not the fairy tale: 'hello darling, thanks Doc' images that were shown on these programmes for the masses to believe, when a single electric shock brought someone back to normality in minutes.

(Jamie got even more infuriated in years to come when James Bond was shown to defibrillate himself and then be fit enough to drive a sports car to chase villains, just minutes later. Worse still, he went back to give the beautiful heroine come villain, a come to bed look and take her there just a few hours later).

"He is at peace now." Jamie said customary words, but wasn't sure this was the best choice, for someone who had shaken every second of his life, for at least the last 5 years. He was however, relieved that he hadn't used either of the alternatives: 'rest' or 'still'.

Once done with the necessary condolences, Jamie went into the office to write the records for both Mr Jamieson (deceased) and Mr Rigson.

Liv had a cup of tea ready for him. Sister Hunter had just returned from what must have been a lengthy lunch break. Jamie knew she would have been relieved to have missed the action. Sister Hunter was tall and thin and clearly still smoked herself and whilst she ran a tight ship, she wasn't one for being knee deep in the action herself. There was a lingering odour of stale cigarettes in the room.

Jamie's parents had both smoked all his life and he understood the difficulties of giving up addiction. However, he was appalled by the staff who continued to smoke, whilst working on the lung wards, with the vivid truth of death from lung cancer, chronic bronchitis and emphysema or those on the vascular wards, looking at the amputations or gangrenous feet, all caused by smoking. It amazed Jamie, the huge numbers of staff at every level of seniority, still smoked and worked in the environments, when he was a junior doctor.

"Are you ok Jamie?" Liv was asking him, when he was lost in his thoughts.

"I've just about recovered!" Jamie replied with full honesty.

"Do you not like resuscitation? Or is talking to the family that's the problem, though you do it so well?" Jamie realised she hadn't worked out what his meaning had been.

"Actually, it was trying to concentrate on the tasks, whilst watching you, that I've only just recovered from." He looked up and caught her blue eyes and watched her blush. The room was L-shaped and she was stood near the door.

"It's the easiest way I find to do it, with being so short. I can't get an output if I stand by the bed, the angles are just wrong."

"Don't stop for me, but bear in mind, I will be running even faster the next time there is an arrest on here." Jamie laughed carefully. He didn't want to change her style. "I'll want to ensure I get the head end action every time, where the angles are just perfect."

"Well, I've achieved something today then, Dr Carmichael, if I can make you run faster to arrests." She turned and headed down the ward, pleased and smiling at her own riposte.

"More than you imagine!" Jamie said under his breath, mostly to himself.

"She is engaged to a very nice man!" Jamie was startled by the voice. She was around the corner of the L shaped room and Jamie hadn't seen Sister Hunter there and was mortified that she had heard the entire conversation.

"Sorry, Sister Hunter, I hadn't realised you were there."

"Glad I was, just in case Liv wants to press sexual harassment charges." Jamie knew Liv wasn't offended and that Sister Hunter had a playful tone to her voice too, but it made him think of his reaction to Wayne.

"Fair cop!" he replied, hoping Sister Hunter was actually just teasing him.

Chapter 34
The SHO Years: More Crazy Resuscitation Attempts

Although on-calls were fairly busy and Jamie didn't have a House Officer when on-call, the pressures overall were not quite as intense as at Stockport.

On his next on-call weekend, Jamie had been quiet enough, to make a foolish mistake of risking having a bath, mid-weekend.

The Baguley Hospital mess, didn't have a functional bar, perhaps more because there was a pub almost within the grounds of the hospital at the time, not that Jamie fancied the spit and sawdust style.

The mess, did have a snooker table though, but also a bath, that was enormous and the water supply was endless.

The bath was run in minutes and Jamie had just soaked and cleaned himself, but was still wallowing in the water, when his next arrest call bleep went off.

Jamie had never tried to put clothes on in a rush, when wet before. It was a greater challenge than he had imagined, even ignoring the underpants and socks, pushing them in his white coat pocket. He buttoned his shirt as he ran, his white coat in his teeth at first.

The call was for B7 ward. This ward was a converted sanatorium and all the beds were in single or double rooms off a long corridor. You could easily spot the changes in structure, where the outside wall of the rooms had been walled in and windowed.

In their original form, the wall opposite the corridor would have been open to the elements.

Jamie had already learnt much of the history from Dr Coleman. It was believed forty or fifty years before that fresh air helped heal tuberculosis. There was no lasting scientific evidence for this, or really for any of the treatments that were tried for tuberculosis (TB), before antibiotics came along. The first effective antibiotic was called streptomycin and allegedly was one of the most painful injected treatments to date and had to be given into deep muscle. However, almost from the start of this treatment through to the modern oral agents, tuberculosis became a curable disease from being a largely incurable one. Sadly, for many reasons, multi-drug resistant strains may change this in the mid twenty-first century.

Jamie had, had the pleasure of meeting some of the sanitorium survivors of past treatments, who were mostly under Dr Coleman, who appeared to have acquired a large cohort of such cases.

Jamie loved talking to them when they were inpatients and hearing of their stories of being in this hospital or other sanatoria.

His favourite story was how they climbed out of the open windows and shinned down the drain pipes to sneak off to the chip shop a mile away, buying 'a poke' of chips for as many of the 'inmates' as they could carry.

One of the other beliefs about TB in the mid twentieth century, had been that if you could rest the affected area of lung, then the TB would heal. This led to intriguing surgical attempts and procedures, that caused some of the most fascinating X-ray changes, Jamie would ever see.

His favourite purely because of the name (derived from French) was called 'plombage'. Small balls about the size of table tennis balls were surgically inserted under the ribs, squashing the lungs down, in the area of lung, where the TB was active. On the X-ray, one lung and the ribs all looked normal. However, there were the visible rings of the balls creating white circles beneath the ribs, just looking exactly as you would imagine, from the description of the treatment.

Other of these approaches, included the process of breaking 4 or 5 ribs at the front and the back and essentially twisting the ribs around 180 degrees, still in their position. The result was the ribs bent inwards rather than arcing around. This again squashed the lung in the affected area and was called 'Thoracoplasty'. These patients, had deformed chests and it was intriguing that they also later developed scoliosis as a result of the loss of symmetry of the chest.

Finally, and the rarest to Jamie's experience (in survivors), was the use of the technique of artificial pneumothorax. A needle was placed through the chest to find that narrow space between lung and chest wall (between the two layers of pleura). Next air was pumped into the space, to create a medically induced pneumothorax. The intention was again to squash the lung down, this time temporarily as it would resolve over time.

The repeated procedures, resulted in trickles of blood dripping down the back wall of the inside of the chest from where the needle went in. Over time this caused some calcium to form, within the blood spots. The final effect of the calcified spots could be seen on the X-ray as a permanent mark of this treatment approach. The little calcified drops, were given the delightful and descriptive name of 'teardrop calcification'.

Dr Coleman, had a wonderful collection of X-rays stored from these patients, which Jamie loved perusing as well as listening to Dr Coleman's and his patients' stories.

****

Jamie ran to B7, still wet through, looking at the changed architecture as he approached.

B7 had been converted into a standard respiratory ward and actually comprised 2 wards (B6 was below). Jamie had to run up the stairs and along the corridors as the auxiliary, who had been allocated the role, pointed him in the right direction for the side room of interest.

Jamie was still dripping water from his hair, as he ran around the corner of the doorway. The medical SHO and house officer had not surprisingly beaten him to the scene. The first thing Jamie saw, was that the enormously obese patient was lying on the floor.

Jamie skidded on a huge puddle of fluid as he ran in the room. The medical SHO had the enormous patient's chest exposed, defibrillator paddles were in place. Most concerning was the fact that the patient was on the floor, lying in the fluid, which Jamie had skidded in and now realised, that it was a very large volume of vomit.

Jamie guessed, that the patient had, had a gastric dilatation, caused when the stomach doesn't empty. The volume of food and fluid (mostly fluid in this case) becomes substantial. What Jamie didn't know is whether the vomiting of the entire contents of the stomach had provoked the arrest, or whether the vomiting was secondary as the patient crashed to the floor.

The medical SHO, two nurses and the medical house officer had started resuscitating the patient, where she lay, in the vomit. The SHO was kneeling in the fluid, the house officer and one nurse, were stood leaning over, getting ready to fire the defibrillator.

Jamie did two things instantly.

One was to take a single stride and followed it with a forward, double pike, with a twist. This manoeuvre, brought him neatly to rest on to the window sill effectively clearing himself of direct contact with the vomit.

The second, was to scream 'STOP'. He screamed it louder than any voice he had ever used, outside of his visits to Maine Road, where Manchester City played football in the 1980s.

Jamie wasn't offended by the vomit, for the record. Well, it wasn't his prime motivation, let's say.

"What, why?" shouted the medical SHO nearly as loudly as Jamie' voice. She was not happy to have Jamie arrive and shout at her so vehemently.

Jamie didn't know her, but in that minute, he realised that he didn't want to. She might have passed exams, but even when challenged, she couldn't work out how dangerous an act she was not just considering, but was just about to execute.

"If you press that defib, you will electrocute everyone in touching distance of the fluid and you are the one kneeling in it!" Jamie's voice still urgent, but he had dialled back the decibels.

The two nurses, immediately stood back and the one nearest to him even came and joined Jamie on the windowsill. The second looked at the floor and backed away out the door until she was fully clear of the puddle. Jamie knew her as Michelle, they had gotten on really well in the first few weeks, as Michelle was the life and soul of the ward and had an incredible way of chatting to the patients, with professionalism and fun combined.

"Imagine petrol and a lit match." Jamie used a recently experienced analogy to try and help. "However, it's your call, but you are on your own!" Jamie looked straight at the remaining doctor, who was supporting her senior, but looking like she had split loyalties.

"But the resus guidance says we should shock her." Jamie rolled his eyes at the response.

He came to hate the word 'guidance' and all they came to stand for, during his full medical career. They were always written with the best of intentions, specifically to standardise practice. Over time, medical professionals, started to give up on intelligent thinking and interpreted 'guidance' as if they were 'rules'. Rules never to be broken, even when common-sense told you in that moment, that they were incorrect and even dangerous. Jamie knew this arrest moment, was a very good example of why guidance was indeed guidance. (Cambridge

English Dictionary abbreviated definition for 'guidance': 'Help and advice about how to deal with a problem').

"The **laws** of physics, tell you not to press that button! Still your call, though!" Jamie stressed the 'laws' word. He already knew any attempt to save the patient was long gone, the time delay caused by the impasse had taken away the final 0.01% of a chance the patient had in the first place.

The SHO was by now paralysed with confusion. She wanted to follow the guidance, which she believed 100%, this part was clear. Jamie however had challenged her and the nurses had followed his lead.

Jamie decided to offer an olive branch and an escape route for her.

"If we put her up on the bed, then you can defib her, to make you feel better, though she is clearly dead and as I will be doing the death certificate, I'm going to time the death as at least 5 minutes ago!" The olive branch wasn't given sweetly.

The SHO took the compromise and they agreed to get the patient on the bed. Just as they were getting the patient on the bed, the anaesthetist on-call arrived. She was a senior anaesthetist and Jamie wondered if they had other emergencies going on at the same time.

****

Fifteen minutes later, when the Medical SHO finally accepted defeat, they started to pack up. The anaesthetist who had spotted the fluid on the floor asked Jamie, if they had tried to 'shock' her on the floor.

His medical colleague was still in the room, so Jamie used a sidebar voice, though he was sure his new enemy would still have heard his words.

"No! I stopped that, I was a bit late arriving, as I was in the shower."

Jamie said shower rather than bath as it was accepted that showers were necessary even during a 48-hour shift, which this weekend was for Jamie. Bath's might have been considered an unnecessary luxury.

"Thank fuck! You would have blown yourselves up." Jamie didn't speak in response to the anaesthetists take on matters, but was naturally pleased an independent referee had come into the argument unknowingly and sided with himself. Silence was now the right approach.

"I'm off to ring the 'relies'." Jamie filled the silence and went to continue the necessary jobs.

He was nearly done, when Michelle brought him a coffee.

"That's for arriving on a white stead. I'm glad you did. We hadn't thought of the vomit."

"Sorry I was late, I was actually in the bath, so I was wet anyway and even more sensitive to the risk," Jamie replied to the grateful nurse.

"Glad you told me that as I wondered why you had a pair of boxer shorts in your white coat. I thought it might be a new fashion statement." Michelle was giggling through her announcement.

Jamie looked down and, couldn't believe that one of the legs of his boxers, were actually hanging out, with his stethoscope.

"Oh my god!" Jamie was mortified. He rapidly pushed the pants and socks to the bottom of his pocket below the stethoscope and other paraphernalia.

"Thought that bitch was going to press the button anyway." Michelle, spared his blushes and rapidly changed tack. The words were said with real venomous feeling.

Jamie didn't want to support the defamation of a colleague, but he couldn't disagree entirely.

"I thought she might do it anyway. Just goes to show you can pass all these fuckin' exams, but you can't teach common-sense." Jamie resorted to indirect criticism. These final words he went on to speak on many occasions during his medical career.

He tidied up the notes and then went back to his on-call room, to do the same to himself.

Chapter 35
Getting Covid: Having Covid Day 1

"Hope all is good and it is just a mild dose. It should be you are fit and slim." If Jamie had had five pounds for every time someone had commented on his physique in the last four hours, he could have sent Colonel Tom, quite a sizable donation to his charity.

This was Akila Kismal, one of the physician associates. She had worked with him on the Covid wards and was personally responsible for keeping them open, during the first phase. The 'wise owls' in the patient flow office had decided, to juggle wards around at six hours-notice.

The new additional Covid ward, which Akila was going to work on, was vacated by surgery. The previous tenants stripped the ward bare of computers, oxygen points and even the drugs trolley. This left the new ward team, four hours to get the ward equipped for the arrival of patients.

No porter time had been allocated and none of the additional computers, drugs trolleys or oxygen points had been ordered, let alone arrived.

There wasn't even a doctor's office, as the surgeons used their own offices nearby and weren't giving those up, even in a time of crisis.

Akila had come to the rescue, with all of her organising and persuasion skills. The ward was almost safe to use, when it was officially opened. A cleaner's cupboard was transformed into a doctor's office with 3 computers, which Akila had 'acquired'.

No one other than Akila, knew how she had got them and had them installed in just three hours. She even set the printers up herself as IT were 'overwhelmed'.

Patient flow in all their wisdom, then moved ten patients into the ward from other functioning wards in the middle of the first night, so there was 'a spread of empty beds'. This meant that a ward that had been staffed as a low dependency non-covid ward, admitted ten sick patients within a two-hour period, in the middle of a night shift. One trained nurse working with only support workers, had to shoulder the burden, single handed.

The next day, Jamie and Dan had been the only ones to create a fuss and describe the decisions and actions as both 'highly dangerous' and 'nonsensical' in an email to the chief executive and medical director.

The email 'requested', that lessons were learnt and a similar event must 'never happen again'.

Jamie received no reply to his email from the senior management team.

Sadly, no lessons were learnt. Just three months later, a similar switch of wards was done again at zero notice, involving the same ward team.

Jamie was even more irate the second time. In incandescent rage, he had even threatened to inform the BMA, the Nursing Professional Councils, for the individual Matrons, who had made the decisions. He also hinted that he might even inform the media. The latter was a dangerous threat and indeed Jamie would himself never have involved the media. He despised and distrusted the media, far more than senior management, but he hoped the latter didn't know this.

Whilst Jamie's colleagues watched with partial amusement and gave him moral support, middle management reacted in horror. Jamie had to go alone the second time. It was much easier to make waves when you were about to retire. It wasn't going to be in Dan's interests, to be seen as a trouble maker at this stage of his career.

Indeed, this action of patient flow, was the final straw for Jamie's career and within a fortnight he had decided on his date for final retirement in May 2021, when he calculated the second wave would be over.

He had long intended to 'retire and return' to part time working for up to two years before stopping completely, but the pandemic delayed this plan, with the onset, coming almost right on the date of his original planned partial retirement date.

Naturally both he and the Trust didn't want a senior respiratory doctor, reducing hours at that precise moment. After the first wave, the plan was further scuppered by some paper work issues, that were proving very complex to sort, in order for him to be signed-off for the new contract at reduced hours.

He had worked substantially more than full-time in the last year, with the extra shifts required to cover colleagues off with covid, or with contacts testing positive.

The year of working beyond full-time, combined with the progressive stupidity of patient flow controlling the hospital, was enough and Jamie realised it was time to go.

In Jamie's ongoing battle with patient flow, the main verbal support he got was from the ground troops and junior doctors. Akila, was particularly proactive in supporting his actions.

They had observed Jamie as being the one senior staff member to stand up for them, even though the juniors had no idea of the actual content of Jamie's letters and High Incident Risk reports.

One of the things Jamie talked endlessly to his colleagues about, was how in the first two months of the pandemic, when all the difficult work was being done preparing for a 'war-zone', that no one could imagine, then it was the doctors and nurses at the front line who made all the decisions.

During this early crisis phase, senior management was almost entirely absent from the wards or clinical areas. Certainly, any 'leadership' activity, was entirely made from the bunkers and was not seen, where the doctors and nurses believed at the time, that they were putting their personal and families' lives on the line.

Further evidence of this ludicrous mentality was demonstrated to Jamie, when the vaccine roll-out came to the hospital.

The first individuals to be vaccinated in Jamie's hospital, were the senior management and patient flow team.

'It is critical we keep effective management as our priority', was the rationale, published in the weekly blog. Jamie was offered his first dose of vaccine more than 6 weeks after the chief executive, chief nurse and medical director, allegedly had theirs.

Jamie was too embittered at this point to make a fuss. The junior doctors on the covid wards and ward nurses, were even later still.

"You do know, Dr Carmichael, it is you who inspired all of us, to keep going through all the craziness of the first few months?" Akila started telling him on the phone, when she had heard he was off with proven Covid.

"I can't believe that, Akila. You were just awesome!" he responded, turning the praise back to his junior colleague.

She carried on, undaunted. "You might not remember that Monday, when it all kicked-off. You were just back on our ward cover for a week. You gave us this rallying call about us going into battle against a foe, we cannot yet imagine or see the whites of its' eyes. But you said: 'it is what we had trained for and signed up to'. You said it was 'our duty, to do the very best job we could at every moment in the months to come'." Akila was almost crying as she talked so passionately about something, that Jamie had indeed forgotten very effectively.

"We all remembered it and still talk about it, to this day," she added and Jamie was genuinely wiping away a tear himself. Fortunately, she changed the subject, "Anyway, I was the designated one to ring you, when we heard the news. We are all rooting for you. All the Nurses and Juniors wanted you to know."

Jamie could barely speak to thank her. "I will be fine. You know I am tough as old boots!" He was rolling out the old cliches with every phone call of good wishes he got.

****

In these early hours after his diagnosis, Jamie had lots of organising to do. He left Tom and Shanaz in charge of the clinical side.

He had been particularly impressed by the efficiency of the virtual ward. A team set up and run by Bushra, his office colleague. Her skill had always been in organisation and quality improvement and it was no surprise to Jamie that a service that didn't exist ten months ago, was the pride of the North West and just about to win a box full of awards.

Bizarrely, Jamie didn't have his own pulse oximeter. He of course needed one, at home on this Monday morning, when his flow test came up positive.

He rang the virtual ward and the one piece of equipment he needed, was with him within an hour. It was delivered by a sensible taxi driver, who put the box down outside the 'leprous house' and ran. Just waving long enough to be sure he had to delivered to the right address.

Jamie wanted the oximeter. He wouldn't take any specific treatment unless or until, he was admitted to hospital. However, the oximeter would allow him to plot his clinical status over the coming days and give hm some advance warning if he was in the danger territory with low oxygen levels.

He would also be able to judge the right time to admit himself, if he was one of the unlucky ones who got bad enough to need admission.

****

Jamie loved patterns. Patterns of symptoms, signs, observations or blood results.

So many of Jamie's colleagues looked at absolute numbers, high/low, positive/negative, acid alkali…to name but a few.

Jamie saw the patterns of results as massively more useful and though he had hated the change from paper records/results to computer ones at first, he later saw the huge advantage of looking at numbers by trends on the computer.

Picture graphs gave this information vividly and Jamie insisted on using the older of the 2 computer systems available at his hospital, as the graphs, that could be pulled up at the click of a button, were visually clearer and therefore more helpful.

The juniors got used to this foible and after a few interesting cases, where the graph, gave an answer that a single result couldn't, they were largely convinced.

Today, he wanted to study his own pattern of oxygen levels. He even contemplated finding some graph paper and making his own day-to-day chart, so any trend over time was visually clear to him. He made do, with jotting numbers down for now.

Jamie knew that Covid-19, had not played by the rules. In the first few months, just about everything you might have predicted, if you used other viral illnesses such as influenza as the model and then applied logic: it pretty much all later proved to be incorrect.

Jamie had expected and shared with colleagues his prediction, that the steroid arm of the early trial of treatment options would do worse than nothing (because it supressed the immune system), but it turned out to be the winner.

They had also as a team, expected that their severe asthma patients would do much worse than the average, age and sex matched individual, just like what happened, if they got flu.

This prediction for their patients was clearly incorrect from their observations, even early in the first wave.

Long before any data came through (from trials and huge datasets), Jamie and his colleagues had changed their minds and reported the low incidence of severe Covid outcomes in their own asthma patient cohort. The combination of their own observation and the protective benefit of Dexamethasone when the first trials were released led Jamie and his colleagues to postulate, that perhaps inhaled steroids had a protective effect against the worst outcomes from Covid-pneumonia.

Later in the year, the epidemiologists from all over the world demonstrated a reduced risk of hospitalisation, death and ICU level care being needed for individuals with asthma. Indeed, this data, suggested that asthma was the only chronic disease, where there appeared to be a protective effect against the worst outcomes of covid. Many authors, were by then postulating a protective effect of inhaled steroids.

It amazed Jamie, this data had never really made headline news. It was another example of how only bad news got reported on the front pages or in the main news bulletins. Good news was buried.

Finally, a study of giving inhaled steroids to individuals who didn't have asthma at the time of the diagnosis of Covid was performed. Half the participants got inhaled steroid and half got inhaled placebo in this study. The risk of hospitalisation was reduced 10-fold, in the group who had the active steroid inhalers, when compared to the placebo group. This staggeringly positive, if small study, merited a couple of paragraphs in one of the broad sheet newspapers only and as far as Jamie could work out, that was it, in terms of media coverage.

He tended to know what was trending in the newspapers or social media, not because he read it himself, but because, he got asked a question 15 times in a single day, by clinic patients whenever such news was trending.

Looking back at where trends had helped him, Jamie openly admitted he was cynical when the first reports of 'proning' as a benefit came through. (The phrase 'proning' was coined during the pandemic to describe getting patients to lie on their tummy when breathless and hypoxic with covid).

Once he tried it on new admissions, it only took 2 patients' computer graphed observation charts to demonstrate the pattern of improved oxygen saturation levels and Jamie was convinced and used and promoted it aggressively.

Jamie noticed another pattern, that didn't get the same, widespread support. It appeared to Jamie that the more supplemental oxygen that was given to a breathless patient, the faster they deteriorated. Jamie was convinced to keep target oxygen levels for patients in the lower reaches of the normally recommended range was the ideal aim.

There was one previous medical equivalent of this concept, which had been scientifically confirmed. Jamie remembered well the patient he looked after as a registrar who had a condition called 'Bleomycin lung'. This rare condition was a fibrosis reaction within the lung, which occurred in a small percentage of people receiving a cancer chemotherapy containing the agent Bleomycin.

It had historically been used in children for certain brain cancers. When Jamie was a student/junior doctor, one of his senior Manchester colleagues had done research, showing the interaction between the drug induced fibrosis and high oxygen concentration, which made the fibrosis worse.

A few years later Jamie had been on-call and was visiting the cancer hospital as a respiratory consult for advice, it was the one and only time he made this diagnosis. The patient had received Bleomycin for a form of lymphoma and was in his forties at the time.

The only options for treatment Jamie had, was to stop the Bleomycin and try giving steroids, though there was no evidence the latter influenced the course of the disease. The key treatment was to use either no oxygen or as little as possible, if this was a rare reaction to the drug. Naturally, medical and nursing staff, normally correct low oxygen levels aggressively and aim to get the percentage of oxygen saturation in the blood, up to those of a normal individual.

The concept of not following this normal behaviour was almost unique and was therefore, very hard for staff to stick to.

Jamie had to actively visit the ward, during every nursing shift for the next 72 hours, to explain, why they were not following normal protocols and giving oxygen to fully reverse the hypoxia. Jamie had engaged his patient, who he later called 'Dan the Harley Man' (he rode Harley Davidsons as his hobby). Jamie managed to keep him off oxygen completely initially, despite Dan being breathless. Later, Dan became temporarily more breathless, so that a little oxygen was needed for a short time. Jamie gave the lowest possible level of additional oxygen.

Despite his regular visits, four times in two days, Jamie came back to find the nurses or cancer doctors had put the supply of oxygen back up, going against his extensively written instructions.

Jamie counted Dan as one of the cases, where he had genuinely saved a life. Dan survived, but still had quite extensive permanent lung damage. He went on to complete chemotherapy, obviously without further Bleomycin and was later cured of his lymphoma.

Jamie had later taken over his case, when he became a consultant as Dan had sequelae of the fibrotic damage that required long term follow-up.

Despite the restrictions on his life, Dan and his wife, knew they had been given an extra 20 years, during which Dan 'got on his bike and rode' many, many times more. He had finally died of heart disease, just a few weeks before Jamie's illness. Jamie would have gone to Dan's funeral if there was an option, they had become more than just Doctor and patient over the years.

Remembering Dan's case was perhaps the reason Jamie considered this possibility of further deterioration with more oxygen supplementation.

Jamie even postulated his theory, to his ICU colleagues. He argued it was possible that this fibrotic enhancing effect of oxygen, could be the reason, why those who got to ICU took a very long time to reach a disease plateau and if lucky, to come off life support machines. That is, if they were in the small sub-group lucky enough to survive at all.

Jamie managed to modify the normal oxygen guidelines within his trust during the first wave. He convinced his colleagues that aiming for 'normal' oxygen levels as they would do for other 'pneumonias' or immune conditions (other than Bleomycin lung), was at the very least delaying discharge, as well as using excess oxygen, for which supplies had been a concern. These arguments held partial traction, even if everyone wasn't convinced that it was improving chances of survival.

Jamie was convinced enough by his observations, that if he was admitted himself, he would want to control his own target saturations and take the lowest amount of oxygen he could get away with. Patient autonomy, would be his weapon. Giving him a treatment, he didn't want (more oxygen), would be considered as assault, if done against his wishes. At least until he was unconscious, Jamie would be in control, but Jamie didn't fancy his own chances if he lost autonomy, because of the need for anaesthetic for invasive ventilation. Survival once admitted to ICU was frighteningly low in overall percentage terms and much lower than they saw with standard pneumonias or flu for example.

Another pattern Jamie spotted early in the first wave and later convinced all his local colleagues when national and international data supported the view, was the huge amount of blood clots that occurred in people with covid pneumonia.

Most of the ones they saw in their respiratory wards were not surprisingly pulmonary emboli as a complication of Covid. However, the vascular surgeons were also seeing infarction (loss of blood supply due to clot in arteries) in arms and legs in the post covid setting. Other Physicians, were seeing clots in relation to Covid infection in arteries, in other parts of the body as well. These rates much higher than the rare events occurring post vaccination.

These clots in lungs legs and other parts of the body, were occurring in people even on preventative anticoagulation. Jamie had told every one of his colleagues, that if he was admitted, he wanted to be fully anticoagulated from day one. Jamie knew well the very small and rare negative risks of anticoagulation, having needed such treatment prior to a heart procedure a few years ago. Fortunately, at that time, Jamie only needed anticoagulation for a few months. However, it gave him clear personal insight into the genuine, but statistically low risk of anticoagulation.

On the contrary, the risk averse culture of modern medicine, meant that a medically induced complication carried more negative weight, than the risk of disease associated complication. As a result, the decision on how much anticoagulation is given to patients during Covid infection, remained controversial.

Jamie, would go against guidance, if the worst occurred and he needed hospitalization. It wouldn't be the first time for sure.

Chapter 36
The SHO Years: Specialist Respiratory Clinics

Jamie got to do clinic every week for the first time. He had done them occasionally with both Dr Lorimer and Dr Firman, but getting to them was dependent on how busy the wards were, in his earlier years.

He enjoyed the patient load most in Dr Carey's clinic, as the patients were mostly those with allergic asthma.

The patients, were initially, never keen to see Jamie. He knew he still had the look of a student, age-wise; rather than an experienced doctor. Whilst Jamie wasn't in his own words 'experienced', he was very keen to test his skills in the clinic environment. He worked hard to engage the patients from the start, always shaking hands and making strong eye-contact.

As he later taught students, the medical information gathering started, as soon as the name was called. He watched the body language, the pattern of breathing, the way they walked (gait), even in those few seconds as they crossed the waiting room.

Then the shake of the hands was the next moment of significant information gathering. The strength of the grip, any tremor, the warmth or even heat and possibly nervousness or anxiety from the timidity and clamminess, could all be felt at that first physical contact.

The handshake also started the bond with the patient.

Christine French was one of the first patients Jamie met in specialist clinic. She clearly loved Dr Carey and was openly disappointed, when Jamie called her name from the waiting area.

"I will go and discuss you with Dr Carey and who knows, he might pop his head in." Jamie was already instinctively anticipating his boss. She worked in retail and Jamie was particularly pleased to hear she specialised in hosiery.

He chatted about her job and how her asthma affected her. Her employer loved her and didn't mind when she took a few days off, with a flare of her asthma.

Like so many patients, she hated the steroid tablets. "Those little red tablets, that make you fat," she described them as.

"When Dr Carey gives you them, do you actually take them?" Jamie asked an inspired question.

"Oh, don't you dare tell him. I do take them, but not them all, just a few. I've a draw full of unused ones at home if you need any! I'd be the size of a house if I took them all."

Jamie wasn't sure at the time what to do with this information. She was a glamourous lady in her late thirties, with an expensive hairdo, beautifully manicured nails and subtle but good-looking make-up. Who knows, she may have done all of this just for Dr Carey, or perhaps she did it for her job every day? Jamie couldn't decide, which to believe!

However, her asthma was troublesome, it was clear with lung function that had bounced up and down, but on today's test it was actually quite good for a change.

Jamie wondered, if she didn't take her oral steroids in a crisis, whether she was really taking the inhaled steroids on a day-to-day basis. Jamie took the time to discuss the difference between oral and inhaled steroids. Something he had already started researching in the medical literature, even before working with Dr Carey.

"We are really sure, the inhaled steroids, don't put weight on you, you know?"

"Dr Carey told me that too, but the 'Intal' inhaler doesn't have any steroids. Am I right?" She was clearly checking that Jamie was going to say the same as Dr Carey. He was careful never to say anything direct to a patient, that disagreed with one of his bosses.

"Quite right, but your asthma would be controlled best if you take both the steroid inhaler *and* the 'Intal'. Then you would almost certainly need less of those nasty red pills." He could tell this argument had hit home. Christine was a very open lady, who wore her feelings on her face.

"Do you know Dr Carey is taking part in a trial of a new treatment for asthma? It's like the blue 'Bricanyl' inhaler, that you are on, but instead of lasting for a few hours it lasts 12 hours and you just take it twice a day like your brown one. You could take part in that study if you like."

Jamie was aware of Dr Carey's research interest in asthma and allergies. Jamie had already spent a day assisting in a study where the volunteers were exposed to house dust mite and had their lung function measured all day after that. The idea was to see how the asthma attack developed and how the drop in lung function came in two separate waves. The early phase came on quickly but passed after half an hour. The second phase, came on a couple of hours later and was sustained for four to six hours if no rescue treatment was given.

Jamie had read about these types of trial in his own time, since his daughter's anaphylaxis and loved working with an expert involved in the research.

"Is Dr Carey running the trial himself?" this sounded a little more important to Christine French, than the outcome of her asthma.

Jamie used the possibility for a double win.

"Absolutely. He is one of the trial investigators. Shall I mention that you might be interested as I chat to him?"

"Yes, but don't tell him, I don't take all my pills. He would be so disappointed in me." This was the bit Jamie was most concerned about. If he told Dr Carey, and he talked about it, Mrs French might not want to see Jamie ever again. Not telling him, would be withholding information, that mattered in terms of her long-term management to the doctor in-charge of her case.

Jamie left his own clinic room and went to wait until a patient left Dr Carey's clinic room, before going in, to discuss the patient Jamie had seen.

After waiting a few minutes to go in, Jamie explained the discussions he had gone through with Mrs French. He talked about the failing to complete a course of oral steroids, but also that she asked for him not to mention it.

"It is possible that no-one finishes a course of treatment, we prescribe." Dr Carey said very relaxed and affable. "Let's try and get her in the trial, I will come and see her." Jamie noticed that his eyes were twinkling even more than usual.

Dr Carey, completed the job of persuading Christine to take part in the clinical trial. The lack of completion of taking oral steroids, was not discussed with her again that day. Jamie did revisit it a few years later when he was back in the same clinic as a more senior grade.

In the same clinic, Jamie met one of the Manchester Air Disaster survivors, that Dr Carey was following-up long-term. Jamie didn't talk to the patient, at all about his premonition. He used as much time as possible to ask about the day, the feelings the survivor had now and the implication for her job as a nurse herself, working in the same hospital they were currently sat in, with her lung limitation, caused by the damage of smoke inhalation.

Jamie had checked the lung function using the machine in his clinic room. The measures had been low and generally fixed ever since the smoke inhalation she suffered (in the minutes prior to escaping). There was just enough variability in the measures to call it asthma, but the pattern compared to Christine French, was so different. Jamie recognised it was foolish to imagine it as the same disease, even though the top line of the diagnosis 'asthma', was the same for both patients.

"Do you not want to listen to my chest?" the patient asked Jamie.

"Not sure if it will tell me anything and I've used more than my time allocation asking you questions. I need to explain how you are to Dr Carey, but I can't think we will do anything different today. But of course, Dr Carey will keep an eye on you long term, as we don't really know what happens after the sort of injury your lungs suffered."

"Thank you for listening to my story, Dr Carmichael, even Dr Carey who is lovely, has never actually asked me how I feel you know? Certainly, none of the other doctors I've seen appear at all interested." Mrs Colina, was giving Jamie one of his best compliments to date.

"Well, I apologise if I was intrusive, as a little bit of me, was just being nosey, but I am absolutely sure not all the damage you suffered was physical," Jamie was in uncharted territory and was picking his words carefully.

"Do *not* apologise!" the survivor, stressed the 'not' word. "I really appreciated it."

Jamie learnt a very positive reinforcement lesson. If you asked a question that the patient readily answered, or did even after hesitation, it was likely you were doing some good and potentially opening doors, for further input or support in the future.

One of the great things Jamie found working in this area of Manchester was the huge range of social class. On one side of the hospital was a very affluent area, where the bankers, lawyers, accountants and even doctors all lived in the 1980s. Some of these occupational groups were ousted by the professional footballers and their agents as time went by. On the other side of the hospital, was one of the UK's most deprived areas. It brought a huge diversity of social class and therefore information and educational needs associated with the same medical treatment.

As an example, relevant to Jamie, was that all patients were being encouraged about taking inhaled steroids as the optimum approach to treat asthma. The data over the negative aspects of 'blue' inhalers and how if used alone they made asthma worse and increased the risk of dying of asthma attacks was already clear in the medical literature. On the other hand, the positive benefit of inhaled steroids, was already clear too, from the papers Jamie had read, even in the mid 1980s. This data got progressively more indisputable over subsequent years.

How you gave the message to an individual patient, to take the treatment focussing on prevention with the inhaled steroid, rather than waiting until it was too late and the asthma attack had started, varied enormously. The ability to understand this information, varies dramatically with both the existing knowledge and the educational understanding ability of each individual and their capacity to comprehend new concepts.

As a simple example, there was a huge surge to use written information and leaflets to back up the data spoken by the doctor. This was all well and good, unless you were unaware that the patient you were talking to, was actually illiterate, in which case you would potentially alienate them, with a leaflet. One they may take from the doctor, just out of embarrassment.

****

The following week, Jamie was working in the satellite clinic, much closer to the City Centre. As with most of the clinics, he was allocated a nurse, to be with him for the duration of the clinic, not just being called in when needed. She prepared request cards and did the lung function test and blood pressure if needed.

There was a good opportunity to chat in between patients and Jamie was in full flirting flow with Pauline. At first, he wasn't sure why a young and apparently smart young nurse would choose to do a clinic job, which must be so relatively boring. That was until Pauline told him she had school age children. Jamie had expressed disbelief, but she told him she was pregnant at fifteen. It all made sense. Ward shifts were not conducive to raising small children as a single parent, even with decent grandparent support. Ward nurses, were doing a 5-day week of shifts: 6 p.m. until 2 p.m.; 2 p.m. until 10 p.m.; or nights from 10 p.m. until 6 a.m. Not easy to get child-care starting and finishing with these timings, except perhaps for permanent night workers.

Their next patient was a tiny man (Mr McNab) with emphysema. Jamie thought he was probably only six stone wet through. Again, he had a barrel shape chest, but Mr Rigson could have gotten this gentleman's lung volumes inside his own barrel chest, three to four times over.

Jamie elected to listen to this patient's breath sounds even though he knew it would be largely unhelpful. He regretted this decision.

Pauline came with Jamie behind the curtain, which they pulled closed just in case anyone inadvertently came into the clinic room. Mr McNab had already unbuttoned his shirt, but Jamie asked him if he could lift his shirt right up, which also required him to release his braces to the side, which were holding up trousers, that were clearly wider waisted than Mr McNab's actual dimensions.

Mr McNab did as requested. His trousers slipped down. Suddenly, both the nurse and Jamie got a view of this elderly gentleman's boxer shorts.

Jamie made a fatal flaw and looked up and caught Pauline's eye.

What had made him check was to see if she had noted the incongruity too. Here in the stone and wood surroundings of a tired old hospital, was an 80-year-old man, in his last few years, desperately breathless from the ravages of a life of smoking.

The boxer shorts he wore had a logo: 'Thomas the Tank Engine'.

Jamie lost his professionalism for perhaps the only time in his career. He was heaving with silent guffaws, staying directly behind Mr McNab whilst pretending to listen to the breath sounds and trying desperately to recompose himself.

Pauline held a sympathetic smile for Mr McNab and was doing the talking, asking for the deep breaths in and out as she knew Jamie couldn't have gotten the words out.

Jamie slowly managed to pull himself back, taking his time to percuss the chest, even following Pauline's lead and feeling for the vibration called 'vocal fremitus' after Pauline had asked Mr McNab to say 'Nine, nine, nine'.

"I'm not sure how I didn't lose it as well!" Pauline was understanding. Jamie was by now mortified. They were speaking for the first time after Mr McNab had left.

"I hope he didn't notice. It makes sense of course he is so small. You wouldn't get adult sized undies to fit," he explained.

"Yes, but you can get *plain* children's boxer shorts, as I know well," Pauline was the arbiter in this argument.

Jamie thanked Pauline profusely for saving his embarrassment further. Jamie did the reflection of his unprofessional behaviour as it was always done at that time. Talking to mates in the pub.

He vowed, that such an incident would not happen again. He was not aware how much provocation he would get in such a regard over the years to come, but he managed to stay good to his personal promise.

Chapter 37
The SHO Years: Second Year SHO: Who Is Dating Whom?

"How is it going with Helen?" it was Jamie who asked the opening question of Duncan. The two of them were sat having lunch together, with Raj, all in the doctors' dining room. Unusually, it was quiet enough for them to chat without eavesdroppers.

Duncan, they knew, was dating a nurse from the cardiology ward having given up on Sally, especially when he heard of the flowers trick and how badly it had gone wrong.

Jamie had found out Duncan was involved in a new relationship by chance a couple of weeks ago.

Jamie had come from the doctors' residence shortly after a fire alarm had gone off in the nurses' residence. It was three am and Jamie, who was on-call, was heading from the on-call room to the wards to see a patient who was suddenly more breathless. As was usually the case, the fire turned out to be a false alarm. Someone probably burning the toast. However, the evacuation had happened and Duncan was one of half a dozen male doctors, who were stood in the huddle waiting for the fire-crew to give them the all clear, along with 50 or more female nurses.

Jamie gave Duncan a friendly wave! As Jamie was on-call, he knew therefore that Duncan was not, nor did he live in the hospital.

The next day Duncan had given up on pretence under questioning and had told them who it was he was dating and the fact they were going away for a weekend in the lake district together.

"Yes, she is lovely," said Duncan, unusually effusive.

"How's the sex?" Raj as always was direct and wanted the gory details.

Duncan was unusually reserved and it took them quite a few probing questions to start to get something of interest.

"She needs a bit of kick-start, but then she gets really enthusiastic and howls like a banshee, when she is cumming." He eventually warmed up into the responses to his grilling.

"Bet the neighbours love that!" Jamie was more subtle, commenting to keep the discussion going, but not adding more direct questions. Jamie and Raj had developed an excellent, good cop, bad cop interrogation style, with Duncan.

"Does she give good head?" Raj unsubtle again. Jamie shook his head, thinking Raj had gone too far and Duncan would clam up.

Instead, Duncan laughed.

"Oh! Now that is interesting," Jamie knowing the unexpected response was meaningful.

"Well, she won't touch it with her mouth normally. However, last night she got me to put peanut butter on and she was a magician."

Jamie was stunned with the clarity of the information and the image. He was speechless.

Raj spoiled the moment.

"Chunky or smooth?"

****

Alongside the gossip of Duncan' success, the three of them had witnessed the developing flirtation between Kali, a Greek origin registrar, with stunning brown eyes and olive skin `and one of the consultants, Dr Brierley.

The latter was married with two daughters. Kali was single.

Jamie had noticed that her original conservative wear had changed, rather unsubtly over the first few weeks from trousers, to skirts. Then heels were added, little kitten ones at first, but eventually ones that were a bit 'cloppy' and not like normal medical wear.

With the approach of Christmas, her skirts had gone higher too and she was wearing hosiery you might normally save for a special night out. Dr Carey's patient, Mrs French, whom Jamie had met in clinic the week before, might even have been responsible for their presence in the large department store in nearby Altrincham.

Jamie at first wondered, with mis-placed self-importance, if he personally was Kali's interest, but knew of course that he was too young.

The other two registrars other than Kali, were both married and very conservative. Charles Harris was devotedly religious and said 'god-bless' every time he rang to check in before midnight when he was on-call. The other was a devout catholic.

"It couldn't be them," Jamie was chatting to Liv.

Over-time, it became more obvious that the dress code was much more provocative on the two days per week, when Dr Brierley was on his ward rounds. The ward rounds had also gone from an hour fifteen minutes maximum, to nearly double that. This wasn't good news to Jamie, but the entertainment value was worth it.

Buried into the time period in question, Jamie's wife had popped into the ward one day, when she was taking their daughter to a vaccine appointment. Diane had bumped in to Kali and had 'clocked' the dress code and had gone as far asking Sister Hunter if Kali was having an affair with Jamie.

When Sister Hunter told Jamie this discussion, he had asked what the ward sister had said in response.

"Are you kidding? She has bigger fish to fry!" Sister Hunter had told Jamie's wife.

Jamie was relieved his wife hadn't met Liv, with whom his relationship had become increasingly flirty.

The rumour mill had suggested they were more than flirting, but it was wrong as often as it was correct and on this occasion it was inaccurate.

The Christmas party was upcoming and Jamie wanted to watch events and manage his evening with Liv, with sobriety on his side.

Jamie had decided to drive and stay sober. As he had expected, Liv stayed quite close to him during the dinner and the start of the dancing.

At one point, Jamie had been literally pinned to the wall, trapped between the buxom cleavage of Emilia, who had also decided he was a target for the night.

Jamie had mouthed 'help' to Duncan and Raj, when Emilia was distracted. They both just laughed at him and gave him rude signals of what to do.

Liv was the one, who came to prise him away from his junior doctor colleague.

"Come and dance, Dr Carmichael, you are being dull talking medicine all night!" Jamie was enormously relieved to have escaped the enormously sized breasts and irritatingly perfect accent.

After a tiring set of dances, Jamie sat down. Liv sat on his knee, briefly.

Jamie nudged her off after a few minutes and she sat opposite him instead, putting her feet up onto the seat next to him.

"I can massage them if they are tired?" he offered.

Liv flicked her shoes off and put the feet on his knees as the only reply. Jamie got to work, fluctuating between soft swirling motions, followed by deep pressure of the thumbs into the sole of her petite feet.

Within sixty seconds, she was fast asleep. Jamie carefully lifted her feet off his legs and left them on the chair. He took the opportunity to ensure he danced with as many of the nurses and staff as he could. He also got the opportunity to watch from close-up, the dancing between Dr Brierley and Kali, which was protracted and indisputably smoochy.

Liv finally woke up, just before the end of the evening, having slept for at least an hour.

"Wow, that was a deep sleep in a noisy place!" Jamie commented.

"Your touch was too good," Liv replied and then looked up at him coyly. "Are you driving me home?"

Although engaged, she still lived with her parents. They talked briefly in the car, outside her house when they pulled up. Liv, probably more than a little worse for wear from alcohol invited him inside, saying they would be able to sneak past her parents' door and get to her bedroom. "They sleep soundly!"

Whether it was the sobriety, or the memories of past guilt, but Jamie declined and left her at the door, after just a kiss. The rumour mill would have increased after their interactions at the party, but it would remain permanently incorrect.

Chapter 38
Having Covid Day 2: Low Oxygen Levels

Jamie sat at his kitchen table, sipping tea, talking to the dog and measuring his saturations. He thought about how hard this was for patients to understand.

Low oxygen must be bad for you.

Well, it is, if it is protracted and you are suffering with the breathlessness. However, Jamie had once taken a pulse oximeter on a plane, just to see what happened. He was not surprisingly normal at 97% saturations, sat on the plane at take-off.

For most of the journey, flying at altitude, his saturations measured between 92 and 94%. To put this in perspective, the cut-off for being admitted to his hospital with Covid is at this level of saturations and you are sent home if saturations are 94% or above. However, for the duration of any flight above eight thousand feet, blood oxygen levels will be within this range, whilst you sit at your seat, sipping beer or gin and thinking positively of your holiday.

The observation that surprised Jamie, was when he got up, to walk to the toilet on the plane. His saturations had dropped to 85% for around five minutes. Similarly low levels of oxygen are likely to be experienced, but ignored, by people exercising at altitude. The obvious example, is your average ski holiday!

Those people with normal lungs do not feel breathless at these moments of flying, even walking back to their plane seat. Whilst skiing any breathlessness is likely to be put down to the exercise alone. However, the oxygen levels are low in all of these situations and demonstrates that it is not low oxygen itself, which makes people experience breathlessness.

Interestingly, the body sensors are normally set to detect high carbon dioxide levels, (the waste gas of the body). It is levels of this gas that the body senses and responds to, by increasing the rate or volume at which we breath.

It is very late in diseases such as pneumonia, (and Covid), when carbon dioxide levels start to rise.

Doctors, world-wide were familiar with the concept of the hypoxic, but comfortable patient during the Covid pandemic. This meant, at least at rest, the patients could be sat comfortable and not distressed, despite having low levels of oxygen. For a while, this was a good thing, but on a negative it meant, they could go very quickly from coping to being unable to cope as deterioration developed.

Interestingly and perhaps of relevance, is that it is also known, that the low oxygen levels on a plane contribute to the increase in blood clots caused by flying. This is one of several risk factors for blood clots associated with flying and many people will be aware that immobility is another of these. The dehydration caused by excess alcohol consumption is perhaps less widely known as a third.

When Jamie taught these facts to his medical students, a key question was often asked, "Why don't they pressurise planes to ground level oxygen concentration?"

"Good question!" Jamie would say, having hoped one of them would ask. "It costs too much fuel, to keep a plane fully pressurised. You could do it, but the furthest a plane can fly, with full tanks at ground level pressure is perhaps 2 hours. That's a lot of stops to get to Australia."

The link between low oxygen levels and blood clots, in Jamie's view was another reason to consider early anti-coagulation in patients admitted with significant Covid pneumonia.

Jamie checked his 'sats' and for a short period they were down at 94%. For the first time he went to lie on his tummy to 'prone'.

Isla watched him with a quizzical eye.

Chapter 39
The SHO Years: Wrong Diagnoses

Jamie was attached to Dr Carey for a three-month block and enjoyed the chance to explore in more detail, the world of allergy and asthma. Not all the work was of course asthma and allergy related, as the random distribution of admissions when on-call, ruled what was seen on the firm for each team on any given day.

During this period, three events of patients with the 'wrong diagnosis', would influence Jamie's long-term approach to medicine.

Unlike the case of Roger Walsh with the unilateral pulmonary oedema, Jamie did not consider these wrong diagnoses as an error in his own personal judgement. Each case had a meaningful impact, despite this.

The saddest case haunted him for some time after. The sixty-year-old female patient had been admitted with progressive breathlessness, weight loss, anorexia and malaise.

Duncan had admitted her and was suspicious an ultimate diagnosis of metastatic cancer was going to be made.

X-rays and scans of lung, abdomen and especially the liver showed lesions scattered around the body, including the brain, bone, lungs and especially the liver. The ultra-sound scan of the liver, kidneys and pancreas had been specifically reported as 'multiple metastases', but added 'no sign of a pancreas or renal primary'.

The patient was experiencing the odd moments of fever, but this also happens in malignancy (*pyrexia of malignancy*) as well as infection and some inflammatory disorders. Attempts to confirm the diagnosis, including a needle biopsy of the liver had all failed to find any cancer cells. Jamie had been responsible for co-ordinating all of the above investigations.

The patient's health was deteriorating rapidly, including her mental state and eventually Dr Carey after discussing at the weekly clinical meeting with all the respiratory consultants, surgeons and radiologists present, decided to stop all treatment and further investigation and proceed to palliative measures.

The patient, whilst fit enough to have the 'capacity' to understand and the family were fully informed and included in decision making discussions, throughout.

When the patient inevitably passed away, Jamie wrote the death certificate as 'Carcinomatosis' as had been the agreed plan from the joint clinical meeting. 'Unknown primary' was added. Jamie had an additional meeting with the family and asked if they would allow a post-mortem to be held, as most importantly, this would enhance the medical understanding of such cases, where some doubt persisted.

The family agreed and confirmed they were fully supportive of the medical team.

Jamie attended the post mortem. It took a few more days to confirm the final diagnosis, but the pathologist immediately didn't think the lesions in the liver, lung and brain looked like tumours, when he cut into them. "They look like small abscesses more like," he had said in the moment to Jamie.

A little later, when he then explored the heart, he found a heart valve, destroyed by an infection. This infected valve had been sending off showers of infected clots around the body, causing hundreds of infected abscesses to spread to all parts of the body. Whilst on the scan, these little abscesses looked like tumours, they were in fact infection.

Samples taken at the time of the autopsy, later identified the infecting organism as staphylococcus aureus, the skin bacteria, with which we are all covered.

Dr Carey, reported the results back through the consultant body as a lesson case.

He also took on himself to do the difficult conversations with a family who were grieving their relative, who would then know, she had died of a curable disease.

Jamie rationalised, that the diagnosis would have needed to have been made weeks before as reversing 'endocarditis' (infection inside the heart) was challenging. The treatment would have been 6 months of antibiotics of which the first 3 months would have been given intravenously and therefore at this time within hospital. Survival would have been very uncertain, but if they had made the diagnosis correctly, at least she would have had a chance.

The case taught him and reaffirmed the view that he should never believe a single result of a test if it didn't fit the overall pattern. The things that went against cancer, were the fever, (though this does happen) and the negative biopsies. Jamie used to explain to patients, in the days when biopsies were done blindly. It's like putting a needle into a scone and trying to get a raisin. Sometimes you just get cake! This analogy was very accurate to this case. Later in his career, it became practice to scan and do the biopsy at the same time, so you could watch the needle go into the 'raisin' and take the bite from the right place.

Very rapidly after one of Jamie's saddest experience a second memorable case, with a clearly more positive ending reminded him of this same principle.

Jamie was called to the cardiothoracic surgical ward: 'to write up the drugs', was the surgical request. Firaz, had moved from Stockport to Baguley at the same time as Jamie did and was just starting as a Cardio-thoracic, surgical registrar at the time. It was Firaz, who had called for the lung physician team.

Sajid Iqbal was a thirty-two-year-old Asian man. He had a six-month history of unilateral chest pain and weight loss. The X-ray had shown a collection of fluid, with what appeared to be thickening of the lining of the lung. Jamie would describe to patients and students alike, that the lining of the lung was a layer of tissue stretched over the surface of the lung. A second layer sealed the inside of the chest muscles. These two layers looked and behaved to all intents and purposes, as being like cling film. Perhaps pleura was slightly stretchier, but otherwise pretty identical. In the space between the two layers of cling film, fluid could collect in disease. In health, there was just a few millilitres of natural lubricant oil in the space, which allowed the cling film layers to slide over each other with no friction.

In Mr Iqbal's case, it looked like there was a sizeable collection of fluid, but also some really thick lining, that would have the physical properties of orange rind. As a result, the lungs wouldn't stretch open during breathing.

Mr Iqbal had been diagnosed with mesothelioma (a cancer of these pleural layers, with a very bad prognosis). The diagnosis was made from both the radiological appearances, but also a needle biopsy.

The issues that didn't fit the normal 'pattern' for this diagnosis was Mr Iqbal's young age. The cancer was almost always caused by exposure to asbestos. The lag period (time that elapses) between exposure and diagnosis, is a minimum of twenty years and maybe thirty years or more.

There were parts of the world, where naturally occurring asbestos in soil and mud was sufficient to cause Mesothelioma in young people. However, Mr Iqbal, didn't come from that part of Turkey. Indeed, he was from Pakistan and had come to the UK at the age of 12.

The fact that saved Mr Iqbal's life, was that his sister was not only a nurse, but she was a smart and pushy one too.

Mr Iqbal, had undergone the correct X-rays and scans in the work up to a lung biopsy. The biopsy was done using a needle-based approach and was successfully achieved as the lining of the lung was thick enough for it to be a success and get relevant tissue from the thickened pleura.

The pathologist had diagnosed it as mesothelioma, based on the number of mesothelial cells (the 'cling film' cells), that appeared reactive and growing.

Mr Iqbal had been given the diagnosis, and told that nothing could be done for him. They gave him 4 to 12 months life expectancy. He would have died in that time-frame if his sister hadn't intervened.

She pushed hard for a second opinion at the Specialist Lung Centre at Baguley. Mr Dermapolous took the case on and was open-minded enough to offer Mr Iqbal a second biopsy, but this time with a full surgical approach to get 'a bigger piece of the pie' as Jamie saw documented within the clinic letter back to the original hospital.

Mr Dermapolous, knew the correct diagnosis, the moment he opened up Mr Iqbal, Jamie could tell from reading the surgical notes. The material inside was not hard enough for Mesothelioma. Mr Dermapolous had taken the biopsy and closed the wound. A piece of the biopsy was sent for what is called a 'frozen section', where the pathologist does a quick look, but does more formal stains later.

In the rapid staining, the pathologist suggested the diagnosis given to Mr Iqbal two months before, was initially wrong and because he could demonstrate the presence of the bacteria, he confirmed Mr Iqbal actually had tuberculosis of the pleura.

With six to twelve months of antibiotic therapy, Mr Iqbal, would now have a normal life expectancy.

Jamie had come so quickly to the ward to see Mr Iqbal after getting Firaz's phone call, that the surgeons hadn't even spoken to Mr Iqbal and Jamie got the dubious pleasure of breaking 'good news'. Jamie was familiar with breaking bad-news. He had no such experience in breaking good news.

He expected to have an enthusiastic response of huge relief. Instead, though perhaps not surprisingly once he had given himself time to reflect, the response Jamie got, was that of anger. Jamie had not been prepared for it, nor to be on the receiving end of it.

Relief for Mr Iqbal, would surely come later, when he also had time to reflect. Jamie realised how important the patient's sister, her nursing background and sharp mind had been in saving the patient. Untreated Mr Iqbal would have had a deterioration and death, which would have looked, very similar for untreated tuberculosis compared to a progressive malignant mesothelioma.

Such events are rare in medicine, but it was another reminder to Jamie, to always keep the mind open. Even when a diagnosis has been made by a biopsy, which doctors, normally accept as the 'gold standard'. If there is something not quite right, the diagnosis should always be reviewed, preferably with a fresh pair of eyes.

Much later in his career, Jamie was involved in a case he thought similar to Mr Iqbal. At the time, Jamie was doing medico-legal reports for diseases caused by occupations. His own research led him in this direction.

The lady was in her late thirties and had similarly been diagnosed as having a mesothelioma, from a similar small biopsy procedure.

She was then referred for a trial of chemotherapy, as part of a trial of a new treatment approach for mesothelioma. Jamie's legal case only had one or two treatments, before declining any further rounds of therapy, because of the side effects.

However, her fluid and thickening slowly resolved and eventually disappeared completely. Jamie was involved only at the medico-legal stage, where she was claiming compensation for getting a potentially fatal disease from her employer; a chain of hairdressers.

The alleged exposure to asbestos, was from the asbestos paper in the old hair driers, that only the more mature reader will understand. They looked like a coloured space helmet, covering half the head. Asbestos paper was used to limit the risk of heat burns from the heaters going through the metal. The hairdressers had to brush the grill from time to time, in order to clear hair from the grills.

The hygienist working the case (*a specialist who looks at exposure to dust and chemicals*) claimed some asbestos fibres may have been released and inhaled, during this brushing procedure as the asbestos paper was disturbed.

Jamie was being asked to provide the medical report on the diagnosis and prognosis, but was also asked to comment on 'causation'. Having discussed all the rights and wrongs in the case, Jamie had to give what he believed was the right answer, on the basis of 'the balance of probability'.

Even though he was working for the lawyers of the lady making the claim, Jamie had to say what he thought was more likely as there were only two theoretical options in his opinion.

One was that a miracle of biblical proportions had occurred, whereby two cycles of chemotherapy had cured an incurable disease. Of side relevance, was the fact that in the trial for this new chemotherapy, for all the other patients who were involved, were reported as showing no beneficial effect of the chemotherapy at all.

The second possibility, was that the diagnosis was wrong in the first place and the lady never had mesothelioma. The resolution of whatever had been going on, was probably coincidental and not even related to the chemotherapy. Making this argument, though, Jamie would be unable to give a new diagnosis, as that was beyond his remit as only being involved at the legal stage.

To say yes or no on the 'balance of probabilities' in a civil case, means that the 'medical expert' only had to have over fifty percent conviction of an answer. Jamie was obliged to call the answer one way or another. Having made the arguments for both theoretical options over several pages, his conclusion was that the wrong diagnosis was actually the more likely event (by substantial more than fifty percent).

Nobody was happy with Jamie. The solicitors had wasted time and most importantly (for them) money on the case and the 'client' didn't get her pay-out, that she was banking on. The fact that a person who had a fatal diagnosis hanging over her, had this removed, did not appear to be of any relative comfort.

Just as it was not immediately at least for Mr Iqbal.

****

Jamie got involved in the third case with what was a wrong initial diagnosis and it became a field of real interest. Leanne was a seventeen-year-old young lady, who had spent nine months out of the last twelve months in hospital with her 'asthma'.

The local physician in Cheshire, had referred her to Dr Carey for a second opinion. She came across on intravenous infusions of both 'aminophylline' and 'terbutaline'. These drugs were used as desperation therapies for asthma at a time when treatments other than oral steroids were yet to be developed.

Jamie had taken the full history on the first day that Leanne Cooper came to the ward.

Leanne had a teddy bear, that also had a cannula in and Leanne appeared to have acquired some 'drip' tubing to it and bandaged its arm up. Otherwise, a kindly nurse might have done it for her. The bear's name was 'Napoleon'. It had another bandage over one eye. Jamie noted that, Leanne's vision was normal.

Leanne was however, distressed with a noisy breathing sound and was clearly working hard to breathe. The noise was like a wheeze, but when you listened carefully it was present on both the breath in and the breath out. In most cases of asthma (but not all), the wheeze is more obvious in breathing out only.

Jamie's immediate response in his gut was, that whatever Leanne had, it wasn't all asthma.

The following night Jamie was on-call and although he hadn't been rung to attend the ward, he did anyway in the middle of the night. He crept to Leanne's bedside, and listened carefully, whilst she slept.

To Jamie's surprise the noise was still present. He had in his own mind, expected it to have disappeared completely. However, what was different in Leanne's sleep was that her respiratory rate (number of breaths in a given minute), was very normal at about eight breaths per minute. It also wasn't laboured. The latter two were at odds with what Jamie had witnessed, when he had seen her during the day.

The following day, Simon Orton, who was doing a research project in the department, took Leanne to lung function and between him and the lead for the lung function (Neil Carter), they tried to do lung function tests.

They were abnormal, but they weren't typical of 'asthma'.

Jamie went off to the library, to do some research.

****

Dr Carey, Simon Orton and Jamie sat in Dr Carey's office.

"So where have we got with Leanne?" Dr Carey started the discussions.

"Allergic to house dust mite, cat and dog; negative to fungus. Eosinophils were normal at 0.01," Simon was first to start.

Jamie had learnt since his arrival at Baguley the importance of the eosinophil cells. They were responsible for the development of asthma episodes. They could be switched on by allergies (allergic or atopic asthma) or through an unknown mechanism (intrinsic asthma). These cells are active in people with asthma, hay-fever or eczema in most cases. Their role in asthma had been known since the 1950s.

"Normal eosinophil count is against it being active asthma!" Dr Carey responded.

"Her lung-function isn't right either, it isn't typical of asthma obstruction. Indeed, it looks more like a large airway obstruction." The three doctors, reviewed the lung function pictures that Neil had managed to get, though they had clearly been a challenge, because the patient was so breathless.

"Oh, we better bronchoscope her, she could have something in the trachea," Dr Carey was interested in the findings.

Simon started again first as Jamie tried to get started.

"I think Jamie has some ideas. Having seen them I am inclined to agree with him for the most part," Simon conceded.

"Ok go on, Jamie." Dr Carey sat forward.

"Firstly, just to explain I called onto the ward last night, whilst Leanne was asleep and although she still had the 'wheeze', which I suspect is more of a stridor, she wasn't actually struggling to breath at all. Indeed, in her sleep, her respiratory rate was about eight breaths per minute. I do think though, the fact that she is still making the noise is really important." Jamie had started fast as he was excited by what he had found.

"I think she has a condition best called 'Paradoxical Vocal Cord Motion syndrome'. There are a number of case reports of similar cases around the world." Jamie jumped in with his conclusion. "Look this one even shows the lung function a bit like Leanne's. A few years ago, an ENT surgeon in the USA, even referred to it with the name 'Munchausen's stridor'. However, I don't like that phrase as it implies, she is doing it deliberately. But the noise was there when she was fast asleep, so that doesn't make sense."

Jamie paused for breath, but he had both senior doctors' attention, though they were flicking through the photocopies of journals he had printed out in the library.

"The PVCMs description is the best, I think. It just describes what it is. For whatever reason, the vocal cords reverse the normal pattern of opening during breathing in and actually close, almost completely. See the picture in that paper from a laryngoscope. It would also explain, why her voice is so quiet and husky." Jamie stopped and let his seniors take it all in.

"But why is she distressed during the day and not at night?" Dr Carey was on the button with this question and Jamie was pleased, he had picked up detail in what he had said.

Jamie and Simon, both started together, but Jamie persisted.

"I'm not sure, but if your airway is closed and you are conscious, it may well make any of us scared and then panic on top. Or perhaps the throat relaxes enough during sleep so that breathing is easier, but not enough to take away the stridor."

"I think she is just crazy. Have you seen that Teddy she clutches?" Simon had interjected. Jamie and Simon disagreed here.

"I'm not saying, that there aren't psychological issues as well, but she has been in hospital for nine months. She is bound to be affected by just that, let alone the frightening aspects of her breathing that no one can sort out."

"She smiles all the time though and seems to like being ill," Simon wasn't giving up.

"I agree and she certainly is getting lots of attention, because of it," Jamie couldn't explain her outward affect. He didn't want to try right now, it seemed more important to find out the diagnosis and work from there.

"Ok," Dr Carey held his hands up in a soothing gesture. "We might not solve this bit today, but we do want to see if you are both right with the diagnosis. What are you suggesting we do?"

"Look at her vocal cords," Simon first.

"Agreed." Simon and Jamie agreeing on this was a bonus.

"ENT?" Dr Carey asked, meaning asking one of the Ear Nose and Throat surgeons, doing the procedure.

"Reading the papers, we need to be careful, because it might be function that actually matters. The surgeon might only look at things to cut out. It won't be good if we divert away from asthma and a surgeon says 'normal'."

Dr Carey pushed Jamie, "C'mon Jamie what are you suggesting, you've obviously looked at this a lot in the last two days?"

"Sharon Warrington is the Speech and Language Therapist here. I spoke to her and she has actually heard of this condition, which beats the three of us. She works with Mr Smith, the ENT surgeon and they do lists together. The other option is Simon does a first look in a bronchoscopy list. He does a list with Dr Brierley this week." Jamie had finished.

"If we get Dr Brierley involved, he might just try and run with this and you might be on to something big here." Dr Carey didn't want a colleague, taking the glory for something he and his team were driving.

Simon interjected, "And *he* will call her mad! To her face as well! Though, he is away this week, I'm doing the list alone."

"Shall we do it alone first? Even ask Sharon if she wants to come down and have a look, with the training head on the scope." Jamie knew that the training head was a new teaching piece of kit at the time, which allowed two people to see the images at the same time, rather than just the person doing it looking down the single fibre-optic eye-piece.

"We better tell Leanne the plan. Do you want me to do that?" Dr Carey was now getting excited himself, which he didn't outwardly show very often.

"Jamie is the one who gets on with her, I'd get him to start, then you follow in behind for the kill boss," Simon suggested an approach, that Jamie was pleased with.

"I'll wait 'til one of her parents are there, as she is really defensive when they aren't around. I might say, we think this is on top of the asthma to start with, if that's ok with you. Changing the diagnosis completely and getting the drips away might be too big a deal for one day?"

****

The next day, the first diagnosis of what was then called PVCMs was made in Manchester. It took another 3 months before they got all the asthma drip treatments away from Leanne. Slowly her life normalised.

In response to the new diagnosis, Jamie coined a catch phrase: 'All that wheezes, is not asthma' The phrase never left his career from that day forward.

The greatest pleasure for Jamie, however, was seeing Leanne's life almost normalise, slowly over many years. Leanne went on to be highly successful in her own professional career. Jamie ended up seeing her about once per year, largely to ensure, there was no relapse or regression to a bad clinical state, as there were subsequently large numbers of these cases and in some, they couldn't achieve full recovery.

The credit for her improvement went to Sharon Warrington and the speech therapy techniques that gradually allowed a more normal function to return. However, it was like learning to walk again after a major brain event. It was a slow and painful process.

Chapter 40
The SHO Years: Bad Times at the End of a Good Year

Around the time of his success with Leanne's diagnosis and the early part of her recovery, Jamie had a run of major blows to deal with before the end of his year.

He was working on Cardiology and despite listening intently to a heart, he missed a soft murmur. Dr Beardsall, called him out on the ward round.

"Not many synapses connecting there, Dr Carmichael." It was the most openly insulted and upset he ever was in his career. He felt it was unnecessary, as well as medically inaccurate, as it was the pressure and probably too many synapses firing, that made him miss the very soft sound through the stethoscope.

Any thought of doing cardiology, was completely obliterated. He hadn't enjoyed the attachment on the cardiology wards anyway. The consultants were not friendly with the junior doctors and treated them more like worker ants, than colleagues. Jamie had no time for this approach, having been shown by Dr Firman, how to work a team to maximum benefit of all concerned.

He also took his multiple-choice membership exam twice and failed both times. Jamie had passed exams with ease until this point and it was devastating to his morale to find an exam difficult to pass.

He was in a low point with his confidence for the first time.

Three weeks before he finished the year at Baguley, his mother had her second stroke. It was a massive one. This time she was admitted to Baguley hospital itself, having been in a different hospital for her first stroke, when Jamie was still a student.

Only at this admission, did the doctors looking after her, notice that she also had a soft murmur in her heart, just like the one Jamie didn't hear.

It was later confirmed, that she had mitral stenosis. If this had been spotted at the time of the first stroke, she would have been anticoagulated and the second event would likely never have happened.

Jamie knew the narrowed valve and an electric rhythm called atrial fibrillation, in combination caused a clot to form in a dilated chamber of the heart and eventually dislodge and head into the arterial circulation. This one had blocked a large artery in the left side of her brain.

Jamie's mother was only sixty-five. He knew she had been cheated of the last decent years of her life. She had only survived a year after her husband had died and was building a positive single life for herself.

Jamie knew, even on day one, that she wouldn't get out of hospital, such was the density of the stroke, in combination with it being a second one. Just to complicate matters, Jamie's next job was in Leicester and he was leaving in three weeks.

Dr Carey had advised Jamie to spend 'at least' one year out of Manchester and he took the advice willingly. He applied for and had got the job, a few months before his mother's event.

Chapter 41
The SHO Years: SHO Year 3: Life in Leicester

Jamie and Diane had rented out their Manchester house and decided to stay in hospital accommodation in Leicester. The cost of which matched their Manchester rental income. This decision turned out, to be a potentially expensive error, as house prices doubled in Leicester, during the single year Jamie and his family moved there. The reason was the train line from Leicester to London was electrified and opened in that year, taking the commute into London down to barely an hour.

In retrospect, moving house would have just been too many life events together, so there were no real regrets.

Unfortunately, Jamie started travelling back every weekend from Leicester to Manchester and at least once per week in between, to visit his mum.

This was exhausting when placed on top his frequent on-call shifts. On one occasion, he fell asleep on the motorway, waking up as the car tyres vibrated on the rumble strips for the hard shoulder. This event terrified Jamie, who thought like many young people that he was indestructible, but that day realised he had come very close to disaster.

Like many doctors at the time, Jamie became addicted to coffee, by necessity.

The hospital accommodation they moved in to, was excellent from a practical perspective. The fact, that all Jamie had to do was walk across two football pitches from the house, to the back entrance to the hospital was a quality-of-life benefit, that was never matched, thereafter.

He could listen to the birds twittering and smell the fresh morning smells of cut grass, whilst being only a few yards from the major city trunk road.

Jamie however, found life in Leicester somewhat unusual, with the locals being rather insular for the most part. All of the friends they made as a family, were the travellers and temporary residents of the 'province' of Leicester.

Work wise, there was a lot of tuberculosis to see, because of the large Asian population in the city. Jamie hadn't seen a great deal of TB in Manchester other than the case of Mr Iqbal.

Jamie was determined to get his membership exams completed as his priority. Having failed the first part twice, he was already behind the curve, compared to his peers, but had another opportunity in September. Having a child and an ill mother, meant spare time was at a premium. He had even given up on playing football, his one personal relaxation, until membership was completed.

On a positive, Jamie's two consultants for the first 6 months were both interesting. Bill Bentham was an academic, interested in hypertension. He got Jamie briefly involved in some research, having known of Jamie's long-term interest and the fact, Jamie had already published a case report in a medical journal, based on the case of PVCMs.

The second consultant, Jamie felt must have been a model for one of the characters in the film 'Carry on, Doctor'. Lord Flimley-Martin had bought a 'Lord of the Manor' title, so rumour had it.

He drove a Rolls Royce and before the hospital moved from an old barracks style building to a multi-purpose single building, it was alleged that Dr Flimley-Martin, drove from ward to ward, during his ward rounds, taking his secretary with him 'to keep notes'. There was a rumour, that the 'Roller' had a sherry decanter inside, which was used between wards, whilst the junior doctors ran between them to keep up.

He was a huge man, with large handlebar moustache and a voice that resembled that of Brian Blessed. He had some old-fashioned styles of treatment especially for asthma, to match his demeanour. Jamie tried to keep the patients on modern therapy as best he could. He tried to achieve this as subliminally as he could, for both in-patients and in clinic.

Jamie was given a lot of autonomy as a third year SHO. His registrar, Alan Thompson, though minimalist with words, was supportive of Jamie, but was also keen on the 'anything for a quiet life principle'.

The ward nurses generally, were very friendly with the doctors and Jamie found his style of ward interaction translated from Manchester to Leicester seamlessly. This was despite the fact that the senior team he worked for, was considered 'challenging' to the nurses. Jamie worked out, this was because of their old-fashioned style (Lord Flimley-Martin) and their academic style (Dr Bentham), which were practically very different. Jamie's job was to keep the peace and iron out the glitches. A task he warmed to, very quickly.

In regard to gaining the trust of the nursing and senior colleagues, Jamie had a success early in the year, which sealed his positive reputation.

The Asian patient involved (Mr Khan), had been admitted, with an acute confusional-state, which rapidly slipped into unconsciousness. There was great concern over the diagnosis, because of the speed of the rapid deterioration. Of key relevance was the presence of a low-grade fever, which after some of his past learning lessons, Jamie didn't ignore.

As with many Asian families and something that seemed to Jamie particularly apparent in Leicester, was the great tumult of family commotion and wailing, that was part of the ward experience. There were sometimes 30 or 40 relatives at a time, waiting in the corridors and stairwells.

Additionally, there were family members from all over the world to talk to, who were 'Mr Khan's cousin'. One, a specialist in neurology in New York, whilst another was a rheumatologist in Mumbai or Toronto.

Jamie did the necessary communication and worked tirelessly for 3 days to do every test known to man on Mr Khan.

The atypical pieces of this jigsaw, were the profound unconsciousness and yet a normal brain scan, excluding a stroke, a brain bleed or brain tumour. Following this, Jamie did the lumbar puncture himself and the CSF pressure was normal, with no sign of infection. Cerebral or meningeal tuberculosis, which was one of the early diagnostic options, were also excluded.

The only abnormality from the CSF had been a marginally high protein level, which was found to be more globulins, rather than smaller proteins.

This led to a focus on the immune system and immune tests showed a high titre of first ANA, which Jamie knew pointed to an immune disorder, but didn't narrow the diagnosis down enough.

At this point, Jamie and Alan together persuaded Dr Flimley-Martin to allow them to give Mr Khan massive doses of intra-venous steroids, more as a desperation measure to see if they could get a response. Tuberculosis and other infections had been effectively excluded, meaning it was a safe 'trial of treatment'.

The morning after the first dose, Mr Khan was responding. He wasn't normal, but clearly had got partial consciousness back.

There was great euphoria and an upsurge of the emotion amongst the masses of family members lining the ward corridors, waiting rooms and even the stairwells that day. Jamie knew there was an improvement in the morning, long before he got to see Mr Khan. His insight came from the number of times he had his hand shaken or had been patted on the back on his walk into the ward. He had the bruises to show for it, for a week.

Jamie rang the immune laboratory as his first job at 9 a.m., to check the outstanding immune result he was waiting for. Strongly positive 'double stranded DNA', the 'strongest the laboratory had on record' was what he was told, by an excited laboratory scientist. Jamie reckoned it was the only time in his career, when he had spoken to an emotionally excited laboratory worker, at least until he got involved in research.

Systemic Lupus, with cerebral presentation, had been one of Jamie's guesses after the lumbar puncture. It was reported in the literature, but presenting as loss of consciousness was almost unheard of, from his library research.

Jamie had rung and spoken to the rheumatological team including the consultant before Lord Flimley-Martin turned up late for the ward round shortly before 10. They were based at a different hospital across town.

The rheumatology team wanted them to move Mr Khan immediately to their specialist ward. Jamie was keen having seen the benefit of specialist care, in his last year at Baguley. The rheumatology consultant agreed with Jamie's presumptive diagnosis on the basis of the new results and wanted to carry on the intravenous steroids. He suggested they might also do a treatment called plasma exchange, to remove all the damaging antibodies, which were causing the impact on the brain. They also said they would probably need to give him some form of chemotherapy.

In response, Jamie told them that 'his boss', was on his way to do the ward round and he would have to get permission to do the transfer, but hoped he could get it sorted before lunch time.

The ward round commenced a little late as Dr Flimley-Martin had the same issues in getting to the ward as Jamie. Initially, he wasn't keen on the idea of transferring their case.

"Oh, this is such an interesting case. We have already made him better and the family clearly love us. Surely, we can get the plasma exchange done here. We might want to write the case up in the medical literature."

"Neither of us have looked after plasma exchange, Dr Flimley-Martin," Alan's approach was very medical and practical.

Jamie had already worked out his new boss and reckoned there might have to be something overt in it for the consultant, to persuade him to do the right thing.

"Another thing, talking to the relatives is taking Alan and I up to an hour a day and now we have the diagnosis I am sure there are going to be Professors of Rheumatology from Singapore to Timbuctoo come out of the family woodwork. They are likely to want to speak to the consultant in-charge too, now we have a diagnosis." Jamie prayed his tactic was subtle enough and he wouldn't be completely transparent.

"Ah yes, there is that!" Dr Flimley-Martin was seeing the rationale in Jamie's argument.

However, no decision was made until they went to see the patient. Jamie counted 28 members of the family either in the room, in the relative's room, or sitting on the corridors or outside the ward as they proceeded to Mr Khan's bedside. This was their first time for the family of seeing the very grand senior consultant and they all wanted to shake his hand and thank him. Jamie had knowingly used the 'Lord' title for his 'boss', on a couple of occasions, to ensure the patient's enormous family knew they had a very 'erudite' doctor in charge of the case.

An hour later, they made it back to the doctor's office to start to see the rest of the patients. Dr Flimley-Martin broached no discussion.

"Jamie, get Mr Khan across town. Do it now, Alan and Emma (their house officer) will finish the ward round, whilst you get on with that task," it was a very curt command. "Tell those 'rheumies', that we want at least one name on the case report if they write it up."

"It should be Jamie's really boss, he has done all the work." Jamie was astonished that Alan had been so magnanimous, but he was right, especially in terms of dealing with all the family interaction.

Jamie almost welled up. Although short for words, Jamie knew Alan had a great brain already, now he realised he had a solid heart inside too. Another lesson to learn for Jamie. 'Share out the medals of war and don't accumulate them for yourself'. Sadly, this was not a lesson, learnt by all his colleagues!

"Thanks, Alan," Jamie managed with genuine gratitude as he scampered with the notes to the nurse's station.

Mr Khan was in an ambulance by lunchtime.

"Jamie walks on fucking water," it was Jane, one of the SEN nurses. Jane had a voluptuous figure and exuded sex appeal. She had a mane of black hair, that she tied up in a bun for work, but let down to play with several times during a shift when she was sat at the nurse's station.

Jamie was transfixed watching the way she ran her hands through her hair and thew her head back, closing her eyes as she playfully twisted her fingers, through the coils. Jamie thought it almost looked like she was masturbating, her movements were so sensual.

"She eats junior docs for breakfast," Alan had whispered in Jamie's ear one day, when he had obviously caught Jamie staring at the hair manipulation.

"Always fancied being a bacon sandwich," Jamie responded, relieved he hadn't said 'sausage' instead. The imagination was already overdoing itself.

Jamie found her visually sensual, if not dangerously so. He had even if anything, tempered his flirting with her a little, such was the intensity of the sex appeal. It looked like she might be hard to handle, if the interest was reciprocated.

He did have second thoughts about resisting the flirting, when one day he noticed that her two legs had a slightly different tone of black nylon hosiery, meaning they were indeed stockings. Jamie's weakness for nurses in stockings, had not abated in his first four years.

"Well, thank you, I try my best!" he said to her, in response to her gratitude at his success. Throwing his musings of her sexuality away as she needed a response.

"Why does Jamie walk on water exactly?" it was Julia, a tall attractive nurse from the coronary care unit, who had just brought them a post myocardial infarction patient, who would be Jamie's responsibility.

Julia was smiling warmly at him. She had kind brown eyes, with a gentle twinkle to them.

"Nothing that impressive, I've just managed to crowbar the patient with the zillion family members into an ambulance across town," Jamie responded, keeping his medical achievement out of the discussion. Although it was the medical success, that he was personally prouder of. Clearing of the corridors and day room, which relieved other people, was as far as Jamie was concerned, more of a collateral benefit.

"Well, if you mean getting rid of all those wailing Asian family members hanging off the handrails on the stairs? That I agree, is a massive achievement," Julia was now praising him and Jamie wondered if he should move location to finish off the paperwork.

"He will get his reward, one party night, married or not, I will see to that." Jane was certainly not frightened to call herself, for her openly sexually behaviour.

Jane started to tie her hair as Julia handed Jamie the notes for the new patient. As she flicked her head, the partly tied hair landed on Jamie's shoulder. Jane then wrapped it into a coil and the hair trail left Jamie, the heat hadn't left his shoulder as she got up and went to answer a patient buzzer. A strong floral scent persisted.

Jamie looked up to ask Julia for the detail on the new patients. Her eyes were staring at him. "Careful, you might get more than you bargained for with that one!" Julia said quietly, not breaking eye contact.

Jamie had to change the subject the intensity of Julia's eye contact was too much, particularly on top of the sexual assault of Jane's hair.

Chapter 42
The SHO Years: Traumatic Times Ahead

Success followed success as Jamie passed his part-I multiple choice exam for membership at the third attempt in September. He immediately applied for part II, despite his mother's illness.

Mr Khan and his family came by the hospital, with a huge cheque, which went into the endowment charity account. There were flowers and chocolates. Mr Khan had made a near full recovery and the family were also hugely grateful.

A medical paper was eventually published. Jamie had written the clinical presentation part of it and given it to the rheumatologist, but due to delays in finishing the writing it took over a year to get in to print. Jamie had left Leicester, by that time.

When it was first published, Jamie's name wasn't on the list of authors. He wrote to the rheumatology consultant after some consideration, very politely explaining that he thought, that he should have been acknowledged at least. The consultant apologised profusely and got Jamie's name added as a full author, over another year later. Jamie's CV was starting to pad out, however and he knew this could be important for his career.

****

The negative aspects of life, undermined the positive achievements very rapidly. His mother progressively deteriorated.

The medical team in charge of her case, had decided at the outset not to anticoagulate her initially as they thought there was likely to be some bleeding as part of the stroke, so large was the infarct. They also felt that she was so unlikely to recover decent mental function, that it wasn't necessarily in her best interests to prevent another stroke, if one was going to happen.

Jamie completely and unreservedly agreed with these views and explained them to his brother and family.

His mother had always said: "I don't want to be a vegetable. Don't let me live as one." Jamie had immense guilt that medically there was nothing he could do, to live up to this plea.

She had recovered a degree of consciousness, before he left for Leicester and when Jamie took his daughter one day to see how she would react, she clearly cried and tried to push Jamie away with her one hand, with any function.

Jamie felt, his mother was telling him, she didn't want her grand-daughter seeing her as she was. He would never know, but it was the most emotion his mother had shown and made Jamie realise, she had awareness of her terrible predicament, even though she couldn't speak and didn't or couldn't try and follow commands.

The only time Jamie saw a vague smile was when he took her out of the hospital building in a wheel chair and showed her flowers. She tried to point at a rose specifically, with her one arm, that had power.

Jamie didn't know if she was trying to say how beautiful it was. However, Jamie's instinct was that she was trying to remind him, that her declared wish had been to be cremated and have her ashes buried under a rose bush. She had told him this instruction on several occasions after her first stroke. He guessed she feared carrying on, being as she was now, more than she feared death. Jamie had always known, she and her side of the family, were characters of enormous inner strength.

Just around the time Jamie was trying to organise a long-term nursing home for his mother, she had a further blood clot, come off her heart. Rather than causing a further stroke, that might have seen the end come more quickly, this one went into her femoral artery in her leg, cutting off the blood supply to her lower leg completely.

Anticoagulants were now started to try and reduce the impact of the clot in the leg. Jamie wasn't sure he believed even that was the right call. Jamie was certain his mum wanted to die and anything that prolonged her life now, would just make things worse for her.

Amputation was the other consideration. To remove the leg, which was now dead. It would be another disfigurement, but she would survive longer if it was performed. Doing nothing, meant that she would deteriorate as her leg went gangrenous and the poisons from the leg slowly took over. The pain however from a gangrenous leg, could be horrendous.

Jamie had these discussions with the medical consultants in charge and his brother. Jamie had already worked out the Hobson's choice they had, with implications both immediately and for a moderately longer term. It helped his brother understand, when the consultant in charge, explained that there wasn't an easy right or wrong answer.

His brother was smart and understood these and Jamie's medical explanations and what things might look like in a week, then a month and then even a year (the latter only if she had an amputation).

"Can the pain be controlled?" his brother's question meant, that he truly understood, this impossible choice.

"Yes, in theory, but it is going to be really hard to work out whether she is in pain or not as she doesn't communicate consistently well enough for anyone to really know." Jamie couldn't remember whether it was the medical team or himself who spoke out loud, but his thoughts were these, whether he or the medical team had voiced them.

In the end, they decided that amputation was not in their mother's long-term interests and they should have a go at least at first at pain management as the key strategy.

Jamie recognised, it was difficult for the medical team to deal, with Jamie. He was only a junior doctor, but they all knew him personally from his time at Baguley. He got on particularly well with Nina, who was one of the staff nurses at the time.

The case was on the border of ethics and ten years later, the guidance would have implied that the medical team should take the decisions in the patient's best interest and could completely ignore the relatives' view, medic or not.

Jamie for his part only tried to suggest rather than request, any change to the treatment plan and the only time he really pushed, was when he felt his mother was in pain and not getting enough pain killer. In this phase, he wondered if he had badgered them, to finally put her on a morphine pump, a little too hard.

Sometimes when he visited after the leg clot and being on the pump, she seemed to sleep through the entire visit. Often when awake she was just more and more agitated.

Jamie knew his mum would want him to push the syringe through and put all the drugs into her in one go. She would want him to finish the job and put her out of her misery. It was nearly 25 years later and in a different country, before this approach would have been allowed for humans.

"We put our pets down, because the suffering becomes worse than what the vet or the owner believes is the quality of life left for the animal. We can't do that to our loved ones, in the name of 'religion'. Whether, we or the suffering loved-one is religious or not. That is an irrelevance of course," Jamie would explain to anyone who listened.

Towards the end of his career, Jamie did wonder if he had the energy or the political skills, to be part of the group attempting to get a euthanasia facility approved and licensed in the UK. He had many nurses and colleagues, who would help, but it would need someone towards the end of their career to be the figurehead. Ideally the leader would have no family. It was very likely that anyone seen to be driving the process would be subject to harassment of potentially very serious proportions, with such a controversial undertaking. In the end, he decided he didn't have the energy, but more importantly, neither the political skills nor sufficient patience, to be the right person for this task.

Chapter 43
The SHO Years: Inexplicable Events

It was a late Monday morning in November. Jamie was working on the wards with Emma, his House Officer and Alan.

He had been back in Manchester over the weekend. It was 4 or 5 weeks, since the leg infarcted and the area of demarcation between the living leg and the dead gangrenous section had become very well defined. The doctors, wondered if the foot would amputate itself.

His mother's pain control had improved on the pump and Jamie was as settled as he could be, that she was in as little pain as was realistic. Her condition was static.

He had come back to Leicester on Sunday evening having had Sunday dinner with his in-laws. They loved the time with their grand-daughter. Even when she was being a little monkey, which she did often.

"I have to go home," Jamie said it before he had even had a thought about it in his head.

Emma responded first, "Of course if you need to. Do you mean, to your house here or Manchester?"

Jamie had never left work early for personal reasons and in the four months of his mother's illness to date he had not left early to go and see her.

"Manchester. I don't know why, but I have to!" Jamie had this sudden overwhelming conviction, but had no idea why at 1045 on this Monday morning.

"Sure!" said Alan, short with words as always.

"Go, Jamie. Trust your instincts." Emma had become a really good friend to Jamie and he had told her of his Manchester Air Disaster experience. She took his hand and squeezed it, even though they were stood in a patient's side room together. She pushed it away from herself, even though she was looking at him intently.

"We can manage just fine. Let us know how you are later. Bleep me!" Emma was almost shouting at him as he turned and fled. Jamie had bought a mobile phone for the first time when his mother was ill, but they were still not widely used and Jamie didn't even know, if Emma had one.

He ran across the football pitches. Diane was amazed to see him. Siobhan giggled loudly and lifted her arms for Daddy to pick her up.

"I'm going to Manchester."

"Why, what's happened?" Diane asked the obvious question. She saw the anxiety on his face, which hadn't been there at breakfast.

"Nothing I know of, they said she was comfortable when I rang at eight. I just know I need to go."

"Shall I ring your brother?" she asked, understanding his anxiety was out of the ordinary.

"No! Not yet. Let me get there first. He would just worry for the two hours I'm driving if you rang him now." Jamie still had time to be practical.

"Ok, let me know, if you want me to do it."

Jamie ran upstairs and threw a few clothes into his overnight bag, which was getting a good work out in the last 4 months.

"Shall we come?" Diane shouted up the stairs.

"No. If I have lost the plot, I will be back later, anyway." He kissed both his girls and ran out of the house, car keys in hand.

It took on average two hours to get from their rented hospital residence to the hospital in Baguley. On a really good run, he had done it in an hour and forty-five minutes. It didn't seem to make that much difference which route, though the motorway was quickest if he did it late at night or very early in the morning. He only used the motorway now, when he did an early evening trip and when he wasn't feeling tired. He stuck to the minimum motorway driving, when he was tired, as driving the A roads over the 'tops', kept him alert.

He didn't risk the motorway through Birmingham on that Monday morning, there could be any number of incidents. He headed North and crossed the country at Chesterfield and did it in an hour and fifty minutes.

Arriving at his mother's room, he anxiously went in. He had met Nina, as he arrived and she said, nothing had changed but it was fine for him to go down. All the other patients were still eating lunch, and there was typical smell of poor hospital food drifting along the corridor. His mother was in a side room, so he wasn't disturbing anyone else, coming outside of visiting hours.

In the single room, there was a large window, which looked over a grass filled quadrangle. There was nothing different. Her breathing was the same as yesterday. He peaked under the sheet that was lifted up on a small frame to keep the pressure of the blankets off the gangrenous leg. The leg looked the same.

"Hi, Mum! Something gave me a fright and I had to come back and check." He held her hand.

"Alan and Emma told me they would cover for me." He had chatted about all his colleagues and even some of the patients to her, as something to talk about whenever he was there, reaction or not. She wouldn't be taking much in with the brain damage and the toxins and drugs rolling around her blood stream, but he wanted her to hear his voice.

He wasn't sure how long it was. It couldn't have been long because he hadn't started telling her what was on the national news. His mum loved politics, being a staunch Tory, despite their working-class upbringing.

It was the sound he noticed first. There was no breathing sound coming from her. He looked in her eyes and they had already glassed over.

Just like that, in a matter of minutes of his arrival. She had gone as peacefully as you could ever wish for.

"Go and find Dad and your family! The pain has gone and it will all be better there." He didn't believe in a god-like being or heaven, but thought there was something more than just nothingness.

The tears fell, but he wasn't really sad. He was just relieved. Relieved she was out of the misery, that she had dreaded all her life and had had to suffer for way too long.

If he had any relief for himself, it was that he now didn't have the burden of guilt to carry, for not being able to end the suffering sooner for her. The intensity of that guilt, came to him over the next few days. He hadn't talked about it to anyone, not even his brother; and might never do so, but it had weighed him down. The travelling and visiting were nothing by comparison.

As Jamie sat holding her hand, lost in his thoughts he didn't hear the nurse come in the room.

"Your brother wants to speak to you," she said, as natural as if she was asking him if he wanted a cup of tea.

Jamie turned and when he should have said 'she has just passed', to the lovely caring nurse he knew as Avril, instead he said the thought, that sprang in to his head like a rocket exploding. "How does he know I'm here?"

Avril looked more than a little non-plussed by the question, which for her was unanswerable. Instead, she responded to the unspoken words.

"It looks like she has gone!"

"Sorry. Yes, a few minutes ago. Literally just after I got here. We were just having a quiet moment, before I was going to come and tell you."

It later crossed Jamie's mind, that the doctors and nurses, might have wondered if he had done something, such was the coincidental timing between his odd arrival in the middle of the day and her demise. He supposed, he could have had a syringe full of neat potassium and diazepam, but he didn't. A couple of times on his visits, he had given the plunger on the syringe driver a little squeeze, not because it would finish her off, but just so he could remember her for the next few days at least, at peace, at the moment he left her.

Jamie gathered himself from his thoughts.

"He is holding on the phone in our office. Do just go in." Jamie hadn't thought about how long his brother had been waiting, but made his way quickly down the corridor.

He had broken bad news so many times in his job, but this wasn't really bad news. Not for his mother at least.

Just like trying to do medical management out of your own environment, breaking the news to his brother took his skills and confidence away and he was still unprepared completely when he picked up the phone.

"Hi, Boss!" (The nickname Jamie used for his elder brother). "How did you know I was here?" the second time in 2 minutes, he had asked that question.

It was possible, that Diane had decided to speak to his brother. Jamie knew she hadn't by his brother's non-plussed response, but one Jamie had been half expecting.

"Errr, I don't know, I just knew I had to speak to you, that's all."

When they talked about it, years later, Jamie's brother didn't remember much at all of these word and moments. Jamie on the other hand, remembered it all like it had just happened. He remembered everything about the strange morning and how he knew he had to get to Manchester. Knew something important was about to happen. His brother had, had a similar unexplainable urge to speak to Jamie and had not rung his mobile phone or the hospital in Leicester and bleeped him as he had done so many times. He had rung the ward in Manchester and asked for him, even though it was unexplainable that Jamie was actually there.

No voices, no spirits. Just a complete and overwhelming certainty, that Jamie had to follow these instincts and his brother to ring him when he was there.

His brother never tried to analyse the inexplicable events. He was a pure scientist and only believed in the things that science knew.

Jamie realised, his brother suppressed the memory of that morning and probably how clumsily Jamie had told him, that their mother had just passed away. Passed away within minutes of Jamie arriving after a two-hour drive, when he should have been working. Perhaps passed seconds before the 'boss', picking up the phone to ask to speak to his brother.

It was nearly 3 years since the Manchester air disaster and nothing similar had happened in between, that Jamie was aware of. At this time, he didn't know, that they would happen again and again in his future, but with very irregular and distant frequency.

****

After doing the necessary hospital paperwork and saying goodbye one last time to his mother, now visibly in peace, Jamie went to his parent's apartment.

Liv the respiratory nurse he had got on with so well, rang him by chance that afternoon. After hearing what had happened, she came straight over and had a cup of tea with him at his parents' apartment, held his hand and let him cry in silence.

She asked him, if he wanted her to stay the night. He really wanted her to, not because he wanted any sexual interaction, but he didn't like the thought of being alone in his parent's apartment, with the ghosts of both his parents to think about. He knew that her staying, would be wrong and he would feel totally awful the next day, so he asked her to leave him on his own, but thanked her and hugged her hard. They would stay friends.

His brother arrived the next day and they organised everything in a few hours. Jamie took one day off work when his father died, plus the day of the funeral. He took 2 days off when his mother died. He was the younger son, but the burden of the medical organisation, the registering of the death and planning the funerals was all his responsibility.

His brother took on the tasks of managing the financial affairs. Months later, Jamie could look back and realise his brother had taken the short straw in reality and that he (Jamie) had gotten off very lightly indeed.

The day after his mother died, there was a football match at Maine road, an evening kick-off.

Jamie had no plans to go, but with his brother there and the day done, they decided it would be good distraction therapy for them both. It was a surreal match. Manchester City were not a great team at this time, in the middle of a barren spell of no trophies. That night they played Huddersfield Town and had their record win in a competitive game in recent history, winning ten goals to nil, with three of Jamie's favourite players all getting hat-tricks.

Jamie never said it, but he reckoned the 'Angels' who had got him to his mother's side, to hold her hand as she passed, had stayed around to give him a little something to cheer.

Chapter 44
Getting Covid: Illness, Day 4

Jamie was thoroughly bored. He had filled his time doing jobs, he should have done before.

He actually wrote his own Soliloquy and sent it to his youngest daughter in a file headed 'not to be opened'. He wasn't going to have some minister, who knew nothing about him, sum his life up in five minutes and miss all the gags out!

It was half-serious, half-funny, but brutally honest in all aspects. All the important people in his life got a mention, not just the ones who would have been politically correct to mention, at the time of his passing.

He had long ago chosen, the key music. He would let his daughters choose one piece and a poem, but he had written one of his own too.

He should have done his will too. This required the involvement of an outside person. He decided he wasn't ready to divulge his fear of impending demise, to anyone at this moment. Consequently, that most important job got shelved.

Jamie certainly had to acknowledge he had symptoms now. He was coughing and breathless on exertion and he could feel the crackles inside his chest when he breathed in. His 'sats' were hovering at 94% to 95% at rest, but dropped to 90 on any exercise.

He was still walking the fields with Isla, who couldn't believe her luck to have Dad at home all day.

As well as doing the morbid stuff, he was also planning the details of his retirement. May 3rd, was his last official day.

Chapter 45
The SHO Years: Life & Career Progression

The next life event after his mother's death, was for Diane to tell him, they were expecting number two. She had known for a few weeks, whilst saving Jamie from worrying about another event as well as his mother's illness, so she was a good way on.

Jamie felt stupid for having not noticed his wife's very regular periods had stopped. It was 6 months away, but just before his year in Leicester would end and he had no definite plans for the year after.

Jamie had to think about his future. Respiratory medicine was clearly the answer by now, but he had always had a hankering for living in Cornwall or Devon. The Royal Devon and Exeter Hospital had a great respiratory department. However, he had his connections with Manchester already set. Dr Carey had briefly talked about research options, before he had left Baguley and the possibility of coming back to work with him as a research fellow.

Jamie had to keep an eye on the job market for next year, but he knew he needed membership completed before any interview was scheduled. That meant he had the February exam, with interviews later in the month.

Jamie applied for jobs in Exeter, Manchester and Preston, when they appeared within a few weeks of each other in the jobs section of the British Medical Journal.

****

His clinical membership exam was in Glasgow and he bizarrely enjoyed the experience, that most hospital doctors remember only with unearthly dread.

The exam comprised of one 'long case', where the candidates got an hour to take a history and examine one allocated patient. They were then interviewed (grilled), by two consultants on the story, potential diagnosis and then what would be the management plan.

Jamie's long case, was an interesting Glaswegian, who had travelled to South Africa. On return, he had liver disease it was clear. The patients were usually told, not to tell the candidates the diagnosis. Jamie waited until his very last question. He tried and succeeded in getting the answer. It rocked him as he hadn't even thought about the diagnosis that the patient told him, his consultant team had made.

"Aye sonny, my consultant thinks I have 'Brucellosis' an infection I picked up in Africa," the accent was broad and Jamie had taken the first few minutes just to tune into it.

Brucellosis was an infection you get from cattle, and was unheard of as a diagnosis in the UK. His patient hadn't been anywhere near cattle in terms of his job, but Jamie guessed he had been in areas, in which Brucellosis was endemic.

To make it harder, Jamie had never seen a case and it certainly hadn't been part of his last-minute revision. He really knew very little about the illness and in real life, if he was faced with this situation, he would have been ringing his hospital ('phone a friend') microbiologist, but this was definitely not allowed in the exam.

Jamie had five minutes to work out how he would handle this, when he went in for his grilling. He didn't believe that coming up with it as the lead diagnosis was a good idea.

"So, what is your primary diagnosis?" one of the two examiners asked him. There was a twinkle in the eyes.

"Well, on the basis of common things are common, alcoholic liver disease would be the most likely diagnosis, though I've highlighted already the atypical features." The examiners were quiet and said nothing making Jamie fill the silence.

"Interestingly, the patient actually told me he was diagnosed as having Brucellosis, which I don't know much about to be honest," Jamie went for the honest, open option.

"Would you have Brucellosis as your primary diagnosis then?" They weren't going to let him off without committing.

"Honestly, I don't think I would. I wouldn't even have had it in my differential until the patient told me, what his consultant specialist thinks," Jamie admitted.

The two examiners looked at each other and raised an eyebrow each. "Almost exactly the words you used, Dr Thompson, if I remember correctly!" the lead one said to the other. He then looked back at Jamie and added, "As you can see, we tend to agree with you. Well done!"

Jamie was allowed to finish a few minutes later, having discussed further investigation options and then went and did the short cases with a new pair of examiners.

These are more like spot diagnoses. It was said that getting four or five right in the allocated time was critical. Jamie got through seven cases, but two were ophthalmoscope cases and this was Jamie's biggest weakness. He had a very weak astigmatic left eye and in real life would use his right eye to inspect both eyes, but this meant taking extra time to get the patient lying down, which wasn't the normal method and took time. Time that he didn't want to use up.

Jamie sensed, he got the first one of these eye cases, completely wrong. He was certain he got the five non-eye cases all correct, from the way the examiners reacted, when he gave the answers. He thought the second eye, he was asked to examine looked normal, though he hadn't heard they used trick cases with no pathology.

In the end, whatever he had done was enough and he was awarded his part II membership at the first attempt and became an official member of the Royal College of Physicians. This was an essential exam on the road to becoming a medical consultant and would hopefully be the last formal examination Jamie would sit.

That moment of realisation of the latter fact for Jamie was a very surreal one, when for the last 10 years, it was a moving pathway of 'O' levels, 'A' levels, medical student exams including a BSc and culminating in the MBChB, (which is the medical qualification) and then on pretty quickly to the membership exams.

An MD or PhD require a viva, but it is a viva on the work you are an expert on normally and are not like 'normal' exams.

A healthy celebration was had in the Carmichael household, the day the letter arrived. The following day, he had the expected personal suffering to deal with in response!

****

Jamie had managed to avoid all the hospital parties and events without losing favour, with the ward teams and colleagues he had worked with. It would normally be considered anti-social, not to go to any of them. However, Jamie talked openly about his personal life to nurses and colleagues in the workplace. As such, they knew he had lost his mother and where he was at in his career, trying to concentrate on exams.

His success over Mr Khan, had only partly worn off and certainly Jane, seemed to have decided he was too boring for her and Jamie was aware she had moved in, on more senior staff. There was lots of gossip, but one of the surgical registrars, Jamie had met a few times over consults, was regularly featured. Jamie was relieved, to be out of her interest zone, even though he still admired the sexual power she exuded.

To keep Jamie distracted a clinic nurse called Penny, had taken a shine to him. She was routinely allocated to his room every time he was in clinic.

She always sat behind the patient by the clinic room door and wouldn't help with any administrative tasks or procedures and clearly had belief, she was merely there as a silent chaperone.

Jamie had challenged her about what she wanted to do in nursing. She had dreams, but Jamie realised, they were just that. Unless she engaged in her job, she would achieve nothing.

When there were no medical students, he spent time teaching her medicine and engaged her to be more involved. Jamie flirted with her gently, but kept her as best he could at a distance. She flirted back and seemed more interested in this, than the interest of the medicine until a particular day.

"How would you describe the wheeze?" Jamie was in clinic with a patient not normally seen by Dr Flimley-Martin, but the patient had been allocated the wrong clinic appointment. It appeared to be an administration error, but the patient had come anyway.

Emma Bird was a young and slightly over exuberant 30-year-old, with curly blond hair, red lipstick and a slightly strident voice. In response to Jamie's question, she clutched the top of her chest, before responding.

"Oh, right here, Dr Carmichael!" Jamie sighed inwardly. It was like a scene from a medical television soap programme. She clutched her hand to her chest, just below her throat.

Penny smiled and crossed her legs a little too slowly to be natural. Jamie thought of Kenny Everett's infamous change of leg manoeuvre.

Penny was perhaps mirroring the over dramatic response of the patient, to Jamie's questions.

"And when do you feel wheeze? I mean by this when you breath in…or when you breath out?" Jamie left a pause deliberately.

"Hmmm. I hadn't really thought of that." Both ladies were still for a few seconds. "You know, I think it is mostly when I breath in."

"Interesting!" Jamie replied. "Are you sure about that? I will explain why after the next question?" Penny leaned forward, clearly interested.

"Pretty sure, Doctor Carmichael." Emma Bird leaned forward herself looking intensely at Jamie. She had a blouse on, which was opened at the front with one too few buttons fastened for Jamie's complete comfort. He noticed she had a burgundy/red satin bra on show, as she leaned forward. Jamie's central gaze, never left the patient's eyes, but he had taught himself to see things outside of his central gaze and not look in their direction.

"When your breathing goes like this, can you talk normally or does your voice change?"

"Oh, my husband loves it, as I go all husky. Not that I am any use to him, as I'm too breathless to let him near me." Emma leaned back, whilst she was admitting sex was not an option for her.

"The reason I ask those questions is I don't think these events are actual asthma attacks. I am not saying you don't have asthma though and you still need your treatment, but the attacks that cause that sensation up here…" Jamie mimicked the throat position as if he was strangling himself, before he continued, "…I think are something I have seen before, but is quite rare."

Jamie convinced the patient and later Dr Flimley-Martin. He spoke about speech therapy being the treatment of choice and arranged this, but had the difficult task of also talking to Dr Clayton, the respiratory consultant, who Emma was normally under.

Dr Clayton was a senior consultant and was high up in the lung specialists' organisation (The British Thoracic Society). Jamie spoke to him at one of the departmental meetings and brought a copy of the pack of papers, that he had made up for Dr Carey and the draft paper, that at this stage was accepted for publication in one of the scientific journals, but was yet to be printed.

Dr Clayton, listened with interest and said he would make an urgent appointment to see the patient himself. Jamie was satisfied, he had done all he could.

A month later however, he met Emma again. This time when Jamie was on-call and Emma Bird had been admitted with an 'asthma' attack. As always, during an emergency admission she had been given nebulisers, been pumped full of intravenous and oral steroids and was on a drip. Jamie, observed and documented that the symptoms were exactly the same as he had elicited in clinic and the hoarse voice, was very significant when Jamie saw her. He documented the audible inspiratory stridor, which made it almost certain in Jamie's mind, that this was his second diagnosed case of PVCMs. The wheeze had all the characteristics of Leanne's case.

"Did you see Dr Clayton after I saw you in clinic?" Jamie asked gently at first.

"Yes," Emma sounded a little sheepish, though it was hard to be sure if this was the correct interpretation, when the single word was said as a hoarse whisper.

"And have you seen the speech therapist?" Jamie was starting to feel doubtful of his success.

"Sorry, Dr Carmichael. Dr Clayton didn't think that would help, so he cancelled it. He is my consultant after all, so I have to do what he says."

Jamie had to bite his tongue. He desperately wanted to say: 'well, it hasn't worked very well as you are back in hospital and having a shed load of steroids you don't need', however, it wasn't the right time to pick fights either with this patient or one of his consultant colleagues. He stuck to his promise of never disagreeing with a consultant in front of the patient. Jamie decided with a certain degree of regret, that discretion was the better option.

"Of course!" Jamie moved on to help patients, that it was within his gift to help at this time.

Penny was fascinated, when Jamie recounted the patient's readmission and this seemed to be the trigger for her to start taking an active role in clinic and starting to learn, the specialist skills of an out-patient asthma nurse, much to Jamie's satisfaction.

Chapter 46
The SHO Years: More Interviews

Jamie went on to love the film, sliding doors. His own equivalent moments that he could relate to the film concept, came a couple of times in his later months in Leicester.

The first occurred, when he received his interview invites and their dates for what was to be his first registrar job.

He got interviews, for each of the jobs he had applied for.

Coincidentally, the interviews were scheduled on consecutive days, in a single week. Specifically, a Monday, Tuesday and Wednesday in the last week of February. Unfortunately, the order was exactly reversed, from the preference order Jamie had. Exeter was the Wednesday and this was what Jamie had most wanted, working towards a lifestyle for the future. He dreamt of living on the coast in Devon or Cornwall. Preston, was his least favourite of the three options, as it meant a long commute from their house in South Manchester or possibly moving home again, without the long-term life aim being achieved.

At this time, it was the medically accepted rule and practice, that you are offered the job the same day as the interview. Indeed, most candidates waited around until all the candidates had completed their interviews and the decisions were made by the committee on the spot.

Once offered a job, it was an accept or decline option only. Assuming you stayed around, you obviously wanted the job if offered.

What was deemed unacceptable was accepting a job and then accepting another one later, or just plain changing your mind. Such behaviour would be recorded and shared with consultants even in other parts of the country and a reputation could be lost.

This left Jamie with a difficult decision. He either had to withdraw from one interview or even two, or leave it to fate to decide for him.

Jamie had previously got jobs at his first interview time and therefore had never failed one. This somewhat surprised him, as although good at getting along with people in the work environment, he felt himself inherently shy and certainly was not one of those who were naturally gifted at selling themselves.

He wondered if his success rate came from the passion he showed for his job. Previously, he had only been interviewed for a job he really wanted. Interestingly when he drove down to Leicester, when he had set off, he had been unsure if it was the right move. On arrival, he had 2 hours of time looking around the hospital and grounds and meeting people. Perhaps even from the moment he walked into reception, he felt a connection. By the time the interview had started, Jamie was convinced.

It took a week to formulate what the decision was going to be, after much discussion with Diane.

Having passed (just) his membership exam clinical part at the first attempt, Jamie was in a strong place to sell this and his CV was enhanced, by being the primary author on the case report of PVCMs. He was ticking many boxes, for a first-year registrar job.

Eventually, he made the difficult choice to withdraw from the Preston interviews, but to remain attending the other two.

On the Tuesday, he went to Manchester for the interviews. Dr Carey and Dr Brierley were among the interview panel. If he didn't get this post, he had a very long drive, partly overnight to get down to Exeter for a lunchtime interview slot on the Wednesday.

Jamie was anxious that Dr Brierley was on the panel. He had a nagging feeling, that Jamie's knowledge of the affair between the consultant and his then registrar, which became widely known towards the end of Jamie's year at Baguley, might actually play against him.

After a very long delay, between the interviews and the consultants coming out, Dr Carey appeared first. Jamie was very anxious.

Jamie was invited in first and was offered the rotation, which would start with a year at North Manchester.

Dr Carey, took him to one side and offered him the prospect of starting a research fellow post in a few months. This was an incredible offer. The research was however in the field of occupational lung disease. This was Dr Carey's primary field of interest and the asthma and allergy work, was more of a side interest for him.

The research would be looking at the respiratory effects of cotton dust on the employees in the textile industry in Lancashire. Dr Carey was hoping to have enough funding to support at least 2 years of salary, which would guarantee Jamie the ability to complete an MD thesis, with possible conversion to a PhD (essentially three years).

Either one of these thesis awards, would set Jamie's career up completely. He would then be in a very strong position to be able to get a consultant job, with a degree of comfort and perhaps, be more selective about where he eventually worked. Ideally choosing a big hospital, with research and teaching potential.

A further factor, that made the option so attractive, was that his friend Duncan from last year, had already been appointed as a research fellow and would be getting the research started, before Jamie.

"Will I be able to attend the asthma clinics you run as well as doing the research?" Jamie thought he might be pushing his luck.

"Yes definitely! Also, we will be continuing the trial of Salmeterol you remember from last year and doing more allergen challenge work, that you can get your teeth into, whilst doing the work for your thesis. The thesis work should only be 75% or thereabouts of your week."

Jamie was sold and accepted both the starting registrar post and the potential prospect of research with great enthusiasm. There was no start date for the latter.

Jamie withdrew from Exeter, with a degree of a heavy heart. Lifestyle planning, might have to wait until consultant post time, he explained to Diane.

Only after the events did Diane express a great deal of relief in the outcome, as their second child was due in June and whilst, Jamie no longer had family around to help, Diane's parents were in Manchester and starting with another young child in a new city was not something she had been enthusiastic about. Her own career was also just starting and whilst it would have been possible to move it successfully to the South West, it would have been disruptive. She hadn't told him any of these thoughts, prior to the interview.

****

Jamie thought his career planning couldn't get any better, but shortly after these interviews, his consultants in Leicester, asked Jamie if he wanted to act up as registrar for his last 3 months in Leicester.

This became an option as Alan, had himself been offered a research post in Nottingham and wanted to leave early on the 1st April to start his own career progression through research. The hospital in Leicester, would find it easier getting a Locum to do Jamie's role as an SHO, rather than finding one for a registrar grade, when the job would just be for 3 months. They had already appointed Alan's job, for the following year starting in August.

All the stars had aligned and Jamie accepted readily. Starting as a locum registrar would be great experience and with membership and his future settled, there were no immediate challenges, other than gaining experience and doing the senior job to the best of his ability.

Jamie even restarted playing club football and had an excellent and scoring debut, for the new local team in Leicester, he joined.

Life was all positive.

Chapter 47
Getting Covid: Covid Illness Day 5: Dealing with Fear

Jamie felt he was physically coping, but was getting genuinely worried. The crackles in his chest, were much more obvious. He was struggling to get to sleep, due to the sensation of breathlessness and the nagging cough.

Walking Isla was still possible, but he had cut the distance slightly, taking the one hill out of the route. He was confident, he was not putting anyone at risk being out of the house (purely because of where he lived and the fact, he could go out the back of his house and walk for 45 minutes on fields, without coming within 100 yards of another human being).

Having Isla collected and dropped off for her walk, would be a much greater risk of viral transmission, he rationalised. He was also sure, that immobility itself was one of the contributors to blood clots, complicating Covid, so keeping active, however challenging, was the right thing to do.

His resting 'sats' were by now rarely above 94% and he knew he would use 92% as his threshold. Well in truth, it would have to be below 92% before he went in, as he didn't want to arrive in the Emergency Department and then for him to be told, he wasn't bad enough to stay. That would be the ultimate embarrassment, for Jamie.

He slept on his front, doing his own 'proning' regularly by now. During the day, he spent a couple of hours lying on his tummy too. Isla, was showing some signs of being troubled and sensing her master's unease. She never left his side and wanted to sit on his head, when he got on his front. After a bit of discussion and persuasion, Isla learnt to lie between his legs instead and rest her head on the back of one of his thighs, when he adopted the prone position on the settee.

Jamie even watched a box-set of CD's he had in, which was something he almost never did. He didn't have the stamina for writing all day.

Jamie had experimented with writing Erotica. Four books were already published under a pseudonym. Although it was a success, he had barely earnt a hundred pounds in total. Sometime after his separation from Heather, he had dated a woman, who appeared to have no sexual boundaries and loved to dabble in bondage and they had played scene's out, where she was a dominatrix. Jamie had loved it and whilst their few months were very casual and certainly not a permanent pattern of behaviour, he chose the bondage and submission genre, to be the arena for his writing experiment.

He had done it as a test. He wanted to write his autobiography of sorts when he retired and used the experiment with a literature, which had a much lower editorial bar as a testing ground.

Jamie's secretary had told him that one of his colleagues, Professor Aubrey Wildwood was desperate to find out his pseudonym. Jamie had told nobody, other than the inspiration of the four books. She received half of the income so far, not that it was more than a couple of bunches of flowers worth.

Aubrey, would cause mayhem if he found out Jamie's pseudonym. Fortunately, without hacking Jamie's home laptop, there was actually no way of Aubrey finding out. The pseudonym he had chosen had no link to his real name.

Jamie realised, Aubrey was probably investing quite a lot of time and energy, in trying to find him. He might even be reading different authors, to see if he could spot Jamie from reading text. If true, Jamie hoped Aubrey would enjoy his dip into the seedier side of literature.

Jamie did have a thought, to ask his secretary in a year or so, to let Aubrey's secretary know, that Jamie had actually never written any books at all and only let the story out about writing, knowing Aubrey would get frantic trying to find his pseudonym.

If Jamie did get his 'autobiography' book published, he could put in this, that the 'Erotica' publication was always a myth. Aubrey would be even more troubled by this possibility.

Jamie loved a successful and careful wind-up. He and Aubrey had already crossed swords in playing tricks on each other, on several occasions. Jamie reckoned he was winning overall, but Aubrey had promised one final revenge, for the last one Jamie had played.

Jamie was on his guard for anything that didn't feel quite right.

Aubrey was significantly older than Jamie and Jamie guessed, he was close if not past septuagenarian. He was still working as he loved the politics of medicine, completely the opposite of Jamie. Aubrey had developed so many positive things, for the specialist unit of Baguley Hospital. In his tenure as a leader, they had gone from a local specialist unit, to being one of the biggest in the world. They had a transplant unit, the biggest adult cystic fibrosis unit in the country, Jamie and team were the biggest severe asthma unit in the UK. They were leaders in cancer diagnostics, Interstitial Lung Disease, Aspergillus related lung disease and had a thriving research base, supported by an on-site clinical trials unit, whose success was unrivalled in their specialist field. All this had come about because of the leadership of Professors Carey, until his retirement some years before and Aubrey Wildwood and other colleagues.

Aubrey was mischievous though and loved playing tricks on his colleagues even more so than Jamie did. One Christmas party he had done an impromptu fire-eating act, that could and should have ended in disaster. Aubrey had spent weeks practising, bought all the equipment and did his show after the main course had been served and consumed.

Jamie had got wind of Aubrey's plans and elected to watch events, from the safety of the entrance door. Jamie was convinced the fire eating act in an enclosed space, would trigger the fire sensors and the whole of the department, glad rags and all, would get saturated.

The hotel manager was apoplectic when Aubrey started doing his act and whilst banning the Professor for life, he did allow the other party revellers to continue with their festivities, in more relative safety.

The darker side to this story is the failure of the sprinkler system to go off. Jamie postulated that it was perhaps because it had been disabled for the Christmas party season, for fear of such an event. An activation of the sprinkler system, would have been very costly to the hotel chain.

A real fire could however have been much more costly.

Cynically, Jamie believed the reason the hotel manager could not be assuaged from his fury, was because the absence of a functioning sprinkler system, which had effectively been exposed.

As other examples of Aubrey's mischief, he had also taken a live tarantula to a cricket match between his own team and one of the other Lancashire league teams, he played against. He released the unsuspecting arachnid into the opposition changing rooms.

However, in Jamie, the Professor had met his match, believed the younger consultant.

It was Aubrey who started it. Prior to the first opportune event, they had sparred with words but steered clear of each other, both knowing that the other would be a very dangerous opponent.

Many years before, Jamie had bought his wife, an item, from an erotica store online. Something had gone wrong with the order and they had written to Jamie, to ask him to ring them back to amend the payment by phone-call.

The letter had come to the home address and fortunately Jamie had opened it himself prior to leaving for work. He remembered slipping it in his jacket pocket and taking it to work with him, so his wife didn't see the letter and spoil the surprise.

Jamie had made the call at work to correct the payment error using his mobile phone and immediately discarded the paperwork. Jamie remembered screwing it up tight and putting in his office bin.

A few weeks later, he received a letter allegedly from the chief executive, saying the trust deplored Jamie's use of the hospital to carry out his 'sordid' practice. Jamie was not fooled into believing the letter had been created by the chief executive, for a number of reasons.

The screwed-up paper from the company in question, was attached. It had been very carefully ironed, to try and get the creases out.

Secondly, how would the chief executive had come by this letter, would also be a mystery.

There was only one colleague, who would enter his office and go through the dustbin to see what was there. That would have been Aubrey! Jamie laughed, but the point scored against Jamie, was the image of Aubrey when he found a glimmer of gold he was looking for. The erotica order form and a chance to try a wind-up. Jamie chastised himself for his carelessness as it should have been shredded, not just screwed up and cast aside.

However, the revenge plot was hatched immediately, though Jamie, did and said nothing. He told no-one about the attempted wind-up from Aubrey. Specifically, he didn't let on to Aubrey, that he knew it was from him.

Jamie waited the best part of a year, before seeking revenge. Aubrey had shown a chink in his armour however. Jamie was going to exploit this himself. Jamie waited in part until he had received a genuine letter from the chief executive. The one that came related to a letter of thanks from a patient.

Jamie, saved it, specifically to save all the codes, that the secretary used.

The top of each secretarial letter has initials, which are usually the secretary's initials followed by the Chief Executive's initials. Next came the year, followed by a code number and finally a document number. The latter is just a sequential number of the letters produced by the secretary, within the year.

Jamie created his own 'fake' letter from the chief executive. He invented the concept, that one of the lung consultants had reported Aubrey for going through some files in the personal office. It alleged that the chief executive 'had seen' CCTV footage that the reporting consultant had brought to show him 'clearly demonstrating the intrusion of privacy'. It added that, the chief executive considered it as: 'particularly concerning as the files, that were being inspected, were of a very sensitive procedural data-set'. These were words Jamie chose carefully.

This latter phraseology was to lead the scent away from Jamie himself and point more in the direction of Dr Brierley, who was head of the endoscopy department. However, no consultant colleagues were actually named.

The letter asked Aubrey to make an appointment to 'see the Chief-Executive at his earliest convenience, in order to discuss the accusations'.

Jamie waited and waited after he posted the letter, but heard nothing. No gossip ensued and there were no enquiries to Jamie about the letter. Their (Aubrey and Jamie's) great mutual friend Professor Carey said nothing. Jamie stayed mute. Patience in the long game is the best weapon of a trickster, Jamie learnt from his early attempts.

Finally, three years after Jamie had sent the letter, he was chatting to Prof. Carey about their esteemed colleague and some of his antics, whilst waiting for a meeting to start.

"Did I ever tell you about the time he got a letter asking him to see the Chief Executive?" Professor Carey started, without trace of alternative motive.

Jamie's heart pumped harder and faster, within a second and he had to control his breathing.

"Don't think so, Prof! What was it about?" Nonchalant as best as he could muster. Head position unchanged, both colleagues staring at the screen, where the images would go.

"He had got a letter saying he had been videoed going through a colleague's filing cabinet. Asked him to come and see the Chief Executive about it. When he went up, the CE read the letter and laughed. 'This looks like it came from me, but I can assure you it didn't', he said to Aubrey. Aubrey thought it was Paul (Dr Brierley) apparently," Prof Carey told this story as if it was just a natural story.

Jamie's heart was alive, but the important thing now was still to give nothing away. The prize was achieved. No reason to gloat or open oneself up for retribution.

"How funny. Mind you it could of course have been anyone. He is always snooping on your desk, whenever he gets in your office." Matter of fact, was the tone Jamie aimed for. He hoped it was achieved.

Jamie never spoke to Aubrey or any of his consultant colleagues about this story.

****

Proning, gave Jamie time to think about the autobiography, he was planning to write and the stories about his colleagues and the tricks they had played on each other, just had to form part of the books.

If being ill with Covid hadn't been taking all his energy, he could really have got started with writing the first draft of the first few chapters.

In one bright energy filled moment, he had even tried to write the prologue, to explain why the book was what he was referring to as a 'fictional autobiography'. He couldn't make it sound right and fatigue soon took the better of him.

Jamie was thinking a lot about friends and colleagues, who had passed away. He had made great friends with a larger-than-life character (Paul Letterworth), who worked for the pharmaceutical industry. An ex-professional sportsman who broke his leg so badly his career was over at a young age and he went into pharmaceuticals and sales.

He told incredible stories and got into the most incredible mischief, that Jamie had seen, leading several of Jamie's consultant colleagues in with him.

Paul Letterworth had teased the consultant world, that he was writing a book about the tales of a pharmaceutical rep and the medical profession. 'The names are changed to protect the guilty', was the phrase Paul told the band of consultants at every meeting he attended. Sadly, Paul had died suddenly a few years ago and Jamie wondered if there was any sign of a partially complete or complete book. Jamie went to the funeral and met Paul's wife.

"Was he ever writing a book that you knew of Molly?" Jamie asked the grieving widow, genuinely out of interest. Molly smiled. "No Jamie, he told me he was threatening to, to scare some of you, but I don't think he ever but pen to paper."

"Shame," Jamie had said to Mrs Letterworth, genuinely. "Now that would have been a best seller!"

Jamie passed some of the time of Covid illness, thinking of the stories, that Paul might have written. Fatigue though, was an incredible part of the illness and even for someone who never sat still normally, the concept of sitting down to write for hours and concentrate hard, was beyond Jamie. All he could do was straighten out some of the stories in his head.

He knew Aubrey was going to be a lead character, Paul would follow.

Chapter 48
The SHO Years: SHO Year 3/Registrar: Promotion, Day One

Jamie had two challenges to his new found senior status, very early in his role as locum registrar.

The first was on both his and his new consultant's very first day. The date by chance, coincided with a national research conference. Dr Miller was presenting at this conference. In their wisdom, the rota-master had put the new consultant and his new registrar on-call, on the very first day.

Yes! A manager had taken over from a clinician in writing rotas, so logic and common-sense were routinely absent!

Jamie's new boss had rung and chatted to him the week before and even though Dr Flimley-Martin had arranged to cover for political discussions, Dr Miller had wanted Jamie to ring himself personally to discuss any emergency medical events.

This suited Jamie. Historically, apart from the 6 months with Dr Firman, he always went via a registrar. Dr Firman had been very enthusiastic about Jamie ringing him direct, except when he was on holiday of course.

Dr Miller similarly was very keen to stress to Jamie, that this was conference and not holiday. He was working and therefore should be Jamie's first 'port of call'.

The pivotal patient came in very early on, during the on-call shift. Gary who Jamie had come to know well, working as SHO colleagues since February, was now 'his' SHO. Gary recognised the sick case immediately and called for back-up.

It was a thirty-year-old Asian gentleman, who had arrived in the UK from India just three months ago and spoke very little English.

Mr Hussain was profoundly septic, dehydrated and with a fever of over forty-two, which was as high as Jamie had seen.

Gary had obtained the medical history from the patient's sister, who had lived in the UK, a bit longer. The key parts of the story were that, Mr Hussain had been unwell, with a dry cough for at least 3 weeks, but not the 3 months one might have expected with pulmonary TB. This was always the first diagnosis potentially for someone who had come from India with a febrile illness, but there were many other infectious disease options.

The sister gave the details of the town he had lived in back-home, which Jamie hadn't heard of. He suggested to Gary to ring microbiology to see if it was a Malaria area, because of the height of the fever, though this was an unlikely cause of dry cough.

The X-ray came back at that moment and Gary and Jamie went off to look at it together.

"What do you think Gary?" Gary was planning to be a cardiologist and wasn't as enthusiastic about lungs or X-rays as Jamie.

"It looks normal to me. I was expecting to see a big cavitating pneumonia," Gary replied.

"I was expecting something more obvious as well, but I don't think it **is** normal, actually."

Jamie exaggerated the 'is' word and picked up a piece of paper. Jamie punctured a little hole in it a couple of centimetres in diameter. He held it up to the X-ray at a point where it was mostly just lung markings. He chose the bottom half of the lungs, where Jamie thought the changes, subtle as they were, were slightly more definite.

The trick with the hole in the paper, was something Dr Coleman had once taught him, to look at the interstitial features. This was the background grey haze. In normality, it was created by just small vessels and edges of airways as the only solid parts of lungs that were otherwise over 90% air. The hole in the paper acted like a high-lighting device and allowed the eyes to focus on the very small and subtle changes, ignoring the bigger features on the X-ray, whether they were normal or otherwise.

Gary looked closer and his eyes changed from sceptical to smiling.

"Tiny little nodules maybe?"

"I think so, which is in fact bad news for Mr Hussain, because we are possibly talking about…?" Jamie left the line unfinished, as a question.

"Miliary TB," Gary answered immediately. Jamie knew he was smart. Just misguided in regards to a career in Cardiology, as Jamie often told him.

"It's classical, being more prominent in the bottom half of the lungs, where vessels predominate as the infection is spread through the blood stream, unlike pulmonary TB, where it is inhaled," Jamie recounted from his membership exam knowledge.

"And it is more obvious as you say in the bottom half," Gary was convinced and was moving the paper around the image himself, as he said it.

"Ring Micro and ask them to advise us on which antibiotics to give intravenously on this diagnosis and say we need them now! I'm going to check his eyes," Jamie started setting an agenda.

"Why his eyes?" Gary asked.

"We need confirmation of the diagnosis, if it is Miliary TB, the little abscesses can be seen in the back of the eyes. Mr Hussain isn't fit enough for any sort of biopsy of the lung, which is another way to make the diagnosis. We might get medical illustration to come and take a picture of his retina, for good measure." Jamie explained his plans to Gary.

"Once I've looked, I'm ringing the boss," he added.

"Flimo?" Gary asked with an edge of surprise, using the junior doctors nickname for the Lord Flimley-Martin.

"No, the new-boy! He gave me a pep talk yesterday, didn't expect to be needing to ring him quite so soon." Jamie ignored the slight derogatory implication of Gary's question.

Jamie was excited as remembering the minutiae of the potential diagnosis from a retina, from his membership studies (*it was occasionally useful*), meant they might be ahead of the curve to get treatment in early, giving Mr Hussain a better chance of surviving.

Jamie thought from the memory of his reading, that there might some controversy about whether giving steroids was good or bad. They might in part help to reduce inflammation and also because the adrenal gland could be affected by the infection, suppressing its' function. However, high dose steroids could weaken the immune system and potentially allow TB, to spread more rapidly.

Jamie couldn't remember the current conclusion on the 'pro-con' debate on the subject and what the current advice was. In a way, this helped Jamie, as he would use it as the focus question for his phone call to his new boss.

Jamie struck gold. The tiny little abscesses which were about the size of millet seeds (and gave miliary TB its' name), were clearly visible in the back of Mr Hussain's retina, even for Jamie, who had struggled with the technique of using the ophthalmoscope, particularly in his recent exam.

Jamie had used a standard ophthalmoscope to view the back of the eyeball, but he immediately rang medical illustration to see if they had equipment that could take a photograph.

"How soon do you need it?" Jamie had never met Peter the 'medical illustrator', but everyone said how helpful he was.

"Err, now actually!" Jamie said.

"If you can justify why, I'm dropping everything else I have on, for you, then I could be with you in five minutes?" Peter's question was friendly.

Jamie didn't hesitate, but went straight into explaining the severity of the illness, the need for a confirmed diagnosis and why the picture, would satisfy everyone going forward. It was 'having some hard evidence to hang the diagnosis on', which was Jamie's real requirement. Jamie couldn't think of any other test or procedure, that Mr Hussain was fit enough to undergo right now, that would give great support for the diagnosis he had made.

A CT scan would be interesting, but would just show the same as the X-ray, just in more detail.

Peter didn't wait for Jamie to even finish the first sentence of this explanation. If medical illustration was going to make a diagnosis no one else could make, then Peter was up for that as his priority. He had packed his gear, before he explained this to Jamie.

After securing the aid of medical illustration, Jamie got on the phone.

He left a message on Dr Miller's answer machine. Jamie remembered he was doing a talk on pulmonary rehabilitation for COPD at the conference this morning. He might have been giving the lecture at exactly the time Jamie had tried to ring him.

"I presume you want them developed 'right now' too?" Peter was smiling after taking the pictures, just fifteen minutes after the phone call. Jamie knew he had a new 'phone a friend'.

"Ten minutes ago, would be much better," Jamie quipped.

"Miracles in fucking Leicester? Can tell you come from the North," the banter was in full flow.

"Could you see the little white spots, with the kit?" Jamie asked. He hadn't been able to see, what Peter was seeing with the ophthalmic camera.

"I'm not a doc remember, but my guess is you won't be disappointed. Give me thirty minutes and you can see for yourself."

Peter, shuffled off as fast as his eighteen stone frame would take him.

Just then the desk phone rang. Jamie had left his bleep number and the desk phone.

"Jamie it's only 10.45 a.m. on our first day, you can't have a dire emergency already, can you?" the tone was benevolent as Jamie had expected from yesterday's interaction.

"I'm afraid so, boss!" Jamie wanted to check how much time they had so asked if Dr Miller had finished his lecture.

"Yes, it's coffee break, so tell me what you have!"

Jamie told his new boss the whole story, what they had done for fluid resuscitation, diagnostics and the plan for treatment, once they had a response from microbiology.

"You've managed all that by 10.45?" Dr Miller had 'impressed' laced in his voice.

"Gary the SHO, saw him at 9 a.m. and had it mostly covered before I got here." Jamie was diverting the implied praise. He didn't want to sound like an arse-licker on his first day.

"Promise you, I couldn't have got medical illustration in Birmingham to come like that! Were you flashing your tits or your legs?" Dr Miller was now joining in the banter. Jamie knew his new boss had come from Birmingham, having been a highly sought-after registrar there.

"I don't have either, unless Peter likes flat and skinny," Jamie replied. "I will buy him biscuits, when I'm shopping next, from his look, he will like them better!"

"Leave it to me, I'll bring some shortbread back. The conference is in Edinburgh after all." Jamie liked that the new boss, also got that merited 'thankyous', were an important part of the game.

"Humour me and get a CT scan done Jamie and lets just give him adrenal replacement dose steroids, just in case his adrenal function is limp. Hold off anything in high dose." Dr Miller got to the serious part and the decisiveness was reassuringly Jamie.

Jamie was completely happy to take all this direction, after a stimulating discussion of the practical situation they were in.

Gary was back with microbiology advice and pharmacy action and had new drugs in his hand. Mr Hussain was getting his first definitive treatment by 11 a.m., little more than two hours after he arrived.

The next morning at 8.30 a.m., Jamie was reviewing a slightly improved Mr Hussain, when Dr Miller walked in.

Although they had spoken, they hadn't met, but it only took voice recognition to kick in on the first word.

"I thought you weren't back from the conference until tomorrow?" Jamie asked, once introductions and a summary of progress was completed.

"I decided letting you have all the glory, might not be in my best interests, so I came back this morning. Here, you might as well have these to take to Peter. Is that the name of Medical Illustration?" Dr Miller passed Jamie a heavy bag, full of shortbread with a sign from a store on Princess Street on it.

"I think you should come with me boss. The pictures are amazing. Perhaps, then we can have coffee with Gary unless you have any more pressing matters." Jamie felt so relaxed, with his new consultant, that he had even gone in to organisation mode.

"Sounds like a plan."

The immediate mutual respect between the two, survived Jamie's entire career. Dr Miller became a national leader, both medically and politically. Their paths crossed many times after Jamie left Leicester. Occasionally they were on opposite sides of a political conundrum, but Jamie would always be grateful for the time he met another of his role models, however briefly. When on opposing sides, they would always find a practical way to compromise their political differences, such was the effect of successful bonding over one special case.

Most importantly in this story, Mr Hussain made an excellent and full recovery.

Chapter 49
The SHO Years: More Clinic Events

Leicester had three primary hospitals and some outlying peripheral links to community hospitals.

When Jamie was on-call as a registrar, he was still expected occasionally to attend clinics at one of the other hospitals. This set up, was later withdrawn, but it meant the registrar being off site, when on-call and caused Jamie one major issue early, in his registrar status.

Another unusual protocol at his base hospital, was that patients with cardiac sounding chest pain were brought direct to Coronary Care Unit, missing out the Emergency Department, on the decision of the ambulance crew.

Most of the time, this worked really well and reduced delay from onset of chest pain, to the ability to give 'clot-buster' therapy, which for the patient reduced the amount of heart damage and therefore could improve outcome dramatically.

Jamie was on-call with an SHO from another team called Amy. She was a first year SHO, but the other registrars and junior colleagues all rated her highly.

This Thursday, she rang Jamie in tears, just before lunch on the on-call day, whilst Jamie was doing a clinic at one of the hospitals across town.

"Jamie, I don't know what to do," she managed between sobs.

"Amy, calm down, tell me what's going on!" Jamie had sensed the fragile close to tears sound of her voice immediately.

"35-year-old Asian man, came straight into CCU. Central chest pain, sweaty!" she took a deep breath, with a huge sob. "ECG was abnormal, with ST changes and the history so typical, that we gave him thrombolysis," she sobbed briefly again, before taking a deep breath and continuing.

"But now I can see that he doesn't have 2-mm ST elevation," she broke down at that point and Jamie had to work to get her focused on letting him know.

"Ok, Amy, so we know we have a patient who has had thrombolysis, but if he isn't bleeding then that's not a crisis. Is he bleeding?" Jamie was giving Amy some time to take more breaths and get herself composed. He sensed something more was coming.

"But the X-ray has just come back and he has a pneumothorax on both sides. What do I do?"

Jamie's head raced. He had never seen this situation before, with or without the added complication of a patient who had been given thrombolysis in the last 30 minutes.

The problems indeed were many. The gentleman, would be barely able to breathe with both lungs compromised, indeed Jamie thought he was lucky to have made it to coronary care unit.

The next concern, is whether either side or even both might be under tension. Jamie imagined that having a pneumothorax on both sides, might mean there wouldn't be any 'shift of the mediastinum' on the X-ray, even if one side was under tension and the other not. If there was tension on one or both sides, action needed to be taken immediately, whether there was a risk of bleeding because of the thrombolysis or not.

Jamie could think of no way, that Amy might be able to tell, whether the pneumothoraxes were under tension.

"What are the 'obs' Amy?"

"BP is low at 100/50. Heart rate is 130, 'sats' 90 and respiratory rate is nearly 30." Jamie noted her voice was stronger as he focused her on medical answers, but he was not reassured by the observations. This man was in deep trouble.

Jamie worked out in his head, that despite the thrombolysis, Amy was going to have to do something and do it now, as the man could arrest at any moment. Jamie wouldn't get back across town in time to help.

Jamie had nearly processed what to do, but was completing his rationalisation as he was asking the last two questions.

"Any shift of the mediastinum at all, though I am not sure how we would interpret it, in a bilateral pneumothorax? And who is with you right now?"

"Emma, your house officer, and Julia, the CCU Sister, are sat with me and nothing obvious in terms of mediastinal shift, but it may be shifted to the left a fraction."

"Press speaker-phone, Amy, because I want other people to listen to these instructions as you are so upset." Jamie paused briefly hearing some chatter briefly.

"Don't think about the thrombolysis now as you have to act, or this man will arrest very soon. Imagine you haven't given it," Jamie started and wanted to give very directed instructions.

"Firstly, put a cannula in the second intercostal space on one of the sides. Decompressing the side with tension or the most tension. If you have no clue, start on the right." He paused momentarily.

"Then, as soon as you can after that, put the smallest available chest drain in to the other side. Don't do any dissection as that will increase the chance of bleeding."

"Once the drain is in, then do another X-ray. Emma call any of the on-site registrars, say I asked them to come immediately. Then call cardio-thoracic surgery and let them know the problem and ask them to get there as fast as possible. I will be there as fast as is legally possible, but you have to act now. Do you think you can do it? If not ring Gary and ask him to help."

To Jamie's surprise the next voice was actually Julia's the sister. Jamie had come to know her as a superbly efficient and composed nurse, who he respected greatly as well as liking personally. He had observed her mixing great efficiency with compassion for patients and colleagues alike. She had warm brown eyes, which she used on Jamie, which also helped.

"I've got all that scribbled down Jamie and I am sure Amy can do it, now she has a plan. I will have a chest drain set ready in five minutes. Let's get the cannula in first as it might buy us a few minutes as Jamie said. Emma, you do the calls!" Julia paused the briefest of moments. "And Jamie, your orders. Drive safely! We don't want another casualty. Your plan will be done by the time you get here," Julia taking control, made Jamie feel so much better.

"Ok, thanks, Julia. Amy if he bleeds; firstly, don't worry, less of an issue than the possible arrest. If he does deteriorate before you get one drain in, put a cannula in the other side too." Jamie was talking so fast, but now decided it was time for action.

"Go!" was his final call to action as he shifted the notes of the last case, that he had seen.

Jamie called Gary himself as he was running to the car and explained the situation in very brief summary.

"If she is doing it herself, Gary, just let her. Don't take over unless she isn't coping. Do you get me as to why?"

"Totally, Boss!" Gary had copied, Jamie's use of this phrase as a friendly term of rank, that could be used between friends.

Jamie was hoping Amy would be able to recover the mess, she had gotten herself into. He knew the 'mess', she had got herself into was almost certainly inadvertent, though it would take time for her to see that. However, it would make the next few days better for Amy, if she solved it herself, if at all possible. He then rang his consultant of the day on-call, which was not Dr Miller, but Dr Clayton. It was also his clinic and Jamie hadn't even wasted the time to call in to his room, before heading across town. He briefly explained his rapid exit.

The traffic was bad and even being as aggressive as he could safely drive, it took Jamie over thirty minutes to get to the car-park and another five minutes to run to CCU.

All the way Jamie wondered if he had given the right advice. He hadn't had enough thinking time. Should he have said, decompress both sides with cannula's first, but he really wanted one side, protected with a drain in as early as possible. Decompressing meant you wouldn't be sure there was a space left to insert the drain and a more surgical approach would be necessary. The latter would be more complicated by the thrombolysis.

There were several family members standing outside CCU, crying and talking on their phones in strident voices. Jamie managed to get past them incognito.

It took no time to work out where the patient was within the CCU ward. The ward was a long area, with cubicles on each side, with curtains covering the space where the patient resided. There was good space around all the beds even when the curtains were drawn with this design. As in most CCU setting the lights were a little too low and there was the beeping of ECG monitors from multiple angles.

Gary was standing outside the curtain, peaking through the crack and one of Jamie's registrar colleagues was leaning over him.

Jamie guessed Gary had said 'Jamie's here' as Julia appeared from the other side.

She came out and put her thumb straight up at Jamie, as he closed the space and then changed her hands position, to the code for 'calm'. Both palms pointed to the floor.

"She has done good, Jamie. He is already much better." The words were better than he could have hoped to hear.

"Bleeding?" was Jamie's one question and the fear, that he had all the way across town.

"Nothing more than any chest-drain insertion, that I've seen." Julia was calming him down again, after the frustrations of the journey and the sense of 'out-of-control' having built up, since he last spoke to her.

Gary and the registrar turned to Jamie. The registrar winked. "Typical Carmichael, skiving across town when the action is here." The registrar letting Jamie know that all was calm and in control, by joking rather than giving him the update.

Gary said, "We can leave you with it, now you are finally back. You need to get yourself a TT." Jamie knew Gary had an Audi TT. Jamie had an old Ford Capri, but had gone across town in his wife's car as it coped better with the rush-hour traffic.

"I was in the Orion, not the '2.8i' unfortunately." Jamie was desperate to get inside, to see how both his patient and his distraught junior colleague were coping.

"Thanks for coming both of you, it is much appreciated!" Jamie spoke this sentence loud enough for his voice to carry, he was outside the patient's cubicle and wanted his voice to be fully professional when it was heard, as there was going to be a lot of explaining to do, one way or another.

Jamie went behind the curtain, now with fear and urgency off his face, mostly thanks to Julia's subtle messaging.

Mr Hafiz, was sat up on the edge of the bed. A chest drain was neatly piercing the mid axillary line on the left side and was connected to an underwater seal bottle, that was bubbling moderately, indicating a persistent air leak, unless Amy had only just connected it. There was no obvious external bleeding.

Jamie could tell that Amy had been crying, but he reckoned it wouldn't have been obvious to someone who wasn't familiar with her normal demeanour and appearance. Her curly ginger hair covered her face a little more than usual, her dimples were still there, but without the broad cheery smile she wore almost all the time.

Mr Hafiz, looked better than the picture Jamie had painted from the observations he heard forty-five minutes ago. He was perhaps breathing a little harder than normal, but this could be just the discomfort of having the drain put in.

Still in his chest at the front, exactly where it should be, was a cannula. The needle had been removed, the port end, normally connected to the IV drip was open. Amy had as instructed used this to decompress the pneumothorax on that side if it had been under pressure. This allows the air to come out, but as it has no valve effect, it would not fully treat the pneumothorax on that side. On the contrary, Jamie expected the one with the drain in it, to be a nearly fully expanded and fully functioning lung at least by now.

"Mr Hafiz, my name is Jamie Carmichael, I'm the registrar. Apologies, I wasn't here when your exciting entrance occurred, I was I'm afraid working at the hospital across town."

"Hello, Dr Carmichael. I think you have missed the excitement. Amy here, has I suspect saved my life." His English was impeccable and Jamie expected to find out, he was educated and in a professional career.

"Do you know Mr Hafiz, that may indeed be absolutely correct." Jamie wasn't letting the opportunity go to give Amy the glory.

"Only after Dr Carmichael, gave me the right order in which to do things!" Amy interjected unnecessarily. Jamie suspected she wouldn't want praise heaped on her, when she still believed she had made a catastrophic error. Jamie remembered the feelings when he had got the wrong diagnosis on his patient with viral myocarditis.

"Well let's not split hairs, shall we, Mr Hafiz? I think you wouldn't go back an hour is my guess?" It was a question the way Jamie said the words.

"No, sir I wouldn't." Jamie knew he would have to explain to Mr Hafiz, what treatment he got that he hadn't needed. If he didn't bleed anywhere, there was no negative impacts of trying to treat a possible heart attack, when it wasn't the actual diagnosis.

"Second X-ray?" Jamie asked Amy turning directly to face her.

"They've just been, the film should be back in a second!" Amy was pleased to have got all the jobs done before Jamie had made it, it was clear.

"Mr Hafiz, is it ok if we go and have a look at the X-rays and results and work out what we are going to do, to that other lung? In the meantime, we are leaving that little plastic cannula sticking out of your chest, but it won't be for much longer I promise. Please don't touch it in the meantime, but if you don't mind, stay sat as you are, as we might need to do some more procedures, to get this just right." Jamie wanted to get Amy away before Jamie started to get into any more discussion with the patient. He thought it was likely that now the immediate tasks were over and adrenaline would be ebbing away, that she might get distraught again, when talking to Jamie.

Amy sorted her chest drain trolley, with her surgical kit still on it and then covered it all over with the drape and what had been her surgical gown. In doing so, it was now respectable to push down the corridor to the treatment room, if seen by other patients or relatives.

"Great job, Amy. He is right you know! You've just saved a life. We don't do that very often in a whole career in reality. Most of the time all we do is help them to get better." Jamie started when they were out of earshot.

Amy kept her head down until they were alone in the treatment room.

"But I made such a stupid mistake." She was heading back to tears straight away.

"I'm not sure you did. It looks like one of those massive medical traps, that we get from time to time. Let's go and look at the X-rays and ECG together and have a think about it." Jamie was in calm supportive tone.

Jamie knew he needed to do this with her, it could be done today or left until tomorrow or another day. She was so upset, they wouldn't be able to move on with the day, until it was done. He wondered if he would need to get an emergency cover for the on-call.

Five minutes later they were sat in the office. Julia had got coffee made and left them to themselves. No-one came in, and Jamie guessed Julia had managed that process.

"The ECG does look a bit like an infarct, it would have to be a posterior one though with the ST elevation being there only."

Jamie was not surprised to see the ECG was indeed, a tricky and clearly abnormal one. "Central chest pain, sweaty, low BP, tachycardia…all of the symptoms and signs of heart attack."

"How do you know you gave the wrong treatment first?" Jamie asked with a genuine question tone to his voice, passing her the ECG.

She picked it up and looked at him.

"What do you mean?" she was a little suspicious.

"Perhaps I should say, at what point in the process did you know that you had got the diagnosis wrong?" He was being as gentle as he could with questions.

"Clearly, when the X-ray came back," she said the obvious answer, to an obvious question.

"Absolutely. That's when you knew you were wrong with your original diagnosis."

"But I should have picked up it was a pneumothorax. I did examine him." Jamie was waiting for this line from Amy. He had thought about the clinical signs that would be present during his drive.

As a result, he turned the comment back on her as a question.

"So how would you pick up a tension pneumothorax clinically, in a typical case."

"Percussion note hyper-resonant, reduced tactile vocal fremitus, quiet breath sounds and possibly signs of mediastinal shift, with tracheal deviation and displacement of the apex beat." Her answer was textbook as he expected.

"Correct. However, hyper-resonant compared to what? Quiet breath sounds compared to what?" Jamie was getting close to finishing his argument.

"Normal!" she said immediately.

He responded quickly predicting her answer, but started with a negative buzzer sound from a quiz show, before giving what he believed was the correct answer. "Compared to the other side actually. On a noisy CCU, could you definitely say one side is hyper-resonant compared to 'normal', if that is the only side you can examine?"

"It might be!" she started and Jamie knew she was beating herself up and he needed a change of tack and direction.

"Bollocks! I couldn't." Jamie's favourite medical word was becoming 'bollocks' for making a point. Especially if he reserved it for really important moments.

"Because we anchor our perspective, by comparing one side with the other. Nine hundred and ninety-nine times in a thousand, you have one abnormal and one normal side. You can spot the signs, because there is a 'normal' one to compare with. Problem here is that both sides were exactly the same. On top of that, he looked like an infarct, gave a history like an infarct and smelled like an infarct. He only wasn't one, when the X-ray came back. You followed the protocol you have and gave him thrombolysis, before he had an X-ray."

Jamie laid his argument out and waited and paused. She didn't respond. "But it was a trap! A medical trap. I told you the other day about my unilateral pulmonary oedema trap. It always seems these things happen, when the boss isn't around!" Jamie laughed at this bit of story he hadn't thought about before.

Amy looked at him and smiled weakly for the first time.

"Lastly, what did you do when you were stuck?" the smile faded.

"Lost it!" she said honestly.

"A little!" he admitted, with a smile himself. "But what else did you do?"

"Rang you!" she started.

"Exactly. What you are supposed to do! Ring for help, when you are stuck." He paused a moment, "Then you saved his life."

There was a tap at the door, it was Julia.

"Sorry to disturb, but the X-ray is back and I thought you might want to see it." She looked at Jamie, apologetic, but also with a big question in her eyes.

"Perfect timing, we had just got to the bit, where we realised Amy did everything right, when set a bugger of a trap." Julia almost let out an audible sigh.

"Funnily enough, that was what I had worked out too." Julia first put a hand on Amy's shoulder as she came properly into the room. Amy's head was down, still unconvinced. Julia passed the X-ray to the outstretched hand of Jamie. 'Thank you' she mouthed at Jamie, over the head of Amy.

Amy lifted her head and had a more determined look on her face.

"Thanks to you too, Julia, by the way. You were amazing there with me you know?" There was genuine feeling and a tear finally slipped out of Amy's eye as she said this. It was the first Jamie saw.

"Now let's see what this X-ray shows and what we are going to do with the side with the cannula in." Jamie was back to business.

They looked at the X-ray together. The drain was nicely positioned and the left sided pneumothorax was almost completely resolved. There was no sign of internal bleeding, which had been Jamie's concern and enthusiasm to see the X-ray.

Mr Hafiz could have been bleeding internally into the pleural space, without them knowing, but if he had it would have shown up on the new X-ray. The other feature of the second X-ray, was that the side with the cannula, still had a sizeable pneumothorax, although it had reduced in size from the first X-ray.

"Think we better put a drain in there too. We can't leave the cannula in and it could have been tension originally. Did it hiss?" He turned and realised he hadn't asked Amy this important question.

"It was too noisy to be sure, but he picked up straight away. His 'sats' came up and his blood pressure improved even before I put the drain in." Her answer left it impossible to be 100% certain, but Jamie thought that the speed of improvement would only have happened if there was substantial tension.

"Too noisy not to hear a hiss, but you can tell what is normal, with a percussion note? I rest my case there though! Shall I do the second drain?" Jamie asked expecting her to be relieved.

"No fucking way. I got us in this mess and I've just put one in with no real bleeding. I'm doing it!" It was the first and only time he ever heard her swear at work.

Jamie took all the communication lead with Mr Hafiz, the family and later with their consultant of the day, but left Amy finishing the practical work, that had truly saved Mr Hafiz's life.

Jamie openly acknowledged to Mr Hafiz and the family, how the initial diagnosis and treatment had been incorrect and that is why they were moving Mr Hafiz off CCU. He explained how the treatment had made it a bit riskier to do the drains, but that actually both had gone without a problem.

Jamie finished by explaining that getting the drains in quickly had prevented what would almost certainly have ended in a cardio-respiratory arrest. Essentially Amy had probably saved the life of Mr Hafiz.

All parties were just relieved and the issues that had been a mountain to Amy, seemed like a molehill to Mr Hafiz and his family, who by now apart from having two tubes attached to his side, was back to normal.

Jamie finished off by going to find Julia. "Well done today, by the way. I was properly impressed, when you took charge and got things moving. Not sure if Amy would have gotten through, without your support and strength." Jamie was wholesome with his praise.

"She would! She did great! She just needed your direction to get her going. So glad you got her to put us on speaker though, that was perfect. So, the 'love in' of congratulations and thank-yous, is mutual in all directions. Amy also has great respect for you and how you talked her through the 'trap' as she called it."

"Did she tell you all about our 'chat'?" Jamie asked a little surprised.

"I think most of it. She thinks you walk on water you know? Though she also told me you have the hots for me…is that true?" Julia slipped from one conversation to other without a breath.

"I certainly haven't said that to her, she is stirring with that comment. Anyway, my second baby is due in a week, so I'm pretty much out of the equation and I'm leaving Leicester in a couple of months."

Jamie had been surprised by this conversation, although he really liked Julia and she was certainly very attractive. Nothing else had crossed his mind. He wondered if Julia was searching and making up Amy's comments.

"Ouch, that's me dumped pretty hard." Julia was smiling, though Jamie now worried, if he had been too blunt.

"I'm not denying you're my favourite though!" Jamie thought a safe middle line was his best bet.

"Have you stayed out of Jane's clutches by the way?" Julia was still interested in this issue, now for the second time.

"Yes, most definitely. I'm not scared often, but she has me on my toes somehow." He wasn't sure this came across as he meant it, but he meant he was always aware of her ability to change suddenly and so he avoided his normal flirting in her presence.

"Well, I'm pleased to hear that at least." Julia turned to go, "Thanks again for today."

"Likewise." Jamie felt unusually awkward. She blew him a kiss as she left the room.

Chapter 50
Getting Covid: Post-Covid Day 9: Potential Recovery

Day seven (the start of the critical period for those with covid pneumonia) had come and gone. Jamie was feeling a little better from a viral symptom perspective, with a fraction more energy. He wasn't having to drag himself around the house, but the breathlessness remained.

Jamie filled his time, by writing out notes of the stories to go in his book, when he had the energy to start it.

He expected this to be when he fully retired in May and was living on his island paradise. He did sympathise with his poor colleagues who rang to check him out, as he regaled them with whichever story, he had just made notes on.

Dan was the most recent, who got the timing wrong. Dan himself still wasn't back at work, but was now on the upward curve after his dose of Covid. As a result, he probably didn't mind listening to a 5-minute story, he may have heard before.

"When I was in Leicester, a GP had been to the house of a 90-year-old lady. He declared the old lady dead at the scene and as such the ambulance crew took her straight to the morgue. She was placed on the morgue table awaiting formal identification, covered in a white sheet, when allegedly she suddenly started to move. As the story goes, she sat up on the morgue table, sheet over her head, moaning and wailing."

Dan, laughed appropriately encouraging Jamie to embellish a little as he went.

"So apparently all the mortuary staff ran out of the building in shock. The ambulance was called back and the old, apparently dead lady was taken to ED."

"Just to make it worse. It turns out she was the great aunt of one of the ED consultants, or some such distant relative. They warmed her up and revived her and a few days later she went home." Jamie kept pausing for effect, whilst Dan made encouraging noises.

"Papers got hold of the story somehow and it made the front pages for one very opportune reason."

"Go on Jamie, you haven't told me this one before," Dan reassured him.

"GP's name," Jamie paused.

"Oh no…spill."

Jamie paused even longer for effect. "Dr De'ath."

"Poor fucker. There but for the grace of God, go us all!" Dan started.

"You might not choose to be a doctor though if that's your name, or change your name by deed-pole." Jamie was on practical logic.

"Hey, we have the same issue with our mate, Tim. His name is Coffey and he chose to be a respiratory doctor, despite the name."

Jamie laughed, he had often thought about it, but never teased Tim about it.

"Just as well, he hasn't had Covid yet, we would be calling him Coffey by name…" Jamie left the end of the sentence unfinished. They chatted some more small talk, before Jamie started to close the conversation.

"Thanks for the call, stay safe mate."

"You too, Jamie, you have to or you ruin my career too. I can't be the one who kills Mr Asthma," Dan joked.

****

Jamie had been looking forward to getting back to work when he starting planning it the evening before. He was Day 10 and had hoped he was allowed back to work that day, but NHS England Track and Trace had been on the phone and told him, the following day (Thursday) was the first day he was allowed back.

The trajectory had all been good in terms of his energy, fever, resting heart rate and saturations.

That was, until the middle of last night. He woke with a sweat and palpitations. Jamie put it down to the fact, he had tried a glass or two of wine, to drown his boredom, whilst watching a fan-less football match.

The fake crowd noise irritated him more than silence, so he watched it with the 'crowd off' option.

He could at least get some intellectual pleasure from, listening to which of the coaches said the most sensible and interesting things to motivate the players.

Jamie had long believed football should go like rugby and let the fans hear everything the referees said. If they did, the first season there would be a rash of sending's off for the foul and abusive language and derogatory remarks from the players, being picked up on the microphones and therefore necessitating action. The technology was there and ready. Other sports did it so much better than football. Perhaps because their governing bodies, were less corrupt than UEFA or FIFA, Jamie surmised.

Disturbed in the middle of the night with the change of symptoms though, he sensed his new deterioration wasn't the wine. He only had two glasses after all. Yes, the most he had, imbibed in the last 10 days, but not enough to cause sweats and palpitations.

He got up and made a cup of tea and caught himself, checking all the bags were still ready and in one piece. When he had done his 'sats' in the morning and they were down at 92%. In response, he had lain down prone for an hour and they came back up to 94%.

Yesterday they had been 95% though, increasing steadily from day seven, onwards.

The lunchtime Isla walk across the field, was slow and painful. The cough was more prominent again and the crackles he could feel on the inside, were louder and present through more of the breath in than they had been yesterday.

Jamie found himself taking a deep breath in.

Having got interested through his early case of PVCM, Jamie had continued to realise that illnesses like asthma could trigger patterns of disordered breathing. He described the phenomenon to patients as if the timing on a car had gone wrong. The cylinders were still working, but not in the right order.

An alternative explanation he used for pure hyperventilation was that you are trying to drive on the motorway at seventy mph, but you've left the gears stuck in first or second. 'The revolutions are so much faster than needed for the speed you are trying to achieve, so it becomes inefficient'.

Now for the first time, he realised how easy abnormal breathing control patterns would be to develop. Jamie wanted to take the breath in more quickly than he actually needed to. A deep breath, called a 'sigh breath', is part of normal breathing and should happen every 20 or 30 breaths.

Jamie's colleagues in the Netherlands, had shown how the sigh breath relaxes the tension in the lung. If it doesn't occur, the tension on the elastic materials, build and build and cause breathlessness, with no other abnormality.

Jamie himself, had reported a case in the medical literature of a patient who was taking one normal breath followed by one sigh breath as a couplet. The trace of the recording of the breath pattern had gone on for over an hour and this one normal, one sigh breath had continued throughout the recording, confirming its' chronicity.

As Jamie postulated in the paper, the work of breathing (the total energy consumed by the muscles to enact breathing) was much higher than it should be, so the profound sense of breathlessness was not surprising. Jamie had postulated that the trigger for the patient to develop these, abnormal breathing patterns, might have been a previous experience of breathlessness. It took intensive physiotherapy and breathing retraining exercises to restore some normality.

Jamie would explain this to patients. "When you were little, I bet your mum said: 'Don't pull faces like that, if the wind changes direction your face could stick'?"

The patients would always agree with that comment as presumably every parent had voiced it at some time in the past. "Starting to think about your breathing rather than it occurring naturally, could be the starting point. Then it kind of sticks as the 'programmed' pattern of breathing, as if the wind has changed direction."

Most people knew a little about what hyperventilation was. Jamie and colleagues had described many different patterns of a group of disorders they now referred to in its very descriptive phrase of 'Breathing Pattern Disorder'.

Jamie thought for the first time that night, how he personally could develop 'Breathing Pattern Disorder' very easily in response to the breathlessness he was experiencing right now and how it made him think consciously about every breath.

One of the ultimate fears of every doctor, was coming across as a neurotic. A second was getting a condition, that you were one of the experts in. Like a neurologist getting motor-neurone disease. You knew all the worst aspects of the disease. Worst case scenario.

Jamie had on a single occasion had his own episode of ILO (what he had originally written about as paradoxical vocal cord motion syndrome-PVCMs). It had occurred when he had an episode of acid reflux in his gullet, to the extent that it was almost a vomit. It happened whilst he was asleep. The spasm of the cords in his throat, which occurred as a natural reflex response, to prevent the acid from going into the lungs was dramatic. Once triggered it was terrifying. Even for Jamie, who knew instantly what it was and actually knew some of the exercises to do to try and get the acute event to settle.

It still took 10 to 15 minutes, for Jamie to get his breathing back to normal after the spasm of the vocal cords occurred. The acid taste in his throat and even the nose took, much longer to disappear. That night was the last time Jamie had a late-night kebab and port together. Indeed, he had never had either individually again, though it was perhaps the combination that triggered the severity of the reflux that night.

Jamie had considered and discussed with his colleagues, whether it was possible that some of the symptoms of cases of 'long-covid', were actually being caused by a breathing pattern disorder, developing after the acute phase of Covid. Headache, paraesthesia. fatigue, palpitations and stomach pains were all symptoms of hyperventilation and were common in long covid. Less commonly known, was the fact that people who had other forms of breathing pattern disorder (as well as hyperventilation), also had lots of these symptoms as well as profound chronic breathlessness.

Jamie, wondered if this was the cause of his new symptoms. The only other explanation was worse. That is, he was developing the second phase of Covid pneumonia.

Chapter 51
End of the Junior Years and Sliding Doors: Part II

A week later, Stephanie, their second daughter was born, in a local maternity hospital. It was uncomplicated and both parents knew their family was complete. Whilst they would have been happy with a boy or a girl, second time around, they had agreed they didn't want to go searching for one of the opposite-sex. They could end up with 3 or 4, all girls quite easily.

Jamie had told Diane the story of Dr Lorimer, who had once told Jamie how 'god had told him he was going to have 8 children and his eighth one would be a boy'. At the time, Dr Lorimer already had 3 girls.

"Can you imagine trying to get to 8, just to have a boy?" Jamie had said. Diane had cringed at the thought.

Jamie also remembered getting very comfortable chatting to an expectant father, who already had two daughters. He was expecting twins. This happened, whilst Jamie was doing his obstetric placement as a student.

The twins were being delivered naturally. The father acknowledged, hoping that at least one of the twins was a boy. An hour later, two healthy girls were born. He was delighted, but reserved as he had wanted a boy, it was clear to Jamie.

Something however was wrong as the womb wasn't contracting and there was no second placenta. Another hour later a small but healthy further daughter came along. Jamie felt very sorry for his new friend, who suddenly had 5 daughters, when searching for a son to add to two daughters. Jamie was relieved Diane, had a similar mentality to his own.

They started packing up their rental hospital property. Their tenants in Manchester had already left, leaving a lot of damage to their own home, which was a major blow and inconvenience.

Diane and the two girls, left Leicester early and stayed with her parents for support. Diane had a new born and nearly 3-year-old to look after. This left the last 3 weeks of Jamie's time in Leicester, with him on his own, but doing lots of on-call shifts as swaps, in place of the days he had off around the delivery.

The penultimate weekend of his attachment, Jamie was on-call for the weekend and got back to Leicester on Friday late evening, having taken the day, as holiday to help move the family and some of the belongings back in to their own home.

There was the last mess party of the year that evening and several of the team had asked Jamie to come.

When he got back to the hospital accommodation, he was pretty tired with driving on a Friday, even after only working a 4-day week. Sleep deprivation was returning full force, with a new born.

Jamie had initially noticed the positive benefit of being a registrar and having 2 juniors between him and the coal face when on-call. For example, he was completely clear of doing the early intravenous drug rounds and only got disturbed after midnight if there was an issue that needed a more senior opinion.

Changing his mind three times before finally, getting changed and heading over to the party. 'Just an hour', he told himself, reminding himself that he was on-call first thing tomorrow.

Jamie hadn't been to a mess party all year and wasn't even sure, which room it was held in. He followed the noise and finding the right place wasn't difficult.

The mess was attached directly next to the nurse's residence. Julia, he knew didn't stay in. She shared a house with another nurse called Jade, who worked on one of the respiratory wards.

Jamie walked into a darkened room. The odour of stale sweat and alcohol and the beat of loud 80s electronic rhythm confronted him. He was just about to walk straight back out, knowing the music and mood was not for him, when Jade was the first to stop him.

"Julia would be so disappointed not to be here. She didn't think you would come and she hates the mess parties," Jade said as Jamie was about to walk away.

"Think I'm too old for this stuff too," Jamie answered feeling the words.

"You look seventeen and you are too old for it? That doesn't seem quite right," Jade teased.

Jamie was just about to answer with something witty, when his hand was grabbed and his shoulder almost wrenched out of its socket.

"At last, the great Dr Carmichael, graces us with his presence." Jane almost screamed at him. Jade rolled her eyes as he was pulled towards the heaving mess in the dance area.

"You are so mine tonight, Jamie Carmichael." This time a deep throaty voice, in his ear. She kissed and then bit it as she pulled away her head, throwing her mane of hair back, whilst at the same time pushing her full figure, all over his upright and over tense body.

It was like being drowned in a bucket of warm honey. Her blouse was satin and slithered along his chest. Her skirt was leather and she manged to ride the front all along his trousers in the same move.

Jamie pulled back and looked at her. She had fishnets on and stiletto shoes which were so high, he thought she would fall over in a trice. Instead, she danced sinuously and appeared high as a kite, but stayed very balanced and intricately rhythmic with the music.

She grabbed his hands, did a twirl, keeping one hand in hers. The planned and presumably practiced result she was aiming for, finished with her impressively firm bottom rubbing straight against his crotch, where she wiggled and dipped, giving his already straining bulge a considerably stimulating massage.

Her perfume was heavy and lingered in his nostrils, despite the contrasting smells from the room. He was dizzy in seconds.

He did his best and let go with his hands, so he could at least step back to get some distance between them and at least try and dance in a non-sexual way.

Jane was having none of it and followed him around the dance floor.

Jamie wasn't sure if Jane planned the route for him, or whether he ended up in the wrong place, whilst trying to get out of the disapproving gaze of Jade.

However, two dances later, Jane pulled him firmly to a door, that was close to where they had finished the last dance. It was completely opposite the door Jamie had arrived through.

"Jamie Carmichael, I have something to show you and you must come with me. I insist." She led him through the door, Jamie looked briefly back and made eye contact with Jade, who despite the distance, Jamie imagined had a hugely disappointed grimace.

A key appeared in Jane's hands and she opened up a door to a room, that was clearly her bedroom.

"You still live in?" Jamie was really surprised at this concept.

"Yes darling!" She dragged him in the room. Having entered with only a degree of resistance, Jamie knew he was in trouble, for not trying harder.

She closed and locked the door and repeated the twirl manoeuvre, she did on the dance floor. This time, once she had her bottom on him, she pushed him backwards, continuously rubbing him with her buttocks. He reversed, step by step. He felt the bed hit the back of his calves. She obviously had practiced the distances. As soon as he reached the bed, she pulled her bottom off him and spun around. She lifted her hands up, placed them on his chest and after a momentary pause, she pushed and he was propelled backwards onto a soft duvet.

She followed him down, her full breasts landing first.

Within seconds, she was on top of him, kissing him deeply. Her tongue, deep inside his mouth and then his neck. Her sizeable bosom, tightly wrapped in the satin blouse was pressing his chest and she had got one leg up and placed a large but shapely thigh over his trouser bulge. The lower leg was down his thigh and she embedded the sharp tip of her stiletto in his knee.

Several things happened in a moment, but the impact was a resounding desire to escape the room.

Showing strength of a physical kind and resolve he didn't know he had, Jamie forced himself up, arching his back and rolling Jane over onto her back.

"God yes!" was Jane's response. Jamie imagined, it came from her hope that he was going to fight for, or to take control and command of her.

"Sorry, no!" Jamie made a dash for the door and unlocked it and escaped into the corridor, with ungracious but impressive speed.

He made the disco and headed across, waving a few goodbyes.

"That was very quick or did you actually escape?" Jade was again close to the entrance door as Jamie headed to it.

"She decided I wasn't her type and chucked me out." Jamie thought lying was the best policy.

"Lucky escape!" were the last words he heard, as he ran down the corridor. Once he was away from the party, he looked down for the first time to make sure, that the stain of his orgasm, hadn't come through his trousers.

He couldn't make up his mind, if this counted as virtuous or not.

"Almost certainly not," he said as he crossed the football pitches, to no one other than himself.

****

"I hear you escaped her clutches." Julia was back on shift on the Sunday, when Jamie went to review a patient.

"Apparently so. I believe it is a rare event." Jamie was only allowing half the truth to come out.

"Well done. I'm proud of you again. Jade said she nearly devoured you on the dance floor."

"It wasn't unpleasant, just surreal!" Jamie was keeping as close to the truth as possible. "Two dances later I was dragged to her cave."

Jamie tried to say the same line as he had to Jade on Friday night, about Jane then deciding he wasn't her type.

"Haha! She doesn't have a type and anyway, that's not what she told us!"

Jamie was sunk if Jane had realised what had really made him run for the hills. Maybe she had worked it out.

"Said you tricked her and pretended to take charge, flicking her over, then ran!" Jamie heaved an internal sigh of relief. His secret was safe.

"A man never kisses and tells!" Jamie tried to close the conversation.

"We are both off work on Thursday evening, I've checked the doctor's rota. Dinner at mine, I promise not to try and rape you. Number and address are on this." She gave him a small card with writing on it.

"Let me know!" She walked away, with Jamie too shocked to respond.

He admitted to himself, that he would probably go. He wasn't sure why.

****

Jamie had long left Leicester, when he found out how close a shave, he had the night of the mess party.

Gary had rung him up in Manchester out of the blue. it wasn't just for a casual chat.

"Boss, did you ever shag Jane?" Gary asked and it was clear this wasn't just a question, without a purpose.

"No, I escaped the year without that dubious pleasure. Had a near miss one night but escaped alive and with my virginity intact," Jamie answered with full honesty.

"Think I saw you being dragged off one night, which is why I was ringing. The reason I was, is that seven docs at our hospital, have now tested positive for hep-C and they think she is the source. First case was one of the new surgical consultants, which is how it all started as a bit of an investigation," Gary continued to give him the lowdown on names.

"Public health, are calling her a 'super spreader'. I think they mean of the virus," he paused a moment. "Not the legs," Gary clearly couldn't resist.

Jamie realised he had, had a really narrow escape. Hepatitis-C was career threatening for surgeons, because of the concern over whether a surgeon could give virus to a patient during surgery if a glove was nicked. It could be life threatening for a proportion of people and personal life destroying for all members of a family, when one member of a couple gets this or any sexually transmitted disease.

"Thanks for thinking about me, stay safe mate!" Jamie concluded, when they had finished the small talk.

A few months later, Jamie heard, that the surgical consultant had committed suicide as a result of being tested positive, whilst having a young family and being implicated in the outbreak, became too much to bear.

Chapter 52
Getting Covid: Day 10: Worst-Case Scenario

Jamie was pleased to get Isla back to the house.

If she was upset, her walks were shorter than usual, she wasn't showing it. Instead, she couldn't wait for him to sit down and to take her place back on the settee next to him and rest her head on his thigh.

Jamie immediately rang Rebecca and told her of his concern, that he had taken a turn for the worse.

"Nothing to do right now. Just checking you were ok and able to come for Isla, if things get worse."

It was 3 p.m. Rebecca, knew him well enough to sense the anxiety in his voice, even though his words were as calming and sensible as he could muster.

Rebecca and Jamie had met online dating and whilst there was insufficient chemistry, to work as a relationship, they had enjoyed each-others company so much, they stayed as friends. They had shared interests in dogs and particularly music and had been to many concerts together.

Jamie also rang his work colleague Tim Coffey. He did it in principle to let Tim know where Jamie was at. Specifically, Jamie didn't think he would be back in work tomorrow. Jamie had an ulterior motive. He also asked Tim, who was on-call today.

Jamie wanted to know if it was someone who wouldn't create a fuss, when Jamie asked for anticoagulation properly from the start.

It wasn't one of those colleagues and Jamie was relieved. More importantly perhaps, it was one of the best registrars (Alice), who was on-call. It was going to be hard for her, if Jamie ended upgoing in. She would be professional and Jamie trusted her skills without reservation, but emotionally dealing with your own colleagues, when they were ill, was the hardest thing to do.

His saturations were 91%. He had told himself he would go in if they went below 92%. He disturbed Isla and rolled onto his front on the settee and tried to distract himself with mindless television, but even 'Pointless' was too much of a mental challenge for him to concentrate on.

Jamie flipped back over after an hour and was pleased he was back up to 93%.

Then, the fever hit.

Jamie was amazed how fast it came. Within five minutes, he was shaking with a rigour. His brain was fuddled and his 'sats' were 89%.

Through his brain fuzz, Jamie rang for an ambulance, knowing he was starting with what was known as 'cytokine storm'. It was the second and devastating form of the illness. Classically if it was coming, it came on day 10. It meant he was in trouble.

Then he rang Rebecca and asked her to come and get Isla.

Isla was openly frightened. She was looking at him with wide eyes and wouldn't leave his ankles as he staggered around. He went and opened the front door. Isla didn't even think about going outside, when Jamie went straight back to the kitchen breakfast bar of his living area.

Eventually Jamie sat on one of his kitchen high chairs…and waited, gasping for breath and sweating profusely.

He messaged his daughters and told them he was heading in to hospital. Neither had picked up the message, the last time Jamie looked at his phone.

****

Rebecca was there first. She had done the twelve-minute journey in a little over eight minutes.

"Shout Isla and pick up the bag! Don't come in the kitchen." Jamie didn't want her to see him like this and shouted the instructions, as he heard her come to the front door. It took three breaths to get the few words out.

Isla would normally have run and leapt into a cuddle as Rebecca crouched down, but today, she only moved six steps from Jamie's feet before running back immediately.

"Don't be stupid, I couldn't do that." She had her mask and gloves on though, which Jamie was grateful for.

"Oh fuck!" she said as she entered the living and kitchen area and saw the state of him.

"Thanks, that good, hey?" he managed.

"How quickly did this bad come on?" she asked.

"Half an hour, tops," four words were all he could manage, before another breath was needed.

"Don't move until the ambulance comes." She moved around the kitchen and got some paper towels, wet them and put them on his head.

"Take Isla and go!" Breath. "Please!" Jamie managed.

"I'm going to have to drag her when I do go, but I'm not leaving you until the ambulance is here. Don't bother trying to argue."

Jamie didn't argue. He wasn't sure how long it was before the ambulance came, but it was quite some time. He knew they were busy and he was just sat in a queue.

He knew he needed some oxygen and at times he was getting very blurry and almost losing his thought processing. His 'sats' dropped to 85%, in the five minutes before the ambulance arrived and got an oxygen mask on him.

It was a non-rebreathing type mask, The one with the bag. It gives pure oxygen and Jamie knew he wouldn't want to be on this highest concentration of oxygen for long, but he was relieved that the breathing felt easier, immediately.

He gave himself up into the hands of other health professionals for one of the few times in his life. He briefly recalled, the first time, when he heard words, he shouldn't have heard as he drifted into unconsciousness having a general anaesthetic, for his wrist abscess.

The crew got him on a trolley, strapping his legs and waist in before moving him.

Rebecca had to clip Isla on a lead and drag her away.

Rebecca and Isla stayed until the ambulance doors closed. The panic in Isla's eyes matched the utter fear and panic in Jamie's head.

He guessed despite any efforts he had made to protect his dog from the reality of his predicament and his own fear, as the ambulance doors closed between them, the awareness was evident to the two eyes that loved him more than any living being.